BETWEEN TWO KINGS

BETWEEN TWO KINGS

The Anne Boleyn
Alternate History Series

Book One

by
Olivia Longueville

www.penmorepress.com

Anne Boleyn Alternate History Series
Book 1: Between Two Kings
By Olivia Longueville
Copyright © 2020 Olivia Longueville

ISBN-13: 978-1-950586-47-9(Paperback)
ISBN—978-1-950586-46-2(E-book)

BISAC Subject Headings:
FIC014000FICTION / Historical
FIC032000FICTION / War & Military
FIC047000FICTION / Sea Stories

Editing: Chris Wozney
Cover Illustration by Christine Horner

Address all correspondence to:
Penmore Press LLC
920 N Javelina Pl
Tucson, AZ 85748

DEDICATIONS AND ACKNOWLEDGMENTS

For my beloved mother, a descendant of the old French nobility, and for my dear father. They have always immensely supported and encouraged me in all the work I do as a writer.

For my friend and cousin, Armand, a descendant of the old French nobility, who gave me a brilliant insight into French history and the reign of King François I.

For my friend and cousin, Antoine, a descendant of the old French nobility, who aided me to invent the plot of the story.

For my friend, Coleen, who co-authored with me the Robin Hood trilogy and whose assistance in working on this novel was tremendous.

For my friend, Anne Carolina, a journalist and writer, who provided me with an invaluable insight into Tudor period and encouraged me to rewrite this novel in my new style.

For my friend, Rosalind, a writer, who contributed a great deal to this project by supplying me with a multitude of useful recommendations.

For my friend, Olivia, who helped me generate ideas for the new version of this novel and shared with me her awesome knowledge of French history.

For my friend, Alejandra, who aided me to significantly improve this novel.

My heartfelt appreciation to all of my pre-readers.

In alphabetical order: Crystal, Coleen, George, Olena, Nadège, Nathalie, Sarah, and Philippe.

ILLUSTRATIONS

Coat-of-Arms of Queen Anne Boleyn (in England)

The arms of Anne Boleyn did not include the heraldry of her Boleyn ancestors. She avoided her paternal coat-of-arms because her father, Sir Thomas Boleyn, descended from London merchants. Therefore, she used her mother's and grandmother's arms against the hereditary rules.

Around the time of her marriage to King Henry VIII, Anne adopted a badge of a crowned falcon with a scepter and Tudor roses. In heraldry, the falcon denotes someone eager in the pursuit of an object that is fervently desired. It is a symbol of her successful quest for the English crown.

Coat-of-Arms of King François I of France

The coat-of-arms of the Valois monarchs of France was three gold fleurs-de-lis on a blue shield. The supporters of the royal arms were two angels, sometimes wearing a heraldic dalmatic. After the creation of the Order of Saint Michael in 1469, its collar was added to the royal arms.

Upon his accession in 1515, King François I selected the salamander as his personal emblem. It was a symbol of might, virtue, and strength, which conquers the fires of passion and triumphs over the vicissitudes of life. The salamanders are omnipresent at the châteaux built upon François' orders.

Coat-of-Arms of King Henry VIII of England

The coat-of-arms of the Tudor rulers of England was supported by the red dragon of Wales and a white greyhound. King Henry VII replaced the English lion with the white greyhound, for the latter reminded people of his Lancastrian lineage. A symbol of the Tudor dynasty, the red dragon was added upon the accession of Henry VII; it was later used by King Henry VIII and Queen Elizabeth I. The Tudor rose was the traditional floral heraldic emblem of the House of Tudor.

Coat-of-Arms of Charles V (Carlos V), Holy Roman Emperor

The complex arms of Charles V (Carlos V) showcased his many holdings. The quartered arms of Castile and Leon were quartered with the quartered arms of Aragon and Sicily. After 1520, the Aragon and Sicily parts also incorporated the arms of Naples, Jerusalem, and Navarre. The quartered arms of Austria, Duchies of Burgundy and of Brabant represented the emperor's Burgundian inheritance. In the middle, the escutcheon showed Flanders on the left and Tyrol on the right. At the bottom, there was the Granada pomegranate.

Cast of Characters in Between Two Kings

Queen Anne Boleyn

Anne is the chief female protagonist in *the Anne Boleyn Alternate History series*. She is former Queen of England, who accomplished the unachievable and replaced Catherine of Aragon, a princess of Spain, on the English throne. By a twist of fate, Anne follows in Eleanor of Aquitaine's marital footsteps.

Born to Sir Thomas Boleyn and Lady Elizabeth Boleyn née Howard, she was Queen of England from 1533 to 1536 as the second wife of King Henry VIII. To wed her, the English ruler broke with the Roman Catholic Church, but their marriage was not acknowledged by foreign Catholic nations. In history, Anne was beheaded on the 19th of May 1536 on the orders of her royal husband in his quest to obtain his freedom and marry the Lady Jane Seymour. However, this is an alternate history series, so many historical facts have been altered.

King François of France

François de Valois is the chief male protagonist in this series. He was the son of Charles d'Orléans, Count d'Angoulême, and Louise de Savoy. The first monarch from the Angoulême branch of the House of Valois, François reigned from 1515 until his death in 1547, although in this series his death is delayed.

A prodigious patron of the arts and a humanist, François ushered his country into an era of unparalleled enlightenment – the French Renaissance. He has been called the founder of the French Renaissance and a true Renaissance monarch, as well as *the Roi-Chevalier* (the

Knight-King) for his personal involvement in battles. His reign saw the gradual and steady rise of absolute monarchy in France. Amid the spread of humanism and Protestantism, he did not abjure the Catholic religion. Nevertheless, he was tolerant towards the heretics, although he endeavored to moderate the growing fanaticism.

King Henry VIII of England

Henry Tudor is another chief male character in this series. Born to King Henry VII of England and Queen Elizabeth of York in 1491, he was the second Tudor monarch from 1509 until his death in 1547. He was the first English monarch to rule as King of Ireland.

His reign brought epoch-making changes and marked England's gradual transition from a medieval to a modern nation. Henry is best known for his six marriages and his unprecedented executions of his two wives – Anne Boleyn and Catherine Howard, both of whom were each other's cousins. Henry is also famous for his attempt to have his first marriage to Catherine of Aragon annulled throughout many years. He broke from Rome to wed Anne, appointed himself Supreme Head of the Church of England, started religious reform in his realm, and ordered the dissolution of the monasteries.

Members of the English Court

Jane Seymour. Born to Sir John Seymour and Lady Margery Wentworth, she succeeded Anne Boleyn as Queen of England after her rival's execution. Jane was Henry VIII's third wife until her death of postnatal complications soon after the birth of her son.

Mary Tudor. Born to Henry VIII and his first wife, Catherine of Aragon, in 1516, she survived to adulthood, unlike all of the couple's other children. She was declared illegitimate and stripped of her succession rights after her father's wedding to Anne Boleyn.

Elizabeth Tudor. The daughter of Henry VIII and his second wife, Anne Boleyn, the girl was declared the heir presumptive to the English throne after her birth in 1533. Later, she was proclaimed illegitimate after the annulment of her mother's union with the king.

Charles Brandon. The son of King Henry VII's standard-bearer, he was created Duke of Suffolk thanks to his close friendship with Henry VIII. He also was the monarch's brother-in-law through Brandon's third spouse – Princess Mary Tudor, Dowager Queen of France.

Thomas Cromwell. A baseborn and yet talented man, he built a brilliant career serving as chief minister to Henry VIII from 1532. He assisted his sovereign in procuring an annulment of the king's union with Catherine of Aragon so that Henry could wed Anne Boleyn. Cromwell was one of the most powerful advocates of religious reform in England.

Thomas Howard, 3rd Duke of Norfolk. A prominent and powerful politician, as well as uncle to Henry VIII's two beheaded wives – Anne Boleyn and Catherine Howard.

Henry Percy, 6th Earl of Northumberland. He was once betrothed to the young Anne Boleyn, but he was compelled to give her up when she caught the king's eye.

Thomas Boleyn. He married Lady Elizabeth Howard, by whom he had three surviving children – Mary, George, and Anne. A competent diplomat and politician, he was elevated to the peerage as Viscount Rochford after Henry VIII began pursuing his daughter, Anne. During Anne's rise to power, he also garnered more titles: Earl of Wiltshire and of Ormond.

Elizabeth Boleyn née Howard. Daughter of Thomas Howard, 2nd Duke of Norfolk, she married Thomas Boleyn sometime in the late 15th century. She became Viscountess

Rochford, as well as Countess of Ormond and of Wiltshire during Anne's courtship with the English monarch.

Mary Stafford née Boleyn. Anne's elder sister was one of the mistresses of Henry VIII for an unknown period of time. She is also considered to have been a short-term paramour of King François I, although it has never been proved. She was banished from court after her second marriage.

William Stafford. An Essex landowner, and second husband of Mary Boleyn.

Edward Seymour. The eldest brother of Queen Jane, he became the king's brother-in-law after her marriage. He was created Viscount Beauchamp and Earl of Hertford.

Thomas Seymour. Another brother of Queen Jane, he was created 1st Baron Seymour of Sudeley after the monarch's wedding to his sister, Jane.

Elizabeth Seymour. A sister to Queen Jane, she married Gregory Cromwell, the only son of Thomas Cromwell, after the death of her first husband in 1534.

Margery Seymour née Wentworth. Sir John Seymour's widow, she had several children: Queen Jane, Edward, Thomas, Henry, Elizabeth, and Dorothy.

Thomas Cranmer. Appointed Archbishop of Canterbury in 1532, he led the religious reform in England. He was a staunch ally of Anne Boleyn and the Boleyn faction.

Francis Bryan. A courtier and diplomat, he was one of Henry VIII's friends, who always retained the royal favor, unlike most of his contemporaries. He was also Anne Boleyn's cousin.

Catherine Brandon. She was the only daughter of Maria de Salinas, Catherine of Aragon's most loyal lady-in-waiting and close friend. She was *suo jure* 12th Baroness Willoughby de Eresby. Catherine became the fourth wife of Charles Brandon, Duchess of Suffolk, who acted as her guardian during his third marriage to the king's sister, Princess Mary.

Elizabeth Somerset née Browne. She was Countess of Worcester through marriage to Henry Somerset, 2nd Earl of Worcester. She served as a lady-in-waiting to Anne Boleyn and was the chief informant against the queen.

Anne Bassett. Born to Sir John Bassett and Honor Grenville, she is rumored to have attracted Henry VIII's attention between 1538 and 1540, becoming his mistress.

Jane Boleyn née Parker, Viscountess Rochford. She was the daughter of Henry Parker, 10th Baron Morley. She married George Boleyn, Viscount Rochford, brother of Anne Boleyn. Although many sources claim that Jane lied to Cromwell about Anne and George's incestuous relationship, this has never been proved. As a result, Jane Boleyn's true story has been obscured by propaganda, and she remains one of the most vilified figures in Tudor history.

William Kingston. A courtier, administrator, and soldier, he served as Constable of the Tower of London during much of Henry VIII's reign.

William Sandys. A diplomat and Lord Chamberlain, he was created Baron Sandys of the Vyne in 1519-1520. He is known to have been one of Henry VIII's favorites.

Richard Rich. The monarch knighted him. He became Attorney General of Wales and Solicitor General of England, in which capacity he worked under Thomas Cromwell.

William Butts. He served as the monarch's personal physician at court.

Elizabeth Boleyn née Wood. Through her marriage to Sir James Boleyn, she was Anne Boleyn's aunt. She was one of the five women who served Anne in the Tower.

Anne Shelton née Boleyn. She was the elder sister of Thomas Boleyn, Earl of Wiltshire, and an aunt of Anne Boleyn. She also attended Anne during her imprisonment.

Margaret Coffin née Dymoke and Mary Kingston née Scrope. They were Anne's companions in the Tower. Lady Kingston is said to have been present when Anne apologized to Lady Mary Tudor before her execution, and to have then delivered the apology to Mary.

Gregory Cromwell. He was the only surviving son and child of Thomas Cromwell, and his wife, Elizabeth Wyckes. Gregory was married to Elizabeth, Lady Ughtred, widow of Sir Anthony Ughtred; his spouse was a sister to Jane Seymour.

Members of the French Court

Marguerite de Valois (Marguerite d'Angoulême). Also known as Marguerite of Navarre, she was the Princess of France and Queen of Navarre through her second marriage to King Henri II of Navarre, as well as Duchess d'Alençon and de Berry. She and her brother, King François I, were responsible for the great intellectual and cultural revival in France – they were both godparents of the French Renaissance.

Henri de Valois, Dauphin of France. The second son of King François by his first wife, Claude of France, he became Dauphin of France upon the untimely and unexpected death of his elder brother – François III, Duke of Brittany, in 1536.

Charles de Valois. The third son of François I and Claude of France, he was at first Duke d'Angoulême. After the untimely demise of Dauphin François, he inherited the title of Duke d'Orléans, which had been previously held by his elder brother, Henri.

Diane de Poitiers. Widow of Louis de Brézé, Seigneur d'Anet, she was infamous for her long-term love affair with Dauphin Henri, despite their substantial age difference.

Anne de Pisseleu d'Heilly. She became François I's long-term *maîtresse-en-titre* in 1526 upon his return from his Spanish captivity. She wielded much power and influence at the Valois court. In 1534, the ruler married her off to Jean IV de Brosse, whom he created Duke d'Étampes.

Péronne de Pisseleu. One of Anne de Pisseleu's sisters, she served as her lady-in-waiting.

Catherine de' Medici. The only daughter of Lorenzo II de' Medici and Madeleine de La Tour d'Auvergne, she married Henri, Duke d'Orléans (later Dauphin of France), in 1533.

François de Tournon. He was an Augustinian monk who became Archbishop of Bourges and of Embrun, as well as a famed diplomat, courtier, and cardinal. An influential advisor to the French monarch, he effectively acted as France's foreign minister of the day.

Anne de Montmorency. Born to the ancient Montmorency family, he was a French general, as well as a statesman and diplomat. He became Baron de Montmorency after his father's death. Raised beside François I, he befriended his liege lord in childhood. His military talent, combined with the boyhood friendship of the king, saw him promoted to Marshal and Constable of France. In 1525, he was raised to Grand Master of France.

Claude d'Annebault. A military officer, he was appointed Marshal of France in 1538. He was also governor of Normandy and a powerful figure during the reign of King François I.

Jacques de la Brosse. A cupbearer to the monarch, he was also a soldier and diplomat.

Philippe de Chabot, Seigneur de Brion, Count de Charny and de Buzançois. Born into the ancient Chabot family, he was a companion of the French ruler in childhood. Upon François I's accession in 1515, many honors and estates were bestowed upon Chabot. After the Battle of Pavia in 1525, he was appointed Admiral of France and was known as Admiral de Brion.

Clément Marot. This illustrious Renaissance poet was patronized by King François and his sister, Marguerite. In 1524, he accompanied the monarch on his Italian campaign.

Mellin de Saint-Gelais. He was another far-famed Renaissance poet patronized by the Valois siblings. As a favored court poet, he was expected to compose poems for special occasions. He was also made Almoner to the dauphin and the royal librarian at Château de Blois.

Robert Stuart, Seigneur d'Aubigny. Also Count de Beaumont-le-Roger, he was a French soldier belonging to the family of Stuart of Darnley. He served as captain of the Scots Guard, or *the Garde Écossaise*, until his death in 1544.

Members of the Imperial Court

Charles V (Carlos V), Holy Roman Emperor and lord of many lands. Carlos was the eldest son of Philip von Habsburg and his wife, Juana of Castile, who was a daughter of Isabella of Castile and Ferdinand of Aragon (the Catholic monarchs). He is the chief antagonist in this series. The most powerful figure in Christendom, he is one of France's worst enemies. He ruled the Spanish Empire from 1516 and the Holy Roman Empire from 1519 after his election as emperor.

Eustace Chapuys. A Savoyard by birth, he diligently served Emperor Carlos as Imperial ambassador to England from 1529 until 1545. He was Anne Boleyn's sworn adversary and an unshakeable supporter of Catherine of Aragon and her daughter, Mary Tudor.

Francisco de los Cobos. He was the secretary of State and *Comendador* for the kingdom of Castile during the reign of Emperor Carlos, as well as a powerful advisor to him.

Fernando Álvarez de Toledo y Pimentel, 3rd Duke of Alba. Known as the Grand Duke of Alba in Spain and Portugal and as the Iron Duke in the Netherlands, Fernando was a Spanish noble, general, and diplomat, who was in high favor with both Carlos V and Philip (Felipe) II of Spain.

Fictional Characters

Jean Frédéric Roger de Ponthieu, Count de Montreuil. He is a fictional character, who was a close friend of François I's father and Thomas Boleyn. A French diplomat and nobleman, he served as the French ambassador to the Republic of Venice, where he lived after his retirement.

Eleanor Hampton. One of the ladies who attended Anne Boleyn in the Tower of London.

Father Esmond Belcher. A priest who served at the Chapel Royal of St Peter ad Vincula at the Tower of London.

Other Characters

Andrea Gritti. Despite his old age (born in 1455), he was the Doge of the Venetian Republic from 1523 to 1538, following a distinguished diplomatic and military career.

PROLOGUE

BETRAYED BY EVERYONE

May 17, 1536, the Tower of London, London, England

"The march of mortality has begun, Your Majesty. Now they are all walking to the scaffold." The soft female voice was laced with compassion and melancholy.

Anne Boleyn, the anointed Queen of England, turned her head to the young woman, who stood on top of a chair in front of a small window. The queen saw the sympathy written all over her face, and a smile of gratitude flitted across her own pale features. Although the ladies, who served her in the Tower, had been handpicked by Thomas Cromwell and were his spies, they all treated her as a queen, despite her disgrace, and some empathized with her sufferings.

The announcement tolled a mournful knell and dealt a crushing blow to Anne's soul, a reminder of her own imminent death. "Thank you," she replied as she rose from the bed.

Anne hastily crossed the chamber and stopped near the window. As Lady Anne Shelton climbed down from the chair, the queen took her place and peered out, fixing her eyes on the large crowd that had gathered on Tower Green. Chains of dread began pulling at her spirit.

George Boleyn, Viscount of Rochford, as the highest-ranking man among the condemned prisoners, faced the axe first. Her view was not perfect because of the lattice on the window, but Anne was still able to see Tower Green well enough. His expression without a trace of fear, her brother mounted the scaffold and made a speech before the throng; she regretted that she could not hear his final words.

His countenance tranquil and dignified, George knelt at the block. A petrified Anne watched the executioner practice strokes several times above her brother's neck, then swing the axe high in the air and down, landing with a resounding crack. An instant later, George's severed head fell into a pile of straw, and a spray of blood spurted out of his body.

The queen's features whitened to a ghostly pallor, and her jaw dropped in shock. Waves of unbearable pain washed over her, pummeling her like storm-driven tides lashing a hapless shore. George, her favorite brother, was dead! Anne would never see George again, would never rely upon his support, advice, and consolation. Only two pieces were left of him.

Her throat constricted, and tears pricked at the back of her eyes, all her energy drained away. However, Anne steeled herself against the devastating emotions and watched. She did not move until the scaffold was littered with mutilated corpses, until all of her alleged lovers – George Boleyn, Mark Smeaton, William Brereton, Henry Norris, and Francis Weston – were no longer in the world of the living, caught in the coils of the fiendish conspiracy waged against her.

The universe was now tinged in crimson hues of slaughter, and the deities of death were performing a gruesome dance across the room. Unable to contain her pain any longer, Anne howled with horror, descended from her chair, and collapsed to the floor in a heap. She buried her head in her hands, her screams dissolving into blood-curdling wails of despair.

Anne did not care who heard her. "Why? Why? Why?"

Moved by such awful grief, the queen's ladies, witnessing this woeful scene, cried as well.

Lady Eleanor Hampton approached Anne. "Your Majesty, please..." She stopped speaking, uncertain about what to say until empathy took over. "Let me help you get to bed."

The distraught Queen of England wept and wept. Her anguished heart hurt so much that she wondered how it was possible to still be alive. Anne cried so hard that she could not breathe, releasing the stress of the past weeks in an abysmal lake of tears. Her world was in ruins like ancient Troy.

"We are all innocent!" bemoaned Anne. "I've loved King Henry, my lord and husband, for years! I've never sinned against him with my body and mind!" Her visage contorted as a sob racked her trembling form. "Why did he kill them? Why does he want me dead?"

The others gasped and shuddered in dread, for it was high treason to speak such words.

Anne cried until she had no more tears to shed. Her whole being was fractured with the enormity of the inequitable executions which had just taken place. Finally, she was able to summon sufficient self-control to calm down and stood up. She wobbled to the bed in chilling silence.

"They shall find peace in heaven." The queen settled herself on the bed.

Lying on the bed, Anne struggled to comprehend why her husband, King Henry VIII of England, believed the absurd story of her multiple adulteries, incest, and other acts of treason. Thomas Cromwell had orchestrated her plight. But what was Henry's role in it? Had Cromwell deliberately misled the monarch? Or did the ruler know that all the accusations against her were false, but chose not to care, wishing to end their marriage without another lengthy divorce?

The deposed queen reckoned that Henry had not commanded his chief minister to fabricate the charges; it was all Cromwell's conspiracy against her. Yet, it changed nothing because her beloved brother and the other men were all *murdered by the king*. Anne ruminated on how Henry now fancied himself in love with Jane Seymour and, driven by his lust for that plain, undereducated wench, was ready to go to any lengths to rid himself of his inconvenient wife.

Anne looked across at her ladies, who kept at a little distance from her.

Her lips curled in a bitter grin. "My only fault is that I've not birthed Henry's son, whom he desires to have the most."

"Your Majesty..." one of the women commenced, then abruptly trailed off.

"Leave me be," the queen enjoined. "I'll mourn for them in silence."

They nodded and curtsied; then they retired to the opposite side of the room.

The queen snuggled into rough linen sheets, nasty and uncomfortable. She closed her eyes, endeavoring to block out the harrowing reality. "My God... Why?"

Everyone had betrayed Anne: they had all left her like rats running away from a sinking ship, even her father. Her loneliness was so deep and sharp, as if she had been hollowed out. For the first time, she abhorred her husband with every fiber of her being; Henry's horrendous betrayals embodied festering wounds on her heart, all of them putrid and vile.

"I do hate you with all my soul, Henry," hissed Anne under her breath. "I shall never forgive you for the atrocities you have committed in your quest for freedom from me."

CHAPTER 1

An Unexpected Discovery

May 18, 1536, the Tower of London, London, England

"I'm doomed," Anne whispered to herself with resignation. "They will gladly wash their hands in my blood. Death begins its walk towards us the day we are born, but the fact that one passes away does not prove that they lived. And I've lived and loved like no one else!"

Anne Boleyn, Queen of England, rested upon a bed, its headboard carved with lions, which dominated the sparsely furnished chamber. Her heart was fragmenting with pain, as if the merciless hands of destiny were pulling it apart. Her thoughts reeled like a trapped bird flinging itself against the bars of a cage in vain attempts to regain its freedom, but only succeeding in hurting itself more and more.

Despite it being a fine May day outside, it was chilly inside the Tower apartments, where she had been confined since her arrest. The cold weather mirrored the chill in her soul. The stark reality was dreadful: Anne had been accused of multiple adulteries, of enjoying an incestuous relationship with her own brother, George, and of plotting the English monarch's murder. The latter charge was a veiled accusation of treason because her husband was the King of England.

It was truly ludicrous that the queen, who was always attended by her ladies, could have had numerous secret lovers for such a long time. In several cases, her alleged paramours had not even been present at the places where her prosecutors claimed she had undertaken illicit encounters with them. There was no evidence whatsoever that she had plotted the ruler's death. Her trial had been an unjust farce! Twenty-six peers of the English realm had declared her guilty of all charges, and Anne had been unjustly condemned to be either beheaded or burned according to the king's pleasure.

Thomas Cranmer, Archbishop of Canterbury, entered. Anne rose from the bed and stepped to him, smiling at him; Cranmer could not save her, and she viewed him as a friend.

In the next moment, Sir William Kingston, Constable of the Tower of London, walked in.

The queen's ladies watched their mistress with doleful expressions from a distance. During these weeks, she had been attended by five women, who had served either Catherine of Aragon or her daughter, Mary Tudor. Anne knew that they were all obliged to report anything she might say or do to William Kingston, while he, in turn, informed Cromwell about the prisoner's behavior.

Archbishop Cranmer lowered his gaze. "My lady, I bring word from the king." He sighed. "Your marriage to His Majesty has been annulled." Grief shadowed his expression.

Anne stared at him with unseeing eyes, and her heart compressed into a dense ball of distress. The words of Henry's denial of their matrimony sounded in her mind like the tolling of a funeral bell. How was it possible? Among her turbulent emotions, disbelief overrode all others.

"Has it really happened, Your Grace?" Her universe was breaking, piece by piece, into fragments, and she felt as utterly hopeless as a captain at sea might if marooned without a compass to guide him.

"I'm so sorry, Madame." Cranmer averted his eyes, his dejected sigh wafting through the air. "Your daughter, the

Lady Elizabeth, has been declared a bastard." He veered his gaze back to her.

A ghastly blend of anguish and fear engulfed Anne Boleyn. Questions flew through her mind like arrows seeking a target in the dead of night. Why was Henry treating both her and their daughter so brutally? Why and when did he become such an iron-hearted beast? Even though she had fallen from his good graces, why did he punish their innocent child?

Her inability to find these answers shackled Anne in the chains of endless misery with no hope of liberation. *Why is Henry so pitiless to me? His deeds symbolize the very essence of ruthlessness. I loved him more than life itself, but he ceased feeling anything even vaguely resembling affection for me.* He wanted to cause her more heartache by annulling their union only a matter of days before her scheduled execution. Henry's cruelty was as boundless as the sky.

The *former* queen composed herself with a gargantuan effort. Her fathomless dark pools gleamed with warped humor. "This surprise is the best gift His Majesty could grant me. Of course, he has played his last trump card, but I should have expected that."

The archbishop blanched. "Madame, please."

A semblance of contrition suffused her face. "I don't know what has come over me."

Once more, Cranmer found himself impressed with the self-control she was now displaying. "I promise I'll do my best to safeguard and help your daughter in any way I can."

A grateful Anne murmured, "Thank you very much."

The time for her last confession had arrived. "Your Grace, I beseech you to hear my last confession." Her gaze oscillated between the archbishop and the constable. "I'd like Master Kingston to stay and listen to me when I confess the truth."

She wanted Constable William Kingston to hear everything for an eminently important reason. His witnessing her last confession on earth meant that there was a small chance that in the future, the people of England, including the Tudor monarch, would learn of her innocence.

Kingston nodded. "As you wish, Madame."

Cranmer took a seat, and Anne knelt in front of him. As she focused her scrutiny on him, his heart twisted in helpless agony at the sight of the great woman whom he loved dearly.

"Madame, speak honestly and truthfully," intoned the archbishop.

"Yes." Anne dragged a deep and shuddering breath, as if it were her last. "Before the Lord, I confess my innocence of all the charges brought against me. I swear upon my eternal soul that I've never been unfaithful to King Henry, my lord and husband, although I've not always treated him with the obedience, respect, and humility which I owed him as a wife."

The *former* queen paused for another breath, and then continued in a voice layered with confidence, "God is all-seeing and knows that I'm innocent." She trailed off, leaned forward, and grabbed the Bible from a nearby table. "The Almighty is my witness that during my relationship with His Majesty, never once, by word or look, have I made the slightest attempt to interest any other man in my humble person. I was a true maid when the king first took me to his bed."

A crestfallen silence reigned in the chamber. A muted sadness hung in the air.

Anne proceeded, "I do not say this in the desperate hope that His Majesty will exonerate me of all the phony charges, for I've accepted my fate. Nevertheless, there is something that you must all know." Her eyes blazing with an inner fire of truth, she promulgated, *"I'm carrying King Henry's child."*

A ripple of astonishment flitted through the group of women, who had also heard it.

In these moments of her triumph, Anne felt herself like a messenger of a higher power that had charged her with divine strength. "On the eve of my execution, I've realized that I'm pregnant. Fate has a bizarre sense of humor, don't you think so? I've felt rather unwell during the past few weeks, but I attributed my sickness to the horror of my situation and to my constant stress. Now I have no doubt as to my condition, and I'm certain that a physician shall confirm everything."

"This is the Almighty's holy doing!" A smile of hope illumined Cranmer's face.

All pairs of amazed eyes were glued to the former mistress of their sovereign's heart.

Still on her knees in front of the archbishop, she crossed herself. "I solemnly swear that the king's child is growing inside of me. I beg you to allow it to be born. Regardless of what might befall me in the future, my baby is innocent of any crime – it must live."

"Lady Anne, I shall do everything to aid you, especially now." Cranmer removed the Bible from her hands and then clasped them in his own. "This child is a blessing."

Tears burned like red-hot pokers behind her eyes. "Your Grace, Elizabeth and this child will need friends after my death. His Majesty will not spare me, but my babe must live."

"Madame, I cannot guarantee that..." The archbishop's voice faltered.

Her cheeks glistened with silvery tears that suggested an indescribable heartache. "I'm sorry for the sins that I've really committed. Sometimes, I was callous to those who did not deserve it. However, I do not dread the loss of heaven and the pains of hell, because the Lord forgives those who repent, and my contrition is sincere."

Anne inclined her head after finishing her confession. At this moment, she looked so humble, so gentle, and so honest that her touching beauty tugged at everyone's heartstrings.

Her ladies were now crying. Having heard Anne speak from the bottom of her heart, they no longer believed that their mistress was guilty of the allegations leveled against her.

Archbishop Cranmer made the sign of a cross on the doomed woman's forehead. "Master Kingston, go fetch a doctor and a midwife. As Lady Anne asked you to stay in order to share her last confession with the world, never forget this day and comply with her request."

Kingston stood up and bowed. "You have my word."

In half an hour, the doctor and the midwife appeared in the queen's apartments. After a careful examination, they voiced their conclusion – Anne was indeed pregnant.

§§§

That evening, Anne Boleyn stood near the window, watching an eerie darkness blanket the firmament. It might be her last night on earth. Would God interfere? Would she be saved? She was a realist: the king would no doubt insist that the father of her baby was one of her alleged lovers.

To distract herself from these traumatic musings, she resorted to a mental journey into her early youth: her carefree childhood at Hever Castle with her siblings, Mary and George, and her parents – Elizabeth and Thomas Boleyn, who had been such a loving father back then.

With fondness, Anne reminisced about her years at the cultured court of Archduchess Margaret of Austria. A small girl in 1513, she had been one of Margaret's eighteen *filles d'honneur.* Margaret had hired a suitable tutor to teach Anne the French language and the sophistication of court life; Anne had been so eager to join the various entertainments.

Yet, I preferred my blithesome time at the French court, where, despite my youth, I served to Queen Claude of France, King François' first wife. These were the golden years of her adolescence. Anne had stayed with Queen Claude for nearly seven years, spending most of that time in the Loire Valley, at Châteaux Amboise and Blois, where the queen had resided.

The English court could not rival the far more refined European courts. Thus, Anne had focused on acquiring a profound knowledge of French etiquette and courtesy while having lived in majestic Renaissance splendor in France. She had completed her study of the French language and cultivated her interests in fashions, humanism, theology, music, and the arts. However, Anne's life had not always been public since Queen Claude had spent much time in confinement during her annual pregnancies.

Marguerite de Valois, King François' beloved sister, Anne recalled cordially as she envisaged the Valois woman. *The influence of this highly intelligent, superbly educated, and politically astute woman shaped my personality in many ways.* At the time, Marguerite had been the Duchess d'Alençon; now she was the Queen of Navarre through her marriage to King Henri II of Navarre. Marguerite was a prominent patron of painters, humanists, poets, and even reformers, as well as a talented author herself. She had encouraged her circle to engage in discussions on a variety of topics, and Anne had participated in these. Anne hoped that Marguerite would remember her fondly.

With this comforting thought, a flood of half-hope, half-relief swarmed the condemned woman, refusing to be contained – Anne chortled merrily, as if genuinely amused by something. Her ladies-in-waiting granted her odd looks, but Anne's smile widened, and she laughed again. Nonetheless, burdened by the hopelessness and injustice of her situation, her mood then swerved to one of deep despondency. Staring into the darkness, she swallowed hard, suppressing sobs.

A whole swarm of memories of Henry whirled through her brain, and a wave of dismay assaulted her as she reflected on their relationship. Henry had been so passionately in love with her, and she with him. Her mind drifted through memories of their long, romantic courtship. The monarch's countless professions of love and his promises echoed through her mind like a sardonic snicker, taunting her – by now, each of them had proved to be worthless and meaningless.

Images of her little beloved Elizabeth inundated her head. Henry had been utterly disappointed with the birth of a healthy daughter, but Anne loved Elizabeth with every fibre of her being since the midwife had placed the baby girl into her arms. An intense cold swept over her at the remembrance of how two unborn children had died in her womb. Her second miscarriage had been triggered by the shock Anne had felt upon seeing Henry's adulterous kiss with Jane Seymour, who had been sitting in his lap.

That night, sleep eluded Anne for a long time, and she lay on the bed, staring at the ceiling pretending to be asleep, but listening to her ladies' quiet conversation.

Her two aunts – Lady Anne Shelton née Boleyn, Thomas Boleyn's elder sister, and Lady Elizabeth Boleyn née Wood, Sir James Boleyn's wife, Anne's uncle – sat together at the table.

In a voice colored with total incredulity, Lady Anne Shelton murmured, "What an unexpected and bewildering turns of events! What will happen tomorrow?"

"The execution should be rescheduled, but we cannot guess the outcome." Lady Elizabeth Boleyn's utterance was more in hope than belief that the monarch would reprieve her niece.

Three other ladies approached and settled themselves around the table.

Lady Eleanor Hampton chimed in, "A pregnant woman cannot be sent to the scaffold."

"That would be unlawful," stressed Lady Margaret Coffin.

"Indeed," Lady Mary Kingston concurred. "But her fate is sealed after the birth of the child."

Lady Boleyn heaved a sigh. "It must be His Majesty's babe." Everyone nodded in concurrence.

"That is all so very unfair," muttered Margaret Coffin. Her companions dipped their heads.

Anne squeezed her eyes shut, her world narrowing to concerns about the little creature she already loved. Sliding her palms under her nightgown, she lay them flat against her stomach. *Henry, you would not dare murder a pregnant woman... That would imperil your immortal soul! Or would you?* She then busied herself with praying fervently for her daughter, Elizabeth, and her unborn child.

May 19, 1536, Palace of Whitehall, London, England

The first rays of the spring sun warmed the white ashlar stone walls of Whitehall, the former York Place, which had once been owned by the late Cardinal Wolsey. The building was still being extended and redesigned, and King Henry had invested heavily in this project, planning to make it a grand masterpiece of Tudor architecture to rival the majestic Renaissance palaces of his French counterpart.

It was a little past dawn and several hours before Anne's execution. In spite of the early hour, the court was wide-awake, and a sense of anticipation was palpable in the air.

§§§

The royal apartments were alive with the morning traffic of servants. King Henry VIII had been woken early as Thomas Cromwell requested an immediate audience with him.

"Damn Cromwell," the monarch cursed as he yawned. "It must be something extraordinarily urgent if my chief minister dared ignore the official protocol regarding the rules and hours for gaining an audience with me."

Henry rested upon a large bed canopied with red brocade cloth. The oak furniture, spectacularly ornate and massive, was tastefully arranged around the chamber. The mahogany bedside tables were decorated with marble sculptures. The walls were hung with stunning and expensive Flemish tapestries depicting the lives of Jesus Christ and the Apostles.

An old man, his wrinkled face sharp-chinned, approached the royal bed. His once strawberry blonde hair had faded to a rusty graying color, and now it almost matched his pale brown serge attire. He was William Sandys, Baron Sandys of the Vyne and Lord Chamberlain of the royal household, as well as the king's favorite.

"Good morning, Your Majesty," began Sandys in an official manner. "Which clothes should we prepare?"

The ruler's face split into a grin. "I'll wear vibrant colors today."

"As you wish." Lord Chamberlain aided him to climb out of bed.

With a menacing air about him, Henry pontificated, "History will remember this day forever. The Boleyn witch shall be punished for her odious crimes against God and her sovereign. Neither my court nor I will mourn for her. I've decided to wear the color blood red."

"This color suits you, sire," responded William Sandys, his features shock-whitened. His feelings over Anne Boleyn's execution were conflicted, but it was not his place to decide.

The monarch stood dressed in a red silk taffeta shirt embroidered with threads of gold. His doublet of crimson brocade glittered with rubies and diamonds. Scarlet silk hose were pulled up his legs and fixed to points hanging from around his waist. A purple velvet cap with a red ostrich feather was placed upon his head, and a gold chain with rubies adorned his neck. It was as though his attire symbolized the slaughter of the Boleyn adulteress, which the ruler craved.

Henry marched to the presence chamber, passing many courtiers, who all bowed and curtsied as he strutted forward, but he acknowledged only a few with a slight nod.

Burly and powerfully built, the handsome English ruler inspired sheer awe and yet terror of his power. Not all of his subjects were comfortable when that aquamarine gaze, intense and hard, came to rest upon them. Broad of face, his rather small eyes and a well-formed, yet petulant and not large at all, mouth, sat beneath the short, straight, auburn hair that showed from beneath his cap.

Henry towered majestically a head above most of his court, although his French archrival, King François I of France, was taller, which stirred jealousy in him. Henry had inherited the attractive looks of his maternal grandfather, King Edward IV, and carried the best of the York and Tudor features.

"Good morning, Your Majesty!" his nobles chorused.

The ruler's countenance was like that of a mighty sovereign without earthly peer, which usually impressed his subjects. Yet, today his appearance, tinged with hues of blood red, frightened them. His entire being exuded the savage darkness, which had always lurked within him, and it was now so close to the surface that courtiers could feel the breath of his inner beast.

§§§

As the king stormed into the presence chamber, Thomas Cromwell dropped into a deep bow.

A silence, full of trepidation, reigned. Henry paced to and fro, like a lion caged in an ancient amphitheater. He paid no attention to the room's grandeur and its elaborately carved oak furniture, decorated with figures of Jupiter, the supreme God of the Roman pantheon. On the walls there were tapestries portraying the life of Gaius Julius Caesar. At his feet, a costly carpet of cloth woven with gold threads took the brunt of his relentless march across the room.

Finally, Henry stopped near the marble fireplace and peered at his chief minister. In a voice laced with impatience, he barked, "Master Cromwell, why are you here?"

His guest emitted a sigh. "I beg Your Majesty's pardon, but we have a grave problem."

The ruler growled, "The only problem I know of is about to be removed from this earth. The Tower is where you must be ensuring that this is so!"

The advisor was immensely skilled at masking his emotions. However, the unforeseen turn of events had unnerved him a great deal, making it rather difficult to keep an inscrutable demeanor. "Sire, you have always been clever and shrewd; your guess is correct."

"What is it?" demanded the monarch.

"Lady Anne Boleyn is with child," proclaimed Cromwell.

"What?" rasped a nonplussed Henry, his eyes venomous caverns.

BETWEEN TWO KINGS

At Cromwell's nod, the king's blank façade cracked wide open. Henry blanched as a mixture of shock, bewilderment, anger, pain, and disappointment passed through him.

Questions circled the Tudor monarch's mind like vultures preying upon him. How could Anne carry a child, and who was its father? Was it a dark irony of fate or the Lord's blessing? Why was it happening now, when he was so close to getting his freedom? Was heaven laughing at him?

Anne Boleyn played with me like a toy. She made me fall for her to ensure her family's enrichment and elevation. I was a fool to believe that whore! She wanted only the crown for herself and power for the Boleyns! Such were Henry's scornful thoughts about the woman whom he had once worshipped. She must have been taught by her vile father and her brother how to set herself in his way and to ensnare him. They had calculated every step of their ascent to power.

When an enamored Henry had offered the adulteress to be his mistress, Anne had sworn with soul-stirring fervor that she would give her maidenhead only to her husband. Whatever purity she had brought to their bed, Henry now believed it was sullied, and all of it pretense. Anne had never loved him! She must have feigned her virginity! All her fake amorous words were as poisonous as those siren songs that drew sailors to the rocks and certain doom. Anne's faux gentleness and sweetness had almost ruined him.

To make the harlot his queen, Henry had disposed of Catherine of Aragon, his first wife. He had declared his daughter, Mary, a bastard. Henry had torn the country apart because Pope Clement VII would not grant the annulment of his union with Catherine. His battles with Rome had led to the separation of the Church of England from the Vatican. Anne Boleyn was the driving force of almost everything that had occurred in the country in the past several years.

BETWEEN TWO KINGS

I regret that I married Anne, Henry lamented wordlessly. *That whore made me the laughingstock of Europe when she birthed a girl – not the boy she promised me. Now my fellow kings must be snickering at me because of her illicit affairs.* A daughter was useless: only a son could guarantee the smooth succession and the continuation of the Tudor dynasty. Just as unforgivably, Anne had lost a male child at the start of the year, after she had seen Henry with Jane Seymour sitting on his knee, and then she had blamed him for the tragedy.

The ruler's love for Anne, which had once been the most ennobling expression of chivalric devotion, had evolved into a murderous hatred that consumed his soul. In April, his chief minister and the Duke of Suffolk had reported that Anne had entertained men in her rooms. The investigation had revealed that she had cuckolded Henry with at least five courtiers and committed another abominable crime – incest.

In a voice as sharp as a million of swords, the king snarled, "I crave to spill the slut's blood. Her sins are irredeemable." His wrathful glare slid to Cromwell. "I want Anne dead."

"Your Majesty, under the laws of England, we cannot send a pregnant woman to the block." Cromwell did need Anne gone as soon as possible. He was a man of action and never admitted any hesitation in carrying out the royal commands, but he could not allow a baby of royal blood to die.

After a brief pause, Henry spoke in a more controlled voice edged with a trace of clear distrust. "Anne has always been a good actress. Are you sure she is with child?"

Cromwell bobbed his head. "Yes, I am. The physician and the midwife both confirmed her condition. We will have to wait until her baby's birth. Only then she can be punished."

The ruler flinched at the sudden remembrance of the several nights he had spent with Anne in March despite Lent when his male hunger had overcome him, but he thrust these thoughts aside. Anne could not be expecting his child! Her bastard was of no importance to him. Definitely, Henry would have a brood of legitimate, healthy children with his beloved Jane, who was so lovely and obedient – an ideal wife for him.

The king's face screwed up in disgust. "This baby could be the product of incest."

"It could have been fathered by any of her lovers."

Cromwell had inflamed his anger, so the monarch roared, "Anne is the worst whore ever! She lured me into marriage by means of sorcery! Is this babe not the result of witchcraft?"

After more pacing back and forth, Henry threw himself into a green-brocaded chair. Cromwell stood quietly, smiling inwardly, pleased that his scheming had come to fruition.

The hands of Chronos, the Greek God of time, were pulling the monarch to a point where his life would be changed forever. The Almighty had taken the matter of Anne's death out of his hands, and he could not kill her today, despite his antagonism towards her. Why was everything against her death? As his gaze flicked to a nearby tapestry depicting Julius Caesar crossing the Rubicon, he made a fateful choice.

The ruler sighed with aggravation. "As unfortunately I'm bound by law, I must allow the Boleyn harlot to live until her bastard's birth." A rueful laughter boomed out of him. "I feel as if I were Caesar entering Italy under arms. His close friend, Gnaeus Pompeius Magnus, betrayed him, just as Anne betrayed me. However, Caesar's victory in the civil war put him in an unrivaled position of power. When that prostitute dies in several months, I shall prevail as well."

His chief minister sought to reassure him. "Lady Anne's execution will be a new beginning for Your Majesty. Your life will be long and happy, unlike Caesar's."

"Of course. God has blessed me to rule England for many years." Henry's thoughts went to the keeper of his heart. "I'll wed Lady Jane Seymour as planned."

"It would be better to postpone the ceremony until Lady Anne's death. Then nobody would ever doubt the legitimacy of any future children born in Your Majesty's new marriage."

Reluctantly, Henry saw the truth in these words. "Indeed, my sons must be untainted."

A golden future without troubles stretched before the King of England. A future with his dearest Jane and many male heirs out of her body. How fortunate Henry was that he and Jane had found each other, and soon they would forge a marriage of love and commitment. The rest of his reign would initiate a Golden Age of peace and prosperity for the Tudor dynasty and England, one that would be better than *the Pax Romana* of the first Roman Emperor Caesar Augustus.

In the omnipresent silence that followed, the castle clock chimed a soft melody, marking the time. The course of Europe's history had been altered irrevocably for all time. Yet, was it to Henry's benefit? A strong sense of premonition stole over the monarch, coiling around the edifice of his dreams like the eerie fog that frequently enveloped Whitehall.

CHAPTER 2

Birth of a Tudor Prince

September 30, 1536, the Tower of London, London, England

"I'll be dead soon, little one," Anne whispered to herself, as she stretched on the bed. She placed a hand on her enlarged stomach. "Your father will kill me after your birth."

She had spent many ghastly months in a living hell that was far worse than the nine circles of hell in *'Inferno'* by Dante Alighieri. Anne wanted to breathe fresh air, but she was not allowed to leave the confines of her chamber. She constantly feared that she would not carry the child to full term. Feeling weak and weary, Anne attributed her state to the poor living conditions and to her deep-seated depression.

A midwife usually examined all female prisoners, for under English law a pregnant woman could not be put to death. In Anne's case, this rule had been omitted. Did it occur to Henry that she could be carrying his baby? He must remember that he had bedded her several times in the second half of March; those had been their last nights together. Had the king become such a monster that he was willing to murder his own unborn child? Or was it only Cromwell's idea?

The Constable of the Tower – Sir William Kingston, the king's ageing and powerful servant – took pleasure in carrying out his duties with the utmost severity and even malice. Just as during her previous pregnancies, Anne craved apples, but these were forbidden, and nor was she to receive any special food. These were prohibited on Cromwell's strict orders.

The constable's spouse, Lady Mary Kingston, who was much kinder to Anne, approached the royal bed. "Master Cromwell is asking for an audience with you, Madame."

Anne peered at the woman in bemusement. Why did her arch accuser come to the Tower? She scrambled out of bed, and jested, her brow quirking satirically, "Does the king's chief minister need the permission of a miserable prisoner to conduct an interview?"

Lady Kingston stammered, "My lady... What should I... tell him?"

There was a concerted gasp from all the ladies, who clustered at the other end of the room.

"I don't need anyone's assent," affirmed Thomas Cromwell from the doorway. He had heard Anne's caustic rejoinder and now made his presence known.

Anne's pun was acrid. "Welcome to my humble abode, my esteemed Master Cromwell. High and mighty men such as yourself are innocent of all the evil done by them."

He walked to the center of the room and dismissed her maids with an arrogant wave of his hand. They scurried out.

Cromwell's eyes roamed over his victim's figure. "Are you well fed?"

"As well as you can see, Master Cromwell. You are staring at me so!"

The chief minister perused Anne again. She was garbed in a gray satin gown, with a modestly cut neckline, and a cross on a silver chain dangled from her neck. Oddly, Anne now looked more scintillating than if she had been adorned with jewels. There was a transcendental aura about her, as if impending doom had elevated her to the rarefied realm of martyred saints. *God's teeth, our liege lord's child will be born in the Tower.* His gaze lingered on her swollen belly.

The chief minister commenced in a deadly tone, "That is enough out of you, Madame. There is no excuse for your offensive speeches about His Majesty's most trusted and loyal advisor. Your manners have worsened. Do not try your sorcerous wiles on me – I assure you that they will not work."

Her distress crystallized into anger. "Because you want me to stop? I'll not obey you."

His wintry gaze fixed unwaveringly upon her for several increasingly tense moments before he articulated in an icy tone, "I have power, and you do not, my lady."

Her dark eyes blazing with rage, Anne took a step towards him. "The depth of your wickedness and perfidy is immeasurable! You hatched a plot against me because I opposed your religious plans. Your yearning to destroy the Catholic Church in England pushed you to betray those who aided you to build a political career. The deaths of all those men unjustly condemned are on your conscience."

His lips curled in a cynical smile. "You are in no position to threaten me."

"True, Master Cromwell, I can no longer stop you. You can steal from all of the monasteries and abbeys in the country without caring for the needs of the commoners. However, you underestimate the people's forbearance, and one day, your policy will stir up an unprecedented rebellion."

"The dissolution shall proceed as planned."

Anne's features softened with a twinge of deep sadness. "I cannot help imagining what would have been if our views on reform had not diverged so radically. I could still have been queen, and my unborn child would have been a legitimate heir to the Tudor throne." Her hand slid to her abdomen.

Cromwell surveyed her with a sort of reminiscent wonder. He had not forgotten that they had once been allies, and Anne had encouraged the monarch's decision to break from the Catholic Vatican. Suddenly, a strong tide of sentimentality, uncharacteristic for him, swept over him with such a colossal strength that it almost induced a short-lived feeling of contrition for his conspiracy against her.

He truly admired Anne Boleyn, one of the most brilliant, superbly educated, and most unusual women in England, maybe in the entirety of Christendom. If only the vicissitudes of life had not transformed the English king from an intelligent, virtuous, and celebrated Tudor prince into the mercurial, bloodthirsty, narcissistic monster he had become. Henry could have ruled wisely with his wife's counsel, and perhaps there would have been a grand intellectual revival in England to rival that of the sophisticated European courts.

Nonetheless, now the wheel of fate was spinning in the opposite direction. Anne's intelligence, as well as her willful and outspoken spirit, had ceased being a boon to King Henry. She had made numerous foes, and they perceived her as a terrible nuisance – many wanted her dead or at least banished. The ruler had sought to dissolve his union with Anne, and now Cromwell needed her gone as well.

If only there had been no animosity between us... To this day, Cromwell was not certain that he would have made a move to annihilate the Boleyns, if it were not for his liege lord's eagerness to end his marriage to Anne. However, it was pointless to dwell on what could have happened.

Her voice intruded upon his thoughts. "You pray and read the Bible. Are you not afraid of the Lord's wrath?" She saw the flash of fear in his eyes and rejoiced that she had struck a nerve.

"Everyone faces the Almighty's judgment after death."

Appealing to his finer senses would not work, so Anne tried another tack to unsettle him. "Betrayal begets revenge. An eye for an eye, a tooth for a tooth, and blood for blood."

Cromwell remained unmoved by her tirade. "You will suffer the punishment for your crimes against the Crown once you are delivered of your illegitimate child."

"How dare you call this babe a bastard!" Anne fumed as she stepped towards him. "You, of all people, are fully aware that I'm carrying the king's baby. Yes, you know that well!"

Once again, he wrestled with regret, but there was no way back. "Your father has refused to be your child's guardian, but Lady Mary Stafford intervened on your behalf."

Astonishment manifested on her visage. "My sister?

"Yes. Lady Stafford came to Whitehall and pleaded on her knees with the king to spare your life. Of course, she was escorted from the palace by guards, and His Majesty barred your sister from court on pain of death. He also acquiesced to her request to take the child into her household."

At this moment, Anne felt as if she had been the one to perpetrate the transgressions of all the sinners on earth. She had banished Mary from court after her wedding to William Stafford, a soldier without money and social standing. Yet, her elder sister had forgiven her and now shown generosity of spirit in endeavoring to save her, after even their own father had dissociated himself from them both. *I owe Mary a cosmic debt of gratitude, but I cannot repay it,* Anne lamented.

Cromwell needed to leave – to be away from his victim. "Madame, I bid you goodbye. Be thankful for your sister's benevolence – for myself, I care not." He strode to the door.

"Cromwell!" This compelled him to halt in this journey.

Her eyes shining with a prophetic light, Anne predicted, "Regardless of my fate, my children will rule England after Henry." Her voice rose to a crescendo. "The children of Anne the Harlot murdered by Henry the Tyrant, obsessed with begetting sons, will achieve what their father never will: they shall usher England into a new Golden Age! That is their destiny!"

"Aristotle," continued Anne sagaciously, "claimed that *'Moral excellence comes about as a result of habit. We become just by doing just acts, temperate by doing temperate acts, brave by doing brave acts.'* Who have you become, Cromwell? A villain who betrayed our former friendship and who is now ready to kill me and perhaps my child? How will you face the Lord when He calls you from earth?"

The dumbfounded chief minister felt that her statement had struck a chord of truth. *"When you are offended at any man's fault, turn to yourself and study your own failings,"* he parried. "Epictetus was a wise philosopher as well. Didn't you make your former friends your sworn foes, Madame?"

As he stalked out, Anne's ladies re-appeared, looking at their mistress with trepidation.

Anne's ire magnified into untrammeled fury. Letting out a shriek of rage, she swept the items on a nearby table to the floor with one swift movement of a hand. Then she staggered to the bed and ripped the covers off, grabbed a pillow, and threw it across the room, followed by another.

One of the pillows flew straight at Lady Kingston, who quickly caught it. "Lady Anne, you must stop this madness! Think of your child!"

Her throat clogged with unshed tears, Anne shrilled, "Leave me be!"

"No! We will not," Lady Boleyn and Lady Shelton objected in unison.

Anne banged her fist against the bed's headboard. "You do not understand what I feel!"

"Hush, Madame! You might lose your babe!" Lady Coffin said bluntly.

The ladies all empathized with Anne's woes. During her incarceration, Anne had spent most of the time in bed, reading the books Archbishop Cranmer had sent to her. At times, she talked with them about her youth in France and Flanders, and they always listened avidly to these tales of a larger world.

This statement hit Anne like a lash. "No! *He* shall not die!" She hugged her abdomen, as if protecting her unborn child from her own folly. "*He* shall be born healthy!"

Lady Hampton helped her lie down. "Lady Anne, you should sleep."

After her anger had deflated, Anne wept until there was not one tear left in her body. Her ladies feared a miscarriage or premature labor, an all-too-common occurrence.

As Anne calmed down, her thoughts meandered through her romance with King Henry. She had pushed him to make innovations in England, which had given him the intoxicating taste of unlimited power such as no English monarch had held before. At the end of their relationship, Henry was so callous towards both her and their daughter! Had this cruelty always been hidden within him? Had absolute power corrupted him? Or had that jousting accident caused the irreparable loss of sanity? When had he lost the last vestiges of his humanity?

I ignored the first signs when the king's passion for me began cooling off. Anne had failed to revive the impending corpse of her dying marriage. After seeing Jane Seymour sitting in the ruler's lap, she had lost her second child, and Henry had not even consoled her. Afterwards, he could not bear to look at Anne, not wanting to be in her presence for longer than a few minutes during official receptions. He blamed her for everything wrong in his life and kingdom.

If blinded by anger, Henry could be easily manipulated by others, especially Thomas Cromwell and Charles Brandon, Duke of Suffolk. The Brandon family had always hated Anne. Brandon's third wife – Mary Tudor, Dowager Queen of France and the king's sister – had loathed her to the point of staying away from court to show her detestation. Mary had been loyal to Catherine of Aragon and a devout Catholic, but then she had passed away, a month after Anne's coronation.

Since Suffolk's wedding to his young ward, Lady Catherine Willoughby, his aversion towards Anne had grown. The new Duchess of Suffolk despised Anne because her mother, Maria de Salinas, had once been a loyal lady-in-waiting to Catherine. Brandon's wife might have given Cromwell false information to help him crush the Boleyn faction. The Duke of Suffolk was constantly working to poison Henry's mind against Anne and her family, and doubtless he had participated in her downfall.

Why hadn't the monarch annulled their marriage and then expelled Anne? Why had there been the executions of all the accused? *I would have gone away quietly not to risk the lives of those innocent people caught up in this horror and not to leave my Elizabeth motherless.* The outcome was catastrophic for her, her relatives, and her supporters. She was hollowed out by grief, anguish, and loneliness.

November 21 and 22, 1536, the Tower of London, London, England

When Anne's waters broke in the late evening, mortal terror clasped her with its icy hands. To ward off the dark, her ladies lit many candles and placed them at the bedside tables.

The former queen attempted to pull herself into a sitting position, but she collapsed on top of the covers. The pain increased with every hour; the contractions coming more frequently as hours passed. From time to time, visions of King Henry and her, moments from their courtship and marriage, flashed in her brain like lightning, brilliantly illuminated, then gone, as a new wave of torturous muscle cramps assaulted her.

"Find a midwife," Anne instructed in a weak voice.

"Madame, I will, but let me aid you first." Lady Anne Shelton rushed towards the bed.

"Please," moaned Anne. "Go. It is hurting so much."

Lady Shelton pulled the covers up around her. Anne was shivering, yet her skin was moist and warm. The former queen was ghostly pale, her eyes full of suffering.

"I did not feel such pain during Elizabeth's birth," Anne complained. "I might die today!"

"You cannot give up." Lady Shelton covered her mouth with a hand to hide her consternation.

As she approached the bed, Lady Eleanor Hampton knelt to lend her moral support. "My lady, you must believe that all will be well. You must!"

Anne endeavored to sit again, but she fell back on the pillows. "Almighty Lord, save my child."

The child was still not born by the late afternoon of the next day. The labor complications were caused not only by Anne's difficult pregnancy, but also by her utter emotional devastation and physical exhaustion. The former queen was so weak that she had passed out twice, and they had awakened her by splashing cold water onto her face. Bloodstained sheets lay in disordered heaps around the bed.

At the next onslaught of the excruciating sensations, which were shredding her insides, Anne dug her fingers into the sheets. Her face was white, as if all its color had been drawn into the darkness of her eyes. She murmured something inaudible, and then lay still for a while.

"It is bad." The midwife was shaking her head in despair.

The seemingly doomed woman writhed in agony and screamed, as if she had been stabbed by a javelin. Every once in a while, Anne called for Henry, complaining how he had abandoned her and their baby. More often, she repeated how she could no longer endure this torment.

The midwife advanced from the foot of the bed, and placed her hands upon Anne's abdomen to feel the child. All of the ladies, who stood nearby, looked at the old woman in ghastly anticipation. Anne heard them discuss the lack of progress in the delivery, their whisperings and lamentations sounding like an inauspicious echo of extinction.

"Will she be all right?" Lady Eleanor asked anxiously.

The midwife put the covers back over Anne before replying sorrowfully, "If the baby does not come soon, neither of them has a chance. I cannot work miracles."

Eleanor sat on the edge of the bed and squeezed Anne's hand. "My lady, you must be brave and optimistic. Gather all your strength and push," she admonished.

"I'm dying," Anne muttered. "Henry... Henry..."

The other women shared worried and doleful glances.

"Madame, please do not say that," Eleanor entreated.

A drained Anne closed her eyes, so tired that she could barely draw a breath. The child had sucked almost the last ounce of strength from her. "My minutes are numbered."

"You must live!" Eleanor brushed back the sweat-soaked curls from Anne's forehead.

"Why? Soon he will have me obliterated from the face of the earth anyway." The anguish in Anne's voice, layered with resignation, was gut-wrenching.

Lady Eleanor assured, "A strong woman such as yourself knows how to use all her exceptional abilities – you will cope."

Anne gritted her teeth as a tide of pain swamped her again. "God, save my child even if I have to die."

Eventually, the dreadful labor finished at midnight as a high-pitched wail heralded the birth of the prisoner's baby. Anne let out a smile and then slipped into oblivion.

§§§

Thomas Cromwell paced up and down the passageway near the queen's chambers. Someone periodically came out and notified him about the progress. Upon receiving the news of Anne and her child being in mortal danger, hope for their deaths blossomed in his chest. Time tickled slowly, and when he heard the loud wail of the newborn, he cursed silently.

Lady Kingston walked out in search for her husband, but instead she stumbled into Cromwell.

The chief minister gripped the woman's hand to stop her, and barked, "What is it?"

Lady Mary Kingston apprised, "A bonny and strong boy!"

Cromwell sighed so heavily that it was almost a groan. It would have been so much better if Anne had been delivered of a stillborn child or a daughter, but not a healthy Tudor prince.

"I'll share the tidings with His Majesty." Cromwell was already trembling like a leaf in the wind at the thought of his upcoming interview with his brutal sovereign.

Indubitably, Anne's son would pose a threat to King Henry and his any future children with Jane Seymour. What should the minister do now? He would never attempt to murder this infant, who had Tudor blood coursing through his veins. As he made his way home, Cromwell labored to figure out a course of action, but his mind was moving in ever-decreasing circles, not getting closer to a resolution.

§§§

Regaining consciousness, Anne was grateful that she had been washed and dressed in a simple clean nightgown of brown cotton. She looked around, focusing her scrutiny upon the bundle in the midwife's arms, and an ethereal maternal joy flourished in her soul. Her baby was obviously alive!

Anne inquired breathlessly, "What is it?"

The woman swiveled her gaze to her. "It is a healthy boy, Ma'am."

A jubilant Anne exclaimed, "I've given the king a son in spite of all odds against me! My dear God, thank you!" She had achieved her goal after all the plots against her.

With the outpouring of the woman's glee, the ladies and the midwife fell silent. Their best instincts suggested that they were glimpsing a phoenix that one day could rise from the ashes of Anne's tumultuous and catastrophic union with England's sovereign to scale the heights of power once more.

Anne looked as radiant as the warm sun, her chest full of pure, unconditional love for her son; tears of happiness stung her eyes. "My beloved boy! Is he truly healthy?"

"Yes, he is." The midwife gave the swaddled infant to his mother. "He is a little small, but perfectly formed."

Humming a lullaby, Anne cradled her child in her arms, and kissed the soft hair on the top of his head. Her son was the living image of his father, his red hair and features attesting to his Tudor origins. Yet, the boy's mysterious dark eyes would never allow anyone to forget who his mother was.

"My dear son," purred Anne lovingly.

The midwife stepped away, and Lady Eleanor Hampton approached the bed. Eleanor was Anne's favorite lady among all the women who served her during her incarceration.

"Madame, how will you name him?" Eleanor inquired.

Anne believed that Henry would select the name Edward. She herself would have named her son in honor of her dearly departed brother, but it was too risky, for someone could interpret it as proof of her son's ill paternity. There were many interesting French names, but it was undesirable to give a potential heir to the English throne a foreign name.

A thought popped into her head. If Prince Arthur Tudor had not died, he would have ruled the country, and Henry would have entered the Church, as had been planned by his father, King Henry VII, and his grandmother, Lady Margaret Beaufort. *I'll name him Arthur,* Anne decided, smiling with devilish satisfaction. *It will remind Henry of his deceased elder brother, and of the ancient legend of King Arthur, who saved England from her enemies in the hour of need.*

Anne was fascinated with the legends of King Arthur and his knights. Her child would be considered a bastard due to the annulment of her marriage. In spite of being the illegitimate son of King Uther Pendragon, Arthur became a great monarch, a famous warrior, and an epic hero. Henry VII had called his firstborn son after Arthur Pendragon – the once king of legend, and maybe Anne's son would also escape his current bleak outlook and would accomplish greatness.

Anne switched her gaze to Eleanor. "He will be called Arthur after the famous English hero," she stated firmly.

"My lady, I have to take the child to your sister tomorrow."

"Why so soon? Can we wait a little bit? Please do not do this!" She pressed little Arthur to her chest.

A silent apology flashed across Eleanor's features. "The infant cannot live in the Tower."

"I beg you to let Arthur stay with me for one more day," Anne entreated. Tears misting her vision, her fingers were caressing her son's plump cheek.

Eleanor's countenance was imbued with compassion. "We'd love to allow you to be with your son, but it is not in our power to grant your wish, Madame."

Lady Mary Kingston came to the bed and regarded Anne with pity. "My lady, I beg your pardon, but we cannot do your bidding and go against Master Cromwell's instructions."

In a voice colored with guilt, Eleanor pleaded, "I'm sorry, Lady Anne."

All of Anne's troubles had two male names: Henry and Thomas. The king's name had been a hymn of hope and love only a few months ago, but now it sounded like a satanic curse. The man who carried out all of Henry's dirty work was his chief minister – Thomas Cromwell, her archenemy.

Anne ground out through clenched teeth, "Cromwell! He has destroyed me, and now he is snatching away the last sweet thing in my life." Contempt rang in her tone.

Lady Kingston chided, "Lady Anne, be respectful."

"I'm saying the truth." Turning her attention to the infant, Anne cooed softly, her fury immediately abating.

Eleanor interjected, "Madame, the boy will be delivered safely to your sister."

"Thank you." Anne cradled her beloved little Arthur until he fell asleep. Torrents of heartache were rushing through her at the thought of losing her long-awaited son so soon.

Soon Lady Eleanor Hampton took the baby boy from his mother, who reluctantly let go of him. Anne reclined on the pillows and sobbed herself to sleep. When she came to awareness again, Anne sensed that her son was no longer there, and then she recalled that Eleanor had taken the baby boy away to her sister – Lady Mary Stafford.

§§§

BETWEEN TWO KINGS

By the time Sir William Kingston appeared in the royal apartments, dusk had mantled the earth. He found Lady Boleyn in bed, engrossed in reading the Book of Hours.

"Ah, Master Kingston." Anne flicked her scrutiny to him, and irony curled her lips. The book lay in her lap. "Today the weather is as frosty as your daily demeanor. Yet, in the abode of the condemned former queen, a sense of timelessness prevails at all times, and there are no seasons."

The Constable of the Tower cringed at her nudging the conversation beyond the comfortable repertoire for him. As he approached her bed and sketched a shallow bow, he admired the superbly decorated manuscript in Anne's hands. His wife, Mary Kingston, had told him that Anne's sumptuous Book of Hours had been manufactured in Bruges circa 1450, and that her adoration of illuminated manuscripts had commenced at the court of Archduchess Margaret of Austria.

Anne put the volume aside. "Why have you come?"

Unable to see past her façade of quiet stoicism, Kingston informed, "Madame, His Majesty commanded that your execution is to be carried out on the Feast of the Immaculate Conception. According to the midwife, you have enough time to recover until this day."

At this heinous message, she nearly jumped out of her skin, but Anne maintained an outwardly neutral demeanor. "Master Kingston, do you have any good news?"

"No. You must prepare for your execution." He smashed to smithereens the final vestiges of her hope of a last-minute reprieve and a lifelong admission to a convent.

With his ominous words echoing through her head, the former queen dragged a fortifying breath before articulating in a sardonic undertone, "Traitors to King Henry deserve only eternal damnation for their sins, especially adulteresses like me. No clemency can be granted to them."

"The king's law is God's law, Madame."

The prisoner laughed uproariously with an outlandish lightness that both shocked and appalled the constable. His reaction amused her, and she snickered again. "I thank you for letting me know, Master Kingston. Tell Cromwell that I'm waiting for the day my soul is received by the Almighty."

William Kingston felt his blood run cold as he gazed into her eyes glittering with a strange light, the meaning of which he could not decipher. Was she not afraid of dying? Anne was the most unconventional woman he had ever encountered. A baffled Kingston then departed the chamber.

Anne stared at the shut door. "Henry will never commute my sentence." Even if the king dithered as to how to proceed with her case, Cromwell would somehow accelerate her death.

Fate was taunting her like a predator. *Now my situation is worse than Catherine of Aragon's was after her expulsion from court. Is God punishing me for her unhappiness?* Anne had never liked the 'Spanish woman,' as she had long labeled Catherine in her mind. She loathed the Spaniards, the House of Habsburg, and Spain. This was thanks to the education she had received in France, Spain's bitter rival. What did Anne feel for Catherine and her daughter, Mary Tudor, now?

At the beginning of their long courtship, King Henry had proposed to Anne and assured her that Catherine had come to the altar and the marriage bed tainted by sin. According to him, her union with Arthur had been consummated, and, after his passing, she had lied about her virginal status to the Pope and the whole world because of her desire to be Queen of England. Thus, Anne had always viewed the woman as Princess Dowager of Wales, not as Henry's true wife.

Despite the collapse in her fortunes thanks to Henry's new infatuation, Anne did not regret marrying him. If

Catherine had not been cast aside, Elizabeth and Arthur would not have been born. The 'Spanish woman's' union with the monarch was incestuous and unlawful, so Mary must be illegitimate. Nevertheless, contemplating Catherine's sufferings, caused by the King's Great Matter and her subsequent exile, Anne could not help but feel empathy for her dead rival.

"I was wrong," Anne acknowledged to herself as she again picked up the Book of Hours. "I committed some senseless acts of cruelty towards *both of them*. So wrong..."

Lady Eleanor Hampton's footfall was noiseless. "What is the matter, my lady?"

For a long time, Eleanor stood nearby in silence. Anne sat in bed, with the illuminated manuscript clasped in her hands, while tears coursed down her pallid cheeks from beneath her closed eyelids. Guilt came crashing down upon Anne with the dead weight of all her transgressions.

"What do you want?" Two angry pools of black fire stared at the other woman.

"Forgive me." Eleanor retreated, but then halted.

"Fear me not, Lady Hampton." Scrubbing the tears away, Anne forced back the sobs clawing their way up her throat. "I meant Catherine of Aragon and Mary. I should have been more benevolent to them both." Yet, she could not find any words to express her new, incipient attitude to them.

"Sophocles, that Greek tragedian, said that *'Kindness is ever the begetter of kindness.'* He was right."

Anne's whimsical smile made it seem like she possessed an aura of gentleness that assured the timid and assuaged the weak. "Benevolence is the flower of humanity."

"Please, try to rest, Madame." Lady Hampton inspected her mistress and then left.

A succession of thoughts raced through Anne's head. King Henry's love... Had Anne ever had the ruler's heart? Or had his former feelings for her simply been lust for something that had been withheld for years? Henry had been drowning in romantic sentiments for Anne! He had sworn his undying devotion to her countless times, only now to paint her wifehood in the most dismal hues of hurt and betrayal. Was Henry capable of loving someone other than himself?

Anne opened the Book of Hours on the page with her own poignant inscription *'Le tiemps viendra,'* which in English meant *'The time will come,'* and with her signature. Years earlier, after her recovery from the commonly lethal sweating sickness, she had made this inscription below a miniature of the Second Coming and the Resurrection of the Dead.

Years ago, Anne had showed it to Henry. "The time will come," she murmured. "For my death. Is it God's will?"

Fresh tears were weaving wet, intricate trails down her cheeks. *Henry Tudor must be in love with the idea of being in love, not a real person. He has never loved me with a true, pure, and unconditional love.* Gloom reigned in her soul; there was no star in the firmament of her anguished mind.

Anne scrutinized her own signature *'Je anne boleyn.'* She had inserted the armillary sphere in between the 'je' and 'anne' years ago. The sphere represented the universe; it could be found in the Almagest written in the 2th century by Claudius Ptolemy, the famed Alexandrian astronomer and mathematician. Anne had used it before switching to the crowned falcon holding a scepter and the Tudor roses, which she had selected as her badge before her wedding to the king.

Her tragedy was draining the vitality out of her. "Once I believed that the whole world was at my feet. Yet, I've never been the queen of the universe because I am not immortal."

Anne Boleyn had lost the war with legions of her adversaries. Nevertheless, she would walk to the place of her death with her head held high and her countenance tranquil. Anne would die with the utmost dignity, showing prodigious strength in her last moments. She would never be broken.

"*Le tiemps viendra...*" Anne continued reading the Book of Hours and praying. "The time will come," she whispered, this time in English. The time for her murder...

CHAPTER 3

Burning of the Anointed Queen

November 23, 1536, Hever Castle, Kent, England
The stillness of the early morning was interrupted by the quiet conversation of the two men, who were unconcerned by the cold wind. The sun had not yet risen, so they beheld the dark Hever gardens, shrouded in snow and fog. Garbed in black velvet from their boots to their ostrich plumed toques and cloaks, they looked like a vision from the Greek tragedies.

They were Henry Percy, Earl of Northumberland, and Thomas Boleyn, Earl of Wiltshire and of Ormond. Yesterday, Percy had left London for Hever Castle and ridden for half of the night along bad roads without stopping, through oak forest, to meet with Anne's father.

Thomas Boleyn leaned against the trunk of a bare oak. "Fate works in mysterious ways. Anne gave King Henry a son, but he doesn't wish to see him." Regret crept into his voice.

Percy stood beneath a beech covered with a mantle of ice. "His Majesty does not believe that the boy is his. He will talk neither to you nor to Lady Mary Stafford about Anne."

Boleyn smiled proudly. "My Mary is very courageous! I was amazed that she came and beseeched His Majesty to spare Anne. It was an audacious step to appear at court."

The Earl of Wiltshire scanned his surroundings. In the misty darkness, the double-moated castle loomed in the distance like an enigmatic abode of shadows. Although it was his home, the towers now were a daunting vision against the dark firmament. The snowy lawns were barely disturbed by footprints, and the trees thrust their white branches upward to the heavens, as if praying for his jailed daughter.

This view roused memories Boleyn could not erase from his mind. *My once brilliant life has morphed into a barren wasteland of loss and grief.* All in combination – Anne's imprisonment, George's demise, and his estrangement from Mary after her second marriage – weighed heavily upon him.

Wiltshire's gaze slid to his guest. "Mary will take good care of Anne's son."

"Yes, she will," Percy agreed, touching his toque. "It is appalling how Cromwell manipulates King Henry who does not see that the accusations against Anne are false. His Majesty does not comprehend how much harm her execution might bring to the prestige of the monarchy and the Tudor dynasty. It will tarnish his reputation forever, and there will be rumors that Anne's son is in reality the king's."

"His Majesty does not think strategically."

They both loathed the English monarch for his viciousness and his impulsive rages, although they had to feign their fealty to Henry VIII. In reality, they considered him a tyrant.

Percy let out a bitter laugh. "Henry Tudor will never release Anne. Even if he wishes to spare her life, Cromwell will simply concoct more charges against her."

"We have resources we can command," stated Thomas decisively.

The younger lord nodded. "I have allies among the Tower Guard. Lady Eleanor Hampton is close to Anne and keeps me informed of changes in the conditions of her imprisonment. If we are quick, smart, and brave, we might well be successful, albeit at a significant risk to ourselves." Lowering his voice, he underscored, "Lord Wiltshire, neither of Anne's aunts attending her must know about our intentions."

"Of course not." Boleyn sighed, exhausted; his health was deteriorating since Anne and George had been apprehended. "Did your spies inform you how Anne is coping?"

"The labor was very difficult, but she is regaining her strength by all accounts."

Hoping for her recovery, Anne's father concluded, "The execution will happen at the beginning of December, then."

Northumberland nodded. "My people will let me know the date and time. I have regular meetings with one of them."

A short silence reigned. The grayness of the morning was gradually lifting from the earth.

Thomas Boleyn thought of his children's awful endings. Every day he was buffeted by a cycle of monstrous guilt and self-loathing. Anne's incarceration and George's murder were his entire fault. He had indirectly assisted their foes: during his interrogation, Thomas had not defended his offspring, for he had feared that it would put an end to his own life.

His ascent to power was slow but certain. First, Mary had entered the Tudor ruler's bed, and then his youngest and favorite daughter had won the crown. However, Anne had failed to keep herself in the royal favor, and Boleyn had lost all he had achieved after the years of ingenious scheming.

My poor wife, the Earl of Wiltshire mused. *I shall never forget her bereavement after my return.* In the great hall, a grief-stricken Lady Elizabeth Boleyn had broken into heart-rending sobs, and when Thomas had stepped to her, she had shrunk from him, as if he were infected with leprosy.

"No! Oh God!" Elizabeth had cried, burying her face in her hands. "My beloved Anne and George! I've lost them! You killed them!" Her words were still ringing in his ears.

Soon Thomas and Elizabeth had learned that Anne's execution had been rescheduled thanks to her discovered pregnancy. Elizabeth had made a dramatic scene, shouting at him that Thomas would burn in hell in the afterlife if he did not rescue Anne, and that it was his fatherly duty to act.

Wiltshire had surreptitiously contacted Henry Percy, who, he knew, still harbored amorous sentiments towards Anne. Boleyn also remembered his old friend, Count Jean de Montreuil. He had once saved the man's life while hunting during the time he had been the English ambassador to France. Now the count lived in Venice, an independent Italian republic, which was an ideal place for Anne to live out the rest of her life quietly, if she could be taken away from the Tower.

In the silence that stretched between them, Percy studied the old man in front of him. At sixty, the Earl of Wiltshire looked older: his withered face was gaunt, his dark eyes – so much like Anne's – lifeless, and his thin lips quivered. His grey hair was shaded with fading traces of brown. The tragedies of his children had taken their toll on him.

Percy said, "No French executioner will come to London."

Wiltshire blinked. "Are you certain?"

"Yes. My man went to Calais. He paid all executioners to ensure that they would not travel to London in December. Cromwell already knows that he has a problem."

"They can use an axe," pointed out Boleyn.

A conspiratorial gleam entered Northumberland's eyes. "I predict His Majesty will order that they burn Anne at the stake rather than have her beheaded."

Lines of anxiety mingled with wonder creased Boleyn's wrinkled face. "How will that be accomplished?"

"It should be fine," averred the Earl of Northumberland. "I've spoken to Cromwell several times. I've suggested that Anne should be burned because she is an evil witch who betrayed our liege lord. I've claimed that she seduced our sovereign through witchcraft, just as she ensorcelled me a long while ago, when she could have had no expectations of a royal match and would have been more than content to marry at least the heir to a rich earldom."

Boleyn's lips curved in a grin: the old man admired Percy's courage. "I've heard such peculiar gossip about you."

Northumberland smirked. "They say that I'm afraid of sorcery. I complained, in the presence of many courtiers, that I had become a victim of Anne's sortilege." He smirked. "Of course, I don't believe in witchcraft. I deliberately spread those rumors to ensure that my conversations with Cromwell do not come across as suspicious."

"It is a very dangerous game, Lord Northumberland."

An animated Henry Percy grinned. "Well, the game is worth the candle, Lord Wiltshire."

For the space of a heartbeat, Boleyn was lost in thought, staring impassively at the oak. "If no swordsman can arrive in London from Calais, Anne will protest against her beheading by an axe. This will infuriate the king and Cromwell, and they will order her death by burning." He stilled for a short time, as if holding his breath, and then asserted gleefully, "If my daughter is burned, there will be no proof of her salvation. Nevertheless, I worry that our sovereign might decide to wait until a French executioner is available."

"No, he will not do so. The tyrant yearns to wed Lady Jane Seymour before the end of the year."

"What will we do if His Majesty enjoins to use an axe?"

Percy outlined the plan. "In this case, Lady Eleanor will dissolve some sleeping draught in wine and water. The guards, save those who serve me, and Anne's ladies-in-waiting will be fast asleep. Then my men will stealthily take Anne out of the Tower." After a moment's pause, he verbalized his concerns. "However, in this case, we would not be able to stage Anne's death. We would have to escape from England, for we would be suspected as her accomplices."

"I would be the first suspect," Boleyn surmised, to his surprise undaunted. "I've prepared enough money to leave the country with my family, including my daughter, Mary, and her children. I'll take Mary with us abroad because otherwise, she will be murdered in place of Anne."

"Let's hope that I've successfully manipulated Cromwell, and that the king will listen to him. If Anne is burned, everyone will think she is dead. We will not have to flee."

"I pray that it will be so."

Thrusting away his disturbing thoughts, Northumberland elucidated, "I'll learn of His Majesty's decision in the next several days and will keep you informed, Lord Wiltshire."

"Thank you," uttered Boleyn with respect.

Percy raised his eyes to the vault of the sky, where leaden clouds scudded in from the west; the burgeoning sunrise colored their edges light pink. "God shall assist us."

§§§

As Henry Percy rode on his black stallion away from Hever Castle, the sun rose, not with the hope of a new day, but with the fear of what was to follow. Despite the confidence in their success that he had professed to the Earl of Wiltshire, anxiety gripped him like a vise. To distract himself, Percy reminisced about the sweetest romance of his life.

Years ago, he had met young Anne when she had been a lady-in-waiting to the late Queen Catherine while he had been a page in Cardinal Wolsey's household. Percy had quickly fallen in love with the beautiful and exotic maiden, who intoxicated him with her French fashions and manners. Anne had reciprocated his affections, and he had courted her in secret, but there had never been anything physical between them. He envied King Henry for being Anne's first lover.

Hever Castle was left behind, and now Percy steered his horse towards a road leading to the capital. "Why didn't my parents understand that I loved Anne? If only they had not been so obstinate in their belief that I needed a wife of higher standing, threatening disinheritance if I did not comply with their demand to abandon her... Why did I obey them?"

Snowflakes swirled around him as the Earl of Northumberland galloped ahead. His mind was concentrated on his beloved Anne. One day, Wolsey had informed the young lord that the monarch would find another match for him. A heartbroken Percy had implored the cardinal to intervene on his behalf, but his pleas had fallen on deaf ears. Later, Percy had realized that King Henry had wanted Anne, and that Thomas Boleyn had intended to make her the next royal mistress once Mary Boleyn had been discarded.

Anne had been sent away to Hever Castle. Percy had retired to his father's estates. By 1525, Percy had been married off to Lady Mary Talbot, the daughter of the Earl of Shrewsbury, and this union was doomed. He had not liked her, while Mary had resented him. *Within four years, my wife and I separated, our relationship irreparably damaged. What a fool I was to tie myself to her! My immense love for Anne made my spouse hate me fiercely,* Percy summed up.

The route to London was well-traveled, but few paid the earl any heed. Nobles and caravans of one sort or another journeyed this way often, though more rarely in winter. If he encountered any peasants, they glanced at him briefly and continued on their way to their humble houses. None of those people whom Percy passed were likely to know his identity.

"Anne," fell from the earl's lips. "Your quest for the throne alarmed me despite the king's obsession with you. Didn't you see how inconstant and flippant our sovereign is?"

Percy had predicted that Anne would be unhappy with the egotistical ruler even as his queen. The earl's misgivings had materialized. Yet, Northumberland had never imagined that the king would sanction the murder of the anointed queen, who was the mother of his daughter and now his son. Gossip had circulated that Henry Percy had secretly wed Anne years earlier and consummated their marriage, but there was no evidence to support this. *I am very fortunate that Thomas Cromwell did not accuse me of being Anne's paramour.*

After Anne's arrest, Percy had returned to London. He had skipped George's trial, but he had attended Anne's. After she had been judged guilty, the shocked earl had collapsed in the court. Later, Northumberland stayed in the city and observed her situation. Skilled at pretense, he praised his liege lord in front of courtiers, in spite of his abject loathing for the man.

"I swear that we will save you, Anne," Henry Percy said to himself, his heart hammering in his chest.

It stopped snowing, the wind dropped, but the weather was gray and dull, mirroring the chronic bleakness in Percy's soul. It did not matter that Anne had fallen out of love with him and given her heart to King Henry – Percy still adored her. Thomas Boleyn had later joined his cause, and together they had designed a perilous plan for Anne's daring escape.

November 23, 1536, Palace of Whitehall, London, England

In autumn and winter, royal tennis, or *jeu de paume* as the French called it, was played in an indoor arena inside Whitehall. A long row of wooden benches was set along one of the walls. Courtiers assembled to watch King Henry's contest against Charles Brandon, Duke of Suffolk. Both the monarch and his opponent wore white linen shirts without any ornamentation, loosened for dexterity during the game.

"Bravo, Your Majesty!" Edward Seymour cried from the sidelines.

"You are playing better than ever," commended Thomas, Edward's brother.

King Henry smiled brightly. "Charles, I've won today!"

Suffolk grinned. "Sire, the game was brilliant."

Henry walked over to Lady Jane Seymour. He took her hands in his and reverently kissed them. "Lady Jane, your attendance was a good omen for my contest with Charles."

The monarch studied the woman he yearned to marry. He was enchanted by Jane's delicate beauty, in spite of enjoying random encounters with his new mistresses. In her modest and elegant English gown of white satin embroidered with her favorite pearls and silver, with her fair complexion and pale skin, Jane Seymour resembled a Vestal Virgin, one of the priestesses of the Roman goddess of the hearth. Her girdle of pearls accentuated the gracefulness of her walk.

Jane's appearance was a veritable symbol of purity – a stark contrast to the whore Henry had once been shackled to. Jane's long, light eyelashes, her demure face, her long blonde hair, hidden behind a gable hood, and her slim figure – all these contributed to an impression of her kindness and grace. Her quiet, docile voice was a soothing salve to his heart, scarred by Anne's betrayals. Jane had awakened in Henry a deep tenderness and a knightly desire to keep her safe.

Jane murmured subserviently, "Congratulations on your outstanding victory, Your Majesty. Your prowess at jousting, hunting, and tennis has long become legendary."

Henry was flattered. "Sweetheart, your presence is always like a blessing for me. Only your favor saved my life when I was unhorsed and hit the ground after the jousting incident."

She flashed a modest smile. "You are most kind to me."

The Seymour brothers observed them smugly, satisfied to see this display of their liege lord's affection for their sister. They tensed as Thomas Cromwell entered the tennis court.

Cromwell bestowed an insipid smile upon them and strode over to the monarch. He stopped and dropped into a bow. "My most humble pardon for disturbing Your Majesty."

Henry's brow wrinkled in exasperation. "What do you want, Master Cromwell?"

His subject dithered for a moment. "I bring the latest news of the Lady Anne Boleyn."

"She is no lady!" The king's fury billowed and swelled until it nearly choked him. "She is a dirty strumpet!"

Ignoring Jane, the ruler motioned his councilor to follow him. The two men left the gaming court and marched down the hallway, adorned with portraits of the Tudor family.

§§§

As they walked in the royal private chamber, King Henry hissed, "What about that harlot?" As of late, his mood swings and outbursts of rage were more terrible than ever before.

The royal chief minister fidgeted with his collar. "Lady Anne's son saw the world for the first time yesterday."

A flabbergasted silence followed. Only the cracking of fire in the fireplace and their breathing breached the quiet.

Henry moved to a window and stared out at the snow-laden trees. Why had Anne birthed a male child now? He swiftly put this thought aside, for that infant must have been fathered by one of her lovers. Nonetheless, for whatever reason, in spite of her alleged and diabolical betrayals, it was beyond anger and beyond pain for the monarch to think that Anne had produced a son with another man.

For a brief moment, the ruler felt unable to breathe, as if the walls, swathed in Flemish tapestries of hunting scenes, were pressing against his ribcage. Henry and Anne shared a passion for hunting. A cavalcade of remembrances whirled in his head: Anne and he had once led a grand hunting party in the woods near the town of Windsor, chasing a hart and a hind – 'the royal pair in love,' as Anne had jovially called them after having shot them. Anne had purchased these wall hangings.

A tremor of misery clutched at Henry, as if Anne had left a ghost in the palace behind her to whisper into his ear about their erstwhile contentment. No, he would not think of it.

Turning to the other man, the king nevertheless inquired, "How is Anne feeling?"

The conflicting emotions flashing across his liege lord's features surprised Cromwell. "Your Majesty, she is doing quite well, although the labor was not easy." His sovereign did not need to know that Anne had almost died bringing *their* child into the world.

"Will she recover?" Against his will, Henry could yet be concerned about her a little.

"Lady Anne will be well enough very soon." Cromwell suspected that the news of the boy's birth would make Henry hesitate, but he could not allow Anne to live.

The monarch had to marry Jane Seymour. Too much had been sacrificed due to the king's desire to set Anne aside. If Anne remained alive, some would remember that she was a queen, and rivers of blood would be spilled in revenge for the murders of George Boleyn and the other innocents. And when her bastard came of age, there could be a war for succession, especially if Henry failed to father a son in a new marriage. *My own life is at stake,* Cromwell reminded himself.

The royal voice was choked with emotion as he described his former wife. "Anne has always been tenacious and resilient. Nothing got in her way until I crushed her."

At present, Henry did not crave to spill Anne's blood as insanely as before. Anyway, they had their little Elizabeth! In a fit of ire, he had once called the girl Henry Norris' bastard in front of his courtiers, but he knew for a certainty that the girl was his daughter. In addition, the king's young illegitimate son – Henry FitzRoy, Duke of Richmond and Somerset – had passed away in the summer of 1536, and perhaps this tragedy had softened his savage heart somewhat.

Questions flew through the ruler's consciousness. What should he do? Should he order Anne's execution or send her to a nunnery? He glanced back at Cromwell and blinked, his gaze expressing confusion. "Perhaps..." He broke off.

Cromwell launched a guileful assault. "During the labor, I was in the corridor near Lady Anne's chambers. I heard her cries, some for help and some of anger. At times, the woman lost all her shame and screamed over and over again that she never wronged you, and other untrue things."

A gust of vehement rage rushed through Henry. "What exactly did she say? I must know everything."

"She declared that you, sire, had murdered five innocents to please yourself and marry Lady Jane Seymour, whom she called numerous vulgar epithets too rude to repeat."

Cromwell would ensure that all those who had attended Anne during the delivery would be forever silent. He would convince them by bribing the women who had served her in the Tower, and have them disappear quietly so that they would never repeat her real words to anyone.

"Damn that deceitful harlot!" bellowed Henry as he thumped his fist onto a nearby table. "How dare she call me a murderer? She is a traitor and an adulteress! She should get down on her knees and kiss my boots for letting her live long enough to have her damned bastard." His mouth twisted in abhorrence. "I'm the king, and her life is in my hands!"

The minister barely repressed a smile. "Lady Anne was accused of treason, adultery, and incest. The court tried her and found her guilty. The prescribed punishment is death."

"Yes, the law is clear." Now the monarch's thirst for revenge against Anne could only be satiated by the utter ruin of her. He would punish her for all the years he had wasted on her, for not giving him a son, and for her crimes.

Thomas Cromwell nodded vigorously, while inwardly leering at the situation. Just as the Greek hero Heracles performed twelve difficult feats, the chief minister had outsmarted Anne and emerged triumphant from their battle. Cromwell also comprehended what England's sovereign did not admit to himself. *His Majesty's hatred of Anne stems from his pride damaged by her alleged adulteries, and from his unfading obsession with her,* he concluded silently.

"Did you send for the French executioner?" The monarch meant the same person who had been hired the first time, before the discovery of Anne's condition.

"That man says that he is unable to arrive in December."

"Why?" Henry stomped across the chamber and landed into an ornate, regal chair under a canopy of yellow velvet.

"It might take us weeks to find another. Few Frenchmen will agree to come to London before the end of the year. Some might not be bold enough to cross the Channel in December."

"I'm intending to marry the Lady Jane before Christmas."

The advisor remembered the astounding things he had heard from Henry Percy. "The Earl of Northumberland once said that Anne Boleyn is a witch. He claims that she practiced sorcery on him. He was bewildered that you did not order her burning." He repressed a malevolent grin. "I wouldn't want to see his hateful expression again when he castigated her."

"There is no smoke without fire, Cromwell. I often think Anne ensorcelled me, and many others share this opinion. Perhaps it is true that this vicious she-devil is a witch."

"Percy knows her well. Long ago, they had been betrothed, but their engagement was broken by their families." Amused in a dark way, the minister supplemented, "Northumberland reminded me of the ancient prophecy that a Queen of England would be burned at the stake."

Two months before Anne's wedding to Henry, Anne had discovered a book of prophecy in her quarters, which had been left open at a special place. The page had depicted King Henry, Catherine of Aragon, and her, but Anne's figure had been missing its head. Anne had shown it to him, but despite questioning of anyone who had access to her rooms, they had not been able to find out who had brought the book there. The king had been outraged that someone had dared threaten his beloved. However, Anne had laughed the matter off.

The ruler recollected, "Anne and I discussed this prophecy. She said that even if she were to suffer a thousand deaths, her love for me would never abate. Such empty promises!"

"Words are often fickle and meaningless. The betrayal of loved ones is the worst sin a person can commit." Cromwell was keen to add fuel to the fire of the king's hatred for Anne.

"Henry Percy has a point, and it makes me think that he is right." Waves of hostility were pounding against Henry.

"What should I do, Your Majesty?"

A crucial silence percolated between them. The king did not risk a glance at the tapestries, which could remind him of Anne again; later, he would have them ripped from the walls.

Henry stood up and strode to a window. The ruler looked out into the gardens, where he and Anne had spent many felicitous hours. A fleeting, yet sharp, twinge of melancholy penetrated his spirit. Their relationship had come to this: the bare park resembled his currently absent romantic feelings for the adulteress, one who merited her eternal and most heinous punishment in Tartarus. The cheerless wintry landscape intensified his desire to start his life anew without Anne.

At the noise of shuffling feet, the king pivoted to his chief administrator. "Burn that vile witch! She deserves such a horrendous end! However, give Anne a strong poison before the execution, for the pyre is a lingering way to die. Let it be known only to her family that I'm being merciful, so she will be dead before she reaches Tower Green. I prohibit anyone from mentioning those dratted Boleyns on pain of death."

"As you command, sire."

The minister bowed in obeisance and exited. This new instruction presented another problem: the crowd would know that Anne had died before she reached the stake. Cromwell would have to give special instructions for Anne's head to be covered with a sack, tied at the neck, and then he would set rumors that the prisoner had been drugged to preclude her from cursing their sovereign.

December 8, 1536, the Tower of London, London, England

"I've always feared fire," Anne spoke in a voice heavily tinctured with mortal fright.

The old prophecy that she had once dismissed as baloney was now coming true. Constable Kingston explained that the French executioner could not come to London anytime soon, so Henry had resorted to the extreme alternative, depriving her of the more merciful death by beheading.

For her first cancelled execution, Anne had implored that a skilled French swordsman would be employed. The ruler had initially consented to her request. Apparently, now Henry hated her so ferociously that he had reneged on his word. She had not anticipated such inhuman bloodthirstiness from her former husband. It was unimaginable and inconceivable that her execution was scheduled for the day of the Feast of the Immaculate Conception. Yet, this horror was *real*.

How would Anne stay calm while being burned in front of a bloodthirsty mob? The chorus of their laughter and curses at her would echo her every scream as the flames rose around her. She hoped that her death on such a holy day would make people at least a little sympathetic to her cause. Anne's end would be far more agonizing than the executions of her so-called paramours, the luckier victims of Henry's bestial brutishness.

"Henry Tudor is an ungodly monster." Anne's words shuddered to a halt as her terror peaked.

Anne had not merited such excruciating sufferings. She swallowed conclusively, but the tart taste of betrayal in her mouth was still there. A ravenous bloodlust emerged from some deepest part of her whole being which she had never known existed. If now Henry had been here, Anne would have attempted to commit regicide. That would at least give him a reason to punish her this way!

I was naïve to believe that Henry would love me forever. I waited for years while that beast tried to divorce Catherine, wasting my most fertile years for nothing. Instead, Anne could have wed Henry Percy, who was her first love. She could have had a brood of Percy's children and been happy with him. Or perhaps it would have been better if Anne had remained at the French court and never returned to England.

She remembered the king's numerous mistresses and his latest infatuation – Jane Seymour. At present, Anne hated the Seymours more than ever. In those months prior to her arrest, Anne had been oblivious to the intrigues woven around her; she should have dealt with her adversaries earlier. Jane had a pale mind in comparison to Anne's education, wit, and intelligence, but the Seymours were as ambitious and cunning as the Boleyns. Her enemies must have instructed Jane on how to captivate Henry, and Anne's fatal mistake had been to underestimate the slut and her smart, cold-blooded relatives.

Now the Boleyns had fallen, and Jane, the mousy country girl from Wulfhall, occupied Anne's place at Henry's side. Eventually, Anne had even lost her chance for survival.

Lady Eleanor Hampton tiptoed towards Anne, who stood staring into space, completely lost in her musings. Anne's eyes were two dark pools of hatred as she pivoted to Eleanor.

Dread chilled Anne through and through. "Is it time?"

"Yes, it is, Madame." Eleanor handed to Anne a cup of ale.

The ale had an odd precipitate at the bottom of the goblet. "What is it in the drink?"

"My lady, the king has granted this favor to you."

Anne easily connected the dots. "Poison?"

The other woman nodded, and Anne laughed at such outrageousness.

Caustic vitriol spilled out of Anne's mouth. "King Henry – my murderer – permitted you to give me this poisoned chalice just before my execution. It is a chivalrous gesture to honor the Solemnity of the Immaculate Conception. No one can deny that His Majesty is such a magnanimous ruler." She broke into a funereal, yet sardonic, laugh.

To her surprise, Eleanor sneered, "Well, some kings have a tyrannical sense of humor."

"I hope the poison will not leave any traces on my tender skin." Anne snickered at her own acerbic wit. "That would be too bad to meet Lady Death in a miserable shape."

"My lady, nothing will be left on your face."

"In a few minutes, I'll meet the Lord." Anne slowly drank the bitter tasting liquid. She was comforted that at least she would not die in the flames.

A tide of dizziness assailed her, and, disoriented, Anne sank awkwardly onto the bed. Lady Eleanor rushed over and wrapped her head in a piece of white cloth, entirely covering her face and her hair. Anne attempted to relax, expecting lethal oblivion to enfold her in the darkness of mortality.

Her mind was in a haze, and Anne could not move while feeling someone lift and carry her. The guards must be taking her to the pyre, but she could not hear a throng. All was quiet, apart from the labored breathing of those who were carrying her. The cold air filling her lungs as she breathed confirmed that she had been removed from the Tower.

Drifting in and out of consciousness, Anne felt something firm beneath her body as she was put down, and then a jerk as whatever she had been placed upon moved beneath her. She was now likely to be inside a cart, and it had started moving. Anne endeavored to scream, but only a muffled cry passed her lips, and a hand was pressed to her mouth. Her tenuous grasp on reality was rapidly slipping away as the ale took effect, and Anne plunged into trance.

§§§

The steely gray dawn sluggishly stretched across the charcoal firmament, as if morning were unwilling to come. An ominous layer of mist had spread across the low areas of the city, and a bank of clouds ensured that the rising sun would remain hidden on this godforsaken day.

People who had gathered to watch the execution of Anne Boleyn crowded Tower Hill. Perhaps never before had so vast an assemblage been present in this place. In the freezing air, snowflakes were swirling in a primordial dance of mortality, while the blazing and blood-red flames gradually embraced a well-dressed woman, her face hidden by a white cloth.

"Anne Boleyn ain't screaming!" one of the witnesses shouted.

"She must be dead!" assumed a peasant in rags.

His wife observed, "She ain't writhing in the flames! There is no devil in her!"

A beggar on crutches deduced, "Yes, t'is true! She was a good Christian!"

Someone lamented, "Such a 'orrible end on such a 'oly day!"

The folk chorused, "Yes! Today is the Solemnity of the Immaculate Conception!"

"It is a mortal sin to burn her today!" a rough-looking woman cried. "She was anointed!"

Horror creased the spectators' faces. The putrid odor of burning flesh filled the air, spreading further and further like a cloud of vapor, reaching everyone's nostrils and turning their stomachs ill. Some started coughing until they retched.

The whole of the lugubrious mob were absolutely shocked with this barbaric execution and the victim's silent acceptance of her fate. They were all eminently cognizant of the poignant contrast of the condemned queen's quiet dignity with their sovereign's appalling ruthlessness. Many cried in the throng.

"The king 'as finally killed Anne Boleyn," uttered a voice in the throng.

"I 'eard that she 'as just delivered a healthy baby boy," a woman added.

"Really? Maybe t'is just a rumor," interjected somebody else.

The woman shook her head. "No, t'is true. One person in the Tower told me."

"I 'eard that, too," invaded another man. "But who is the child's father?"

"The boy must be the king's son," pronounced the same woman. "The dates would be right. She were not arrested until the beginning of May."

"How do you know?" a male voice shouted.

She answered, "I'm a midwife. I understand these things."

The folk crossed themselves. Profound sympathy rippled through the women in the crowd: childbirth was dangerous enough, without a vengeful monarch wanting one dead.

"Never!" protested a middle-aged merchant. "That whore was a 'eretical demoness! Her son is a bastard – a vile, twisted creature born of incest and witchcraft!"

Another young woman entered the conversation. "You are speaking with such religious zeal that you must be for popery. Is that why you 'ate Anne Boleyn so?"

The midwife continued, "Whoever Lady Anne was, it is blasphemy to burn a lady so soon after she 'as just 'ad a child" and on this 'oly day." She crossed herself. "God rest her soul!"

In their eyes, their sovereign had committed a *triple* blasphemy: he had burned the innocent anointed queen, who had just given birth to a son, on one of the most important Marian feasts celebrated by the Catholic Church. In any case, it was totally unacceptable for a queen to be burned, for royals were viewed as God's chosen representatives on earth.

Suddenly, a bleak ray of the sun broke out of the clouds overhead, as though blessing Anne's soul.

§§§

Thomas Cranmer, Archbishop of Canterbury, and Henry Percy, Earl of Northumberland, were among the official witnesses. Various words hung on the tip of their tongues, but none of them would dare say anything. Everybody thought that during King Henry's reign, there was only one step from the palace to the prison and another from the prison to the scaffold or to the pyre, just as it was in Anne's case.

As the smoke obscured the silent woman tied to the stake, Cranmer declared, "She who was Queen of England on earth has today become *a Queen in heaven.*"

"May the lady rest in peace," some of those on the official platform intoned, their voices quiet not to be overheard.

Henry Percy tore his gaze from the stake and perused the Archbishop of Canterbury. *A disconsolate Thomas Cranmer is barely recognizable.* A man of average height in his late forties, Cranmer was usually full of energy and vitality. Clad in a marten cloak, which he wore above white and black brocade ecclesiastic robes, the archbishop looked exhausted and frail, as though Anne's afflictions had sucked the life out of him. His careworn face was pale, and his hazel-green eyes sunken, and there was a sorrowful air about the churchman.

Percy crossed himself. "Find peace, my lady." He did not wish to be here at all, but he needed to reinforce the idea of his staunch loyalty to his liege lord and Cromwell.

§§§

Another flurry of snowflakes commenced falling from the heavens. This immaculate white mass was slowly erecting a cathedral of ice around the stake, as if in the murdered queen's memory. A blast of wind blew from the River Thames.

From the mob, somebody shouted, "The king simply wanted to marry another pretty lady, and that devil Cromwell trumped up charges against Anne Boleyn."

"His Majesty changes wives, like 'e changes 'is shirts," a courageous lad joined.

They were swiftly alerted to a potential peril. "These are treasonous words, even if they are the truth."

The horde were becoming restless, and their mood was turning increasingly ugly. To restore order on Tower Hill, a contingent of halberdiers marched towards the pyre, and then appeared a troop of arquebusiers. At the sight of them, a low, irate murmuring rumbled through the folk, and most of them made the sign of a cross, as if in tribute to Anne's sufferings.

The audience stirred into action, and some ululated before dispersing, "Amen!" Soon the area was empty.

In the eyes of many people, including Archbishop Cranmer and other reformers, today Anne Boleyn had won the glorious crown of martyrdom. The archbishop hoped that perhaps, one day, her name would be enrolled among the Protestant martyrs. Those who had once shunned and loathed Anne were now shaken by her demise, as well as horrified by the blasphemous actions of their despotic sovereign.

CHAPTER 4

Death and Rebirth

December 9, 1536, Dover, England

Anne opened her eyes and blinked several times, clearing away the fogginess and black spots from her vision. Her head was heavy, and her temples throbbed, as if her brain was about to burst; she inhaled deeply, holding her breath for a long moment. Her head lay on something quite smooth, while the rest of her body was on a firm, rough surface.

With a series of rapid blinks, Anne tried to pull her surroundings into focus and found herself staring into the smiling face of Henry Percy, Earl of Northumberland. She moved her head and discovered that they were lying within the high walls of a cart, her head on his knees.

"Harry Percy?" Bewilderment was etched into her features.

Her rescuer was dressed in a cape lined with brown marten fur, which effectively barred the cold. A flat cap of black velvet with a white ostrich plume adorned his head.

Raising her arms, Anne noticed that sleeves were those with marten fur cuffs. She realized that she still wore the same clothing as for her execution – a dark gray damask gown with a low square neckline. To keep her warm, Percy had wrapped her in a black sable cape.

"Good morning." Henry Percy smiled encouragingly.

Her baffled gaze locked with his. "Where are we?"

"On the south coast near Dover. The roads are frozen, and our journey has been rather slow. But at least it hasn't been snowing since our departure from London yesterday."

In a handful of heartbeats, Anne comprehended that she was free. She was able to breathe, see, and think. *She was not dead!* Anne touched her face, as if this gesture would reassure her that she was still in the world of the living. "Harry, I was to be executed... I don't comprehend..." she stuttered.

"Anne, you are alive." Percy took her hand in his and squeezed it. "Soon you will sail from Dover to Calais, where you will be met by a man who will accompany you to Venice."

A befuddled Anne muttered, "I am very confused."

Henry caressed her forehead. "I wanted you to live. At the trial, I gave a guilty vote, but it was evident that you were innocent. The king wanted to dispose of you, so all the peers delivered the verdict he desired so desperately." He heaved a sigh as anguish flickered in her eyes. "While you were in the Tower, your father and I masterminded a plot to save you."

"My father?" Her voice was drenched in amazement.

"Maybe Lord Wiltshire had a change of heart," presumed the earl, shrugging. "During our meetings I could see that he still has some dignity left. Probably, after your brother's execution, his conscience refused to be silenced, and he resolved not to let you die."

Anne felt a surge of appreciation for Thomas' actions, but commented, "Perhaps you are right, but it is hard for me to have confidence in my father's affection for me."

"At first, Lord Wiltshire found and asked me whether I could arrange an audience with the king in order to persuade him to send you to a nunnery. I knew from my conversations with Master Cromwell that your sentence would never be commuted. Thus, we devised this plan together."

"Master Kingston told me that the Earl of Wiltshire had refused to be my son's guardian."

"We cannot appear to be associated with you in any way. We must be above any suspicion."

Her jaw clenched, Anne's eyes shot a black fire of hostility towards her former husband, and she growled, "Any word about me is treason in His Majesty's eyes."

"Anne, relax," advised the Earl of Northumberland. "You are free."

"How can I forget the horror I went through? I cannot ignore all the atrocities that Tudor beast did to me and our children. I'll remember this ordeal for the rest of my life."

"You must leave the past behind, or otherwise, bitterness and hatred will destroy you." His hand stroked her hair with a gentleness that belied his slightly brusque tone.

Anne was too stunned to answer. "I don't know."

Her companion searched for a way to convince her. Eventually, he gave up and maneuvered to another topic. "I confess I recommended that Cromwell burn you."

"Why?" Her blood ran cold.

"We decided to stage your death. It was far easier to achieve this if there was no body left. Fortunately, Cromwell was pushing hard to have you executed after the birth."

"I cannot think clearly." She tried to sit up, but Percy would not let her.

"Calm down and lie still for a while. You need more time to recover from the effects of the sleeping draught you consumed yesterday." Concern vibrated in his voice.

"I'm fine, Henry." Anne's curiosity goaded her. "Who was burned instead of me?"

"Another woman had died yesterday, and we dressed her in a gown similar to yours. One of your ladies and two guards from the Tower were my accomplices. Lady Eleanor gave you some sleeping draught, and then my men took you into a side corridor, where your body was replaced with that of the deceased woman. It was hazardous, but we succeeded."

Anne wanted to know the whole story. "Where did you find that poor dead woman?"

"She was condemned to death, but she hanged herself in her cell. We merely took her body."

"Oh, God! How terrible, Henry!"

Northumberland avouched, "Anne, do not fret, please. It no longer matters because everything has changed. The world witnessed Anne Boleyn's execution, and she will remain dead as long as it is necessary. My people are staunchly loyal to me; they are now on the way to my estates in Northumberland."

"Is it really over?" she whispered hoarsely.

"Yes!" asserted the earl confidently. "And I'm so happy that now you are safe!"

Two dark pools met two gray ones. "I can never thank you and my father enough."

A man of lean build and average height in his mid-thirties, the Earl of Northumberland had a handsome countenance, with strong features and kind gray eyes a shade darker than a stormy sea. His appearance had the gentle sadness of a man who had experienced afflictions, but who was resigned to his fate. Percy beheld his former sweetheart with a heartwarming gaze full of perpetual adoration – an expression that made Anne feel as if she were the only woman in the world.

A wave of nostalgia swept over Anne as she scrutinized his face and recollected some of their past gladsome moments. If she had married Percy, Anne could have given him many children, and they would have been a large and happy family. Anne mused dolefully, *Harry has always looked at me with the genuine love shining in his eyes more brightly than the summer sun. However, it is impossible to reverse time.*

Northumberland resembled a medieval knight swearing to love his lady forever. "I did what I believed was right and just. My feelings for you have not changed, and they never will." His tender voice was as intimate as a kiss.

Tears stung her eyes. "I know, Harry. Thank you."

He smiled at her with a subtle grace that was rare in the world of the living. "Love finds you when you least expect it. If it is pure, it does not expect anything, does not demand, and does not fade away. This sensation is natural, gracious, and freeing. Even if a woman no longer returns your affection, this feeling forebears all, believes all, hopes all, endures all, and lasts forever. True love does not demand a reward."

Deeply moved, Anne looked into his eyes which burned with what she guessed was the very feeling he had described a few moments ago. Her admiration for him was growing like a well-watered plant in the sunshine. Henry Percy was a brave man, honorable to the bone, who would safeguard his lady from all perils and rescue her from all evils, just as Lancelot saved Guinevere after her abduction by Meleagant in Chrétien de Troyes' romance 'Lancelot, the Knight of the Cart.'

This speech awakened incomprehension in Anne. Every time she thought of King Henry, she was full of abhorrence, her heart hollow: Anne's passion for the ruler was no longer there, as if it had been ripped from her. If her sentiments towards the king had been her true love, why now could Anne not find anything of it in herself? Had her feelings for

Henry Tudor ever been as pure as Percy's for her? These questions struck Anne like a dart, but she could not find an answer.

Her mind floated to her baby boy. "Do you know where my son is now?"

"The boy is with your sister. Lady Stafford will take care of him, loving him as her own."

Anne's visage brightened. "I'm content that Arthur will grow up with Mary." The sudden trembling of her lips communicated her agitation. "Does she know that I'm alive?"

"No, she doesn't. We decided it was best not to tell her. The fewer people are involved in your salvation, the safer you are. At least for now, it is the best course of action."

Words of contrition poured out of Anne. "I betrayed Mary! When she wed William Stafford, my father cut off her allowance and ejected her from the family. I did not support Mary and banished her from court, just as I was ordered. Yet, despite everything, Mary has now come to help me."

"One day, you will meet and reconcile with her."

"It might never happen as I must escape from England."

Northumberland requested, "Now listen carefully. I fear we are running out of time, as much I wish we could be like this for many more hours. Within an hour, you will board a ship sailing for Calais. You will live with Jean Frédéric Roger de Ponthieu, Count de Montreuil."

"Who is Monsieur Jean de Montreuil?"

Percy elucidated, "Your father and the count are close friends from the time Sir Thomas Boleyn was ambassador to the French court in the late 1520s." He stilled to let it sink in. "The Count de Montreuil lives in Venice, where he served as the French ambassador for years. Fortunately, he does not intend to return to France so far. Your father contacted him, and the count consented to help. Do not worry: he is loyal to Sir Thomas and knows what he is doing."

Anne was now starting to believe that her parent possessed at least a shred of honor. "My father seems to have gone to great lengths to smuggle me out of England."

"That is true, Anne. Deep down, he loves you."

"Despite everything bad he did, he is still quite dear to me." Affection glimmered in opaque caverns.

The earl refocused on the topic at hand. "The Republic of Venice is a safe place for you, for it is neither part of France nor that of the Holy Roman Empire. You will assume the identity of Anne Gabrielle Marguerite de Ponthieu, who was the count's only grandchild."

Anne absorbed Percy's instructions. "Where is this lady?"

He narrated, "Several years earlier, she married a German commoner without the count's permission and moved to the Duchy of Cleves. As Anne de Ponthieu had disappeared from the sight of French and Venetian nobles, her father kept her ill-suited union secret. Five months earlier, she and her husband both passed away, claimed by deadly smallpox."

"So, no one in France and Venice has seen her for a long time," she concluded.

"Indeed," corroborated Percy. "She was your coeval. Your father remembered her well. He was sorry to hear that Madame Anne had died, but it is as though fate is guiding us. She had dark hair and hazel eyes, which simplifies our task – you will look more like her."

The Earl of Northumberland outlined the escape plan. "In Calais, you will be met by a trusted person from Count de Montreuil's household." He extracted two folded and sealed papers from a bag and handed them to her. "These are for you. One has details about the Ponthieu family that you must learn by heart; the other is a letter from Lord Wiltshire."

Anne took these small packages and turned them over to examine the seals. Thomas Boleyn had used his seal as the Earl of Wiltshire, and she wondered how much longer he would hold this title, especially if the monarch ever learned that she had fled from the country.

"I'll read them on the way to Calais." She noticed that the dizziness in her head had evaporated.

"We have prepared gowns, surcoats, undergarments, and other accessories suitable for a French countess, as well as a purse with money and several sets of jewelry."

Anne nodded her thanks with a smile. As her thoughts drifted back to Elizabeth and Arthur, tears prickled her eyes. "But how can I leave my children?"

"Forgive me, Anne, but there is no other alternative."

She was shrouded in a pall of grief over her offspring's misfortunes, caused by their father, and over their imminent separation. "How is Elizabeth? Did Henry exile her?"

Percy answered honestly, "His Majesty sent your daughter to Woodstock Manor."

The blood drained from her face, for Woodstock was too far away. "My poor dear girl! She does not deserve to suffer! She has not wronged the king in any way!"

"You must be strong, Anne. There is nothing you can do for her right now." To put her at ease, he pledged, "I'll ensure that your children will have a life as good as possible."

She muttered, "Thank you, Henry."

The cart ceased moving, and she could hear seagulls crying like souls in torment.

"You are welcome. Now we must go."

Still feeling weak, Anne climbed down from the cart with Henry's aid and stood nearby. As the snow-covered ground was slippery, he stepped to her side to support Anne.

The cold morning was crisp, yet bright and clear. The sky's canvas was bellclear, deepening from a cerulean blue at its apex down to the light pink of fading dawn at the horizon. In the distance loomed the white cliffs of Dover and the smooth expanse of the English Channel.

Anne's gaze dashed to the heavens. "Today, the firmament is such a perfect sight to behold! During the last days of my imprisonment, it was always grim gray and so chilly."

Henry chuckled. "This signifies the advent of a new life for you. Despite the time of year, the sea is surprisingly calm, as though fate blessed your voyage to Italy."

She looked in the direction of the Channel. "This can also be a bad omen. If one is too optimistic, their plans might be derailed, and hopes smashed into pieces."

"Put aside your melancholy."

"Is that really possible?" Her laugh was brittle.

Percy forewarned, "In his youth, Count Jean de Montreuil was a friend of Charles d'Orléans, Count d'Angoulême, who, I was told, passed away years ago. My knowledge of French lineages is limited, and I cannot tell you more."

The realization of the danger Anne could find herself in struck her like a physical blow in the gut. "The Count d'Angoulême was the father of King François. As I was raised and educated at his brilliant court, His Majesty knows me very well, and if I ever meet him, he shall recognize me."

He appeased, "Anne, you are going to Venice, not France. You will need to talk to the Count de Montreuil. He is well aware that you lived at the French court, so he understands the risks he will take upon your arrival in Venice."

Anne's shoulders sagged as her anxiety deflated. "I'll do my best to stay calm and control my emotions."

§§§

At present, Anne Boleyn was a different person with a new name, as though she embodied the Goddess Persephone, queen of the underworld, who ruled over the changes of the seasons and the eternal cycle of nature's death and rebirth.

"The old Anne is dead," Anne Boleyn told herself. "She was burned, but she was then reborn, as if by Persephone's wish."

Soon she boarded the ship with a heavy heart. For a long time, Anne remained on the deck, watching the white cliffs of the English coast grow smaller. She was forced to part with Arthur and Elizabeth by circumstance. Yet, at least now she would get tidings of how they were faring, and perhaps one day, she would be reunited with them.

§§§

Meanwhile, the Earl of Northumberland galloped towards London. Leaving the port behind, he said adieu to Anne, the love of his life, thinking that they would probably never meet again. His conniving mind was busy with forming a plan to prove her innocence and punish her foes. For Percy, it was a matter of duty and honor to assist Anne in any way he could.

At the same time, the people, who had rescued Anne, were traveling to Northumberland, to their master's lands. Their mission was accomplished, and now they were to stay in Henry Percy's estates, hidden from the eyes of the Tudor ruler and his councilors, especially Cromwell.

December 20, 1536, Château de Fontainebleau, France
King François I of France and his elder sister, Marguerite, Queen of Navarre and wife of King Henri II of Navarre from the House of Albert, sat together in the private gallery. The chamber linked the royal apartments with the Chapel de la Trinité. The château was the jewel of the French royal

palaces, and François often stayed here; when he spoke of coming to this place, he referred to it as going home.

"Death is a pitiless damsel." The ruler skimmed through the letter in his hands.

The monarch was seated in an elaborately carved, gilded chair. Candelabra illuminated the chamber, and the flickering flames seemed to dance a slow, plangent pavane in memory of the woman whose illustrious personality dazzled everyone. Once more, he re-read the missive from his ambassador to England – Philippe de Chabot, known as Admiral de Brion.

François turned to his sister. "Anne Boleyn is dead."

"Finally dead," echoed Marguerite in a voice colored with sadness.

The Valois siblings stared at each other, doleful incredulity etched into their features.

Clad in a white-slashed doublet of mulberry velvet, the monarch's rich ensemble reflected his gloomy mood; dazzling accents of sapphires and gold thread could not overcome his somber appearance. His Italian hose of matching velvet displayed the athletic symmetry of his limbs. The handle and sheath of his poniard were studded with gems; his girdle was set thick with rubies and diamonds. His plumed toque of red velvet was ornamented in a similar manner.

Marguerite's fashionable gown of azure and black velvet, with a low square-cut neckline and loose, hanging sleeves, set off her amber eyes and creamy skin. Her long stomacher was of cloth of gold, studded with gems. The hem of her skirt was stitched with gold thread. Set amidst her dark curls, her small skullcap of red velvet was embroidered with emeralds.

He crumpled the parchment. "You cannot imagine how she died, my dear sister."

"Didn't Henry hire a French executioner from Calais as initially planned?"

Thoroughly shocked, François did not reply straight away. He did not pay any attention to the majestic splendor of the spacious gallery, which was his favorite place in the palace. Being away from state and court affairs, he could spend hours here, conversing with his sister, for they were very close and adored each other. He always kept the key with him.

The walls were adorned with figures of mythological goddesses and nymphs in languorous poses, carved in oak. Between them, there were magnificent frescoes by Rosso Fiorentino, each of them framed in richly sculpted stucco and depicting the Gods of Olympus, some of which had François' features to illustrate the king's virtues. In particular, the fresco *The Royal Elephant* portrayed one of the Carthaginian general Hannibal's elephants, which personified the ruler's greatness. Fiorentino's talented hand gave the gallery a sense of refined eroticism.

At last, François shook his head in consternation as he answered, "Henry... God above, that narcissistic monster did not need any executioner. He burned Lady Anne at the stake as a witch." He laughed tragically and then jeered, "What a benevolent and fair monarch sits on the throne of England!"

Crossing herself, a horrified Marguerite gasped, "Oh Lord! Oh my dear Lord! How is that possible?"

His mouth tightened in a firm line. "Maybe the devil cast a spell over Henry."

"Henry really does have a wicked heart." As it was only between the two of them in the room, like her brother, she could not refrain from expressing her true opinion of the man. "Emotions take the best of him, and when he is incensed, Henry can neither think logically nor see the truth."

François objected, "It matters not what effect anger has on my English rival, and it is no excuse. He had no right to burn an anointed queen, even if he believes that she was guilty."

The ruler's sister balled her fists in rage. "Even a blind fool can see that she was innocent. Moreover, their marriage was nullified. How could Anne commit adultery, then?"

The monarch lifted his gaze to the stunning plafond, painted by the best of the Italian masters in France. "I can imagine this incredible woman in heaven among angels such as the ones on the ceiling." His eyes flicking back to his sister, he said with admiration, "She was different from anyone I've ever met and from other women at my and English courts. I'll mourn for her like a painter mourns for a lost masterpiece."

"And so will I." Her voice quivered with anguish. "I've always liked Anne, although I did not support Henry's vicious abandonment of Catherine of Aragon to wed her."

"Margot, I did not suspect that our cousin, Henry, at his worst could act in such a barbaric fashion."

François found in Henry everything he detested in a ruler. Henry was a hedonist obsessed with power and pleasure, and a tyrant who respected no laws but his caprice. Some of Henry's faults, like love for power and extravagance, could be attributed to François as well, but no one would ever say that the French king was less humane than his Tudor counterpart.

They had been rivals since the moment when the young Kings of France and England had wrestled near Calais, on the site that will always be known as 'the Field of the Cloth of Gold' because of the extravagance of the display all those years ago. When the French ambassador had informed François that Henry's passion for Anne had been cooling, he had expected that her marriage would be annulled, but not that his English adversary would sentence her to such a gruesome death.

"What Henry did is..." Marguerite fumbled for words. "It was monstrous, unfair, and from the political standpoint, foolish, too. It is a turbulent time for the English monarchy."

A myriad of visions was teeming in François' memory banks. He remembered a young Anne Boleyn curtsying to him in Queen Claude's apartments. Then he recalled a beautiful, alluring seductress wearing a white mask over her face, who had gracefully danced with him during their last meeting in Calais. Alternating waves of disbelief and regret inundated his whole being.

He whispered, "Anne Boleyn was crowned, even though she was not acknowledged as queen by Catholic nations."

A sense of bereavement was settling in Marguerite. "After Queen Catherine's passing, it seemed that nobody would dispute the legitimacy of Anne's union with King Henry."

"No one, save the King of England," stressed François.

"Indeed, Henry made himself the most powerful man in the kingdom. All those changes that he introduced to enable him to wed Anne gave him absolute power."

The King of France sighed. In spite of his reforms aimed at centralization, he was still dependent on influential French nobles. "Yes, England is now an absolute monarchy."

"Do not envy Henry, brother. Unlimited power might be all well and good, but see how it has led him astray. He sinned against the Almighty when he executed an anointed queen, one who was innocent of any wrongdoing, and the horror of his heinous crime will be felt in heaven."

"That is all true, Margot." His gaze flitted to one of the frescoes on a nearby wall, where the Goddess Persephone was depicted. He smiled at his whimsical thoughts: Anne Boleyn must have become queen in the realm of shadows after her demise. "Isn't it ironic? Those same reforms, which Henry implemented to marry Lady Anne, eventually killed her. You know, when the goal in life is magnificent greatness, the price might be extremely high. We pay it, step by step, as we work towards it. We commit to certain acts in the hope that they will eventually pay off."

Marguerite joined the philosophical debate. "Status does not make people great. History knows many miserable rulers, who tainted the reputation of their dynasties."

François elaborated sagaciously, "Greatness is an attitude, and a lifestyle. It is also the consistency, with which people maintain momentum in heading towards their goals. It is measured by the focus they apply to perfecting their lives, and by the results they accomplish."

"And Anne Boleyn, François? If we follow that definition, she was truly a great woman. She achieved her goal to be crowned as King Henry's consort, and all of her actions were consistent with it. Anne earned greatness in life, yet in the end, she paid too extreme a price for it."

"There is greatness in death as well," supplemented the Valois ruler. "Probably, Lady Anne became greater in death: now she is a martyr in everyone's eyes. She died at the pyre due to Henry's lust for another woman, and England will remember this forever. It gives her an air of tragic legend."

François paused as he mulled over the ramifications of the recent events in England. "The English people might consider Anne's execution an act of tyranny, one which warrants resistance to Henry's reign. A monarch ought to be wise and forward-looking when it comes to choosing methods to demonstrate his authority. Henry has long abandoned the humanism that influenced his youth. He has been corrupted by power and greed, having demonstrated that he is capable of oppressing and murdering anyone who does not approve of his policies. He is so fickle, and his temper too volatile."

The Queen of Navarre let out a sigh. "We are in agreement, brother. Tyranny is now in Henry's blood."

"Lady Anne birthed the king's son," he reminded. "Henry has deprived himself of a long-awaited male heir. It must be his child. I don't believe any of these ridiculous accusations."

"Did the ambassador write about this motherless infant?"

The Valois ruler leaned forward in his chair, as if poised to reveal a bit of confidential information. "The baby boy was taken into the custody of her sister, Lady Mary Stafford."

"Henry committed blasphemy," pronounced Marguerite as she crossed herself again. "The English folk must be perplexed and simultaneously exasperated."

François leaned back in his chair. "Philippe reported that the people of England have been keeping silent so far, but many of them blame their king. They did not expect that Lady Anne would be executed so soon after her child's birth and in such a bloodthirsty manner. Many doubt the charges leveled against her, but they are afraid of speaking it aloud."

"I would not have anticipated any other reaction."

"The Seymours and their supporters are both pleased and gleeful because their power has strengthened. Henry is going to wed Lady Jane Seymour before the year is out."

Marguerite frowned. "That would be so distasteful and indecent. His haste convinces me that Henry is an immoral person who does not respect the Lord."

His expression evolved into an icy stare as the vision of Henry's face formed in his brain. "Henry has become a brutal despot. His policies pose a threat to the peace and stability in England. I wonder how long Lady Jane Seymour will be allowed to remain his queen if she does not produce a son."

"She will also be set aside, if she fails to have a boy and has nothing but miscarriages."

"Yes, sister. His English Majesty is so unpredictable and bad-tempered that the courtiers walk on eggshells around him. Ordering Anne Boleyn's death by fire shows that he is capable of inhuman cruelty. If Jane Seymour disappoints him, he might kill her on false charges."

Marguerite bristled. "Enough about Henry!" She then redirected the conversation. "Brother, what are you going to do with your miserable marriage? You pay no attention to your queen, to the exclusion of official occasions; you have never visited her bedchamber."

"Ha!" François gritted his teeth and barked a short laugh. "I refuse to sleep with Eleanor of Austria. She is a sister of my mortal enemy – Carlos the Fifth, Holy Roman Emperor. Moreover, I'm not attracted to her at all." A flamboyant smile blossomed on his face. "I've my Anne who knows all ways to please me. Many other beauties are eager to warm my bed."

The Navarrese queen rebuked him sharply. "François! Madame Anne de Pisseleu is only your mistress. Eleanor is your wife, and you cannot ignore her forever."

"Why not? I'm the king, and I can do whatever I want."

Marguerite spoke sympathetically. "Eleanor is merely a poor woman, the emperor's pawn in his contest for power in Christendom. Carlos dreamed that you would sire a child on her when he compelled you to marry his sister." She released a sigh. "It has been almost seven years since your wedding. I'm aware of your distaste for Eleanor, but you must change something. Eleanor has been neglected by you and everyone at court – your wife is not liked here, and she is suffering."

"I shall not consummate my marriage," declared François in a categorical voice edged with the animosity he felt for the Habsburg family. "I cannot risk getting her pregnant. If my sons do not have any male progeny, and if I have a son with Eleanor, Spain will have much influence over France, and I shall not let that happen.   No Habsburg will ever rule our great country! If one day the Valois male line goes extinct, then it is better to have the Bourbons on the throne."

"Then, you must keep Eleanor at arm's length."

"That is the reason why I'm always coolly courteous with her while remaining very aloof.   I'm relieved that my behavior seems to have crushed her dream of being happy with me."

"Brother, I understand you, but I pity her."

Rising to his feet, the sovereign strolled to a monumental fireplace at the gallery's western end, which was decorated with bronze statues, copied from classical busts in Rome.

His gaze latched on to the statue of the Goddess Hera, Zeus' wife. "At least I've enjoyed amours with fewer women than the number of Zeus' lovers.   Eleanor is distressed because of being a neglected spouse, but that is the emperor's entire fault. I hope her infatuation with me will fade."

"François, you have to find a way out of this matrimony."

"Very soon." The king leaned against a nearby wall, his enigmatic gaze directed at his sister. "I'm fed up with the number of Imperial and Spanish spies at our court."

She shot him a worried look. "What are you planning?"

A sense of triumph gripped the monarch as he pictured sending his wife back to Spain. "Sister, I'm not Henry – I shall not murder Eleanor or lock her up in prison. According to canon law, a forced marriage is null and void. If the Pope grants me an annulment, it will be better for both of us."

Marguerite grinned at the prospect of his escape from an unwanted union. "Of course, you and Henry are as different as day and night." Yet, anxiety ripped through her gut. "But if you discard Eleanor, the emperor will be in a towering rage. He might launch a new campaign against France."

His mouth quirked. "My dearest sister, you have always been politically astute. What has happened to you today? The Habsburg-Valois wars are seemingly endless since Charles the Eighth of France invaded Italy all those years ago. My annulment will contribute very little to the further escalation of my conflict with the emperor."

She bobbed her head. "You are right, brother."

François pointed towards the depiction of Hannibal's war elephant. "It embodies the might and strength of France and her sovereign. Emperor Carlos, that Habsburg devil with a protruding lip, must not forget one important lesson of history: although many of the elephants Hannibal led across the Alps perished, the surviving animals aided their commander in crushing the Roman cavalry at Trebia." Narrowing his eyes, he sneered, "That Spanish thug captured me once, but I survived, as did the hardiest of those elephants. And I'll crush Carlos at the first available opportunity."

Marguerite omitted that the remaining elephants had also later died after being struck by a violent thunderstorm in Italy. "Sometimes, Lady Luck is a fickle friend."

"The Roman Emperor Marcus Aurelius, a celebrated stoic philosopher, believed that virtue progresses while fortune is fickle. At least, I'll no longer be tied to my sworn foe's sister."

The Queen of Navarre had never been fond of Eleanor and loathed the Spaniards. "Pope Paul the Third is well-disposed towards you, and I hope you will be free of her soon."

Having filled their goblets with wine, the siblings raised a toast for the king's divorce from his Habsburg spouse. They chatted in generalities about how they would defeat Emperor

Carlos and deliver the Duchy of Milan from the bondage of the Spanish overlordship. François and Marguerite were both descendants of Valentina Visconti, so given that the House of Sforza, which had ruled Milan for about a century, had gone extinct, now only the descendants of the Visconti family, who had been lords of Milan before Sforza, had the right to govern the city. François was determined to press his claim to Milan in the future. Victory seemed within their reach, vengeance was the French monarch's to take, and they were committed to seeing this course through to its conclusion.

CHAPTER 5

Condemned to the Shadows

April 5, 1537, Palace of Whitehall, London, England

"Another boring day in my life," muttered King Henry under his breath.

Queen Jane flicked her gaze to the monarch's face as her heart rate increased with worry. Why was Henry saying that? "Is everything all right, Your Majesty?"

For one panicked second, Henry was at a loss for words. He had spoken his thoughts aloud! "Nothing," he said coolly, at last. As he averted his gaze, he did not see his wife flinch.

The ruler of England sat on his massive throne on the dais in the great hall. On his left sat his new wife, Queen Jane, and his daughter, Lady Mary Tudor, occupied the seat on his right. Thomas Howard, Duke of Norfolk, and Charles Brandon, Duke of Suffolk, stood to the monarch's right behind his daughter; Edward Seymour and his brother, Thomas, were on Jane's left.

His melancholy evaporating, Henry glanced back at Jane affectionately. He was content to be married to her. Jane deserved to be loved, for she was pious, docile, and humble – she was everything that Henry wanted in a wife, and Anne's opposite. Even her motto was *'bound to obey and serve.'* He loved his Jane even more than either of her predecessors.

Upon their marriage, the monarch had gifted his *third* wife more than one hundred manors and many forests. Although her father, Sir John Seymour, had passed away in December 1536, Henry had categorically refused to postpone their wedding, not letting Jane mourn for her parent. Archbishop Cranmer had conducted the ceremony in the privacy of the queen's closet at Whitehall. On the same day, the wedding procession had passed through the streets of London. Later, Jane had been introduced to the court as Henry's consort, and then days of feasting and jousting had followed.

The monarch was not disappointed in the slightest. Jane had proved herself a good wife in every sense of the word: she had quickly conceived after their marriage. Now she was over two months along in her pregnancy. An overjoyed Henry was convinced that God had blessed their union.

Determined to eradicate Anne from the canvas of his life, Henry had enjoined that the carved initials of 'H & A' be removed from all his palaces and hunting lodges. Her clothes and personal possessions had been burned; the jewels he had gifted her had been melted down and made into new ones. Any reference to or hint of the harlot could be construed as treasonous. No one would ever forget the scene of the king trampling Anne's badge of a crowned falcon with his feet.

Breaking from his memories, the ruler refocused on the present. Jane was clothed in a gown of white velvet, set off with gold lace, her stomacher encrusted with diamonds. An elaborate silver and pearl necklace glittered in the hollow of her throat. Today, her headdress was a white velvet coif, adorned with rows of pearls, and confined by a circlet of silver.

Henry asked, "Sweetheart, how are you feeling?"

"I'm perfectly well, Your Majesty," answered Jane timidly.

Jubilation seized Jane. *I'm carrying the future King of England. My marriage to His Majesty is valid and blessed by the Lord,* she reminded herself. The Boleyn strumpet had fornicated with the ruler, and the Almighty had directed His wrath towards Anne for her sins, denying her a son. At present, Jane was deliriously happy because she was the wife of the glorious and handsome English monarch.

Since catching his eye, the regal air about Henry had utterly captivated Jane. Their courtship had been short but romantic, save the time when she had endured the whore's insults and temper tantrums while serving Anne as her lady-in-waiting. She was grateful to her mentors – her brother, Edward, and Sir Nicholas Carew, another of the harlot's foes – for teaching her how to ensnare the king. Jane loved Henry and was convinced that he reciprocated her feelings.

In an exhilarated tone, Henry proclaimed, "Soon we will have our dear son in the new silver cradle I've commissioned. I'm looking forward to having him in my arms."

"Me too." Although she smiled at him wanly, her eyes had a certain harried look. Inside Jane was shuddering at the mention of the male heir her husband craved.

He eyed the necklace on the queen's bosom. "Do you like my latest gift, Jane?"

"It is beautiful, I love it very much. It will always remind me of you."

"Sweetheart, you will give me the most precious of gifts." Henry's gaze meandered from Jane to the Duke of Suffolk, so he did not notice the flash of fear in his wife's eyes.

The monarch was briefly distracted by thoughts of his children and his heirs. The Second Succession Act of 1536 had been passed by Parliament, so it had been declared that only Henry's children by Jane would be legitimate heirs to the Tudor throne. This document also confirmed the illegitimacy of the Lady Mary Tudor and the Lady Elizabeth Tudor.

Jane had reconciled King Henry with his eldest daughter, Mary, who had returned to court before Christmas. By signing the Oath of Supremacy, Mary had repudiated the papal authority and acknowledged her parents' union as invalid. Since then, Henry was doting on her, as if she had always been the pearl of his world, with no years of separation for them and forgetting the shame of her living as Elizabeth's servant. It seemed that their relationship had been repaired.

Elizabeth had been ejected because she reminded the king of her mother. Her intelligent eyes, dark and enigmatic, were like Anne's, burning him with the same fire with which Anne had ensorcelled Henry. Elizabeth's elegance and grace, so rare for a little girl of only three and a half years, irritated and pained the ruler, for they were another memento of Anne.

Jane's answer intruded into his musings. "I'm praying for our son every morning and every evening."

The monarch let out a smile. "I'm lucky to have such a pious queen, one who is a paragon of benevolence and virtue."

"I'm trying to be a good spouse to you, sire."

His countenance morphed into seriousness. "I do need a son, Jane. Make the child in your belly a boy." At this, her skin prickled with a dread that chilled the queen to the bone.

Henry scanned the assemblage of nobles, who chattered boisterously, ate ravenously, and danced merrily. Everything was totally routine to a point of boredom that made him wish to leave the feast. He coveted a fire of lust and vitality that

Jane was unable to give him. It occurred to him that there had been many lively and festive banquets, fêtes, and masques when Anne Boleyn had been his consort. Angry in his mind, he forcibly redirected his thoughts to the present day.

The king's gaze landed on a raven-haired woman attired in a French gown of pink velvet with a low, square-cut neckline. The girdle, studded with precious stones, encircled her small waist. Her hair was worn in the same fashion as women did at the Valois court: neatly arranged rows of dark curls around the face and at the nape of the neck. *She is vivacious, wistfully appealing, and simultaneously tempting,* Henry observed silently. *Her contagious laughter is as melodious as Anne's had been.* In the next instant, he cursed the dead harlot.

Henry turned to the Duke of Suffolk. "Charles, who is that lovely lady? I've rarely seen her at my court."

Brandon intercepted his sovereign's gaze and blanched. The girl's continental fashions and her flirtatious demeanor were similar to those of the Boleyn slut. Her sardonic humor and sharp tongue were famous at court, although it could not compete with the whore's unparalleled wit. The similarity to Anne made Brandon wonder whether his liege lord still had feelings for the Boleyn woman.

"Does Your Majesty mean the lady in a pink gown?"

"Yes," confirmed the monarch.

A knowing smile twisted Brandon's lips. "She is the Lady Anne Bassett. Two months earlier, she arrived at court to serve as the queen's handmaiden. Do you need my help?"

"She is so feminine." His gaze undressing her in a single sweep, Henry decreed, "Inform this stunning creature that I'll be waiting for her in my chambers tonight."

Charles nodded. He often helped his king in arranging extramarital affairs, but this task discomfited him, for the Lady Bassett was similar to the dead Anne in some aspects.

§§§

On this night, King Henry bedded Lady Anne Bassett for the first time. As a ruler, he could have as many paramours as he wanted, especially if his queen was with child.

"Oh, Lady Bassett," crooned the monarch against his lover's lips. "You are a gorgeous, amatory nymph who makes the blood of all men boil with indecent desires."

"Your greatest Majesty," his paramour purred between kisses. "England's most glorious monarch!"

Henry grinned conceitedly. "And most powerful, too."

Her mouth travelled down his throat to the hollow in his neck. "Undoubtedly, sire."

"You are so young," he moaned. "Yet, you are not a virgin."

Anne lifted her gaze to him. "Are you disappointed?"

Outside, the shadows of the evening had spread across a slumbering earth. The lovers reclined on a large bed canopied with red brocade cloth. In the light from an array of candles, their bodies glowed a soft gold.

He fondled her bosom. "It is fine for a mistress to be experienced in physical love." His mouth captured her nipple, alternating between both breasts. "But not for a wife."

She quivered with bursts of pleasure. "Your Majesty! I'm honored that you have chosen me to be your lover, and I need nothing else, save your passion."

His loins swelled with unbearable hunger. "I cannot wait any longer, my dear. I must claim you now!"

Anne laughed jovially. "I want you more than my next breath, my king."

The monarch positioned himself facing Anne. Wrapping his large hand around the back of her thigh, he draped her leg over his hip, opening her body to him. With one hard stroke, he penetrated her. He began thrusting into her with all of his might, impaling her with every bit of his throbbing manhood. Reality blurred as primeval desire took hold. He feasted kisses upon her neck, while his hands roamed over her well-curved form. Their experiments were tinged with unrestrained debauchery. Henry rolled onto his back and marveled at her audacity as she straddled his hips and expertly rode him, as if he were a prized stallion.

"You are an exquisite little thing," praised the ruler in a husky voice, his eyes closed.

She leaned down and kissed his torso. "Your Majesty is most virile and most handsome." Her mind briefly detoured to her first lover – young Thomas Howard, Earl of Surrey. Her heart still ached from his abandonment of her, but she had been merely infatuated with him.

He forced her to change positions, rolling so that she was under him. "Now you are mine."

Enfolding her legs around his waist, she chortled. "Yes!"

King Henry pounded into her with reckless abandon. "All women in England belong to me."

Their moans and groans mingled, and their bodies were coated with a thin sheen of glistening sweat. Anne observed her royal lover: he was tall and burly, with an attractive broad countenance, yet there was the hint of a sinister threat lurking in the depths of his aquamarine eyes, even though they were currently dazed with lust. *The king is rather corpulent,* the mistress mused. *Yet, he is still athletic in bed.* She compared his stout appearance to Surrey, who was slimmer and more pleasant to touch. The smell from Henry's ulcerated leg irritated her senses, but Anne compelled herself to ignore it.

After their wanton adventures, Anne Bassett fell asleep next to him, and Henry perused her. His paramour was an unusual beauty: like Anne Boleyn, she was dark and seductive, and most men found her intriguing, although she did not have the deceased Anne's larger-than-life personality. Henry took this woman twice in a vehement and lewd dance, because his need for salacious fire suddenly returned with the fury of a colossal tempest. Neither wine nor sleep could quell it, so he ravaged his lover's body until he had no strength left.

The air in the room was pressing in on the monarch. At one time, everything in his chambers and in every corner of the palace – from the ceiling beams to the embroidered covers – had symbolized his union with the harlot. Although his quarters had been refurbished after her arrest, he could still feel Anne Boleyn's spirit in Whitehall. When he thought of her, his entire being was wrapped in a pall of his eternal animosity towards her. But in the next moment, his hostility vanished as if by enchantment, and a tremor of longing ran through Henry.

His eyes riveted on Lady Bassett's face, Henry released a sigh. "She is not that whore. That traitor is gone forever!"

However, it seemed that the dead adulteress would always haunt the ruler from the world of shadows. He plunged into a fitful sleep where visions of Anne Boleyn dancing at the Château Vert pageant swarmed his mind like wasps around a nest. When the word 'Perseverance' slipped from his lips, his lover's eyes flung open, and Anne Bassett's pretty features contorted in displeasure at the realization that he was thinking of the dead Anne.

April 15, 1537, Palace of Whitehall, London, England
Thomas Cromwell smirked to himself as he read through the parchment in his hands. It was the list of the

monasteries he would close down within the next year. For the first time in over two years, he felt secure about his future. *Now my position is stronger than ever,* the minister enthused. *The king praises and trusts me more than his other councilors.*

A male voice moved Cromwell out of his reverie. "Do we need to rush the dissolution?"

The royal chief minister lifted his eyes from the document and glanced at Sir Richard Rich, who sat at a nearby desk. He could not read the other man's expression, for Rich was as skilled at concealing his real emotions as he himself was. The previous year, Rich had been appointed chancellor of the Court of Augmentations, which had been established for the disposal of the monastic revenues. Thus, the two of them would have to collaborate in all the religious projects.

"Yes, we do, Master Rich. The sooner the corrupt religious houses are demolished, the better it will be for the nation's soul and for the Royal Treasury."

Thomas Cromwell was a tall, sturdy man in his mid-fifties, clad in sumptuous robes of black brocade wrought with threads of gold, a cap of black satin atop his greying head. His shrewd, hazel eyes looked straight into Rich's discomfited soul, piercing him like a rapier's thrust to the heart.

Richard Rich sighed apprehensively. "If we act too quickly and handle things roughly, the population of England will be appalled. Many commoners and nobles still remain devout Catholics who yearn for the past. They will not stand by and watch the desecration of churches, convents, abbeys, and chantries, as well as the defacement of their monuments. An uprising against the king might take place."

Cromwell dismissed his concerns. "They love His Majesty. Everyone signed the Oath of Supremacy, and in doing so, they recognized him as Supreme Head of the Church of England, empowering him to freely exercise his rights in that capacity."

"Master Cromwell, many people still want to restore the English church's allegiance to the Bishop of Rome."

"His Majesty will never bow to Rome."

"Of course, he will not," replied Rich. "Many signed the Oath, but in reality, they abjure the reformed Church. The religious upheavals will enrage them, and their response will be a mass protest, God forbid. Any hasty action upon our part will provoke them to act equally precipitately."

"They will not dare," Cromwell repeated, but his voice lacked conviction.

"I'm counseling caution." Rich stilled for a moment, his countenance thoughtful. "I cannot help but think that Anne Boleyn's warning about a possible revolt was right."

The chief minister sniggered. "Anne is dead! We are no longer facing any opposition and can proceed with our plans. Even if the commoners are unhappy, they will obey the king."

Cromwell dropped his gaze back to the parchment. Nobody and nothing would deter him from his obsessive goal to demolish the Roman Catholicism in England.

At the beginning of the reform, Cromwell and Cranmer had both thought that if Catholic and Protestant beliefs were combined, a compromise could be achieved. Now the Church of England was neither Protestant nor Catholic – it was *the Henrician Church*. It would never work, and Cromwell must make it purely Protestant. *I hate the idolatry of popery,* hissed Cromwell in his mind. *I've launched the destruction of statues, roods, and images at the monasteries and abbeys.*

Once Parliament had passed the Suppression of Religious Houses Act, this had enabled the dismantlement of the corrupt monasteries. A year earlier, Cromwell had dispatched commissioners to inspect religious houses of all kinds. He had closed many small monasteries, confiscating their wealth for the Crown. He advocated the all-out dissolution of both large and small monasteries because of the feckless and ungodly lives of the monks. In the months to come, he would send more men to the abbeys, each of them strictly loyal to him. Many nobles and commoners were Catholics, but that did not matter because the king supported Cromwell's plan.

Cromwell prided himself on an excellent understanding of the monarch's mind. He could effortlessly anticipate what his sovereign wanted, and zealously worked for the welfare of King Henry and the realm. His secret of personal success was that he let his liege lord enjoy and exercise absolute power while surreptitiously and craftily manipulating him.

Anne Boleyn, Cromwell hissed wordlessly. *I contrived to have her killed because she evolved from being my ally into my archenemy and an obstacle to the king's reforms.* Years earlier, he had supplied Anne with some forbidden books by the reformers Martin Luther and William Tyndale. She had showed these texts to the monarch, which had led to Cromwell's appointment as royal secretary and chief minister.

However, later they had disagreed about the way funds from the dissolution were to be used. Anne had refused to support his stance that all the monies from the liquidation of abbeys belonged to the Crown. She had claimed, despite the people's distaste for her, that the monasteries gave vital help to the poor, the needy, and the sick. Their arguments had escalated; Anne had vowed to send him to his death, should he decide to follow his plan, and she had not jested.

That had been her fatal mistake! The clever chief minister recognized that as the ruler's wife, she had become a threat, which had forced him to act. Even though her marriage had been wrecked beyond repair, Anne had still been queen. If she had turned against him, then Archbishop Cranmer and the Boleyn faction would certainly follow in her footsteps.

Many English nobles despised the royal chief minister due to his rise from his low birth, secretly opposing Cromwell and his ideas. Furthermore, they disliked the idea of the Anglo-Imperial alliance, which Cromwell supported, and hated the disbandment of religious houses, despite the significant enrichment which it could bring the nobility and the gentry. In general, the Boleyns had stood in the way of Cromwell's political ambitions, for Anne had preferred a French alliance.

Long ago, Cromwell had learned that assuming power meant being fearless and ruthless with opposition. It was a fact that either he or the Boleyns must win – the losing party risked everything, even their lives. So, the chief minister had joined forces with the Duke of Suffolk. Together they had spread rumors about Anne's infidelities, and these had duly reached the King of England's ears. When Henry had ordered to investigate the matter, Cromwell had manufactured charges against Anne; his initial assumption that the monarch would believe her guilty had been correct.

Studying the sheet of paper clasped in his hands, Cromwell laughed gleefully. Ruthlessness and fearlessness! One had to possess a combination of these qualities to climb high and then survive at the volatile Tudor court, as well as accumulate more power and wealth. The minister had long realized that.

April 23, 1537, Venice, the Republic of Venice
Dusk descended and shrouded the city of Venice in a veil of gray mist. Count Jean de Montreuil and Anne Boleyn

dined in a room on the ground floor. Three walls were swathed in tapestries of hunting and maritime scenes, and the fourth was decorated with Titian's frescoes. He was seated at the head of the table, while she occupied the place at his right. The walnut furniture was lavishly inlaid with gold and silver.

Anne brought a goblet to her lips and sipped. She then commented, "I've been studying the history of the Ponthieu family the whole day. Now I know it by heart."

"I'm glad. What else were you doing today?" inquired Jean as he finished off his drink.

"I read Boccaccio's '*Decameròn*.' I love this book."

"His style is fabulous. Were you reading it in Italian?" he asked casually as a servant refilled his cup.

"Yes, I was. I've not forgotten this lovely language." She broached the subject that interested her the most. "Monsieur Jean, do you have any news from England?"

"Grandfather." The count gulped wine from his goblet.

"I'll remember it," she promised with a smile.

Several months had passed since Anne's arrival in Venice. The most dangerous part of her journey had been the time spent in France, where she could have been seen and recognized. It had been an enormous relief when she had crossed the French border and entered the Duchy of Savoy.

Anne was fascinated by the '*City of Water*,' which was located on a group of small islands separated by canals and linked by bridges. Venice was one of the most beautiful Italian cities with its grand palaces, cathedrals, and water all around, which gave the place a romantic air.

She had settled at the Palazzo Montreuil – the residence of Jean Frédéric Roger de Ponthieu, Count de Montreuil. He had greeted Anne warmly and seemed to have accepted her, although he was still cautious around her. Nevertheless, they were slowly starting to trust each other.

Jean's only son, Guillaume, and his daughter-in-law, Beatrice had both passed away years ago. His orphaned granddaughter, Anne de Ponthieu, had been placed in a convent to receive an education while her grandfather had served as the French ambassador to the Republic of Venice. At twenty, she had journeyed to Venice for a short time. After her clandestine affair with a German merchant, she had eloped with him, much to her grandfather's shock, and then she had lived in the Duchy of Cleves for a year before dying of smallpox.

Henry Tudor's betrayal had condemned Anne Boleyn to a life in the shadows. It was a stroke of luck that Jean had no surviving relatives, and that few French and Venetian nobles had ever seen Anne de Ponthieu. Fortunately, the count kept only a few servants, all of whom were absolutely loyal to him. However, there was still a risk that she might be recognized by a visiting French noble who had seen the adult Anne Boleyn in Calais with King Henry.

Jean's voice snapped Anne out of her musings. "You are pensive again, Anne."

A chunk of venison poised on the tip of her knife, Anne replied, "I'm trying to use thoughtfulness and kindness in my interactions and think before I speak."

"These are useful qualities." Having finished a dish of broiled pheasant, he apprised, "I've received a letter from my old friend."

The count meant her father. "How is he doing?"

"He is staying at his estates; he hates the countryside and wants to return to court where his life brims with intrigues."

Her eyes hardened, betraying her rising temper. She was afraid that Thomas Boleyn would use her son, Arthur, for his personal advancement. After all, Anne, along with her siblings – Mary and George – had been Boleyn's pawns in his avaricious quest to gain new titles and positions.

She changed the topic. "Is there any other important news?"

"My friend's grandson, little Arthur, resides at his eldest daughter's household. The boy is hale and hearty. His aunt loves him dearly and patiently mothers him."

A sigh of relief escaped her lips. "It is God's blessing when children are healthy."

"The French ambassador to England wrote to me."

Anne shot him a questioning look. "What did he say?"

As a servant refilled his goblet, Jean took a sip. "King Henry married Lady Jane Seymour ten days after the death of his second wife, Anne Boleyn." He paused, his eyes never leaving her face. "A week afterwards, His Majesty summoned Parliament. He made a long speech and stressed that despite all his marital misfortunes, he had ventured to marry again."

"How did the Parliament react?" She disguised her anger with a brittle smile.

"One of the speakers, Sir Richard Rich, compared King Henry's justice and prudence to Solomon, his strength and fortitude to Samson, and his beauty and comeliness to Absolom."

She spat, "They are disgustingly servile, which manifests the lack of their self-respect. For honest rulers, servility is the forewarning of a potential traitor."

"That the English king remarried with such haste was hardly unexpected."

A certain part of Anne missed the time when she had wielded power as queen and presided over festivities and jousts. These days, she rarely smiled, and if she did, it was a cold smile that was like a frosty wind blowing across an icy lake. Her dark eyes did not sparkle unless the former queen was engaged in some captivating discourse or deliberation about her absent children, who were only referred to obliquely.

Jean took a hearty swig of his wine before continuing, "Queen Jane encouraged her husband to reconcile with Lady Mary Tudor, who has returned to court."

"What about the monarch's youngest daughter?"

"King Henry does not acknowledge the Lady Elizabeth as his child, despite her surname being Tudor. Unfortunately, he stopped paying for his daughter's household, so Queen Jane donated money to cover the girl's expenses. Several relatives are reported to be supporting her financially."

A gust of primal rage ripped through Anne. "How can a father treat his own child in such a savage manner?" At this very moment, she hated Henry with every fiber of her being.

"I don't know because I loved my family dearly, but there is nothing you can do for the girl at this point."

She threw all caution to the winds. "I cannot be calm when my daughter is suffering at the hands of her own father!"

"Lady Mary and Queen Jane will take care of Elizabeth. Your family and friends will help her, too." The count alluded to the secret support of Thomas Boleyn and Henry Percy.

"I hope so. I'm praying for my Lizzy every day."

"I've also learned that the Earl of Northumberland has befriended the Archbishop of Canterbury."

"That is interesting news." Her former fiancé had told Anne that he would endeavor to prove her innocence; maybe he would ask Cranmer to disclose her last confession.

Their conversation paused for a time, and they ate in silence. Anne eyed the Count de Montreuil. A man of sixty-five, Jean could have been her natural grandfather. Tall and of slender build, his face was narrow, with hazel and deep-set clever eyes below a forehead made broader by a receding hairline. His grizzled hair had been light brown in his youth.

Over the months, they had frequently discussed music, the arts, literature, and fashion, but politics was his favorite topic. Admiring her stellar education, Jean was proud that the French court had helped Anne become so cultured, and to her, he was an epitome of the best of French aristocracy.

After her arrival, the count had hired seamstresses to create new clothes for Anne. As a result, now she had a multitude of fashionable gowns in the Venetian style, as well as many stunning headpieces and expensive jewelry. While in the Tower, she had worn only plain, dark gowns, and her only jewelry had been a silver cross suspended from a simple chain around her neck. Delighted with her new wardrobe, Anne was exceedingly grateful to Jean for his unexpected generosity.

In a philosophical tone, Jean averred, "Nothing happens without a reason." He emptied his goblet. His voice layered with wisdom and encouragement, he added, "Reality is harsh. Sadly, most people turn a blind eye to the afflictions of others, especially the poor, so they can enjoy life to the fullest. But Henry Percy is not one of them, and that will be to your benefit, Anne."

A smile tugged at her lips. "Lord Northumberland has loved the lady of his dreams for years. That is why she is not dead yet." She drank her wine slowly, savoring the taste.

He understood her hint. "Everyone needs compassion to thrive." He sighed, anticipating her reaction to his next piece of news. "Queen Jane is with child."

"Procreation is the main reason for marriage," affirmed Anne, her gaze stony, giving away nothing of her inner tumult. "I hope she will have a healthy daughter."

Despite her antagonism towards Jane Seymour, the exiled woman did not want her to suffer a miscarriage or bear a stillborn child. Children were innocent of their parents' shortcomings. *Yet, I cannot bear the thought of Jane having Henry's son while my own boy has been rejected.*

Sympathy shone in Jean's eyes, for he could imagine her feelings on the matter.

The count swallowed his food before asking, "Have you heard about the ongoing Italian war?" At her nod, the count added, "Currently, King François is spending much time in Provence, Piedmont, and Lombardy."

As her hands had begun trembling, Anne set her goblet on the table. "Will he come here?"

"Perhaps. France is interested in an alliance with the Republic of Venice against Emperor Carlos. Nevertheless, for now, the King of France is quite busy in Piedmont."

She fidgeted with her hands. "What should I do?"

"You are unlikely to see him even if he travels to Venice."

"If our paths cross, it shall be a disaster for me."

"It would be useful for you to meet with His Majesty."

A puzzled Anne fixed him with a skeptical look. "Why? Monarchs ally with other rulers only if it is beneficial for their kingdoms. And I can do nothing for the King of France."

"King François hates the English monarch as much as he loathes the emperor. They are both his mortal foes."

"Sovereigns still ally with each other, if it serves some purpose." After a short pause, she went on. "There has always been fierce competition and dislike between Henry and François. But such strong antipathy?"

"My liege lord has compelling reasons to feel so."

Anne did not pursue the topic further, for apparently Jean would not elaborate on the matter. As Queen of England, she had woven intrigues, but she had grown immensely tired of the deadly games of court, where lives were governed by gossip and deception. Her current interest in politics was tied only to her children's future in England, and for this reason, she craved to learn more about the enmity between the two kings.

CHAPTER 6

Attempted Regicide

May 2, 1537, the Vatican, Rome, Italy

On the Feast of St Athanasius, the early morning in Rome was sultry, windless, and hot. The sun blazed down upon the city's inhabitants as they hurried back and forth to attend to their daily business. However, many paused to watch a cavalcade that was moving away from the grand St Peter's Basilica, which was built in the Renaissance style and located in Vatican City.

First appeared a dozen trumpeters, blowing flourishes. Next came a squad of halberdiers, whose leader proclaimed in accented Italian, "Make way for the king's grace!"

Then followed Sir Robert Stuart, Seigneur d'Aubigny, on his black stallion caparisoned in azure velvet, and bearing the Valois royal standard. He was captain of the Scots Guard, or *the Garde Écossaise*. This elite force had safeguarded the French monarchs since King Charles VII of France, called the Victorious (*le Victorieux*), had founded the group in 1418. Many armed men trailed their captain.

Everyone's attention was focused on a sumptuous litter in the middle of the procession. It was swathed in cloth of gold and drawn by four brown palfreys. Blue and white damask, ornamented with fleur-de-lis and Valois escutcheon, was draped extravagantly across the horses' flanks, and it brushed the pavestones as the litter passed. It was shadowed by more guards, all of them vigilant and disciplined.

The several occupants of the litter, who were comfortably reclining against its plump cushions, included King François I of France, whose hand was linked with that of his long-term *maîtresse-en-titre* – Anne Jeanne de Pisseleu d'Heilly, Duchess d'Étampes. They were joined by François de Tournon, Archbishop of Bourges and Embrun, a French diplomat and a cardinal high in royal favor.

"It is an amazing day today, isn't it?" questioned Anne de Pisseleu d'Heilly. "Your Majesty's freedom is a glorious fire consuming me entirely. Now we will always be together!"

King François grinned back at her. "Yes, my Venus."

"Your Majesty," began Cardinal de Tournon in a mighty tone, briefly touching his four-cornered red cap. "Accept my congratulations on the annulment of your second marriage."

The monarch replied, "Thank you, Your Eminence."

"We got what we wanted," the cardinal spelled out.

The King of France's secret meeting with Pope Paul III had resulted in the much-desired nullification of his unfortunate union with Eleanor of Austria, born Archduchess of Austria and Infanta of Castile from the House of Habsburg, the elder sister of Carlos V, Holy Roman Emperor.

The disastrous marriage had been part of the terms of the treaty after the Battle of Pavia on the 24th of February 1525. The defeated king had been captured and held prisoner in Madrid for a long time in awful living conditions. Eventually, François had been released, but in exchange for his sons – the late Dauphin François and the current Dauphin Henri.

To secure the release of the princes, Emperor Carlos had forced his Valois archrival to make degrading concessions to him, one of them his marriage to Eleanor. However, François had never consummated his matrimony with his second wife and preferred Anne de Pisseleu, who had been his constant paramour throughout the past eleven years. François' two hapless sons had spent several years in Spain in similar bad conditions before finally returning home in 1530.

At present, King François had a large, well-trained army. As France had broken away from Spain's control, he appealed to the Pope to end his farce of a marriage. The forced nature of the monarch's union and its non-consummation were the compelling grounds for the nullification. It was surprisingly easy for François to get the Vatican's support, despite the Pope's fears that Carlos V could again command his troops to sack Rome, as had happened in 1527.

The ruler recalled his meeting with the Supreme Pontiff. "I heartily thanked His Holiness for his help. Now Her Highness Infanta Eleanor ought to return to Spain to her evil brother." He referred to Eleanor by her Spanish title, as if she had never been his wife. The king did not have strong aversion towards Eleanor, but he had never been able to overlook the ferocious hatred he felt for the House of Habsburg.

The cardinal gave a nod. "I'll see to it."

François grinned with devilish satisfaction. "The emperor will be infuriated like an angry Minotaur."

Anne sniggered. "Now Your Majesty is like King Henry of England because you disposed of your spouse."

The monarch's incredulous gaze turned into a glare. "You are wrong, *ma chérie*. I did not murder any of my wives." His rigid features relaxed. With a faint echo of his usual humor, he said, "Ladies are like flowers and should be treated most courteously. They need tender care to blossom and be happy. Affection, kindness, respect, and tenderness are as the sun for them. Most definitely, no man should be allowed to harm a woman physically, let alone murder and torture them."

Realizing her mistake, the royal mistress defended herself. "I only implied that you are a man who cast his unwanted wife aside, just as His English Majesty did."

Tournon interjected, "King Henry annulled his marriage to Lady Anne Boleyn. If they were never married, then there was no adultery, which the whole of Europe is discussing."

The ruler slipped into melancholy. "I knew Lady Anne in her early youth. She was too clever to betray Henry; she did love him, I saw it in Calais." He sighed. "God rest her soul."

The cardinal crossed himself. "Let her rest in peace."

"That Tudor tyrant killed her to remarry," assumed Anne.

King François gazed out of the litter's window. "No doubt Thomas Cromwell's plot destroyed Anne Boleyn. It is a great pity that she is dead."

A jealous Duchess d'Étampes regarded him irritably. "What, Your Majesty?"

The monarch veered his gaze to her. A smile of peculiar, undefinable expression flicked at his mouth as he again remembered Anne Boleyn. "Exactly what I said." He switched to another topic. "Soon I'm intending to meet with the Doge of the Republic of Venice."

"Is it so urgent?" she queried.

François inclined his head. "We must secure as many new alliances on the Apennine peninsula as possible."

"Does Your Majesty want to be friends with Venice?" the cardinal asked.

The ruler intoned, "Yes, I do. We must assemble as many Italian allies against the emperor as possible. I expect Your Eminence to aid me with negotiations in Venice."

"Of course," obeyed the councilor.

"Your Majesty, am I traveling with you?" Anne reached out, took his hand in hers, and then placed it on her breast, but he gently pushed her away.

A long silence stretched between them as King François appraised the green-eyed blonde. Her small-framed body, clothed in a crimson velvet gown, ornamented with rubies, with an indecently low crescent décolletage trimmed with lace, was sculpted like an ancient Roman statue of Venus.

The chief royal mistress had a face that was classically beautiful with a small straight nose, delicate chin, and rosy mouth; it was too perfect to behold without experiencing unchaste stirrings of spirit. There was a seductive air about her, despite the gold chain with a cross dangling from her neck. Anne wore a matching elegant and small red velvet hat that had a pair of long and white plumes, which dipped and bobbed about her shoulders in the breeze.

There were many incredible things about Anne d'Étampes: from how her eyes sparkled with a lascivious fire to her small-boned feet in rich velvet slippers, from her great education to her strong intelligence. She walked like a temptress: her feet glided across the floor, as if she were floating, with her hips swaying like the leaves of a trembling tree in the wind.

My mistress enjoys being at the center of attention, especially if she is an object of male adoration, the monarch remarked to himself. Everyone collectively leaned towards her when Anne entered, and a pert tilt of her haughty head communicated her sense of superiority over others. When Anne smiled at men provocatively, they held their breath and had the impulse to submerge themselves in her flesh.

A daughter of a Picardian nobleman who had not been wealthy, Anne de Pisseleu d'Heilly had come to court in 1526 as a maid of honor to François' late mother, Louise de Savoy. When the King of France had returned from Spain in 1526, he had been drawn to her at first sight and forthwith dismissed his first long-term favorite – Françoise de Foix, Countess de Châteaubriant, taking Anne as his replacement *maîtresse-en-titre*. Anne had been all too eager to warm his bed.

The Duchess d'Étampes had faced no competition from the former Queen Eleanor and acted as if she were the Queen of France. She was always at François' side, and the monarch had even been faithful to her in the past several years. With the exception only of his sister, Anne de Pisseleu was the one woman with whom the ruler discussed politics from time to time. She was described as *"the most beautiful among the learned and the most learned among the beautiful."*

King François scrutinized his paramour once more. Anne regularly gave him colossal carnal pleasure and entertained him with clever conversation. However, lately, he began yearning to have a relationship on a spiritual level, albeit with an equally beautiful and intelligent woman. His lover was incapable of fulfilling this need, and, thus, he did not feel as strongly for her as he had felt a few months ago. Certainly, he did not want her company on his trip to Venice.

"Madame, you will return to Turin," instructed the ruler. "You will wait for me there, Anne. I'll be very busy in Venice."

"I'll obey Your Majesty," a chagrined Anne muttered.

The duchess struggled to maintain a demure façade. *If I protest against François' order, he will rebuke me harshly,* she inferred. Anne de Pisseleu always used everything and everyone to her advantage, calculated every word and step, and endeavored to manipulate the monarch, though rarely successfully. She had influenced some of his decisions, and the ruler had encouraged her to advise him about various courses of action, but the final word was always his alone.

Anne fancied herself in love with François, being proud that during the past few years, he had not bedded anyone else. Yet, sudden terror slithered through her like a coiled snake: did their separation mean that the monarch would have some Italian mistress? If the king discarded her, she would lose not only a lover, who could be replaced, but also all the power and prestige that came with being his royal mistress. *I want to be the only woman in François' bed!* Anne moaned silently.

The monarch shifted his scrutiny to Tournon. "Your Eminence, you and Monsieur de la Brosse will come with me. Monty will stay in Piedmont with our army."

The cardinal nodded; he appreciated the high royal favor and trust. He was an experienced courtier, skilled at keeping the king's secrets and preserving state interests.

Anne tilted her head to the side, exposing the delicate skin on her neck to her lover's view. "Will I have a chance to spend some more time with Your Majesty before you leave?"

A primitive male desire for Anne seized the Valois ruler, but there was no love in him. "Of course, Anne. Tonight we will ravish each other with all the fervor we can muster."

Not wishing to ruin the intimate moment, Tournon grinned to himself and looked out. He contemplated the people hastening through the streets of Rome.

Her cheeks bloomed like a tender rose. "You will never be disappointed, *mon amour.*" Her hand brushed her lover's knee, a whiff of her violet perfume hovering in the air.

"You are immodest, Madame, but too attractive," drawled François. "Never disappointed in you?"

Anne forced a laugh, but she tensed. Her hollow laugh sounded normal to Tournon, but not to François who knew her too well. "Never ever, Your Majesty," she swore.

May 21, 1537, St Mark's Basilica, Venice, the Republic of Venice

Lady Anne Boleyn sat on the multicolored silk cushions in Count de Montreuil's private gondola. Her mood elated, she was enjoying the breathtaking views around her.

The gondola was passing through the Grand Canal with a slow, rhythmical splash from the oar. Soon they landed at the quay that led to the city's central piazza. A thrill of wondrous excitement ran through a fascinated Anne as, once again, she beheld the immense, pink, arcaded bulk of the Palazzo Ducale – the Doge's Palace, which was her favorite building in Venice.

Stepping out of the gondola, Anne strode in the direction of the Piazza San Marco, dominated by a grand cathedral at the eastern end. She mingled with the people who crowded the square. She moved slowly and often paused as there were many pigeons cooing and strutting about, some of them circling about her, as if blessing her with their silvery wings.

Anne entered St Mark's Basilica and headed to the left transept of the church. After slipping into the Mascoli chapel, she sat on a wooden pew near the altar; she was glad that she was alone for this bit of time. It was a Catholic church, but Anne, who was a devout reformer, had no other choice if she wanted to pray, for the Republic of Venice was Catholic.

Anne prayed fervently. "Gracious God, I beseech you to protect my beloved children, Elizabeth and Arthur."

She crossed herself and stood up. Her gaze fell on a cycle of stunning mosaics by Michele Giambono, portraying the life of the Virgin Mary – the Birth and the Presentation. As today was the Feast of the Ascension, Anne glanced at the wooden cross of Jesus Christ on the wall. She silently commemorated the bodily ascension of the Lord into heaven.

O Christ God, You have ascended in Glory,
Granting joy to Your disciples
By the promise of the Holy Spirit.
Through the blessing they were assured
That You are the Son of God,
The Redeemer of the world!

After another prayer, Anne crossed herself and pivoted. She spotted a swarthy Italian man, dressed as a merchant, who surreptitiously drew a dagger. Evidently, he was preparing to throw it at a rich Italian nobleman, who stood nearby deep in prayer, oblivious to all around him.

The victim's clothes were of extraordinary richness: a white taffeta shirt with a standing band collar, hose of black silk, as well as an azure brocade doublet lavishly embroidered in jewels and gold. His toque of white velvet was encircled by three black ostrich plumes. There was a thick air of power and authority about him, an almost visible aura of leadership. He towered at least a head above everyone else, including Anne, who was above average height.

Audaciously stepping forward, Anne apprised in Italian, "Signor, watch out! You are in peril!" Her words reverberated throughout the chapel like warbling birdsong.

Warned about the danger, the target man spun around. He blinked, his countenance dumfounded. "Anne Boleyn?" he spelled out with intense amazement. "Impossible!"

Her mouth falling agape, she instantly recognized King François I of France. Having spent some years at his court, she could not mistake him for another.

The French ruler was the sheer epitome of knightly, yet saturnine, handsomeness, his stature lofty and imperial. His oval face was decidedly masculine, with his strong forehead, his full, sensual, lips, and his long Valois nose. The monarch's high cheekbones set off his almond-shaped, amber eyes, sparkling vivaciously and cleverly. His thick and straight chestnut hair fell over his ears from beneath the toque. François' whole being emanated a peculiar blend of fire, benignity, intrepidity, and indomitability, as if imbued with the dazzling light of medieval chivalry.

The full weight of horror hit Anne like a gale wind: the Valois monarch knew who she was. Her heart skipped a beat and started racing like that of a gazelle running from a lion.

"No! No! No!" she murmured in a shaken voice.

Anne was about to say something else, but she failed. Everything happened too quickly: a flash of metal as the assassin threw the dagger at King François, but the man missed. The weapon struck Anne in the side, and a blast of white-hot pain surged through her body. She let out a cry and tumbled to the floor; a cloud of gloom enveloped Anne, and she passed out.

The monarch swiftly closed the gap between them, knelt down, and checked her pulse. "She is breathing," he muttered to himself, a wave of odd relief washing over him.

In a few moments, several women appeared in the chapel, looking to discover the source of the shout. When they saw Anne, a cloak of panic settled over them, overwhelming and swift; their gasps, screams, and lamentations filled the church, the sound piercing the air.

"Oh my God! What is going on here?"

"What happened to the signora?"

"Poor signora! She was stabbed!"

"Quiet!" François roved his eyes over the frightened women, who clustered in his vicinity. He put a finger to his lips and murmured, "Shhh! Control your emotions."

A hush settled. The ruler glanced across the oratory, searching for his retinue. "Guards!"

Usually, the King of France was accompanied by the Scots Guard, but today, he wanted to have some solitary time in the church with the Creator. In the next moment, Cardinal François de Tournon, Jacques de la Brosse, and members of the Scots Guard stormed into the chapel.

They all cried in unison, "You Majesty!"

"To me! I was attacked *again!*" beckoned François, his eyes immediately darting back to his savior.

Brosse ordered, "Capture the assassin!"

"He could not have run far," conjectured Tournon.

"We shall find the villain," replied Sir Robert Stuart, captain of the Scots Guard. Some men stayed in the chapel to ensure the monarch's safety; others ran out.

Looking at the still scared parishioners, Brosse enjoined, "You are all dismissed. Leave the chapel. Now!"

The women were gone within a minute. For a moment, a perfect silence, pulsating with fright, ensued.

Encircled by the royal guards for his protection, King François knelt beside the injured woman. His bewildered gaze traversed the figure of his savior in a slow sweep. In her lovely gown of green velvet decorated with pearls, her stomacher wrought with threads of silver, she appeared to be an Italian noblewoman. Some of her long, raven tresses had become loose and fallen over her neck and shoulders. A black velvet cap, embroidered with emeralds, now lay on the floor.

For a series of heartbeats, the ruler thought that his mind was playing a trick on him. Nonetheless, he was not hallucinating: his savior bore a striking resemblance to Anne Boleyn. The unconscious noblewoman, who could pass as the dead queen's twin, looked as vulnerable as an injured lark abandoned in the wilderness to fend for itself.

Tournon's question shook him out of his reverie. "Is she alive, Your Majesty?"

François noticed a blood stain, spreading on the side of her gown. "She has been wounded and needs urgent medical help," he concluded without taking his eyes off her.

Brosse and Tournon flicked their gazes to the woman's face, and confusion painted their features.

The king enjoined categorically, "No questions; not now." They could only bob their heads.

June 2, 1537, the Palazzo Ducale, Venice, the Republic of Venice

King François stayed at the grand Palazzo Ducale with the Doge of Venice. He was lodged in spacious and luxurious apartments, and his councilors were similarly accommodated.

"Good evening, Your Majesty," greeted the Doge Andrea Gritti, bowing low to his notable guest.

The monarch made an elegant bow as well. "I'm always delighted to see you, Messer Gritti."

François gestured towards the living room that was part of his quarters. An old man of eighty-two, Gritti walked with a cane, so the ruler followed him slowly.

Despite his age and his fragile health, Andrea Gritti had a sharp and quick mind that could nimbly resolve political conundrums and devise crafty plans. In spite of his short stature, he was a stately man with a wrinkled oval face, bright piercing eyes, and a disarming smile, although his expression was solemn for the most part. He was clad in an auburn velvet doublet, the placard of which was worked with gold, and his grizzled head was covered with a red velvet cap.

"Your Majesty has not left the palace in the past week," commented the doge in Italian. François was exceptionally skilled in the language and conversed easily in it.

"Indeed, Messer.   I've been preoccupied with French affairs of state.   My sister has long acted as my supreme regent in my absence, but I always keep in touch with her."

Gritti lauded, "Queen Marguerite of Navarre is both a remarkable patron of the arts and a politically astute woman. She is a great credit to France and the House of Valois."

François added, "And to my friend, King Henri of Navarre, and the House of Albert. We are both proud of her, and we love her dearly." He gestured invitingly to the right.

The two men seated themselves into matching gilded armchairs, between which stood a low marble table piled with parchments and papers.   The interior's superb decorations were all in the Venetian style.   The walls, paneled with black marble, were hung with artworks by Titian, Giovanni Bellini, Giorgione, Tintoretto, and Paolo Veronese.   On the vaulted ceiling, there were a series of mythological frescoes painted by Titian, who called them 'poesies,' or 'poems.'

François leaned back in his seat and observed the art.   "I regret that Titian is not in the city now."

"Yes, it is a great pity," concurred Gritti. "Messer Tiziano Vecelli had left for Florence several months before Your Majesty arrived in Venice. It would have been good for you to meet him, but I must warn you that he is the official painter for the government of Venice."

"Yet, he is given commissions in other cities," countered the ruler. "They are in Italy, so he travels frequently. I know that Messer Tiziano is unlikely to accept the offer to work at my court, even if my commissions are very lucrative."

"Indeed," the doge acknowledged.   "He always comes back to his native Venice, where everyone loves him."

François studied the other man's face. "How can I help you tonight, Messer Gritti?"

Gritti inquired with concern, "Your Majesty, have there been any other attempts on your life?" As the king shook his head, the doge continued, "We are all saddened that someone tried to kill Your Majesty in our peaceful and beautiful city. We are also happy that you are unharmed. The security measures inside the palazzo have been strengthened."

The assassin had been captured in the Piazza San Marco while endeavoring to make his escape. The man had been apprehended and interrogated, but he had not confessed to the emperor's complicity even under torture.

The Valois ruler knew that Emperor Carlos had compelling reasons to eliminate him. He stated, "I'm fully convinced that the villain was working on Imperial orders."

"And so am I," Gritti uttered sadly. "It was difficult for me to believe that Emperor Carlos could be capable of such a horrible deed, but I've come to the same conclusion."

"At present, Infanta Eleanor is on her way to Spain with her ladies-in-waiting from Castile. Carlos is already aware that our marriage was annulled, so he is trying to retaliate."

"I'm sorry." Gritti's voice was compassionate.

François flashed a smile of gratitude. "I am alive because it is the Almighty's will."

The Doge of Venice opined, "The brave woman who saved your life in the cathedral deserves many accolades."

"Ah, God bless her!" exclaimed the king, his amber eyes twinkling. "She was as courageous as Jeanne d'Arc."

"Will Your Majesty reveal her name?" Yet, Andrea Gritti knew the answer in advance because François had refused to give any comments when the doge had asked him twice.

The king's sly eyes were as evasive as a fox's. "*La Sauveuse du Roi-Chevalier*! That is enough for now."

"I've heard people invoke this name for this mysterious lady." The secrecy around her identity puzzled Gritti, as well as Venetian government officials and aristocrats.

More than a week had passed since the attempt on the King of France's life in St Mark's Basilica. It was a shocking event, to say the least, in particular because it had happened in a cathedral on the Feast of the Accession. Many rumors were circulating in Venice, and moral condemnation of the crime was deeply ingrained in any discourse about the matter.

The tale of the king's miraculous salvation had spread like wildfire. Everyone wondered who his courageous savior was, but nothing was disclosed. François was called *le Roi-Chevalier*, or the Knight-King thanks to his personal involvement in battles, so the unknown woman was proclaimed *la Sauveuse du Roi-Chevalier*, or the Savior of the Knight-King. The legend was borne that she had come to the church because God had ordained her to save François. People viewed her as a heroine, one who was capable of sacrificing herself for a foreign ruler.

Only three persons had more than a suspicion of the royal savior's real identity, including François himself. The king had carried Anne away from St Mark's Basilica. Cardinal de Tournon and Jacques de la Brosse had also seen her. Having met Anne in Calais, both men were stunned by this woman's resemblance to the late Queen of England.

Andrea Gritti apologetically admitted, "I have no right to meddle into Your Majesty's affairs, so please forgive me if my questions are annoying."

The King of France replied, "On the contrary, I'm very grateful for your concern, Messer Gritti."

Soon the Doge of Venice retired to his chambers. Then the monarch summoned his councilors to his rooms.

§§§

Between Two Kings

In the antechamber, the ruler sat at the head of a table, with Cardinal de Tournon and Jacques de la Brosse occupying places nearby. The table was covered with an excess of food: dishes of sauce-drenched meats, roasted meat, partridge, fish with sliced eggs, capons, cooked vegetables, veal, and venison. Pine nut cakes and sweet cup custards were served. Tournon refilled three goblets from a decanter of red wine.

After handing the full goblet to his sovereign, Tournon continued eating a piece of fish. "How does Your Majesty propose to deal with a threat from the emperor?"

King François took a long swallow of wine. "The assassin will be executed soon." A look of anger slashed across his face, and he slammed his bejeweled goblet back onto the table. "We cannot prove that the half-Flemish, half-Spanish thug was the culprit. Yet, I know Carlos wants me dead!"

Having a ravenous appetite tonight, Jacques de la Brosse put morsels of roasted meat on his platter. "The nasty rumors about the emperor's involvement will harm his reputation."

"Yes, they will," agreed the monarch with satisfaction.

"We must proceed with caution," declared Brosse. "We will double the number of your guards, Your Majesty. We must prevent any further possible assassination attempts."

François sipped from his goblet. "Thank you." He studied Brosse and Tournon. "Neither the name of Anne de Ponthieu nor that of an English queen must be mentioned."

"Yes, Your Majesty," chorused Brosse and Tournon.

The monarch supplemented in a commanding tone, "You must ensure that no one speculates about her identity."

His advisors nodded. Yet, the cardinal inquired bluntly, "Will you contact the English ambassador in Venice?"

François glowered at the officious Tournon. "King Henry's adversaries are my friends."

Brosse assured, "We will obey you in everything, my liege." He refilled his cup and gulped more wine.

"I'm very sorry for displeasing Your Majesty," apologized Tournon. "As your loyal advisor, I'll always support you in any decision you make. At the same time, I'll always work to assess all risks and to have them eliminated or reduced to safe levels." He sliced a chunk of venison off the roasted haunch, and then he stuffed it into his mouth.

The sovereign of France pointed an emphatic finger at the ceiling, referencing to a higher authority. "God has a plan for all of His children, who have to let it all fall into place. He chose me to be the King of France and endowed me with wisdom and magnanimity. He also required that I rule with justice and righteousness. It is my duty to serve the Lord and to carry out His will." He hinted that the Almighty had spared Anne's life and chosen her to rescue him.

For some time, François did not speak as he recollected the recent events. When they had been in the basilica, one of the parishioners had mentioned that she was the granddaughter of Count Jean de Montreuil. All the women had been paid for silence by François' men. So far, there had been no hint as to her identity, just the epithet *La Sauveuse du Ro-Chevalier*.

Anne had been taken to the Palazzo Montreuil. The count had been speechless when the monarch had entered the great hall with Anne in his arms. Jean's physician had been fetched, and Anne had been delivered to her quarters. Then Jean de Montreuil had spoken with his liege lord for a short time, but he had not confessed yet to who she was.

According to the doctor, her injury was dangerous. Anne had lost a lot of blood and was weak, but her recovery was expected soon. Since then, she had been slipping in and out of consciousness for days, as fever ravaged her body. To his relief, today the page François had sent to the count's house had returned with news of an improvement in Anne's health.

The diners redirected their attention to their personal thoughts, and the meal was finished in silence. The cardinal snapped his fingers, summoning a musician. As the shadows of nightfall enclosed the city, candles were lit to illuminate the chamber, frescoed with Titian's allegorical paintings.

"Your Eminence, you have arranged some entertainment," observed a pleased François.

"It will lift Your Majesty's spirits," Tournon promised.

The king leaned forward and slapped the cardinal across the back in a friendly manner. "Splendid! I love music full of soul and intensity. It always makes my heart beat faster."

The musician began playing, and the tune changed from a plaintive chanson to more exotic music. A mood of relaxation settled over everyone, a cocoon in which the outside world had no place. François, Tournon, and Brosse spent the remainder of the evening talking about the arts and drinking wine; no other serious topics were touched upon to avoid tension.

CHAPTER 7

A Marriage Deal

June 8, 1537, the Palazzo Montreuil, the Palazzo Ducale, canals, Venice

When King François arrived at the Palazzo Montreuil, Jean de Ponthieu invited him to his study. The interior was fascinating: the wall tapestries were woven with gold thread and portrayed scenes of Italian city landscapes, including the piazzas and palazzi of Venice. However, this luxurious setting was not soothing the count's apprehensive mood.

"It is such a delightful morning!" François blindly stared out of the window overlooking the canal, frantically endeavoring to bring his disjointed thoughts to order.

For a short time, they sat quietly by a window in matching chairs, embroidered with silver thread, their dark walnut arms scrolled with hand-carved designs. There was a walnut table between them, laden with books and parchments. The king politely declined any refreshments.

The bright disk of the sun blazed like a great ball of orange fire in the firmament that was a cloudless azure. The warm weather was incongruent with their demeanor: they both were ill at ease in each other's presence for the first time in their lives, for the monarch's relationship with the elderly count had always been close, amicable, and respectful.

The ruler directed his train of thought to the former Queen Anne of England's incredible survival. *Jean de Montreuil is an old friend of Thomas Boleyn's,* François recalled, his gaze fixed on the count. *They still correspond. Boleyn clearly arranged Anne's rescue and then helped her vanish to Venice.*

"Monsieur Jean, you may confide in me," began François in a voice that was polite, but layered with insistence. "Anne de Ponthieu is the same person as Anne Boleyn."

Sighing, Jean assembled his courage. "Your Majesty, I'll answer all your questions as far as I can."

"You were my father's close friend and mean a lot to me, too; fear me not." The monarch arched a brow. "I do not believe in coincidences. My savior is either the allegedly late English queen, or someone so much like her. I'm fully aware that Anne Boleyn did not have a twin, and I remember her very well. Besides, you are the Earl of Wiltshire's friend."

Jean dipped his head in acknowledgement. "You are right, Your Majesty. If I may ask, what are you going to do now? Will you send her back to England?"

"That is the last thing on my mind. Or do you think that I'm a dishonorable man?"

A dart of guilt pierced the count's vitals. "No, of course not! I've never thought so! Please, forgive–"

"Don't apologize," interrupted François. "Be at ease, Monsieur Jean. You have my word that I'll keep the Lady Anne out of harm's way."

"God bless Your benevolent Majesty!" exclaimed Jean in the most cordial tones.

The king climbed to his feet. "I think my fortuitous meeting with her was a good omen for both of us. It was the Lord's doing that she rescued me from that scoundrel."

"Our Holy Father speaks to us when we face trials in life and need His protection."

"The Lord has spoken: I'm alive, and so is Anne Boleyn."

The King of France had received reports that the count's granddaughter was feeling better, understanding that soon it would be time for them to meet. He departed shortly and returned to the quay, where Cardinal de Tournon waited for him; then they were rowed to the Palazzo Ducale.

§§§

The royal gondola glided along the aquamarine, glass-like water canvas of the Grand Canal. A light breeze broke the morning's heat, carrying with it a hint of coolness. The sunlight merrily danced on the wavelets, as if weaving a golden tapestry.

"I'll meet with him before his execution," King François announced, staring at the vast expanse of the canal ahead of his gondola, his countenance devoid of emotion.

"Your Majesty, are you sure?" asked Cardinal de Tournon.

"Yes. I wish to talk to the man who tried to kill me."

"Please, forgive me my curiosity, but why?"

The monarch smiled ever so slightly. "Your Eminence, you would not be who and what you are if you were not filled with questions about everything that might affect my life."

"The duty of all your subjects is to give our lives for you if necessary."

"Your loyalty helps me feel safe and elated." As visions of the attempted regicide in St Mark's Basilica flashed in François' memory, the blood drained from his face. Jumping back to their topic, anger simmering in his veins, he answered, "I'll tell him that I know who his master is."

"He will not confess to anything."

"I read somewhere that looking death in the eye makes you free. When my time comes, I'll soar in the air like a bird." The king's joke was a sign of his improving spirits.

Between Two Kings

Reclining on the blue silk pillows in the gondola, the monarch was lost in thought, but this time, Anne Boleyn was on his mind. She was alive! For some reason, he felt a bubble of relief in his chest. How had Anne avoided death at the pyre? What could the ruler do with her? In spite of the uncertainty gnawing at his gut, there was one thing François would never do: he would not send an innocent woman back to the brutal and sadistic Henry, who would surely murder her.

François sorted through the available options. If he did not interfere, she would remain Anne de Ponthieu and live in Venice until her dying day. Or he could take her to France, but the courtiers, who had met Anne in Calais in 1532, would see her striking resemblance to the "dead" woman.

A proverb echoed through his head. "The enemy of my enemy is my friend."

He did not doubt that Anne considered Henry her sworn foe. The English king had destroyed her life! Most definitely, the thirst for vengeance must scorch through her blood, as it did through his own. François hated Henry since his spies had discovered that English gold had allowed the emperor to hire mercenaries for the Italian campaign of 1521-26. He abhorred the duplicitous Henry for making this secret alliance, while Cardinal Thomas Wolsey had positioned himself as a loyal friend of France. Henry Tudor was the bane of *their* lives.

Anne could become a valuable political ally. In the future, one of her children with Henry – Arthur or Elizabeth – could ascend the English throne. Even if it did not happen, they could step into a new era of real, lasting friendship between England and France, perhaps even stand against the powerful House of Habsburg together. Anne's role in the religious reform in England would also enable François to create an anti-Spanish coalition with the German Protestant states.

Tournon's voice interceded into his musings. "Your Majesty, we are close to the central plaza and will disembark in a few minutes."

François smiled absently. His eyes swept over the picturesque palazzi on either side of the Grand Canal; their colorful stone façades, of lime, larch, and ochre with whimsical tracery and ornamentation, open loggias, and arcades, dominated both sides of Venice's main thoroughfare.

His mind was again diverted to the problem of what to do with Anne. How could he, the King of France, have any relationship with this former Queen of England?

How could their alliance be shaped? He could promise Anne to help prove her innocence. But if they had only a secret verbal agreement, he would not gain any influence over England's politics and could not openly promote the royal succession through her children. That could be achieved only through matrimony. Marry Anne Boleyn? *Sheer insanity!*

Nonetheless, François silently admitted to himself that he wished to take this opportunity. *Our marriage can be kept secret until Anne's name is cleared. Henry will never recover from the painful shock he will get upon learning that Anne became the Queen of France and my wife,* François leered in his mind. This would be the most satisfying revenge imaginable upon his English rival! And Anne was even more beautiful in maturity than the girl he had once known.

Now the woman, who had been wounded by the dagger meant for the king, was admired as the Savior of the Knight-King. Once the news of the attempted assassination reached France, it would infuriate his subjects. His people needed a patriotic boost, and the idea of battling for the monarch and his brave queen would instill in them a sense of unity against the Spaniards. *My people will see my marriage to my savior as a matter of divine providence,* François concluded.

The king snapped out of his reverie as Tournon apprised, "We have arrived, Your Majesty."

The gondola nudged the steps up to the large piazza. François scanned a multitude of palazzi on both sides of the canal. They had different exteriors, although many possessed a large set of central windows, as well as semi-circular arches, large pillars, columns, and arcades. Soon they faced the Palazzo Ducale or the Doge's Palace, which had been built in the flamboyant Venetian Gothic style; it was one of the main landmarks of the city.

"The Gothic style was once the pinnacle of design," reflected the monarch, examining his surroundings. "See those thin pillars, the pointed arches, the lobed ones – and there," he pointed and continued, "the ogee arches. They all exhibit such elegance! Yet, I much prefer Italian and French grand modern buildings. They have such perfect symmetry, such exquisite proportions, and a fine geometry of parts. To my mind, a single round-arched window, its columns done in the three classical orders, would far exceed any of these in its beauty and perfection."

The cardinal thought that it was impossible not to admire the immensely cultured French sovereign. He complimented, "Your Majesty is a true modern connoisseur."

§§§

They left the gondola moored at the quay. Escorted by a contingent of the Scots Guard, they stepped ashore and strolled to the Palazzo Ducale. Brosse moved closer to his liege lord's side, always on the alert for danger, as they steered through the crowd on the Piazza San Marco.

Inside the palace, King François and others headed to the famous Venetian prison known as the 'Piombi.' Reserved for those accused of political crimes, the prison was comprised of many dirty, stinking, and tiny cells, which were barely lit by torches. The place was so damp and extremely wretched that the visitors screwed up their noses in disgust.

A banging arose from somewhere nearby, along with shouts and clanging sounds.

A male voice screeched in Italian, "They are escaping! Stop them!"

Tournon prompted, "Your Majesty, we should leave."

A scowl darkened the monarch's brow. "I'm a knight, not a coward!" He rushed towards the sound, closely followed by his companions.

They entered a corridor illuminated by burning torches in a yellow glow. A moment later, a mass of fighting men appeared in sight, and a cry resonated in Italian, "Stop these worms!"

Ten prisoners were being slowly driven back by a greater number of guards. The prisoners' reactions and reflexes were becoming slower, and some of them were injured. Yet, they still resisted a horde of Italian soldiers as desperately as they could, determined to die in battle rather than be captured and executed. Swords slashed, blood gushed, and men fell.

Among them, François noticed the same person who had tried to take his life in the church. A wave of hatred for both the emperor and the assassin surged up inside him, something raw and primal. Acting on impulse, he unsheathed his sword and charged forward, his focus being on the criminal. Brosse drew his weapon from the scabbard and rushed hotfoot behind his liege lord. The French men followed suit and joined in the battle, endeavoring to protect their sovereign.

Jacques de la Brosse impaled a short, stout, swarthy prisoner who came dangerously close to his master. "Your Majesty, retreat. I beseech you not to put your life at risk!"

This fell on deaf ears, and the incensed monarch roared over the din, "You will not evade retribution!"

King François was ramming his way through the men to get to the nefarious assassin, who battled his opponents with desperation. Unencumbered by a warrior's armor, François moved lightly and swiftly, and an aura of bloodlust flowed from him like vapor from ice. Yet, it was directed only at the assassin, and he did his best to avoid injuring others. One of the prisoners almost caught the king on the shoulder, but his battle-honed instinct threw him aside just in the nick of time.

"Surrender," pronounced François in Italian. He halted a small distance from the assassin. "I shall not allow you to flee. And I'm tempted to slaughter you like the cur you are."

The assassin's features contorted in mortal terror as he recognized the King of France. "Never!" he snarled, holding his sword at the ready. "I would better die!"

The man heard a quiet sound of movement to his left, but he didn't spin around, and in a heartbeat, it was too late. To his horror, he spotted François in his peripheral vision, as the ruler brought the hilt of his sword down on the base of his skull, and darkness encompassed him. Soon the criminals were all forcibly subdued, only half of them still alive.

Cardinal de Tournon explained to the Italians who the two men wielding swords were and why they had come here. Stunned, the guards tipped their heads in acknowledgement of the Valois monarch; then they manacled the survivors to take them back to their cells.

The king pointed at the unconscious assassin with his sword point. "Leave this man here."

"Signor, he is a vicious criminal." One of the jailors then tried to vindicate himself. "We don't know how he managed to contrive an escape plan and incite others to partake in it."

"Leave him here for the meanwhile," repeated the ruler with authority.

All of the prison guards again bowed, and then attended to their duties. In the span of a few minutes, the whole area was cleared of the shackled men and corpses.

The assassin opened his eyes when one of the French men roughly prodded him with a boot. "Wake up! Learn your position: you are a prisoner condemned to death."

He lifted himself up with effort. Feeling the chains around his wrists, he gritted out, "At least I tried to rescue myself from the execution. I have nothing to regret in my life."

François had to ward off the urge to gut him right now. "But you did not kill me, you scum."

Cardinal de Tournon and two royal guards flanked the monarch and stood at attention.

"Burn in hell, you French rascal!" the assassin ground out.

Tournon's expression convulsed with fury. "Shut your mouth, you damned swine!"

The cardinal ran to the criminal and struck the assassin hard across the cheek. The man's head snapped back and then fell forward; the blow left a thin trail of blood in its wake.

The ruler regarded his fallen foe with contempt. "It seems that the demons have not been kind to you today. There are no avenues of escape, and your hours are numbered."

Abject loathing was written across the bandit's features. "What do you want?"

With an effortless haughtiness, King François pontificated in an affable tone, "I do not need your confession: I know that Emperor Carlos ordered you to murder me. Did he want the Knight-King to die in a church, becoming a sacrificial lamb on the altar of Carlos' ambition?" His mischievous air vanished, and severity took over his face. "The emperor and those who serve him are a surly, arrogant lot. If I told you outright what I'm planning for him, you would not believe me." His voice taking on a higher octave, he ended with, "I vow that Carlos von Habsburg shall eventually be defeated and captured!"

The ruffian was then dragged away, his chains jingling and rattling.

One of the Italian officers approached the Frenchmen. "We learned that several Spaniards disguised themselves in our uniform and infiltrated into the Piombi to break him out."

A rush of disdain overwhelmed the king. "This proves that thug's allegiance to Spain and Emperor Carlos."

The officer questioned, "Your Majesty, these people are dead. What do you want us to do now?"

Spinning on his heel, the monarch advised, "I suggest you ensure that he does not see another dawn." He then strutted away, his entire retinue trailing after him.

§§§

As the French exited the prison compound, everyone breathed easily. The sun kissed them with its gentle warmth.

Cardinal de Tournon chided, "Your Majesty! You should not be so reckless!"

King François walked next to his advisor. "Indeed, Your Eminence." His countenance brightened. "This incident has pushed me to make a decision that will change everything."

Tournon pulled nervously at his lower lip. "What is it? Another visit to this place?"

"No! I meant that someone would aid me to retaliate against my adversaries."

The ruler's mind rested on the unforgettable face of Anne Boleyn. The emperor had never acknowledged her as Queen of England, and he had fiercely resisted Henry's annulment of his union with the late Catherine of Aragon. Carlos was not only François' enemy, but also Anne's – another common foe in addition to Henry Tudor. Fate instigated François to act.

The monarch's resolve to take his vengeance against his two mortal adversaries – the Holy Roman Emperor and the King of England – solidified into steel. He would opt for a course of action that would allow Anne and him to join forces in their mutual quest for revenge and to benefit from their alliance. François would offer Anne *a marriage deal*.

However, a union with Anne could lead to ruin. But was François not a risk taker? In the Italian wars, he had experienced both victories and losses. After the Battle of Marignano in 1515, he had subjugated Milan, but he had then lost it. A year ago, he had conquered Piedmont and the Duchy of Savoy. François gambled on the battlefield and in politics, not always successfully. Over time, he had learned patience, caution, and clear focus in pursuit of his goals.

Her image was engraved on his mind since her early youth. François had first met Anne when she had served as a lady-in-waiting to Queen Mary Tudor, the third spouse of Louis XII of France. Of course, he had seen her when she had been a maid of honor to his first wife, Queen Claude of France. The young Anne had aroused everyone's interest, including his.

And their meeting in October 1532... In Calais, Anne's entry had happened in the middle of the banquet given in his honor by King Henry. She had appeared with her face covered with a golden mask, dressed like a Greek goddess, followed by ladies in gold-laced overdresses of white taffeta, ornamented with an intricate pattern on silver cloth. Each of them had chosen a Frenchman to dance with; François had been invited by a masked beauty and admired her dancing skills.

After the dance, Henry had removed her mask, and François had realized that his partner had been Anne Boleyn. Her exotic, enigmatic loveliness shone and beckoned, and he had been smitten by her irresistible wit, charm, elegance, and intelligence. He had even felt a twinge of envy that Henry had been loved by such a phenomenal woman. During a private conversation with Anne, François had expressed his support for her union with Henry, but later, he had withdrawn it.

His relatives – the late Louise de Savoy, Marguerite of Navarre, and the long dead Queen Claude of France – were all strong-willed, intellectually gifted, and able to rule. *Anne is another woman capable of becoming a truly great queen.*

Picking up his pace, the monarch broke into a vainglorious tirade. "The biggest risk is not taking any risk. My new motto should be: *'A salamander can withstand fire. I take risks and win, for I'm unaffected by flames of failures.'* My courtiers and my subjects would love it!"

Cardinal de Tournon eyed him with a great amount of curiosity. "Would they?!"

June 12, 1537, Venice, the Republic of Venice
The sovereign of France arrived at the Palazzo Montreuil at sundown. The Count de Montreuil met him in the great hall and dropped into a bow, from which he was quickly dismissed.

His tone cautious, Jean started, "Anne has already been notified that Your Majesty wants an audience with her."

François quizzed, "Monsieur de Ponthieu, how is she feeling?"

"Her life is no longer in danger," the count assured with obvious relief. "However, the physician prescribed that Anne stay in bed for another week. The wound in her side still throbs, and the pain increases if she moves. The fever has drained her strength, and now she is rather thin."

"She needs a plenty of rest," the king surmised.

Jean nodded. "Anne is aware that during her illness, Your Majesty visited us and enquired after her."

"She has nothing to fear from me. I'll prove it to her."

Jean smiled. "I love her as my own granddaughter."

François patted the old man's shoulder in reassurance. "I shall help Anne." His gaze fell on the fresco depicting a battle with the participation of the Venetians. "I'm the Knight-King, and Anne will be the queen of my noble kingdom."

A confused Jean arched a brow. "Your Majesty?"

"You will learn everything soon, Monsieur Jean." The ruler then marched to her bedchamber.

I've wanted to see Anne, a surprised François admitted to himself. He had spent the previous days attending meetings with the Doge of Venice and discussing the alliance treaty.

§§§

Anne awaited the King of France in her bedroom. At the thought of facing him, a frisson of apprehension coiled in her chest. Footsteps in the corridor sent a rush of panic through her. She inhaled deeply, struggling to regain her composure.

"God, protect me, I beseech you!" Anne crossed herself. "François is too chivalrous to send me back to Henry..."

Outside the door, the monarch paused and rehearsed the speech that would alter their future forever. When he walked in, his gaze was stunned by the vision of Anne, who rested upon a large canopied bed, wrapped in tawny silk sheets and holding a book in her hands.

As her eyes met the king's, her countenance was as impenetrable as granite, although her nerves were tangled into knots. François was dressed in luxurious Italian attire: a doublet of light blue brocade beaded with lapis, rubies, and jade, and black Venetian hose. It matched to perfection a feathered toque of a darker blue hue. He had made his tailors copy the latest Italian style. His girdle was set with gold and sapphires, as was the handle and sheath of his poniard.

As always, Anne marveled at his height. To his foes, the King of France was unnaturally tall, as if his body had been stretched on the rack. In his friends' eyes, he embodied a magnificent French titan, born to bring enlightenment and prosperity to erstwhile medieval France.

François flourished a bow to her, and his lips curved into a grin. "Good afternoon, Lady Anne," he commenced in French, for she was pretending to be a subject of France.

A pang of fear hit Anne. He referred to her as Lady Anne, not as Madame Anne. "Your Majesty, forgive me for not rising from my bed," she replied in flawless French.

"Only if you excuse me for not coming sooner," retorted the ruler good-humoredly.

She flashed a faint smile. "Would you like to take a seat?"

"Yes." He landed in a whimsically carved chair near the window facing the courtyard that had flowerbeds of roses, a natural lawn, and benches. "Thank you, Madame."

As his eyes locked with hers, the monarch was almost breathless, as if fearing that Anne were a phantom, not a woman of flesh and bone. He had not forgotten her unique appearance, and it still took his breath away: Anne's striking dark eyes which perused others with a soul-subduing light, the long and elegant line of her nose, as well as her luscious and full lips which spoke smart, witty, or flirting things and the next moment smirked with a peculiar mocking twist.

When I see her, François mused, *I yearn to be lost together with Anne in a romantic forest.* The alluring, yet graceful, bearing of hers was like that of a dryad living in mythological woods. Anne attracted men unintentionally, and the King of France was no exception; he suppressed his carnal desires.

"I hope you are feeling better today." His formality belied the look of interest in his eyes.

"Thank you for your concern, Your Majesty. My health has improved."

"What are you reading?"

"It is Machiavelli's *'The Prince.'* It is the finest book on political philosophy."

"It was printed five years after Machiavelli's death thanks to Pope Clement the Seventh. You are lucky to be in Venice, for it is difficult to find it in France."

Astonishment flickered across her features. "I didn't know that it is not available there."

François chuckled. "Perhaps I should become a more enthusiastic patron of the arts."

She cried, "Your Majesty has done so much for France!"

"I'm happy that you enjoyed the time you spent at my court, Lady Anne."

Anne put the book down in her lap and folded her hands over it. *I need patience and poise to treat His Majesty politely and yet indifferently, not showing any vulnerability.*

A strained silence spun out until the ruler broke it at last. "I must express my most sincere gratitude to you for saving my life in the cathedral. I would have been dead without you."

She tensed like an arrow laid against a bowstring. "My duty was to save you, sire."

"If only everyone had thought so... The emperor believes that he has the right to murder another monarch. Carlos fiercely hates me and tried to dispose of me several times. Two other attempts on my life were prevented in Piedmont."

Mingled bewilderment and sympathy tinged her visage. "I'm sorry to hear that. Thanks be to God that you are alive."

François grinned conceitedly. "Madame, I'll not die! Have you forgotten that my royal emblem is the salamander in the midst of flames, demonstrating that they are immune to fire? I'm sure you know that it is a symbol of immortal glory. So, my enemies shall not destroy me, and the most devastating wrath of God shall befall them in punishment."

Relaxing, she allowed herself a grin. "Salamanders are also a symbol of bravery, and Your Majesty is widely known as the courageous and chivalrous Knight-King."

His laugh reverberated throughout the air. "I'm foolhardy, too." His voice lowered, as if he were sharing a secret with her. "Perhaps you will think so when I offer you a deal."

"I would be happy to serve you."

François affirmed matter-of-factly, "My lady, I know who you really are." He discerned the flash of panic in her eyes, and his heart swelled with compassion towards her. He spoke in a quiet and very gentle voice. "I'll not inform King Henry that you are alive. On the contrary, I'm going to help you. In return, you will assist me in accomplishing something."

Anne's slender fingers covered her slim throat in a protective gesture that shielded her from an imaginary executioner. "I do not understand you at all."

There was a promise in those riveting amber eyes as he assured, "I'll aid you to clear your name in England. It must be Thomas Cromwell who designed those phony charges."

"Yes." The intensity of his gaze cut through Anne.

"I do not like Cromwell because he champions an Anglo-Imperial alliance. Besides, I hate King Henry, and, of course, I do not appreciate the emperor's villainous behavior." He brought a finger to his chin for a brief moment. "Do you know what Henry did to me?"

She shook her head. "No, I have no idea."

François revealed bluntly, "Henry supported the emperor financially in the Italian war ten years ago, which ended with my defeat and subsequent capture at Pavia."

"I did not know about that," asserted Anne honestly.

An air of suppressed fury whirled momentarily about him. "My spies unraveled Henry's betrayal about a year ago. He had managed to keep that small fact secret."

Startled, she commented, "Cardinal Wolsey always favored France in public. Even when he incurred Henry's displeasure after the Legatine Court of Blackfriars in 1529, he still supported England's alliance with Your Majesty. Yet, he was also as hypocritical as an old fox. I knew that he was a cunning man, but I underestimated his guile. As a man of the cloth, it was surprising how he seemed to have been capable of using every weapon available to attain his ambitions."

He tipped his head. "Exactly."

"His Majesty and Wolsey must have done it to coax the emperor into supporting the annulment of his first marriage. But the Spaniard took money and deceived them."

François smiled at her astuteness. Unlike other women, Anne was capable of thinking strategically, rationally, and long-term rather than being swayed by fashion, emotion, and the trivial concerns of the day. "Lady Anne, you are correct."

His expression was funereal for a split second before a bland mildness settled over his features. "My two sons spent several years in captivity in Madrid." He paused and, as she nodded, he resumed, "After their release, my eldest son, François, never regained his health, and he died about a year ago. That is why I shall never forgive Carlos and Henry."

Anne's expression was one of compassion. "Sire, please accept my sincere condolences." Anne averted her gaze to conceal her heartache. She knew the agony of losing an unborn child, a sorrow that would never stop haunting her. Yet, losing a child whom you had raised was worse.

The monarch sighed. "Thank you, Madame."

"Was your imprisonment in Spain so horrible?"

"It was the darkest time in my life."

"I apologize; it was improper of me to ask Your Majesty about it."

The King of France appeased, "It is fine, Lady Anne." He flashed a reassuring smile. "My captivity in Spain was a turning point in my relations with Emperor Carlos and in my life. While being there, I was treated not only with a gruesome ruthlessness unsuited to my rank, but also with a callousness that was inhuman." His voice thinned at the end of his speech.

A waterfall of tormenting memories tumbled through his head. "The emperor locked me in an old castle, where living conditions were extremely poor, and I stayed there until I contracted a severe fever. Although Carlos initially denied me an audience, he came to my cell when he was apprised of my grave illness. He feigned pity, barely concealing his joy that I was suffering and humiliated. In actuality, Carlos feared that my death would diminish Spain's triumph over France, so he pledged that he would do everything to procure my freedom in the near future. I was moved to a better place."

Anne reflected on his confession. "Did he keep his word?"

His candor surprised her a lot. "No, the emperor called me his friend and brother, but it was an act of pure duplicity. It was rather naive of me to believe my enemy's promises, but Carlos seemed so sincere at the time. At first, I assumed that he was a man of honor."

Anne loathed the Habsburg ruler wholeheartedly. "It is clear that Emperor Carlos does not possess any integrity. I recall what he and the vile Constable Charles de Bourbon, who betrayed Your Majesty, did over ten years ago when Carlos permitted his troops to sack Rome. The emperor was in Spain when his soldiers plundered the city and raped civilians, but he is still responsible for this act of barbarity."

Nodding, he admitted, "It is not easy for me to remember my cousin, Constable Charles de Bourbon, who was once my friend, but who then betrayed his country and conspired with my worst enemy to invade my realm and partition France."

"I did not mean to cause Your Majesty any discomfort."

"The past must remain in the past." François smirked half-bitterly, half-painfully. "Once my health improved, Carlos showed his true colors: he reneged on his word, and his determination to keep me prisoner solidified." He stilled, more of his harrowing memories resurfacing. "Once such despair seized me that I was close to abdicating the throne of France in favor of my eldest son, the late Dauphin François. Fortunately, my sister, Marguerite, came to Spain to take care of me and to negotiate the terms of my release with the emperor. She dissuaded me from such a course of action, and I had to make concessions to Carlos."

She had never suspected anything of the sort. "Sire, I'm sorry that you and your sons had to endure so much. I'm glad that Madame Marguerite was with you at that time."

"It taught me a number of valuable lessons." François maneuvered the conversation to the most important topic. "One of those was to be careful in where I place my trust. With that in mind, Lady Anne, I wish to make you an offer that will confound our enemies."

Confusion suffused her face. "What do you mean?"

"My marriage to the emperor's sister was annulled. Now I want to wed you."

This announcement was like rubbing salt in the gaping wounds of her soul, because long ago, another monarch had proposed to Anne. "What do you want to achieve?"

"Our union will be a political bargain."

Anne's heart tumbled like a stone dropping down a bottomless well. "Could Your Majesty please elaborate?"

In an imperial voice, the ruler promulgated, "It is a matter of politics and mutual benefit for us." He then outlined his sophisticated plan while she listened in awed amazement.

June 15-16, 1537, Venice, the Republic of Venice

"What have you decided, Anne?" asked Jean de Montreuil.

His pretend granddaughter lay in her bed, propped up by crimson silk pillows. "I don't know," she wearily confessed.

Jean lounged in an elaborately carved chair near the bed. "Your marriage to His Majesty will give you the opportunity to accomplish things you cannot achieve living in Venice."

In a forlorn tone, she lamented, "I narrowly escaped death at the behest of one king. How can I place myself, my future, and my very life in the hands of another monarch?"

The count's eyes shone with compassion. "I understand your hesitation."

Silence pulsating with doubts ensued. Anne glanced in the direction of a window; the sun was high in the sky.

Memories of Henry's cruelty plagued her, piercing her soul like thousands of swords.   The Moira Clotho was spinning the thread of Anne's life in the most mysterious of ways.   Her whole universe had morphed into an incredible fairytale, one in which she now had the chance to become the Queen of France.   It was as though her destiny was to be royalty.   Yet, she had no desire to live at court again and to be involved in its webs of intrigue and deception.

Anne's mind drifted to her distant days in France. "Once, when Queen Claude accompanied King François to a banquet, I heard him say, '*A court without ladies is like a year without springtime, or a spring without roses.*' Ah, all women love his high-spirited speeches!"   Her voice was colored with disdain. "I considered it poetic until he seduced my sister, Mary."   An acrid laughter erupted from Anne. "Such charming words!   François probably did not mean Mary! He not only abandoned her, but he also defamed her during the Field of the Cloth of Gold all those years ago. François called her '*a great whore, infamous above all,*' which utterly destroyed her reputation."

Jean remembered this vulgar epithet about Mary Boleyn. He defended his sovereign. "Back then, His Majesty was a young and impulsive man, and he lacked maturity. Perhaps these words were spoken when King François and King Henry were both inebriated. I recall that wine flowed like rivers during the Field of the Cloth of Gold. As for your sister's affair, if Mary had not wanted to be with His Majesty, nothing would have happened between them."

Anne could not refute it. "When we lived in France, Mary was enamored of François.   She was so elated after her rendezvous with him that she praised him as her Adonis."

The unsavory facts about her sister's amours moved to the front of Anne's mind.   Mary had sacrificed her maidenhead to be with François, but he had soon discarded her, leaving her disgraced and heartbroken. At their father's behest, Mary had later slid under Henry's sheets, and soon she had become infatuated with the English king. Once more, Mary had been set aside, her soul traumatized again.

"The fickleness of kings is horrible!" spat Anne. A worm of disgust twisted inside her. "Will François call me *'his English harlot who escaped the flames'*? Will he cast me aside if my name remains ruined forever?"

She continued to imagine the worst. Would François tell his friends that he had married an English slut who had slept with two kings? Or would he invent something more eccentric and coarse for Anne? Would he wed Anne, claim her, and then annul their marriage, ruining her life absolutely? Such questions tortured her like the notes of discordant music.

Jean commented, "Years have elapsed since your sister was his mistress. His Majesty has matured after experiencing hardship and heartbreak. Your fears are exaggerated."

She said nothing, lost in thought. Jean waited in silence.

Anne Boleyn was officially dead. The new Anne was a living incarnation of Nemesis – the ancient Greek Goddess whose pursuit of justice and vengeance symbolized her own quest for retribution. But Anne had tasted power and did not want to forgo the pleasure of having it again, for power was addictive. Her marriage to the King of France would be perilous, but it had been his idea, Anne consoled herself. She also assumed that it would be less hazardous since she did not love François.

Again, she recalled the French ruler's illustrious tirade: '*A court without ladies is like a garden without flowers.*' His words blazed through her head in a torrent of recollections.

If she wed King François, Anne would be the wife of an infamous royal philanderer. Unlike her matrimony with the

Tudor monarch, she would not care about his dalliances, nor throw tantrums of jealousy in front of the Valois court. She had learned a valuable lesson in England.

Anne speculated aloud, "The people of France will worship me as their beloved king's heroic savior. According to my father's letters, the English people now view me as Henry's victim, and I'll earn their sympathy when it is revealed that I've been falsely accused." She paused for a moment. "I shall have to prove myself continually useful to François. Then he will be unlikely to set me aside. I must also be very cautious."

"So, you will agree?" the count hopefully asked.

Anne made up her mind. "I do not want to spend the rest of my life in obscurity. I wish to see my children again. I yearn to avenge George's death and my own sufferings."

Jean climbed to his feet. "It is the right thing to do. Even though you want to marry His Majesty because you crave revenge, your feelings will change over time."

She threw a frosty look at him. "Never ever!"

He said wisely, "Only God knows His children's future, Anne." Then the count exited the bedchamber.

Anne snuggled under the covers and pondered the king's offer again. The vision of her sitting on the throne at François' left seemed both fatal and fabulous. The main motive for this marriage would be vengeance. *Henry will be in mental agony upon learning that I've married his rival, and that I've never betrayed him.* This solidified Anne's decision.

§§§

The next morning, King François paid Anne another visit. They exchanged greetings tinged with tense anticipation.

The monarch eased himself into a chair near the bed. He wasted no time in addressing the urgent matter that lay between them. "Anne, will you wed me?"

His personal tone surprised and simultaneously discomfited Anne. "Yes, I will, sire," she stated.

He sent a jocund grin to her. "I'm delighted to hear that. Undoubtedly, we will be great allies and plotters."

Her synopsis of her former husband's behavior was brief. "King Henry persuaded himself that I was guilty, because it was convenient for him. He always blames others."

"One day, he shall open his eyes to the truth."

Anne shrugged uncertainly. "I do hope so."

The ruler took her hand in his and kissed it. "Anne, if our plan falls through, you will still be treated as my savior. In this case, I'll proclaim that I married Madame Anne de Ponthieu."

Her brows jerked up. "Marriage under a secret identity?"

"Yes. I'll never confirm who you really are. In France, those who think you resemble the late Queen of England are not many, and it has been years since they last saw you at close quarters." His face split into a broad grin that conveyed supreme confidence. "But we will win. That I promise you."

Anne flashed a smile. "I pray that it will be so."

Unbeknownst to her, François thought that it was the most enchanting smile he had ever seen. He was mesmerized by those bewitching dark pools; a man could drown in their immeasurable depths. They beguiled him with a vision of their glorious future, of joining with Anne in holy matrimony, and for the time being, everything else receded from his mind.

CHAPTER 8

A Secret Wedding

June 23, 1537, the Palazzo Ducale, Venice, Republic of Venice

"I'm marrying Anne Boleyn, once Queen of England and wife of my enemy."

King François spoke to the full goblet of wine sitting on the table in front of him, in an attempt to soothe his lingering doubts. He was alone, lounging in a princely oak armchair decorated with carved lions and scrolls of acanthus leaves.

Truth be told, the ruler was still hesitating to some degree because the marriage was a huge risk. Nevertheless, in his privileged and charmed world where no one dared gainsay him, François was fairly confident that this plan would work. He resolved to quash all of Anne's foes, a task to which he was prepared to commit himself with unswerving enthusiasm.

Cardinal François de Tournon paused in the arched doorway. He cleared his throat to attract the monarch's attention, and when François trained his eyes upon him, he entered. He crossed the study to where his sovereign was seated at a heavily carved, mahogany table.

As his subject stopped and bowed, the ruler beckoned, "Your Eminence, I've been waiting for you. Take a seat." He gestured towards an armchair at the opposite side of the table.

Having eased himself there, Cardinal de Tournon released a sigh before broaching an alarming subject. "Is Your Majesty indeed going to wed the Count de Ponthieu's granddaughter?"

François nodded. "Yes, I am."

The cardinal was momentarily flummoxed, but he swiftly recovered his voice. "It is none of my business, but Your Majesty knows that she resembles Lady Anne Boleyn, who was a driving force behind the religious reform in England."

The ruler looked at ease, as if Tournon's speech did not worry him in the least. "Lady Anne understands well that I'll never let the ideas of reform spread and flourish in France. She will have to keep her true religious beliefs to herself. Anne is too clever not to realize that, as Queen of France, she can practice heresy neither in public nor in private."

King François favored religious tolerance. Only once had he turned sharply against the Protestants – after the Affair of the Placards. On the night of October 17, 1534, anti-Catholic posters had appeared in public places in Paris and several other French cities; one poster had been discovered on the door to François' bedchamber at Château d'Amboise, which had shocked the monarch to his very core. In the aftermath, most of the perpetrators had been captured and punished, but the incident had led only to a brief persecution of Protestants.

"That is enough for me," responded Tournon.

"Moreover, Lady Anne has been blamed for things she has not done. If King Henry did not want to abandon Catherine of Aragon and to separate the Church of England from the Bishop of Rome, nothing would have occurred. Ultimately, it was the English sovereign's decision, not hers."

"That is true." His concern somewhat alleviated, Tournon refocused on the agenda. "Lady Anne Boleyn is dead in the eyes of the world. Will you wed Madame Anne de Ponthieu?"

"Just Lady Anne, or Madame Anne. My bride's name will be kept secret until we can disclose it. Even my children and my sister do not need to know the truth at this point."

"There will be a declaration about your wedding, with no mention of her name, then."

The ruler drained the contents of his goblet and placed it on the table. "The official reason for secrecy is that we must safeguard my queen from all dangers. After all, several assassination attempts on my life have taken place in the past few months. No doubt my adversaries would take great delight in removing a new wife from my side."

"A plausible explanation." The cardinal looked pensive for a moment. "There are political reasons for you to wed her. However, France and Your Majesty will only benefit from this deal if her name is cleared," he remarked pragmatically.

François smiled with a confidence that belied his last vestiges of doubt. "Your Eminence, I'm planning to achieve that in a crafty way. Undoubtedly, Cromwell engineered Lady Anne's downfall, and he shall pay for his transgressions."

Tournon's face creased in a grin. "I'd like to watch it."

"Once her innocence is proved, I'll announce that Anne Boleyn is my consort. My subjects will worship her as my legendary savior. Probably, the English people will not grow to love her, but they will be sympathetic to her sufferings at the hands of my homicidal cousin, Henry."

It is unpleasant that the Tudor tyrant and I are distantly related, François ruminated. They were descended from King Charles V of France known as the Wise (*le Sage*):

François from his son – Louis de Valois, Duke d'Orléans, while Henry from Charles V's granddaughter, Catherine de Valois, who had married King Henry V of England – a ruler whom French patriots all loathed for his attempts to subjugate the kingdom of France and to deprive the Valois dynasty of the French crown. Henry of England also shared Capetian blood with François because Isabella of France, a daughter of Philippe IV of France called the Fair (*le Bel*), was Henry's ancestress.

"As Your Majesty knows, they already blame him for Lady Anne's burning so soon after the birth of her child."

Tipping his head, the monarch fell into contemplation for a short time. "My marriage to Lady Anne is an important political step, through a risky one. France would benefit from having a friendly England in the future and from establishing solid alliances with the German Protestant states." He then emphasized, "Only you, Your Eminence, and Jacques de la Brosse will know the real identity of my new wife."

"Of course. When are you intending to marry her?"

"The wedding will take place here, in Venice, after Lady Anne's recovery."

"A strictly private ceremony?"

An affable smile lit up François' visage. "I trust you like no one else. You will organize the ceremony of the French Zeus and his Hera, whose realm is far larger than Mount Olympus."

Tournon smiled at his sovereign's comparison of himself with the mythological Greek King of the Olympian gods and goddesses. "It will be an honor for me to serve you well."

A sudden thought struck the ruler. "My sister is regent of France in my absence, as always. Marguerite has contacts with many artists, poets, and humanists. One of them is Clément Marot, who has prominent ideas about

Reformation. Inform her that I need Marot to prepare a book criticizing the policies Cromwell has implemented in England. We want him proclaimed as culprit for that barbaric act – the burning at the stake of an innocent, anointed queen."

"Anything else, Your Majesty?"

The king grinned knavishly. "You could suggest my sister orders the poet Mellin de Saint-Gelais to prepare amazing incriminating pamphlets about Cromwell."

"Are you going to distribute the book and the pamphlets once they are ready?"

"Of course," answered François. "The pamphlets will be made available both in England and in France, and we will watch Cromwell's and Henry's reactions. Our scheme will have the added benefit of distracting Henry from conspiring with the emperor." As he envisaged the furious face of his English counterpart, he grinned acrimoniously. "Commoners are so lucky! They will have free tickets for the extraordinary spectacle, in which Cromwell will be the main actor."

His councilor guffawed. "It will be entertaining."

"Ask Philippe de Chabot and our spies to provide me with the list of the names of all those who were interrogated during the investigation against Lady Anne."

"I shall contact Admiral de Brion, then."

François had never met Cromwell, but he knew enough about the man. "Cromwell is a ruthless, guileful, and smart politician, but his Achilles' heel is his assumption that no one is more cunning and intelligent than him. Without this man, England's foreign policy will better suit our interests."

"Certainly, it will be less radical, Your Majesty."

The monarch's lips twisted into a wolfish smile. "Ah, I am in deep mourning! Cromwell's days will be numbered once the pamphlets and the critical book appear on English soil."

Tournon sniggered maliciously. "It will be his well-deserved punishment for heresy and other crimes."

François spoke in the voice of a judge announcing the verdict. "The Greek gods condemned Sisyphus to ceaselessly roll a rock to the top of a mountain, thinking that there was no more terrible punishment than such futile labor." A malevolent grin tugged at his mouth. "Our plan will sentence Cromwell to the hopeless mission of attempting to conceal his plots from Henry. What a futile task it will be! Eventually, this heretic shall be executed on Henry's orders."

"Let's hope it will happen soon."

"You may go," the monarch dismissed.

"Just another moment, please," requested Tournon. As the king nodded his permission, he enlightened, "We will have to secure a papal dispensation. I beg your pardon, but I have to remind Your Majesty of something: long ago, the Lady Mary Stafford née Boleyn was your mistress. According to canon law, your relationship with her is an impediment to your marriage to the Lady Anne Boleyn."

"Affinity." A sigh erupted from François. "Officially, the marriage is taking place with Anne de Ponthieu. We can procure the dispensation later, before we announce her true identity, even if I have to pressure the Pope. Once we are in a position to reveal her name, we will obtain this document as if it had been granted to us before my wedding. We must ensure that my enemies will never be able to question the validity of my union with the Lady Anne."

"When the time comes, I'll take care of it," promised the cardinal.

"Your Eminence, I'm sure you will not fail me."

Cardinal de Tournon stood up and bowed to his master. With a lighter heart, he left the chamber, for the king had convinced him that his union with Anne was worth the effort.

June 29, 1537, Venice, the Republic of Venice

The wedding day of King François I of France and Lady Anne Boleyn fell on the Feast of Saints Peter and Paul. It had a dreamlike, incredible quality, as if the world itself were surreal. It had been decided that the ceremony should take place in the Church of San Silvestro, located far from the city's center, in late afternoon when there were few people around.

Count Jean de Montreuil and Anne approached the chapel just as the king and his party arrived. Both François and Anne were dressed in dazzling white attire, like another couple long ago – Anne de Bretagne and her third husband, King Louis XII of France. Cardinal François de Tournon and Jacques de la Brosse stood several respectful paces away.

The ruler was enchanted by Anne's fabulous appearance. "Madame, your attire is so grand! I should start saving money in the state treasury to cover your wardrobe expenses."

Anne wore a magnificent gown of dazzling white brocade with a low square-cut neckline, a long train, an ample skirt, and a stomacher worked with gold. The front was ornamented with diamonds; the collar and the sleeves were trimmed with white lace. Her Venetian headdress hid a mane of long, glossy, dark hair that was arranged in an elaborate chignon. A large, oval cut diamond necklace adorned her bosom, a pair of matching diamond earrings in her ears.

In a half-serious, half-mocking tone, his bride countered, "Your Majesty, I'll feel guilty, for you will offer your subjects less succor to buy more gifts for me. I'll better sell my jewels so that they can afford at least one decent meal every day."

"That is not going to happen." He boasted, "France is a rich country; the collected taxes cover all the court expenses."

Anne suppressed the urge to snort. Were all kings similar? Did François resemble Henry in some ways? Immediately, she threw this dark thought away. There could be no ruler in Christendom with the same tendencies: ruthless, narcissistic, hedonistic, egotistical, and extremely volatile. No one could match Henry Tudor for cruelty. Yet, François de Valois was a monarch: in her life with him, Anne would have to navigate uncharted waters. Anne would be caught *between two kings*.

She riposted, "Your Majesty loves your subjects the most."

"That is true. But you are the Knight-King's savior, which makes us both special."

Deciding she had nothing to lose, she murmured, "You can still stop it."

Breath caught sharply in his throat. "You want me to do it, don't you?"

"I accepted your proposal, and I'm glad we have met in Venice."

"Do you want to be my queen and live separately, just as Eleanor of Austria did?"

"I'll not be offended if you walk away now, Your Majesty. You are taking high risks by marrying me. This gamble might backfire, and you can easily lose this throw of the dice. But if you are confident, despite the unfortunate circumstances in my life, then I'll be your wife."

"That is honest of you, Anne. Nevertheless, I'm not going to renege on my offer."

They shared smiles and relaxed, relieved to have dealt with this awkward topic.

Her eyes flashing impishly, she retorted, "Your clothes are so splendid that I fear the Crown's expenses will skyrocket. Your subjects might after all go hungry."

The king wore only the color white: a taffeta shirt with a standing band collar edged with lace, puffy brocade hose, and a low-necked brocade doublet. An impressive mantle of white damask, trimmed with sable and ermine, partially concealed his costume, decorated with diamonds and gold. His flat cap of white velvet was crowned with a gold braid, festooned with two white feathers, and jeweled with an affiquet. A girdle of white velvet, enriched with gems, encircled his waist.

François beamed. "I'll certainly give my beloved people a glorious future. My mission in life is to thrive with immense passion, humor, and style, motivating others to do so."

The monarch escorted his bride inside the church; the others followed them. As they passed down the aisle, yards of white taffeta flowed behind Anne, the long train of her gown sweeping across the marble floor. The king experienced an unconventional feeling of wonder how enticing she was.

The ceremony was conducted by Cardinal de Tournon; Jacques de la Brosse and Count de Montreuil acted as witnesses. The candle flames flickered and set the nave aglow. The bride and bridegroom knelt at the altar; their hands were linked under a black and white silk bridal canopy embroidered with fleur-de-lis. A sense of unreality lingered during the ceremony, as if the most fantastic miracle were taking place.

As Mass was spoken in Latin, Anne stood still, her emotions akin to a black void. Her brain registered the King of France's steady voice and her own replies as they exchanged their marital vows. As remembrances of her wedding to King Henry thundered through her consciousness in a calamitous torrent, a tremor of fright and pain clawed through Anne. In a heartbeat, Henry's image faded when François slipped an exquisite golden ruby ring onto her finger.

"I pronounce you husband and wife," stated Tournon.

"This is the most welcome news," murmured the king.

François gave Anne a kiss that barely grazed her lips, and she froze; it symbolized their entangled fates. When he pulled away and gazed at her, Anne was cognizant of the burgeoning excitement within her, which she could not comprehend.

The monarch averred, "Now you are the Queen of France and my wife."

This sent her heartbeat scampering madly, and Anne echoed, "Your wife."

"You are *Anne de Valois*." Their hands touched, fingers laced together." He reiterated, "*Anne de Valois*."

Incredulity flashed in her eyes. "Is that true?"

François squeezed her hand slightly. "Calm yourself, Anne. When you trust God as the highest divine authority, you will never cease to see wonders in your life."

As they sauntered down the nave, Anne discerned a flicker of lust in his gaze, and a long-forgotten passion thrummed in her blood. Her cheeks heated up under his intense gaze. In an instant, it was quenched by a mental reminder that there was no place for affection in her new life. *François is a womanizer who takes women to his bed and leaves them brokenhearted as soon as he is satisfied,* she told herself.

Accompanied by a squad of sword-bearing guards, the small procession walked down the street along the Grand Canal, where gondolas plied lazily back and forth. After half an hour's sail in the royal gondola, they safely arrived at the Palazzo Montreuil, where soon they were served a sumptuous dinner and wine; Tournon and Brosse then left the house.

§§§

When the moon ascended the firmament in gorgeous night splendor, Anne retired to the quarters that had been prepared for the newlyweds. She regretted that she would no longer occupy her old apartments. The thought of being alone with François made her ill at ease, as if he were a feral animal.

"He is not Henry Tudor," Anne repeated to herself. "I am François' wife, so I must be with him tonight."

The walls of the luxurious bedroom were hung with ivory, gold, and silver brocade. They were frescoed with scenes set in ancient Greece and Rome. In the center, a wide walnut bed boasted cross-matched veneer panels flanked by a pair of tapered, fluted, and carved columns on each corner. The canopy was an ivory and gold tapestry; the bedside tables were inlaid with marble and shell. Several golden velvet-clad chairs were placed on large Italian carpets.

The maids removed Anne's headdress, followed by the rest of her bridal ensemble. They bathed her in aromatic lavender water and assisted her in putting on a white silk night attire.

When the undressing ritual was over, the girls curtsied and retired, casting curious glances at her before exiting.

Anne sat on the bed, holding the point of her chin between two fingers. *Holy Mother of God*, she gasped. Anne had evaded thinking of her wedding night until this moment. The only man to ever be in her bed was King Henry, whom she had loved, yet he had betrayed her. Anne was now tied to his rival only by means of a political marriage. Would she be able to sleep with François without loving him? Nonetheless, love matches were a rare luxury for aristocrats and royals.

She could still retreat to her former rooms, leaving her husband alone tonight. Anne snickered at herself: she was not a coward to flee like a terrified hare. She also feared that later, François could try and annul their marriage if it had remained unconsummated, and if something went wrong.

Unbidden, thoughts of the English monarch recurred. At present, the plain Jane Seymour was Henry's queen and warmed his bed, just as his mistresses did. Throughout their marriage, Henry had strayed to many other women, and this remembrance stirred Anne's spirit with vindictive energy. *I'll pay Henry back with the same lustful coin,* Anne fumed silently. *I'll use every opportunity to take my revenge.*

A French baritone intruded into her musings. "I hope I did not make you wait for long."

Anne turned her head as King François strode over to her. He was dressed only in a robe of black silk embroidered with gold thread, and she blushed like a virgin on her first night.

She sprang to her feet and sank into a deep curtsy. "Your Majesty." She rose slowly as he waved his head.

The monarch led her to a marble table in the corner that was draped with a white lace-edged cloth. François lifted the cloth and dropped it to the floor. Her gaze rested on stunning jewels which lay on small, crimson silk pillows.

There was a glittering array of necklaces, all to her taste. Anne counted nine pieces in total, made of diamonds, rubies, topazes, emeralds, sapphires, and pearls. Near the table with necklaces, on the Italian cassoni, she saw three brooches: one diamond, one sapphire, and one black pearl. Three diamond, ruby, and pearl bracelets shimmered in the candlelight.

"Are these the Crown Jewels?" queried a bewildered Anne.

"Indeed, Your Majesty," François addressed her with a roguish smile. "These luxurious pieces are only a small part of them. Now, as my spouse, they belong to you."

Amazement engulfed Anne. "Why are they in Venice if you have spent months in Italy?"

He elucidated, "Cardinal de Tournon arranged the delivery of these items from Paris. No one has worn them before you – neither Claude nor Eleanor or anybody else. A year earlier, the collection of the French Crown Jewels was expanded."

"Thank you very much, sire."

He smiled at her bemused expression. "Do you like them?"

"Yes, I do, but this gift is too generous."

"You are my wife and have every right to wear them."

An awe-inspiring hush ensued. There was something intimidating about him as François towered a few feet away, emanating sensuality, charm, and vitality. Anne resisted the pull of attraction, which was tugging at her, but she was not immune to it and averted her scrutiny. The silence deepened, and she sensed that she was the focus of his attention.

At last, Anne garnered the courage to look up at the ruler. François observed her all this time, and his countenance gave no clue to the interior of his soul. His gaze traveled over her with the warmth of a caress, and a blush tinged her cheeks at his blatant regard.

Experienced in matters of the heart, the monarch guessed Anne's feelings. Beyond ensuring that his paramours found their couplings pleasurable and not a chore, he also thought of what was going on inside a woman's head. *Tonight, Anne has failed to guard her emotions. Her body wants me, but not her mind and heart,* François inferred. He comprehended her: they had met in the past, but he still remained virtually a stranger to her; perhaps she saw him as a threat.

"Anne," he called in a velvet voice. "We can wait." Physical love was an art that had to be learned by a man to please his lady, but any encounter needed to be mutually consensual.

His wife dropped her gaze, feeling exposed, scared, and embarrassed all at once. Uncertain whether to be relieved or irate at his suggestion, she heaved a sigh. Admiration for him won: *François is not the kind of man who will pressure a woman to sleep with him. There is some goodness in him.*

She trained her eyes on him. "We have to fulfill our marital duties tonight."

"We do not have to do this today. Are you sure?"

"Yes, I am, sire."

Anne stepped forward, and the quiet sound of her footsteps marked her assent. She paused near the bed and waited, her skin tingling with the awareness of his nearness.

François strolled across the room and extinguished all of the chamber's candles, beginning with the ones on the bedside tables. He knew very well that women, in particular newlywed brides, felt far more comfortable in the darkness.

"This unforgettable night belongs to us," spelled out the King of France. "Your wish is my command, Madame."

"Why darkness?" Puzzlement tinctured her voice.

Beams of silver moonlight filtered through the window, letting them make out each other's outlines. As their eyes locked, his smile broadened, warming the contours of his face.

"Your beauty is more enigmatic in the moonlight," averred the ruler. "The moon is the reflection of your inner world."

The monarch approached Anne and gathered her into his arms. At the sight of the amber fire in his eyes, her heart thudded with prodigious strength, like tempestuous waves crashing into the shore. His mouth tentatively descended to hers, but his lips, at first, only brushed hers.

He touched his forehead to hers and cradled her face in his hands. "You are so beautiful, Anne. I shall not hurt you on purpose, and I want you to believe me."

"Your promise is much appreciated," Anne murmured.

The ruler put a finger to her lips. "Shhh," he whispered.

François eyed his queen in the moonlight. Her illness had taken its toll on her: her figure was thin and quite petite, and although she was rather tall, he felt like a giant next to her.

Their mouths met in a gentle kiss, his arms tightening around her, and she arched up closer, her eyes half-closed. But Anne would not return his kiss, feeling that if she showed an eagerness for anything beyond acceptance of him, her passions could be enflamed even without love.

His knowing lips slid leisurely down her throat, and his tongue found the spot where her pulse was palpitating wildly. François chuckled at the confirmation that she wanted him, and his heart sped like a chariot drawn by mighty horses. He helped Anne pull off her nightgown, and then disrobed himself; all of their garments were now strewn across the floor. His arousal was flagrantly revealed, and he pressed closer to her until, suddenly, Anne stiffened in his arms.

With a sigh, the monarch released his wife. After a few moments, he took a step towards her, but she danced away dexterously. François heard her sigh deeply and cursed in his mind: he had tried not to display his hunger and not to act too boldly so that not to frighten her. *Anne must be afraid of being with any man after Henry,* François figured out.

Between Two Kings

The silvery glow of the moon shimmered on their naked skin, scattering patches of pale light all around them. Their gazes intersected, and in her eyes – those enigmatic and dark spheres which hypnotized men – François distinguished a glimmer of trepidation. It was a tantalizing moment: they were together, but neither of them was certain of the outcome because of Anne's hesitation. As a gallant man, there was only one thing François could do in this situation.

"I think it would be better for me to leave." His deep voice echoed through the chamber.

"No! Do not go!" She stepped to him.

"Do you want me to stay?" Confusion lined his brow.

"Yes." Anne glanced at the fresco of the Goddess Hera presiding over the wedding of her daughter Hebe, the goddess of youth, to Heracles, the greatest of the Greek heroes.

François closed the gap between them. With a mixture of reluctance and fear, Anne permitted him to carry her to the bed. He drew back the covers and laid her onto the feather mattress, his own body swiftly following. As his mouth caught hers in a featherlight kiss, her eyes fluttered shut.

The king coveted to submerge himself in the deep river of his spouse's loveliness. It was excruciating, his voracious hunger for her spreading through his body in agonizing, yet exquisite, tides. He nevertheless held it in check not to devastate his consort with any wanton display of passion.

Anne opened her eyes and glanced at the famous amorous monarch. She hated Henry for making her feel so perturbed on her own wedding night. Then her resolve solidified: Anne would sleep with François, and it would be her vengeance upon her former husband. She leaned closer to François, and her tongue outlined his lips, as if prodding him to reach for her. The ruler did not need any further signals and crushed his lips, firm and hot, into hers.

His caresses were of lyrical tenderness, and she barely noticed his gentle invasion into her body. An amazed Anne peered into his eyes like a doomed bird trapped beneath him, but his endearments soothed her frazzled nerves. His gaze overflowing with emotion, François smiled cherishingly, and his mouth again landed on hers, his lips and tongue relishing her sweetness, his hands delighting in the feel of her tempting body. He lavished kisses on her eyes, ears, and neck.

Hera, goddess of marriage and family, smiled from the wall fresco on the couple. François was thrusting into his spouse with a languid slowness. Into and out – such ordinary motions of lovemaking, yet so new for Anne. The moonlight cast a whitish glow onto their entwined bodies, heightened the intensity of her sensations. At last, a maelstrom of marvelous pleasure rushed through Anne like a celestial deluge, and a whimper of rapture slithered from her throat.

Reaching the pinnacle, François thrust into her harder and deeper once more before covering her body with his, letting out a rumbling groan. As their first bedding was over, he rolled off of her onto his back. Anne pulled away to her side of the bed, as if he were the bearer of a contagious disease.

He took her hand and kissed it, then held it near his lips. "How are you feeling?"

"Your Majesty should not worry about me."

"Why not?" The king sounded amazed. "You are my wife."

"Yes," she whispered. "Are you... concerned about me?"

François connected the dots. "Anne, I understand why you feel uncomfortable. Every day your mind tells you that all men are womanizers and villains, but that is not true."

Apparently, he had alluded to Henry. "I swear by all that is holy that I've never thought that you might be evil. I respect you a great deal, and I'm grateful to you, too."

"I'm not *him*, and I swear to God that I'll never cause you any physical harm."

At this, a perplexed Anne rose from the bed and donned her robe. A blush suffused her cheeks at the thought that he could see her naked in a shaft of the moonlight. She dropped a hasty curtsy and scurried to the balcony, where Anne leaned over the railing and scanned the dark canal below. The night air was fresh, and the smell of the salt water was familiar to her, as she had already spent half a year in Venice. Above her, the stars winked like diamonds on ebony velvet.

"Good that it is summer now." The ruler appeared on the balcony; he stayed a short space behind her. "I've been told that there is the distinctive smell of freezing seaweed here in winter. I don't want to spend the next winter in Venice."

"Where will you go, sire?" questioned Anne quietly.

"To Turin or to France, depending upon circumstances. Naturally, you will travel with me, Anne."

"Your Majesty's wishes must be obeyed."

Paying no heed to her formality, François neared Anne. He kissed her on the mouth, his arms encircling her. For a breath-stealing moment, she tensed as if a vise had squeezed the air from her lungs, when visions of Henry whirled through her head, but the monarch did not hurry. His lips warm and persuasive against hers, the contact with his body sending waves of odd relief and nascent sensual yearning through her.

He carried Anne away from the balcony. "Madame, let's have another amorous dance. I want to be with you while the moonlight envelops us like a blanket of contentment."

As he placed Anne on the bed, the monarch coaxed her raiment from her form. His lips explored her throat and the pure line of her jaw, while his hands fondled her breasts. Anne's senses were spinning as he slowly slid into her. This time, it was different: for him deeper, more sensual, and more emotional, while for Anne, there was less awkwardness and discomfort. The world transformed into a blissful blur, and everything flickered as sunlight does on waves.

As the amatory deities flew away, Anne disentangled herself from his embrace. Yet, just before she could move away, François found the scarred flesh on her side. He felt her tremble as he brushed his fingers over the injury she had received deflecting the dagger meant for him.

"Does it hurt you now, wife?" She had not heard that wonderfully silken tone from him before.

"At times the scar throbs, but it has not happened tonight."

François kissed the top of her head and drew her closer. "I shall ask my physician to examine you tomorrow so that we are confident that your health is not in danger."

"It is not necessary, Your Majesty. I feel well."

Her eyes flickered shut. Anne thought that she had known what it felt like to make love, but her experience with François was totally new for her. His kisses were unfamiliar, yet fantastic; his tactic was not an assault, but a long torture, exquisite and delicate. His innate tenderness had touched a chord within Anne and penetrated deep into her soul against her will. Her encounters with Henry had been so different: a battlefield of passion, love, and, later, hatred.

The new Queen of France guessed that François had not given his desire free reign so as not to scare her, and she was thankful for it. She had not said anything about her previous bedding experience, but he seemed to care about her and put her first, which was the opposite of the lustful Henry – a man whose selfish passion had brought her to the edge of ruin. Anne had no romantic feelings for François, and she doubted her ability to feel passion for any man again.

Her initial expectation that François would take Anne for his own pleasure had been wrong. The French king was a superb lover, his expertise rivaling that of Eros, so their lovemaking was satisfying for Anne, despite her passiveness and his deliberate restraint. Her gratification must have been borne out of a primitive need. Yet, a warning rang in her head: *François is a typical Frenchman with infidelity in his blood, and he will cheat on his wife regardless of who she is.*

The ruler's voice, a lilting tenor that evoked the beauty of sacred music, broke Anne out of her reveries.

I do feel the lurch and halt of my heart
When I stare right into my Anne's eyes,
Full of enigma and beauty of my sweetheart,
Almost mythical contents I can see in them,
As if she were a creature of magical sunrise.
Yet, my Anne's eyes are two brown pools of fire
That burns me with their intense, fine art –
Art of the majestic mystery of my sweetheart,
I discern in them my own Gardens of Eden,
My golden future and our long reign in France,
I'm hooked to my wife's eyes which I adore.

Anne's heart sped. "Did Your Majesty write this poem?"

"I did." François kissed her on the nose playfully. "It is my small wedding gift. I write often, and you will be my Muse."

"It is lovely, thank you." She was aware that the King of France had composed poems for beautiful women whom he had pursued in the past, one of them her own sister.

The monarch stroked her cheek. "I am delighted you like it. Now sleep, Anne. It was a very long day."

As Anne slipped into the arms of Morpheus, the ruler observed the gentle fluttering of her eyelashes. It took a colossal effort on his part to suppress the vehement hunger for her. He was bewildered as to why he had experienced not only lust to possess her, but also a tender longing for his new spouse. *Why do I feel like Anne is my treasure? I do not love her, but I did greatly enjoy being with her. Doubtless she has touched my heart in a way that no one else ever has.*

François had even been inclined to apologize to Anne if he had caused her any discomfort, but he had not, for he was a monarch. And there was such a winsome aura of vulnerability about his exotic consort! The odd sense of possession and protectiveness, intertwined with his desire for her, puzzled the king, for he had never felt anything like this for other women.

CHAPTER 9

Marital Landscapes

July 18, 1537, Venice, the Republic of Venice, the Palazzo Montreuil

"You have a magnificent intelligence, Anne," lauded King François. "It is to be admired and treasured."

Anne stared at the king with astonishment. A smile of joy crossed her expressive features. "Truly, Your Majesty?" she breathed eagerly. "Or are you flattering me?"

His heart hummed with delight: his wife had just flashed him her first felicitous smile since their wedding. "Of course, Madame, I value it greatly. Or do you doubt my word?"

With endearing innocence, she replied, "I'm very glad."

Cardinal de Tournon flicked his heedful gaze back and forth between the royal couple. They were all seated together in fine matching chairs by a window in the study.

The negotiations with the Republic of Venice were temporarily put on hold until the French envoys returned from the Ottoman Empire. After his defeat at Pavia, the French monarch had needed powerful allies to fight against the hegemony of the House of Habsburg. As a result, in 1536, a controversial alliance had been established between King François and the Turkish sultan Suleiman the

Magnificent, much to the surprise and shock of the Christian world.

Now the Valois ruler resided at the Palazzo Montreuil, and it was officially said that he had moved to the residence of his father's old friend. François had made a public declaration about his new marriage. His spouse's background remained unknown, but the announcement stressed one important thing to cultivate the image of divine intervention – the mysterious Queen of France was the one who had taken the dagger meant for the monarch, and saved his life.

Throughout Christendom, it was known that the King of France had wed this lady soon after the nullification of his union with Eleanor of Austria. The Spanish were infuriated; the French were astounded and intrigued; the English waited for clarification. Everyone wondered about the identity of the Valois ruler's third wife, placing wagers as to who she was.

When the smile had faded from his spouse's face, François concentrated on the agenda for the day. "We need to revive the *'Auld Alliance'* with Scotland for our safety."

The friendship between the countries had been ratified and supported by many past treaties, marriage contracts between royals and nobles, and economic privileges. François needed to strengthen France's old diplomatic and political connections with Scotland, whose land borders provided a springboard from where to harry his English enemy.

As François remembered the late Princess Madeleine, his fragile daughter, his heart plummeted like a stone. Her death of consumption at the age of sixteen had broken his very soul into countless smithereens. *I've lost several children, both legitimate and illegitimate, and I shall mourn for each of them forever.* Some had not survived infanthood, others had succumbed to infections, whereas his late son François had died because of his weak health after the Spanish captivity.

In 1536, King James V of Scotland had asked him for Madeleine's hand in marriage. At first, François had refused, fearing that his daughter's poor health would deteriorate in the harsh Scottish climate. Nevertheless, Madeleine and James had fallen in ardent love, and François had reluctantly consented to the match, despite his fears. Before the arrival of the newly wedded couple in Scotland, Madeleine had already been gravely ill and soon wilted like a dying flower.

Tournon nodded. "That is an excellent idea."

Anne inquired, "Are you intending to achieve it through matrimony?"

The monarch confirmed, "King James needs a new wife."

"France does not have a princess of suitable age," noted Tournon.

François speculated, "We can offer Marie de Guise, Duchess de Longueville. She is a young widow who has already proved her fertility – she has a son of three summers."

The cardinal ruminated, "The Guises are a wealthy and powerful family, but they do not belong to the French royalty. Will that not be an impediment for the King of Scotland?"

The ruler raked a hand through his hair. "King James urgently needs a French wife and an alliance with France." His gaze flicked to his wife. "Anne, what do you think?"

The queen speculated, "The House of Guise are members of a royal dynasty, though with no real sovereignty. They also enjoy the rank of foreign princes at the French court. I heard that Madame Marie is beautiful and young, and if her dowry were as large as that of a princess, she would become a sought-after royal bride. Why would King James not wish to wed her?"

François let out a smile of pride. "You apparently grew up at my court, Anne! You are fully aware of the intricacies of the French aristocracy and of our political background." His gaze shifted to the prelate. "Your Eminence, if possible, the marriage contract should be finalized by the end of the year."

Tournon put in, "I'll convey your wishes to Duke Claude de Guise. He is ambitious, so he is highly unlikely to object since his daughter will become the Queen of Scotland."

She questioned, "What other alliances do you have in Italy?"

"The Duchy of Savoy that is occupied by us and the Papal States," answered the king, his fingers drumming on the armrests of his chair. "A year ago, my diplomats established an alliance with the Republic of Sienna against Emperor Carlos. Now it is crucial to sign a treaty with the Republic of Venice, which will be enough for now."

"What about the Republic of Genoa?" the queen suggested.

François grinned ironically. "Genoa would be the first place I would order my troops to attack if I yearned to capture the entire peninsula and undermine Spain's financial power. But they will not ally with us unless there is a huge gain to be made. However, I'm interested only in the Duchies of Savoy and Milan; I do not want any other Italian lands."

Anne was surprised that the king had tamed his appetite for conquests and vainglory in Italy, for in the past François had felt differently. "What is so important about Genoa?"

Tournon explained at length, "Years ago, Admiral Andrea Doria, from a powerful Genoese family, allied with Spain to win the war against France in order to restore the Republic of Genoa's independence. The Genoese bankers have since then obtained significant control of Europe's finances. Emperor Carlos has already borrowed a great deal of money from them to fund both his foreign and domestic activities. Nowadays, the Spanish ship huge quantities of American silver to Genoa, and if the city were ever besieged, this would prevent the silver from being exchanged into the gold which Spain needs. In this case, the emperor's coffers would be empty."

Anne deduced, "If the country lacked a regular income, this would not only derail Spain's massive plans to continue her colonial expansion, but also result in her king's inability to pay to soldiers and purchase provisions for them."

The queen's quick grasp of Genoa's situation impressed Tournon. "In addition, Emperor Carlos spends massive amounts on crusading against Protestantism that has got great footing in the German states, in the very center of the empire. As of late, Carlos needs a lot of money."

François scoffed acridly. "One day, the world might see the bankruptcy of the Spanish Crown."

Anne comprehended the political landscape of England, Spain, and France, but she lacked knowledge of Italian affairs. "The Ottoman Empire became France's ally a couple of years ago. If the emperor continues scheming against France, and if we happen to be on the losing side, the Turks will lay a siege to Genoa, which will weaken Spain and, hence, benefit us."

Tournon tipped his head. "Something along these lines."

"What about Florence?" queried the queen, aiming to get a full knowledge of Italian politics. "Dauphine Catherine is a Medici; her family enjoys a solid position in Florence."

The king knitted his brows in annoyance. "At first, we thought that the Medici marriage into the House of Valois would bring France a strategic alliance. A large dowry was offered, including Pisa and Livorno. However, Pope Clement the Seventh died, and the dowry was not paid."

"This union gave France nothing," complained Tournon.

François issued a rejoinder. "Nothing, save a headache."

Anne and Tournon smiled, but the joke did not diffuse the tension gathering due to Dauphine Catherine's matrimony.

In the hesitating voice of a philosopher who doubts some grand theory, the ruler elaborated, "Perhaps I should send a request to Pope Paul to annul my son Henri's marriage to Catherine." He cast a glance at his councilor. "There was no dowry, and it seems that there will be no heirs."

Anne understood why King François was in two minds. Dauphin Henri was not fond of his spouse, and Catherine had failed to produce a son during their four-year matrimony. It was a dilemma for the monarch, for his heir needed a fertile wife. Anne sympathized with Catherine de' Medici, who was under pressure from the Valois family, and the whole country, to produce an heir. *Now Catherine is in exactly the same situation as the one I was in England,* Anne summed up.

François shrugged. "I need to mull over it." He switched to another subject. "Anne, the Medici owe Emperor Carlos for the restoration of their power in Florence after they had been deposed during the War of the League of Cognac. An alliance with Florence will become possible only if something makes the Medici turn against the House of Habsburg."

The queen concluded, "As Your Majesty is not interested in conquering the whole of Italy, it is enough to have the Republics of Venice and of Sienna, and the Ottoman Empire as France's allies. The Duchy of Savoy is occupied by France and is against the emperor. Other political entanglements are desirable, but not much needed at this point."

The king commended, "I see you understand these things very well; not everyone does." He released a sigh. "No one can guarantee that the Pope will always be France's ally."

Anne predicted, "Especially when everyone learns that the King of France married the very woman who, they believe, led King Henry of England to break from the Vatican."

François' sigh was like a storm wind. "Yes."

The cardinal measured Anne with a penetrating look. "It was all King Henry's doing, wasn't it?"

The queen parried, "If Henry had not wanted to establish the Church of England, would I accomplish it alone?"

"Your Majesty is not a simple woman," parried Tournon. "You can influence men substantially, but I agree with you."

François observed her intently as Anne and Cardinal de Tournon began conversing about Spain's growing influence in the New World and her various alliances in the old one.

The Valois ruler watched Anne with a mingled feeling of admiration and awe. *I'm drawn to my clever wife like an art collector, gravitating towards the rarest and most unusual of masterpieces*, the monarch silently remarked to himself. He adored his queen's intelligence, beauty, poise, resilience, and inner strength. Not for the first time, François compared the Anne Boleyn whom he had met in Calais to this new Anne. She was an unconventional beauty, exotic and intriguing, but those striking dark eyes, framed by long and raven lashes, were changed. He remembered their former sparkle, but now, for the most part, they were either muted or blank.

His consort's life had been shattered by cruel betrayal, and now it was shrouded in secrecy. No wonder Anne possessed an air of fatality. More mysterious than ever, she rarely smiled, and sometimes, there was a vengeful intensity about her. For the most part, Anne's exterior was emotionless, as though frozen by the blast of an icy squall. François wondered whether this would ever thaw and be replaced by warmth.

August 1, 1537, Venice, the Republic of Venice, the Palazzo Montreuil

The fading sun was a large ball of vivid and flashing red fire. Dove-shaped clouds, tinged with every shade of crimson and orange imaginable, traversed the darkening heavens.

In the palazzo's art gallery, Anne and François sat on a bench by a window, watching the sundown. Around them, many stunning paintings by Giovanni Bellini, Marco Basaiti, Cima da Conegliano, and Titian hung on the walls. The count's collection contained even a rare portrait by Giorgione inspired by Petrarca's poem about his unrequited love for a woman called Laura. Anne's French "grandfather" was an avid art collector with an eye for genius.

As the sun's disk transformed into a thin crescent, King François shifted his scrutiny to his wife. "Sunrise and sunset mark time, Anne, both of the natural day and of one's life."

Her eyes darting to his, Anne looked as pale as a mere phantasm of herself. Tormenting images of the bloody executions on Tower Green blazed through her head. "The sunset is crimson; the blood is crimson. They remind me of horrors in my life, so I no longer like this time of the day."

The monarch nodded his understanding, and a warmth seeped into her veins. A sense of calm and safety engulfed her, as Anne glanced into his compassionate eyes. During the day, he was busy with his courtiers and the Doge of Venice, and Anne liked these rare moments that they spent together.

The past and the present. Henry and François. Cruelty and nobility of the heart. Darkness and light. *It gladdens me that they seem to be quite different, especially on the inside,* Anne effused in her mind. *Yet, François is still a king...*

In contrast to Henry, François was even-tempered: he was levelheaded, rarely ruled by emotion. Anne treasured that her *second husband* – these words still sounded foreign to her – was far more willing to listen to her opinions than Henry had ever been. François was an erudite conversationalist, positive in demeanor no matter who or what he faced. Highly intelligent and impeccably educated, the King of France impressed Anne as both person and ruler. Moreover, François was the most humane of the monarchs of the period.

"Anne?" the ruler called softly, jolting his spouse from her mental comparison of the two rivals and kings.

She turned to her husband before informing, "I've received a letter from Henry Percy who is my staunch ally in England."

Her husband warned, "Lord Northumberland should talk to Archbishop Cranmer only after the pamphlets are issued."

"I fear that they will enrage King Henry, and he might be unwilling to hear anything about Anne Boleyn." It was an odd sensation to talk about herself as a third party.

François took her hand in his, their fingers entwined like two halves of one whole. "Certainly, Henry will be furious. However, without the pamphlets and the critical book about Cromwell, the Archbishop of Canterbury will not have any plausible reason to disclose your last confession."

"Should I warn Harry Percy about the distribution of the pamphlets in England?"

"It would be the best course of action." He emphatically added, "Inform Lord Northumberland that he may always find refuge in France if his life is in danger in England. Beware of being too clear in your reply of what is planned.

He will know how to act when those pamphlets hit the streets."

"Thank you, Your Majesty." Her gaze flitted to the Bellini painting of '*Madonna and Child.*'

"Do you like the painting?" There was a note of bleakness in François' voice, and a startled Anne pulled her gaze back to him. "I see how you are looking at the Madonna."

"This work of art has impressed me, sire."

"What does it say to you, Anne?"

"The child is so small and innocent. The Madonna's hands seem to be holding my good memories of England and of my childhood, in the same way as she is holding the baby."

He commended, "You have a keen eye for the arts. I have a similar painting by Bellini at Château de Fontainebleau." A furrow formed between his brows. "Looking at it, though, I see only my own dearly departed children."

François meant the late Dauphin François and the late Princess Madeleine, who had both died in the past two years, as well as his two daughters, Princess Louise and Princess Charlotte, who had passed away years ago, in their early childhood. He was still grieving over the loss of his offspring. Anne felt a similar pain about her two miscarriages, but that was where the similarity ended. She at least had two surviving children. It was a different thing to raise a child, to see them grow into adulthood, and then to lose them to death. Her thoughts returned to the English king.

Was Henry shaken by grief when Catherine and I lost his children? He did not mourn for very long! Many beautiful women at court fawned over him, and he bedded them, while his wives wept. Such were Anne's thoughts of Henry, who had always continued leading his usual life of opulence as though nothing had happened. The queen wondered whether he was so strong that he had swiftly moved on, or because he was merely a shallow person, incapable of feeling deeply.

Anne whispered, "I understand what you mean, sire."

"It is not for my own pleasure that I gather these works of art." François shifted closer to Anne and pulled her into an embrace. "Artists create masterpieces which can broaden and enrich the knowledge of all those who see their work. And I want my subjects to know art, for it is through its beauty that people will see the glory of God and His creation."

The ruler reminisced about an extraordinary Florentine whom he had invited to France in 1515. He had long passed away, but François enthusiastically recalled, "Leonardo da Vinci taught me to understand and cherish all aspects of art: the use of color, the logical elegance of proportion and perspective, options for artistic composition, and the choices an artist makes – what to include and what to leave to the imagination. There is a great beauty beyond the outward appearance of a masterpiece; a beauty that is echoed within the soul of anyone willing to fully experience a work of art."

Anne remembered the gentle Italian, with the cruelly gnarled fingers bent by rheumatism and age, but with a mind that was as sharp as a man half his age. "Although I spent much time at Amboise with Queen Claude, I saw Maestro da Vinci several times. I heard that he was a brilliantly educated and intelligent man, truly the greatest genius of all times."

Remembrances inundated the king's head. "I've never known a man as thirsty for knowledge as Leonardo da Vinci. The many hours I spent with him at Château du Clos Lucé and Château d'Amboise are precious memories to me. Although Leonardo's arm was paralyzed in the last years of his life, and he could no longer paint, I enjoyed our captivating conversations and debates. Before meeting him, I could not have imagined that someone could enrich my mind and broaden my education with such invaluable knowledge. That is why I regarded him as the most cultured man in Europe."

"I was at Blois when he died," she recollected.

François ran his bejeweled fingers through his brown curls. "According to a bittersweet story that still circulates to this day, Leonardo died in my arms. The truth is that he drew his last breath at Château du Clos Lucé at Amboise. I was not there, but my physicians attended to him."

"This legend is much loved by the French," said Anne in a voice colored with sadness. "People say that Your Majesty was embracing a lifeless Maestro da Vinci for a long time."

Those amber eyes danced with humor. "Let them think so! Many legends are revered! They are all mysterious and romantic portions of history, whose nature remains unknown to all, except for those who believe in them. Some, like the one about Leonardo's passing, are appealing to the imagination."

Anne discovered a new facet of her spouse's personality. *It is incredible that François is capable of being so impassioned and so romantic, so aflame with creative ideas and jocund, and even a bit sentimental. He is so human in such moments,* she observed silently. Everyone knew of the monarch's high-spirited nature and of his mischievous, sometimes acerbic, wit. Yet, at the same time, King François was regal, arrogant, and slightly pompous in the presence of his subjects.

The ruler laughed mirthfully at his wife's visible elation. Anne joined in his laughter, and the sharing of it felt as a traveler must when returning home after a long absence. A connection was forming between the spouses: their original common link was their desire for revenge, but they shared something beyond it – many interests and passions.

§§§

Once Anne had doubted that she could enjoy intimacy with any man other than Henry, but she had been wrong. Her encounters with François sent her soaring into a breathtaking realm of ambrosial sensations. When their mouths met, she was trembling with the force of the unleashed passion that his touch had freed within her, but she endeavored to hide it. Anne was eager for whatever he would do to her, although she knew that he did not give free reign to his hunger for her.

She did not regret marrying King François in the slightest. At present, Anne Boleyn was the Queen of France! Centuries earlier, Eleanor of Aquitaine's successive marriages to two monarchs had made her the only woman who had ruled both France and England, and at present, Anne was following in her illustrious footsteps. After her coronation in France, Anne would celebrate her complete victory over King Henry, rising like a glorious phoenix from the ashes of his ruthless attempt to extinguish her life on the pyre of his narcissism.

In spite of her optimistic expectations about the future, recurring nightmares still disturbed her nights. Once, when the sheen of dawn washed the sky a light pink, Anne dreamed of her own burning, while King Henry and Jane Seymour witnessed her torments, laughing at her. It was not the first time she had had this dream, but tonight it seemed too real.

"No!" cried Anne as her eyes opened wide. Feeling the cold sweat on her forehead, she stared into the darkness, her breathing as erratic as if she were wheezing.

When François woke, he enveloped his distressed wife into a protective embrace. "Shhh, Anne. It is over."

"Thank you," murmured the embarrassed queen.

The king had never been as tender with any other woman as he was with his new wife. Even so, he had felt her body, at one point, tensing like an arrow poised in the bow. He had noticed this before, during their moments of intimacy, and François wondered if he had somehow caused her discomfort. His heart was imbued with concern about his queen, and this, he realized, was new to him. *Why am I feeling this way? Accepting Anne wholly into my life is utterly life-changing.*

"Was everything to your liking today, Anne? Answer me honestly." He would further restrain his cravings if necessary.

"Yes, sire," her truthful response followed.

"Good. If you do not enjoy something, you must tell me."

The moonlight silvered his spouse's alabaster skin and highlighted her gorgeous mane of long, raven hair scattered across the pillow. It gave her an unearthly charm enthralling any man like a holy vision. François admired his sleepy wife, who seemed especially vulnerable and innocent now.

The ruler kissed the nape of her neck where her hair fell away. "What was your dream about?"

The queen dragged a deep breath and held it for a long moment before saying, "Nothing serious."

A sigh tumbled from his mouth. She never alluded to the Tower of London, her almost execution, and the tragedies and bereavement in her erstwhile life. At this very moment, the king realized how emotionally fragile Anne was, despite her brilliant masquerade of indifference in the daytime.

He pressed his lips to hers in a chaste kiss. "Try to sleep."

"Yes." Her eyes squeezed shut, and she dived back into the realm of Morpheus.

"Everything will be well, I promise you, Anne." His arms encircled his consort as François lay back on the pillows.

François guessed that his Tudor archrival often came from Tartarus to torture Anne in her sleep, but he was patient, knowing that she had been too traumatized. Fearless of life's fires, like a salamander, François was certain of their plan's success, and a sense of triumph swept through him as he envisaged them presiding over festivities at *their* court. *As our lives are joined, I'm responsible for ensuring the healing of Anne's heart wounds,* the king mused as he drifted to sleep.

August 12, 1537, Newcastle-under-Lyme, Staffordshire, England

Lady Mary Stafford née Boleyn and her second husband, William Stafford, had settled in a small village near the city of Newcastle-under-Lyme in the County of Staffordshire.

Today William, Mary, and Arthur met the morning in the sparsely furnished living room of their modest house. The floors were covered by thickly woven rush mats, the massive oak table, several heavily carved, high-back chairs, and other pieces of oak furniture, giving it a pleasing appearance.

William noted his wife's pensive expression. "Are you happy with me, Mary?"

Lady Stafford was now cradling little Arthur. "Oh, yes!" she enthused. "Never doubt it, you beloved fool! You and our children are my most precious treasure."

He viewed his spouse from top to toe. As if unblemished by time, her mature beauty was as tender as the sighing of a breeze through the trees. His breath caught, and a mere look at his wife sent a shudder through his body. As Mary smiled at William, his heart, filled with amorous longing, hammered like a live creature that had been sewn into his chest cavity.

Mary was slender and shapely, and her silk gown of the palest shade of beige without any ornamentation accentuated her feminine figure. Her face was highlighted by expressive, sagacious eyes of cerulean blue, fringed by thick, brown lashes. Her long, glossy hair – so golden, more halo than hair – was swept up in a chignon. Mary's classic features and her pale complexion, so appealing to men, were a stark contrast to the exotic allure of her younger sister, Anne.

William's entire being was imbued with adoration for the entirety of Mary's loveliness. His wife had evolved into the type of woman who shared his delight in watching a sunrise or admiring the grandeur of fluffy, dove-colored clouds drifting across the warm firmament. His captivating spouse never lacked for admirers at royal courts, and William silently brooded, *I understand why many men, including two kings, wanted her, but now Mary belongs to me forever.*

Her question jolted him out of his musings. "Why are you looking at me like that?"

William complimented, "You are absolutely stunning, my darling."

She flushed a little. "To be beautiful, one must fill their mind with beautiful thoughts."

"You do have them in abundance," he claimed.

Her answer was a melancholic smile. Events of the past paraded in front of Mary in a cavalcade of remembrances.

When several years ago she had wed William, a man far beneath her station, Mary had not cared about opinions of others because she loved him. Mary and William had gotten acquainted in Calais in October 1532 when King Henry and her sister, Anne, had met with King François. One of the two hundred people among the English party, William had served as an arquebusier, but he and Mary had been so overmastered by passion that they had quickly become lovers.

Mary had conceived their first child during their nights in Calais. Upon their return to England, she had discovered her pregnancy. Both shocked and exhilarated, Mary had come to William with the news, and he had offered her to elope. Spirits of elation had been singing in their souls when they had exchanged marital vows in a small church in Dover. Mary had anticipated the condemnation and resistance from her relatives, but not the harsh treatment she had received.

Upon learning about her scandalous marriage, Anne had banished her sister from court on King Henry's orders. Her father, Thomas Boleyn, had disinherited and expelled Mary from the family. Her eldest children by William Carey, her deceased first spouse – Catherine and Henry Carey – were estranged from her. They had been taken away to be raised in the Carey family household because, in their opinion, their mother had disgraced herself by marrying a commoner.

Betrayed and humiliated, Mary and her new husband had left London. A woman of strong character, kind heart, and principled convictions, she had not begged any of her many relatives to give her money or food, even though she had been literally thrown out into the street.

In early youth, Mary had been light-hearted, merry, and flippant. Peitho, the Greek goddess of seduction, had enticed her into having affairs. Enamored of King François, Mary had become his paramour while living at the Valois court. After her return to England, at her father's behest she had been a mistress of King Henry, who had charmed her and then broken her heart, just as François had done before. Her first arranged marriage to Sir William Carey had been unhappy.

Over time, Mary had realized that her sentiments towards both of these kings had been nothing more than infatuation. There was only one man for whom her feelings were deeper than a blend of passion, physical attraction, and admiration.

He was Claude d'Annebault, a powerful figure in France. Several months after François' abandonment of her, Mary and Claude had suddenly become entangled in a web of passion, and he had proposed to her out of pure love.

I'm very sorry, Claude, that I could not be with you, Mary lamented silently. *I was recalled back to England and obeyed my father. What else could I do?* Thoughts of what might have been swirled through her head like a tempest, spelling one male name – Claude. What if Mary had married Claude and stayed in France? What could their family life have been like? A dart of shame speared her: Mary loved William Stafford, but at times, she remembered about Annebault.

After her union with Carey who had treated her like his property, and after her affairs, Mary had been fortunate to find William. She had matured into a dignified woman, one who now regretted her erstwhile flippancy and easy virtue. However, Mary would not have changed her life because she would otherwise never have met William Stafford, the love of her life. *I've learned by hard lessons what is really precious in life: it is not riches, power, titles, and royal favor.*

To Mary, relationships revolved around the people she cared about and shared experiences with rather than the activities one could afford. Anne had endured an awful lot of unhappiness throughout her short marriage to the English ruler and, in the end, died for crimes she had not perpetrated, while Mary had found her true love. She often remembered her siblings through tears of abysmal sadness; unlike them both, Mary was lucky to have a happy ending.

The Staffords were not wealthy. William's family was only distantly related to the once mighty Staffords who had controlled the dukedom of Buckingham until 1521. However, William was a commoner and only a second son, so he could not offer Mary any wealth and high status.

After Mary had become the guardian of Anne's son, they had been worried that they would not have enough money to sustain themselves. They had two children of their own – little Anne and Edward. When Lady Eleanor Hampton had arrived with the baby Arthur, she had handed to Mary three bags of coins to provide for the child. Their benefactor's name had not been given. Astounded, the Staffords had taken the welcome injection of money to their coffers.

Breaking out of her reverie, Mary lamented, "I still cannot accept that Anne and George are both dead." She looked down at little Arthur lying in her lap.

Despite Anne's difficult pregnancy and her horrible birth ordeal, the baby boy was healthy. At nine months, Arthur had learned to sit and crawl. Recently, he had started trying to pull himself up to a standing position while holding onto furniture or Mary's hand. His intelligent, dark eyes first surveyed his 'mother' and then analyzed his surroundings. In spite of his reticent demeanor, he smiled and gurgled in gladness whenever Mary or William took him into their arms.

William articulated sympathetically, "Mary, they are gone, and nothing will change that."

"I know, but..." Her voice failed her.

The profound sadness in Mary's features tore at her husband's heart. "If Anne and George could see you so distressed, they would scold you for a certainty. You told me that your sister's motto for her coronation had been *The Most Happy.*' They would want you to find peace even without them." He emitted a sigh. "My dearest, please do not torment yourself with thoughts of your elusive guilt and self-recrimination. You could not have saved them."

As she glanced at Arthur who was playing with her gown's collar, a smile illuminated her countenance. "Yes, they would have chastised me." She bounced the toddler, and he giggled. "Arthur has Anne's eyes, but otherwise, he is a fine copy of King Henry in miniature with the Tudor red hair."

William sighed heavily. "Our sovereign believes that he is not his son."

"If the king ever meets the boy, he will realize that he is Arthur's father."

I'll never forgive King Henry for Anne and George's deaths. A blistering and scarlet rage billowed through Mary like a fiery dragon. She had given herself a word that Arthur would know all the truth about his mother's tragic romance with his father and about Anne's murder once he grew up.

"I doubt it will happen anytime soon, given that Queen Jane is pregnant."

Mary winced as Arthur pulled her loose hair that fell freely down her back. "If the queen delivers a girl or a stillborn child, the king may want to meet with Arthur."

William broke her hope into pieces. "He is convinced that Anne betrayed him, and, hence, he does not care for Arthur. At least, now your sister's son is safe with us."

Her eyes were alight with mockery. "Anne named her son in honor of His Majesty's elder brother – Arthur Tudor." Her lips stretched into a malicious grin. "She knew that this name would rub that egotistical monarch the wrong way."

William chuckled. "It would be entertaining to see His Majesty's reaction, if he cares to ask about the boy. I do not believe the king knows what he is called."

Mary envisaged Thomas Boleyn, grimacing in disgust. "Arthur and I mean nothing to my father. He does not wish to see his motherless grandchild." She slanted an affectionate look at Arthur. "But at least, he sent us some money for Arthur's expenses several months ago."

There was a pause while William searched for mild words to express his opinion of Mary's father, whom he despised wholeheartedly. "He is a contradictory man."

A despondent silence ensued. However, as Arthur grinned with a childlike innocence, his cheerful laughter inundated the chamber, creating a moment's repose for the Stafford spouses.

Meanwhile, in Venice, Anne was deluged with those short memories of her dear Arthur, and would have given anything to share their joy of her son for just a fraction of a second.

CHAPTER 10

News of a Royal Wedding

August 20, 1537, Venice, the Republic of Venice, the Palazzo Montreuil

The larger-than-life marriage of King François and Anne Boleyn! It was with a sense of unreality that Count Jean de Montreuil thought about their union. However, he could not doubt what he had witnessed since their wedding: the adoration, shaded by some deeper emotion, with which the monarch looked at Anne, apparently deeply attracted to her.

Jean sat at his desk in an ornately carved walnut chair, decorated with gold leaf, in his study. He had begun to read a book when the door flew open, and Anne walked in.

"Good evening, Grandfather," she greeted as she strode over to one of the shelves. The months of playing this role had made it become her second nature.

"Your Majesty," the count acknowledged her officially. He addressed her by the rightful title, for now Anne was the Queen of France. "Is His Majesty home?"

"No, he is not." She picked out a book at random and turned to leave.

"How is your relationship with King François?"

Surprised, Anne froze in the middle of the room, staring at him. "It is normal." She let out a laugh. "I'm like Eleanor of Aquitaine, who was married to two kings."

"The Duchess of Aquitaine was one of the greatest women in history. But you, Anne, will never be like her: you are wise enough not to rebel against your own husband."

"I'm not insane to dig my own grave." She would never attempt an uprising, even if it were the only way to place her son, Arthur, on Henry's throne. Anne had made many enemies in England, but they all thought she was dead; the queen would never commit the same mistakes again.

"Please, listen to me," Jean appealed to her. "It is by the mysterious workings of providence that King François was in the same chapel at the same time as you prayed there. It was the Almighty's will for you to become the Queen of France."

Anne's fingers clenched around the spine of the book she was holding. "The Lord rules everything, and His children cannot change their destiny."

The count stroked his silver beard. "You narrowly escaped death in England, but here you are: a queen again, married to the king at whose court you became an intellectual diamond in adolescence. That was God's plan for you! King François is different from King Henry. You have achieved what no other woman could, and you should be content."

"I know that I'm a fortunate woman."

"I am certain that His Majesty might fall in love with you, Anne. It all depends upon you. François has always looked for true love with a woman who is his equal."

Anne was so amazed by this unforeseen prediction that she found herself speechless. Could her marriage to François become something more than a political arrangement? At this time, her answer to herself was a categorical, emphatic NO! She was entirely focused on her revenge upon Henry.

"Thank you for the candor. I'll leave you to your business." She stalked to the door and walked out of the study.

The count sat in silence as he considered her reaction. He saw the burgeoning affection in the king and hoped that Anne would not be blinded by her obsession with vengeance.

August 26, 1537, the Royal Palace of Valladolid, Valladolid, Spain

It was late afternoon, and the sun had vanished behind a bank of dormant rain clouds. Carlos V, Holy Roman Emperor, was in his private chambers. His suite was suffused with light from a profusion of candelabra and decorated with the portraits of Habsburg family members.

A collection of maps of Europe was tacked to one of the walls and written over with what could only be routes and directions. The Duchies of Savoy and of Milan, as well as Piedmont were encircled in bold red ink. The top of the desk was piled with many books on war and military strategy. On the other side of the table, there were statues of saints. A large golden crucifix hung between the maps on the wall.

The emperor was so absorbed in his thoughts that he did not hear Francisco de los Cobos enter.

After the fall of Mercurino Gattinara nine years earlier, De los Cobos had been appointed leader of the Council of State and become Carlos' most influential advisor. His expertise in financial matters usually kept him in Spain, which was ruled by Empress Isabella as regent during Carlos' frequent absences as he traveled through his vast lands.

De los Cobos flourished a low, servile bow. "Your Imperial Majesty, I beg your pardon for intruding."

Emperor Carlos was a handsome man of considerable talents, whose features were neither soft nor stern. The hallmark of his appearance was his protruding Habsburg jaw. His face was thin and pale, only redeemed by a fine open brow and heavy-lidded, sly, hazel eyes. Athletic of frame, the monarch's figure was well proportioned, his stature of middle height, his deportment impressive and commanding rather than pleasing. Carlos smiled and laughed rarely.

His austere bearing was accentuated by the severity of Spanish fashion. Today, Carlos was clad in a tight-fitting, high-collared doublet of black brocade, pointed in the front, which was surmounted by a wheel-shaped, stiff collar, making his head appear detached from his body. The collar of the Order of the Golden Fleece, full-length sleeves, knee-length black trunk hose, and sword belt completed the ensemble. A black velvet cap was placed upon his short brown hair.

The ruler swiveled to look at his subject. "Francisco, I was thinking of the Italian war. King François has captured Piedmont, but I'll expel the French from the north of Italy."

"These lands rightfully belong to Your Imperial Majesty."

Carlos smiled at his advisor. In his early sixties, Francisco de los Cobos was a sturdy man with a short white beard and black eyes. His broad countenance had wrinkles, and his still raven brows were fixed in a frown that suggested his worry for his liege lord. Cobos' attire was black damask worked with gold, with a flat cap of brown velvet upon his head.

The ruler enquired impatiently, "Any news from Venice? Who is the woman who saved François and ruined my plans?"

Cobos apologized, "My people checked everything, but despite our best efforts, we have found nothing."

An outraged Carlos snarled, "That Valois blackguard set aside my sister, Eleanor, and had the gall to wed someone mere months after the annulment. My sister fell in love with him, and his lewd behavior of sleeping with his courtesans and ignoring her hurt Eleanor." His voice took on a higher octave. "I'll never forgive François for my sister's humiliation."

Since the annulment, Emperor Carlos had maintained a calm façade in public. Yet, his close entourage and even his wife, Empress Isabella, were the recipients of his wrath. He had not anticipated such audacity on François' part. Upon Eleanor's return to Valladolid, he had scolded his sister for not resisting the divorce proceedings, having reduced her to tears. Yet, his initial anger had been nothing compared to the rage he had felt after learning about his rival's new marriage.

"François has dared insult us, the great Habsburgs!" the emperor blustered. "And he is not even a pure Valois! He belongs to a cadet branch of the House of Valois!"

"Your Imperial Majesty has a far nobler lineage," flattered Cobos. "The current French monarch is a count's son."

"François inherited the French throne by chance," Carlos continued his irate tirade. "King Louis the Twelfth didn't have any surviving male issue. So, he married his eldest daughter off to his cousin – young François d'Angoulême, who was proclaimed Dauphin of France." His mouth compressed into a line of distaste. "François' father was Charles d'Orléans, Count d'Angoulême, with some royal blood in his veins. He is François *the Fortunate parvenu!*" His voice reached a crescendo on the last words.

"He is nothing compared to you," intoned his councilor obsequiously.

The monarch stood up and commenced pacing to and fro. "François never touched her as a man, and my foolish sister allowed him to avoid his marital duties." The corners of his lips twitched sarcastically. "And now, a disgraced Eleanor is sewing and doing needlework all day long."

"How is Her Highness faring?" asked the royal adviser.

The monarch stopped and stomped his foot in fury. "Francisco, how is a woman, betrayed by a despicable husband, supposed to feel? My sister was the Queen of France for seven years, but now her marriage has been dissolved, and she has been thrown out of her kingdom like a piece of dirt. Now the whole world knows that François disliked her so much that he never bedded her." The tendons in his neck and face were stretched taut in a grimace of loathing. "Eleanor has fallen into a deep depression upon learning about François' recent wedding, but she endeavors to hide her frustration." Charles did love his sister and was concerned about her.

"Her Highness is a strong woman," Cobos noted.

"Yes." The emperor returned to his chair and settled there. He stated with pride, "Eleanor is heartbroken, but she is a Habsburg. Thus, she is stronger than others and shall cope."

Francisco de los Cobos broached another subject. "Your Imperial Majesty, many rumors are circulating in Europe that you sanctioned the murder of King François."

Carlos' lips stretched into a vinegary smile. "People will not trust this gossip. Our spies confirmed that the assassin whom we hired for the deed did not confess. Everyone will simply assume that he hated François because French troops invaded Italy and Savoy." He huffed out an exasperated breath. "It is such a great pity that our man failed."

"He was executed, thus ensuring that you are safe."

The ruler nodded. "Francisco, we shall try again. François and I have been enmeshed in intrigues and rivalries since we took our thrones all those years ago. Our enmity shall last as long as we breathe and rule. Now my goal is to get rid of that Valois bastard and his new wife; they both owe me debt, and it will be repaid." His face assumed an intensely hateful look. "I should have killed François when he was my prisoner."

Cobos nodded. Silence fell, thick with unsaid words of the emperor's animosity towards his French archrival, perennial as the leaves on the trees, which come forth year after year.

Someone knocked at the door, and the emperor permitted, "Come in."

"Good afternoon, Your Imperial Majesty," began his guest and friend. "Empress Isabella and... erm... Infanta Eleanor have asked me to tell you that the dinner has been served."

Fernando Álvarez de Toledo, Duke of Alba, was a high-ranked Spanish nobleman, general, and diplomat favored by the emperor. A tall man four years younger than Carlos, he had a powerful physique and stern countenance, with a sharp nose and wide-set, ice blue eyes. He was attired in a white and brown damask doublet worn beneath a short-sleeved black jerkin, adorned with bands of silver-thread embroidery, over which he wore the Order of the Golden Fleece.

At the mention of his beloved spouse, Carlos smiled, his mood instantly improving. "We ought to go now! We cannot make my wife and my sister wait for us for long."

Alba was glad to see his master in a less rueful frame of mind. "Of course, Your Imperial Majesty."

The monarch crossed to the duke. "Any news from France and Italy?" He threw a glance at Cobos over his shoulder, then complained, "Francisco' spies have not learned anything."

Cobos pledged, "I'll order all our agents to work harder."

Alba shrugged apologetically. "I have nothing interesting to share either."

Hiding his disappointment, the emperor prodded, "Let's go. I am quite hungry and eager to see my family."

They headed to the grand chamber, where a small private feast was organized. At present, the Spanish court resided in Valladolid, but they would soon move to the Alcázar de Seville.

September 3, 1537, Palais du Louvre, Paris, France

Dauphin Henri of France and his beloved mistress, Diane de Poitiers, were spending the evening in her quarters. A decanter of wine stood on the table, and she filled two goblets, handing one to her lover and sipping from her own. She then took a pack of cards, and they began playing.

Henri pushed the cards aside and scrutinized his mistress. "*Ma chérie*, you are such an experienced gamester that you always win when we meet at the card-table."

Diane flashed a mischievous smile. "Perhaps I'll beat you again, Henri." She looked through her cards, and her smile widened as she saw that she would surely not lose the game."

He smiled cordially. "Your victory will make me happy."

Henri had become the Dauphin of France after the death of his elder brother, François. He was a handsome young man with wide-spaced, brown eyes. He did not have the Valois long patrician nose. His short, dark hair fell in curls around his face, imbued with youthful naivete, but beneath it, there was the powerful and well-defined body of a grown man.

Unlike his father and his dead elder brother, who both had the stately bearing of kings, Henri lacked a charismatic air. He was an exceedingly serious and strongly principled man; somber and aloof at all times. His frigid demeanor seemed to be an unapproachable wall that was impossible to surmount. The time he had spent in the Spanish prison with his brother had changed his character, but, fortunately, it had not broken his spirit. Consequently, in spite of being barely out of boyhood, Henri was no longer carefree and cheerful.

In contrast to King François and other courtiers, Henri preferred unostentatious clothes, although his wardrobe was grand and expensive. His tastes were highly influenced by the Spanish fashions he had seen in Madrid. Now he was clad in a black damask toque plumed with one ostrich feather, trunk hose, and a black-slashed doublet of brown and gray velvet; the diamonds on the sleeves were the only embellishments.

"Life is a game." Diane was now shuffling the pack of cards fantastically fast with her only hand. "We are all playing. You either win or lose; there is no draw."

Henri did not see a calculative glint in her eyes. "You are so wise and good."

She bantered, "I wonder when you will be bored with the color of my gowns."

Diane de Poitiers possessed the classical and timeless beauty of an ancient goddess, which would never fade. She had full, rosy lips and high cheekbones, although her nose was a little long to be perfect. Her eyes were a brilliant blue, like the pure firmament on a summer day, and her hair was glossy, long and blonde. Her smooth skin was fresh with a translucent quality to it. Diane had a bewitching elegance and a natural charm of the Goddess Aphrodite.

For sixteen years, Diane had been married to Louis de Brézé, Seigneur d'Anet and Count de Maulevrier. Although he was thirty-nine years older, she had given him two daughters, neither of whom lived at court. After her husband's death in 1531, she kept his emoluments and assumed the title of the Grand Sénéchale de Normandie for herself.

As usual, today Diane was dressed in elegant black and white silk. Her gown had no opulent ornamentation, its modest high neckline trimmed with snowy lace. After her spouse's death, she had adopted the habit of wearing these two colors, and this had become her personal hallmark at court. The color of her attire against her alabaster skin was stark and dramatic.

Henri broke into an avalanche of compliments. "Madame, you are the most beautiful lady at court. Other women look like geese while you are a lovely swan."

Diane smiled. "Don't flatter me, Henri."

For a handful of moments, they beheld one another, lost in affectionate worship. He looked at her as if she were a goddess. In truth, this mutual warmth was an illusion: only one of the lovers was baring his heart, the other was safely ensconced behind a mask.

It was a masquerade many years in the making. Diane had been the first woman to treat Henri with tenderness after his mother's death. No less subtly woven than a playwright's tale – one of love, suffering, and mysterious threats – Diane had come into Henri's life as a woman of strong character, filled with grace and kindness, yet one who was beset by unknown perils. It had seemed inevitable that a noble, honorable man like Henri should offer her his protection.

It had been a perfectly orchestrated strategy for the most part, save her initial sympathy to him. Diane was a stunning creature, chilly and distant – the beauty of a cold star. Yet, when she appeared at court, her loveliness overshadowed everyone, save that of Anne de Pisseleu. She did not flirt and tease! Moreover, Diane was not known to have any lovers despite her widowhood. Courtiers gossiped that she had refused to be the king's mistress, which impressed the prince.

All this cultivated Henri's belief that Diane was not like his father's paramours – wanton, egocentric, and greedy for power and wealth. So convincing were these rumors and Diane's appearance of perfect propriety that Henri never bothered to ask François about the matter; if he had, he would have learned that his parent had never invited her to his bed. Diane had circulated this gossip so as to inspire Henri's vision of her as a woman with high moral principles.

Therefore, Diane had plied her craft and ensnared an enamored Henri into her web of charms. The young prince had made her his mistress three years ago, for he saw her as a woman unlike any other he had ever known. Diane felt a deep closeness to Henri and even loved him in her own way. Nonetheless, the passion that always simmered between them like a fierce, unquenchable fire had not lessened with the passage of time, continuing to smolder and burn.

Like most French female aristocrats, Madame de Poitiers was well educated and skilled in music, hunting, poetry, dancing, etiquette, the art of conversation, and languages. Her manners were impeccable: she spoke, walked, and ate with the delicate daintiness one would expect from a queen. Her keen interest in financial matters and her shrewdness were undeniable. Beneath that façade, unbeknownst to her royal lover, she was a calculating and cunning creature.

Diane was twenty years older than Henri. The age gap was not an obstacle to love between them. Life had been kind to Diane, and she did not look anywhere near her real age. Her body was still firm and strong, and she needed no cosmetics to mask her wrinkles. Diane ascribed the secret of her well-kept beauty to daily cold baths. The court had accepted her as the dauphine's mistress, but they did not favor her as much as they did Anne de Pisseleu, her main competitor.

"Wonderful!" cried Henri with a good-natured smile. He opened his cards and put them in the middle of the table.

"*Ma chérie*, I knew you would win, and I'm not angry with you."

"Luck is on my side," purred Diane. "As always."

As he recollected today's events, his brows knitted, and his lips pursed. "I've received a letter from my father. He indeed married someone in Venice."

She arched a brow. "And who is she?"

"He called her '*an incredible woman.*' I do not know her name, and neither do others."

A brief look of wild apprehension crossed her features at the monarch's characterization of his wife. Like the prince, Diane was not pleased with the news because this union could make her life more complicated by introducing a new rival at court. "There is a lot of gossip about this wedding. The people call the new Queen of France the king's savior."

"Indeed, she saved my father's life."

"Maybe the Duchess d'Étampes will soon be set aside."

"That is one of my most cherished dreams!" exclaimed Henri. "I've always loathed that immoral Pisseleu whore. She is superbly educated while being far more arrogant than stunning. She holds herself as if she were a queen. Maybe my father's new wife will put that strumpet in her place."

His lover was not so optimistic with what she saw and forewarned, "We cannot predict how the new queen will treat the royal children. We do not know why your father wed her in such secrecy, nor do we even have the faintest idea of her family or identity."

"She will be only the king's spouse."

"Ha!" she thundered. "Don't be so naive, Henri! That woman might have real influence over the king. His Majesty listened to your mother's opinions and valued them."

"Do not worry, Diane. My father's marriage will not alter your status. The queen will treat you with all the respect and the distinction due your high status."

BETWEEN TWO KINGS

Henri, you are still such a boy! You do not yet realize that everything in France might turn topsy-turvy in a heartbeat, Diane mused. She recalled her crime: the poisoning of the late Dauphin François. She did not regret her part in his death, and she contemplated the roles of her accomplices. They were Count Sebastiano de Montecuccoli and, most importantly, a friend of King François, a man so powerful that she was afraid to even think his name, lest she accidentally betray his confidence in a moment of carelessness.

As for Montecuccoli, he was a fanatical Catholic who had arrived in France as part of Catherine de Medici's Florentine retinue. His motive had nicely dovetailed with Diane's: Henri, Catherine's husband and Diane's lover, was now the king's eldest surviving son and, thus, the Dauphin of France. Although Catherine's elevation to Dauphine of France had been a great boon to the young girl, she had no idea of the conspiracy that had raised her to such an exalted position.

Diane wanted the dauphin to be on the alert, her intuition crying out for caution. "This odd marriage is unexpected."

"I hope the new Queen of France is a devout Catholic, just as my dearly departed mother was. I'm not fond of the policy of religious tolerance. My father is lenient towards heretics because he aims to weaken the Holy Roman Empire, where Protestant princes oppose the emperor's hegemony."

"Indeed, Henri." She eyed his stiff figure speculatively. "When you are the King of France, you will probably have to follow in your father's footsteps in religious policy."

Henri's visage whitened with a burst of fury. "Diane, you know my attitude to the heretics! And you still dare say that?" His eyes glittered with ire under his bristling brows. "It is my duty to rid France of the threat posed by reform that would divide not only the Church, but also the country. If I succeed my father as king, I'll take action against the Protestants."

Diane shook her head disapprovingly, although she shared Henri's views. "Dwelling on these things will keep you from accomplishing what is expected of you as Dauphin of France." She raised her voice to further berate him. "Be careful when you speak about France's religious policy. You do not need any open clashes or disagreements with our sovereign."

The dauphin blew out a calming sigh. "That is the reality in which I must live." He rubbed a hand across his forehead, as his thoughts returned to the war against Spain. "Can you ask Anne de Montmorency how my father is doing in Italy?"

"I'll write Monty. His Majesty is still in Venice."

"Then, we must wait for clarification."

The herald announced the arrival of Henry's younger brother. A moment later, Charles de Valois, Duke d'Orléans, entered with a slow, dignified stride. Crossing the room, his eccentric and conceited character showed in the arrogant swagger his gait developed.

Charles was much taller than an average boy of fifteen, a trait he shared with his father. The attractive youth had almond-shaped, amber eyes, the Valois long nose, and high cheekbones. His smile was breezy, although that easygoing expression could instantly become serious. He was dressed in purple: a taffeta shirt, puffy Venetian hose, and a striped satin doublet lavishly trimmed with diamonds and sapphires. His chestnut hair fell over his ears from beneath an azure velvet cap, adorned with white feathers and jeweled with an affiquet.

Charles was his father's son through and through, and François' favorite. He had many of the monarch's traits: a penchant for extravagance, outspokenness, geniality, and charisma, love for the arts and all things progressive and new. As their tastes in fashion were the same, the design and adornments of their clothes often were similar. Like his parent, he was known for his charming jests and his eccentric manners, which made Charles more popular at court than Henri.

A surprised Henri uttered, "Charles, I hadn't expected to see you here."

The Duke d'Orléans bowed slightly to Diane de Poitiers. "Madame." His scrutiny dashed to the dauphin. "Henri."

The dauphin's mistress rose to her feet and dropped a curtsey. "Your Highness, I'm honored to greet you in my chambers." She then seated herself back into her chair.

Charles nodded and glanced away; it was no secret that he did not respect Diane. His gaze slid to his brother again, and his countenance lit up with an amicable smile. "Henri, you didn't come to play cards, so I decided to pay you a visit."

Henri forced a smile. "Charles, we are already playing."

Charles eased himself into a chair next to his sibling. He loved his brother dearly, but he hated that Henri preferred Diane's company to his own, and that she had such excessive influence over him. Struggling to keep his voice even, he jumped to another topic. "His Majesty wrote to me."

His visage darkening, Henri muttered, "I already know all the tidbits from Venice."

The dauphin's brother effused, "Our father is alive and will soon make a new alliance against the emperor. I'm pleased that he has married again, and I wish him all the best."

"I pray that this secret wife is of the true faith," snapped Henri, furrowing his brows like a thunderstorm. "Only a Catholic queen has the right to sit on the throne of France."

Charles cocked a brow. "If Her Majesty is interested in new religious teachings, like Aunt Marguerite, I see no harm in this. Enlightenment is a key factor in ensuring progress, growth, prosperity, and development of our country."

Henri's scrutiny flicked to his paramour, whose expression implored him to end the argument. Instead, he trained his eyes on the other man and growled, "Charles, you might be indifferent to the queen's religion, but I do care because I love France that cannot fall prey to heretical doctrines."

"Henri, relax and enjoy life." Charles rolled his eyes. "You are always intransigent when it comes to religious policy, but it is not you who makes the final decision – it is our father."

"Enough!" Madame de Poitiers intervened before tensions could escalate. "Brothers should not quarrel!"

"I do not want to argue," concurred Prince Charles. Taking a pack of cards, he proposed with a conciliatory smile, "Henri and Madame Diane, shall we play?"

"Let's not discuss state affairs," acquiesced Henri.

"Gladly, Your Highness," she consented with a faux smile.

Diane de Poitiers sighed in relief when Henri assumed a neutral demeanor. His relationship with his younger brother worried her more than anything else. Watching them play cards, she sighed while considering the differences between them, and how much Charles resembled King François.

Many aristocrats preferred Charles to succeed François in due time rather than Henri. So far, the ruler respected Henri's birthright, although he could change his mind. In theory, King François could convene *the États-Généraux, or the Estates-General*, representing the three French classes: the clergy, the nobility, and the commoners. The monarch could force them to accept his decision to replace Dauphin of France. There had never been such a precedent before, but nobody knew what the future held in store for them. Thus, Diane thought that Henri ought to be extremely cautious instead of dancing on the thin line between disapproving of his parent's policies and openly opposing them.

September 7, 1537, Castello di Rivoli, Turin, Piedmont

"Madame d'Étampes is in the gardens," apprised a servant in Pisseleu livery, bowing to the high-ranking guest who was frowning at him as if he had been slighted.

"Be at ease, lad," the visitor answered. "I believe you."

The man bowed low again and hastened to leave the presence chamber.

Anne de Montmorency smirked to himself. Those who served the Duchess d'Étampes feared him. He suspected that deep down, Anne de Pisseleu was wary of his unshakeable influence over King François and of their boyhood friendship. Maybe her terror had transmitted to her large household.

Stopping near a window, he opened the shutters to find that dusk had descended, and that the heavens had become an awning of purple and blue silk. In Italy, autumn came later, and the park was alive with the violets, blues, reds, oranges, and yellows of the flowers in bloom.

The 11th century castle was a large fortified fortress that clung majestically to the edge of a cliff, overlooking the neighboring mountains. The first owners of the castle had been the archbishops of Turin, but it had belonged to the Savoy family since 1247. It had been one of the residences of the Savoy court, a hub for their political meetings, marriages, and celebrations.

After the capture of Savoy by the Valois troops in 1536, this place had become the primary French residence in Piedmont. A small part of the French court had relocated to Turin together with the Valois ruler and his mistress, as well as some important courtiers and military men.

"No country is as glorious as France," Montmorency spoke to himself.

After closing the shutters, Montmorency perched himself on an armchair by the window and patiently waited for Anne de Pisseleu d'Heilly, Duchess d'Étampes. All this time, she lived in her own blithesome world. Fearful that she would take her wrath out on them, everyone had refrained from telling her about the monarch's marriage. *It is high time for the duchess to learn the truth,* Montmorency resolved.

A laugh reached his ears, and the herald declared that Anne de Pisseleu and her maids had just returned. As the door burst open, Montmorency lurched to his feet.

Several women streamed into the room amidst chatter and laughter. They were a picture of serene beauty with their cheeks rosy and their hair wind-blown after an afternoon outdoors. In the center, Anne de Pisseleu walked gracefully, with all the conviction of her high position.

For a split second, Montmorency was rather mesmerized against his will. The Duchess d'Étampes was a petite, alluring blonde whose eyes had a glimpse of intelligence, craft, charm, and danger in their depths. The soft pink of her rich silk gown, wrought with gold, added to the glow in her cheeks.

Reluctantly, he bowed to the royal mistress, who in turn bobbed a shallow curtsey to him. Anne settled herself in an armchair and motioned for him to take the seat beside her.

As if in a perfectly choreographed dance, all of the duchess' maids swung around in unison and curtsied to Montmorency. They all were the sisters and cousins of Anne de Pisseleu, who had numerous relatives; each of them had to thank the monarch's mistress for their elevations and many privileges.

The Duchess d'Étampes smiled through gritted teeth, their mutual loathing bubbling beneath the surface.

"Monsieur de Montmorency, have you heard from His Majesty?"

"That is why I've come here, Madame." He did not hurry to speak as he eyed his liege lord's lover once more.

A man of war, Montmorency was a gifted strategist, one who would arrive in the hour of the greatest need to rescue his sovereign. He was not interested in women in general, save those exceptional representatives of the sex whose superior qualities made them truly remarkable. He genuinely admired Queen Marguerite of Navarre, King François' sister, and he had a degree of grudging respect for Anne Boleyn, despite her role in the religious upheaval in England.

Anne de Pisseleu d'Heilly is not an extraordinary person, Montmorency concluded. Unlike her, Marguerite de Valois would surely leave an everlasting mark in France's history. The duchess was no more exceptional than the king's other paramours. As he did not possess an amatory temperament, Montmorency did not comprehend why his liege lord favored Anne de Pisseleu so profoundly for years. He had allied against her with several courtiers, including Diane de Poitiers.

"Silence suits you less than war," the duchess prodded.

"Ah, yes!" Montmorency enthused. "But there are things worse than any military confrontation for you."

"Don't quibble and prevaricate. You ought to be gallant!"

"Madame, I bring alarming news. The emperor's assassin tried to kill the king in Venice. It happened *again*!"

"Dear Lord!" she gasped in horror. "How is His Majesty?"

Anne de Montmorency fended off the urge to laugh most venomously. "Our sovereign turned a new page in his life. Several weeks ago, he wed the brave lady who rescued him."

An obnoxious leer tugged at his lips. "Since then, he has been enjoying her company and her bed in Venice."

This cannot be true! The royal mistress narrowed her eyes like a cat about to pounce on a mouse. *Monty, my sworn foe, is lying!* She studied Montmorency: though not attractive, his oval and severe countenance was memorable, exuding a blend of authority, strength, and courage. His rich doublet, hose, and cap were all of a sumptuous brown velvet, stressing his robust health, his tall height, and his martial deportment.

They loathed each other since the first day King François had introduced them at court years ago. When out of the ruler's earshot, they often threw nasty barbs at one another. In 1522, the king had appointed Anne de Montmorency, who was his boyhood friend and his companion in the Italian wars, Marshal of France, and Grand Master of France in 1526. Unable to counter his growing power, Anne de Pisseleu had accepted his presence as part of her life with the monarch.

Do I mean so little to François that he did not even warn me about his hasty wedding? Anne de Pisseleu bemoaned. She struggled to accept that the Valois ruler was no longer a free man. As she roved her eyes over the room, the colorful wall frescoes of ancient gods and heroes by Antonello da Messina and Jacopo del Sellaio did not sooth her distress.

She hissed, "I do not appreciate your jokes."

Her expression of mingled fear and rage caused him to snicker. "Ask others if you don't believe me."

"Who did he wed and why?" Her chin rose defiantly, but her voice cracked with shock. "Why so soon after he regained his freedom? Do you have a letter from His Majesty for me?"

"Madame, I can tell you what I know." He then informed her about the events. He ended with, "His Majesty did not notify his Venus about his nuptials. This is a clear sign that he no longer wants to keep you as his mistress."

Anne shot him an icy glare. "Your acerbic wit is awful."

Montmorency taunted, "You might think that I'm a poor excuse for a mentor, but I recommend that you leave Italy. Your husband, Duke Jean d'Étampes, is not sleeping and eating – he has been so impatiently waiting for you for so long. Our sovereign does not need you anymore, but maybe His Grace would find it in his heart to accept you back."

Several years ago, King François had arranged a marriage of convenience for Anne de Pisseleu. She had become the wife of Jean IV de Brosse, Count de Penthièvre, for the purpose of elevating her to Duchess d'Étampes. The estranged spouses had always felt pernicious animosity towards one another.

Her temper snapping like a dry stick, she jumped to her feet, her eyes glittering with fury. "Leave now, Monsieur de Montmorency, before I command to throw you out!"

He smiled with baleful satisfaction. "I've merely offered you some friendly advice, which might help you a lot."

"Get out!" roared the enraged woman.

The Marshal of France stood up to leave. "His Majesty will be bringing his queen to Turin. While this will be a wonderful occasion for those wanting to meet his wife, it would be a humiliating experience for you if you remain here." He strode over to the door, but paused and added sardonically, "Have a pleasant evening, my dearest Madame d'Étampes."

Montmorency bowed to her maids, who were all shaken by the turn of events. As the door closed behind him, Anne dismissed everyone, excluding her sister, Péronne de Pisseleu.

Feeling as if her heart had been trampled by a herd of bulls, Anne dissolved into tears which spilled down her cheeks in rivulets. "Why did François marry another woman?"

Péronne seated herself in a chair beside her sister. She consoled, "Anne, please don't panic! You are still the king's beloved favorite who means the whole world to him. You are the most beautiful and the most learned lady at the French court and in France. No woman can outshine you!"

The mistress contradicted, "François has already had two political marriages. If he wed so soon after the annulment, it must be a unique union for him." She suppressed her sobs, took a handkerchief from Péronne's hands, and blew out her nose, then threw the handkerchief to the floor.

"What are you going to do?"

"I'll wait for François in Turin," answered the duchess as she scrubbed the tears away. "I need to understand what he feels for his new wife and for me."

"Don't jump to rash conclusions, Anne. Life is a journey of many twists and turns. You must also know that whatever happens, my loyalty is always and only to you."

A benign smile illumined Anne's tearful countenance. "Thank you, sister."

"If you want something, just let me know."

"I need only my François," pronounced Anne de Pisseleu, her eyes blazing with a lurid fire of obsession, like two smoldering coals. She vowed, "I love my king madly! He is mine and mine alone. I'm his Venus, and he is my Zeus! I shall not allow anyone else to take him away from me."

Péronne scrutinized her sister suspiciously, as if she had misheard or misconstrued her words. She was about to say something, but Anne spontaneously embraced her and broke into shuddering sobs. Together they rocked and swayed for a few minutes, caught up in the threnetic rhythms of sorrow.

CHAPTER II

A Canvas of Emotions

September 2, 1537, Château de Fontainebleau, Fontainebleau, France

"Poems and prose carry deep emotion," Queen Marguerite of Navarre spoke to herself as she scanned the document in her hand. "They are the canvas where a poet or a writer uses words to paint the different shades of life with colors of emotion."

The shadows of dusk were falling outside, and the François I gallery was illuminated by an array of candles. The interior decorations by Rosso Fiorentino and Francesco Primaticcio – frescoes, elaborate stucco decorations, woodwork, and gilding – created an aura of artistic magnificence around Marguerite as she lounged in a chair carved with the Valois heraldry.

The Queen of Navarre, the King of France's beloved sister, was reading the pamphlets that contained the poems written by Mellin de Saint-Gelais about Thomas Cromwell. Another poet, Clément Marot, was working on a book about Cromwell's role in the religious reform in England, where he focused on the Dissolution of the monastic houses and listed all the differences between the English chief minister's ideas for how the money should be spent and Anne Boleyn's.

As the two artists entered, Queen Marguerite looked up. "Mellin, these pamphlets speak about the evil done by Thomas Cromwell just as clearly as any painting would."

Saint-Gelais bowed to Marguerite. "Your Majesty, I'm glad to hear that."

She stared down at the book in her hand. "The pamphlets are so easy to read and memorize. Most people will remember the main facts immediately or quickly." Her gaze shifted to Marot. "Clément, when will the book about Cromwell be finished? François wants it to be ready as soon as possible."

Marot flourished a bow to the queen. "Your Majesty, it is already nearly in its final form."

"Clément, I wish to have your draft before the week is out," enjoined Marguerite. "We need time to make changes if we are to finish it by the end of September."

Marot apprised, "I'll bring the current draft of the book tomorrow, Madame Marguerite. Of course, I'll improve it and add whatever you deem necessary."

The king's sister smiled brightly. "Thank you, Clément and Mellin."

"You are most welcome, Your Majesty," chorused the poets.

Mellin de Saint-Gelais and Clément Marot were both famous poets at the Valois court. Patronized by François and Marguerite, the poets were part of their literary court.

Having studied at Bologna and Padua, Saint-Gelais was a doctor, astrologer, musician, and poet. After living in Italy, he had returned to France in 1523 and quickly gained favor of the art-loving King François by his skill in light verse.

Marot had been attached to Marguerite's household since 1519, when she had become his patroness; he also was a great favorite of King François. He had attended the Field of the Cloth of Gold and accompanied the ruler on his disastrous Italian campaign in 1524, but the poet had avoided capture.

Both artists admired their beloved patroness, whom they had known for years. The Queen of Navarre had aged exceedingly well: her attractive face was all soft and smooth, with very few wrinkles. Marguerite's saturnine complexion, with the long Valois nose and smart, amber eyes, was set off by a fashionable gown of burgundy brocade, ornamented with black pearls and sapphires, also stressing her splendidly proportioned figure. A stunning diamond tiara – a gift from her husband, the King of Navarre – adorned her head, her long and chestnut tresses cascading down her back.

Saint-Gelais reported, "The pamphlets will be printed next week."

"It works well for us," pronounced Marguerite. Her gaze flew to Marot. "Clément, if we keep to this schedule, I want the book printed by the middle of October."

Marot assented, "You have my word that there will be no delays."

"These works will create a sensation throughout England and France." In a voice tinged with satisfaction, Marguerite announced, "My brother will be very pleased!"

The monarch's sister had no clue as to why the pamphlets and the book were so important, and why François was set on ruining Cromwell's reputation and life. Another mystery was why he strove to highlight Anne Boleyn's innocence. And why had her brother rushed headlong into another matrimony soon after the annulment of his union with Eleanor of Austria? *What a secret! Did François wed someone so precipitately for political interests or out of love?* Marguerite wondered.

Despite the uncertainty as to François' actions, Marguerite fulfilled her task diligently and successfully, as always. Her brother had commissioned her to prepare these materials because he trusted her to do it in the most efficient way. The Queen of Navarre was a prolific poet, dramatist, and author in her own right. Margot had published a two-volume anthology of her works, and she also wrote 'The Heptaméron,' which was a collection of seventy two short stories written in French.

In his letter, François had said that Philippe de Chabot – the French ambassador at the English court – would arrange the distribution of the pamphlets. Marguerite would hand the pamphlets to one of Cardinal de Tournon's spies in Paris, who would then travel to Guernsey – an island in the Channel off the coast of Normandy – where Chabot's people would collect them and deliver everything to England. Thanks to his sister, the king's orders would be carried out with the utmost secrecy.

September 5, 1537, Hampton Court Palace, Middlesex, England

Two hours had elapsed since sunrise, but it was not cold. A dense layer of drifting, gray clouds blocked the sun, and the breeze turned into a stiffer wind bearing the smell of rain. Not in the least intimidated by the prospect of rain, the Lady Mary Tudor, a bastardized Princess of England, and the Imperial ambassador Eustace Chapuys strolled in the vast gardens.

In their vicinity, other than a squirrel scavenging in the shrubbery, there was no one else in sight at such an early hour. Thus, they could talk without the risk of being overheard.

"I like this place," uttered Mary in Spanish. "The court has become my gilded cage, but this garden is my little glimpse of freedom. Here I can breathe easily and talk about anything."

A week ago, the court had arrived at Hampton Court by water. King Henry liked the redbrick palace built by the late Cardinal Wolsey, whose fall from favor had resulted in the transfer of its ownership to him. Since then, the ruler was implementing the palace's rebuilding, having added the kitchens, the great hall, and the tennis court to the ensemble.

The Savoyard smiled. "I'm always willing to listen."

"Thank you." His friendship warmed her scarred heart.

The garden had been designed to outshine the magnificent park at Fontainebleau. It had individual square plots filled with red brick-dust, white sand, and verdant lawns, which were ornamented with decorated posts surmounted with lions, dragons, unicorns, and other heraldic beasts on poles. Flowerbeds were surrounded by the green and white railings, and the posts painted in these colors; there were many tree-lined avenues for walk. The nip of autumn was barely felt: the trees were green and leafy, and fragrant plants still bloomed.

"Your Highness," began Chapuys in a hushed voice. He always addressed her so in privacy. "What did His Majesty say about your prospective marriage?"

For a handful of heartbeats, Mary's mind went blank; the prospect of remaining an old maid filled her thoughts with sinister gloom. "Your Excellency, my father was furious when Queen Jane asked him to revoke his bastardization of me and to find me a husband."

The ambassador released a sigh of frustration. "The most acceptable match for you would be a Spanish or Portuguese prince. Is His Majesty opposed even to your marriage?"

"It appears that he does not care for my happiness at all."

"That damned concubine's death should have led to your reinstatement to the succession."

Her gaze drifted to the palace looming in the background. Mary admired how its architecture blended the finest features of Gothic perpendicular design and Renaissance ornamental style.

As Mary turned to Chapuys, streams of ire and bitterness flowed from her. "The harlot paid for her crimes against my father and England. Then I signed the Oath and declared my parents' marriage invalid. By doing so, I betrayed my mother! Now I'm a bastard! However, this sacrifice of mine has won me nothing, not even a better standing at court."

"Queen Jane may promote your interests, Your Highness."

She shook her head as they stopped near a flowerbed with roses, violets, and primroses. "Her Majesty will soon have her own child. Hopefully, it will be a healthy boy."

"I have a very deep respect for Her Majesty. She is a noble-minded, pious, and virtuous woman."

Mary gave a nod. She liked Queen Jane, and Mary was grateful that Jane was loyal to the memory of her deceased mother. But her stepmother and Mary could not be described as being close, although it was apparent that the new queen was sympathetic to the king's bastard daughter.

The queen and I have few things in common, Mary mused, *apart from our love for my mother and our Catholic beliefs.* Jane was uneducated and simple, so they could not discuss culture or politics, and had never engaged in an intellectual conversation. Yet, having Queen Jane on the throne was far better than having Anne Boleyn as her father's consort.

The ambassador again redirected the conversation to Mary's future. "Your Highness, Infante Luís of Portugal, Duke of Beja, would be a great husband to you."

Infante Luís was a son of King Manuel I of Portugal and his second wife, Maria of Aragon, who was daughter of Queen Isabella I of Castile and King Ferdinand II of Aragon.

Mary lifted her eyes to the vault of the sky where God was enthroned, as if beseeching Him to strengthen her in order to resign herself to His will. She then flittered her gaze to Chapuys and affirmed, "Your Excellency, if I'm allowed to marry, I'll have my own children, who will be the true heirs to the Tudor throne, and my father would not want this."

"Nonetheless, His Majesty might be interested in securing an Anglo-Imperial alliance. Your union with Infante Luís would serve this very purpose."

"We all favor this alliance, including Cromwell and the Seymours."

"His Majesty might still let you marry Infante Luís. You two are first cousins, which puts you in a prohibited degree of kinship. We will need the papal dispensation."

She sighed with aggravation. "The Church of England is separated from the Roman Catholic Church. I'm very sad that obviously, my marriage to Luís is impossible."

"Don't lose hope, Your Highness," Chapuys encouraged.

A rueful smile suffused her face. "I would rather not dwell on things I cannot have."

The ambassador flashed Mary a smile. "Your Highness is always lovely! A great beauty exists in melancholy of saints."

She managed a smile. "Your Excellency is exaggerating to make me more joyful."

Mary Tudor was a gorgeous creature, with fair features, a straight nose, and a sweetly shaped mouth. Her modestly cut gown of rose velvet, trimmed with gold, still revealed the contours of her womanly curves beneath the tight bodice and skirts. Over her gown, she wore a surcoat of black and white satin. Her long, dark red-gold Tudor hair was swept up in a neat bun, and her Spanish hood, ornamented with rubies, was tightly fastened. Her girdle was embroidered with gold.

Her smart hazel eyes, fringed with dark lashes, reminded Chapuys of Queen Catherine, and his heart constricted. A woman in her twenties, Mary was expected to exude the very essence of life and be jolly. However, a halo of despondency shrouded her whole being, for she had nothing to look forward to in her life. The several years of disgrace, hardship, and poverty as the Lady Elizabeth's servant had damaged Mary's youthful demeanor, though not her beauty.

A titanic rush of implacable hatred flooded Chapuys. Anne Boleyn, "the concubine" or "the whore" as he always referred to her, was fully responsible for Mary's sufferings, and he was happy that she had been burned. *The Boleyn whore was a devil creature. Denied God's love after her death, now she must be burning in hell,* he thought with malevolence.

"Let's go," she prompted.

Mary resumed walking, and the ambassador followed her. They took a narrow path that wandered between flowerbeds, lush lawns, and tall strands of trees, sloping gently down towards the distant River Thames. Soon they reached a hill overlooking the river, where they halted.

Usually, she appeared outwardly unruffled, but right now, she was too agitated and spoke nervously. "Your Excellency, nasty rumors have circulated that my cousin, Carlos, is behind numerous assassination attempts on the King of France's life. The French say falsehoods and want to get away with it!"

The diplomat was inclined to believe that his Habsburg master was guilty. However, Mary did not need to have it confirmed, so he approached the matter cautiously. "Your Highness, the rivalry between Emperor Carlos and King François has intensified in the wake of the annulment of

Infanta Eleanor's marriage. I do not think that His Imperial Majesty ordered someone to kill his Valois archenemy. I firmly believe that gossip was spread by the French."

"King François tries to blemish the emperor's reputation!" cried Mary in indignation. "My cousin would never have stooped so low as to sanction the murder of any monarch."

"His Imperial Majesty is a victim of King François' game."

"Exactly. I've never liked France," she snapped scornfully.

The firmament darkened. Far off, there was rumble of thunder, and bolts of lightning shot across the horizon. Mary and Chapuys hastened away from the park. Picking up their pace, they arrived at the palace seconds before the heavens opened, and the rain poured down upon them.

September 7, 1537, the Palazzo Montreuil, Venice, the Republic of Venice

Anne woke at first light, and tears suffused her eyes. She was awash with relief that François had left their bedchamber, for she would not want him to see her so vulnerable.

She buried her face in her hands. "My beloved Elizabeth!" she sobbed, as if her daughter could hear her. "Today, you are turning four. I'm so sorry that I cannot be with you."

Anne retrieved from under the pillow a small, stunning, single strand of pearls with a gold 'ET' pendant hanging from the center. The strand of pearls was similar to an old necklace of her own, one which had a golden 'B' pendant. She had ordered it for Elizabeth's birthday from a Venetian goldsmith, and he had brought it to her yesterday.

"Your father abandoned you, my dearest girl," bemoaned Anne, clutching the necklace to her chest. "Maybe Lady Mary will come to you, if she can overlook her hate for me."

§§§

At the same time, in England, an exiled Elizabeth Tudor was alone, fighting off tears and dreaming of her mother. Her ladies and her governess, Lady Margaret Bryan, congratulated her on her birthday, but there were no gifts for her. Elizabeth remembered that she had been given a lot of lavish gifts when her mother, Anne, had been alive. Unbeknownst to Anne, Mary Tudor would visit her half-sister in the afternoon and would give her a small sapphire necklace.

§§§

"What lies did they tell you about me, my Elizabeth?" a distraught Anne asked her absent daughter. "Do not ever believe that I committed treason against your father."

As she calmed down, a bout of nausea assailed Anne. She emptied her stomach onto the floor near the bed. She gagged as her body again tried to rid itself of food that was not there.

As the sickness subsided, Anne reclined on the pillows and counted the days since her last period. Her courses had stopped over a month ago, and she felt rather unwell in the past week. She must be with child! She had experienced such symptoms during her previous pregnancies.

The queen put a hand on her flat stomach and caressed it. "Little one, I'm sorry for not loving your father. But I do love you with all my heart, and I long to have you in my arms."

It was a wonder, a treasure, and a terror for Anne that soon she would have a new baby. She had doubted her ability to conceive after her difficult pregnancy with Arthur. Given the tragic history of her miscarriages, at present, the queen feared that she would not carry this baby to full term.

Anne addressed the Almighty. "Heavenly Father, You are the giver of life. You spared me from the jaws of death in England. This new life is in Your hands, and I beg you to cover it with Your love and grace." Her lips quivered, and fresh tears slid down her cheeks. "Do not take this baby away from me! Let this child become a boy or a girl according to Your will."

After the prayer, peace swaddled her mind. Anne had longed for her estranged children. This baby would be like a balm to her scarred soul. *One day, King Henry will learn that I have a child with another king,* she thought with malice.

§§§

Unable to contain her emotion, the Queen of France paced the room. Fighting an onslaught of dizziness, she made her way to the bed and seated herself on the edge until it receded. The sun was fading, and candles were lit in her apartments.

Her gaze veered towards a walnut table near the window. A collection of jewels was laid out meticulously on a strip of black velvet for her selection: a diamond and emerald choker, several pearl, ruby, diamond, and sapphire necklaces, as well as matching bracelets. Near the jewelry sets, there were yards of fabric: golden brocade edged with silver, blue silk woven with gold, lavender silk edged in silver, black and ivory velvet, brocades embroidered with flower motifs, and so forth.

"François lavishes me with such gifts. Why is he spoiling me? He cannot be treating me like one of his paramours."

To distract herself, Anne climbed to her feet and strode to the table, where she took an oval-cut sapphire necklace. She fastened it around her neck and stood for what felt a long time, admiring herself in the gold-framed looking glass set on her dressing table. Her reflection was wonderful: she was glowing in her pregnancy, and there was a regal air about her as well.

At the sound of the opening door, the queen swiveled and curtsied to the ruler. Anne chuckled, noticing that his gold-slashed doublet of blue silk and matching hose complemented her low-cut gown, with its blue brocade woven with gold.

François sauntered over to Anne and stopped behind her. His arms snaked around her waist, and they both stared into the looking glass. As always, his wife admired how tall he was, towering over her like a giant protector.

The king grinned, for their reflection was perfect. "Anne, your unusual beauty surpasses that of the loveliest exotic flower in full bloom, although you are pale."

Her lips lengthened in a smile. "Your Majesty's flattery can turn most women to your will. You are a genius in that respect. But it will not deflect me: I have some news for you."

"Go on." He bent and nibbled her neck.

"I'm with child." Once more, unconditional love for this new life burgeoned in her fractured heart.

His face was alight with exhilaration. "Thank you for this marvelous gift, Anne. Having a baby is like sharing a piece of your soul with the rest of the world and with me."

The monarch was ecstatic that he was to become a father again. After Queen Claude's death, he had wished for more children, but he had refused to consummate his marriage to Eleanor of Austria. In spite of his many amorous conquests, there were not many bastard children, most of whom he had sired in his early youth. Some of his illegitimate progeny had already passed away. *All of my future children with my wife shall be unique, just as Anne herself is,* the king enthused.

"Stay here," requested François.

A bewildered Anne complied. "Of course, sire."

BETWEEN TWO KINGS

The ruler strode to the bureau and pulled out a drawer, gazing at the glittering contents. Since their wedding, he had gifted her several sets of jewelry, as well as various gowns and accessories befitting a queen. As they shared a passion for reading, François had also given her works by illustrious Italian writers such as Ludovico Ariosto, Giannozzo Manetti, Alessandro Piccolomini, and Leon Battista Alberti, as well as books of poetry by Francesco Berni and Antonio Beccadelli.

His fingertips strayed across the sapphires, diamonds, and rubies of the coronet, imagining how stunning it would look upon Anne's head. Above all, he wanted to give her something that she would treasure. Before extracting the coronet, he opened another drawer and retrieved a book. He returned to her with both items, smiling at Anne's bewildered expression.

He handed to her a small leather volume. "I know you love poetry. Actually, we both like Italian and French poetry."

Holding it in her hand, Anne effused, "Ah, this is amazing! '*The Canzoniere*' by Francesco Petrarca! All his poems are a model for lyrical poetry. I adore how the poet's epic love for Laura is expressed in a few words in each sonnet, and yet, there are infinite ways to interpret them."

François observed her with amusement. His spouse was always delighted to receive books and works of art. In such moments, her smile was genuine, unlike the artificial one she wore when thanking him for the gowns and the jewels. *Perhaps Anne is no longer easily seduced by riches and worldly things to meet her selfish desires,* he deduced.

"Poetry is a perfect communion of beauty, heart, and head. It is not only vision, but also the architecture of our lives."

She sighed. "Petrarca believed that love is desired, despite being painful, and that the world's delight is a brief dream."

Guessing that her thoughts were about Henry, François attempted to distract her. He placed the coronet on her head. "I hope you like it. I am more than pleased with what I see."

Anne studied her reflection in the glass, and their eyes met. "Your Majesty is more generous than I deserve. This is one of the most exquisite things I've ever had."

The monarch took the book from her and put it on a nearby marble table. As he came back to her, he asserted, "I thought that you would like to have a coronet."

She arranged her lips in a smile. "Thank you."

The queen pivoted to him, her smile fading. Remembering her pregnancy with Elizabeth, her gaze turned woebegone, and she broke eye contact. Henry had been immensely happy during the months when they had waited for the birth of what they had believed would be a golden Tudor prince. However, Anne had given birth to a baby girl! She would never forget the disappointment in Henry's eyes when he had visited her chambers and looked at their newborn daughter.

Anne put these sickening remembrances aside. Yet, they would soon return to haunt her like ghosts. "I'm sorry."

"Henry?" spewed François with scorn. "Are memories of him troubling you? Or do you find the fact that you are carrying my child unpleasant because it is not Henry's?"

Her eyes flew to his, puzzlement mingled with the hurt obvious in their depths. "How can you say this to me, sire? I love this child, and don't ever think otherwise."

François discerned a light of gladness in her eyes, and his doubts dissipated. Anne wanted his baby, in spite of not loving him, and this knowledge brought him an intense joy.

217

"I am relieved to hear that," he admitted.

Am I developing a strong affection for Anne? the King of France wondered, staring at his spouse as if she were some rare jewel. His mind detoured briefly to his mistress, Anne de Pisseleu, and he discovered that he did not miss her at all. He had not written to his paramour even a single letter!

At the same time, the monarch's sentiments towards Anne Boleyn were simultaneously uplifting and inexplicable. His wife captivated him, as if she were a goddess of love and passion. That he could feel such vehement desire and such deep longing for any woman amazed François, as did the depths of his interest in Anne. It was a sensation unknown to him, almost magical and ethereal. For all his experience with women, François could not fathom what it all meant to him.

September 20 and 23, 1537, the Palazzo Montreuil, Venice, the Republic of Venice

Finally, Admiral Baron de Saint-Blancard and Jean de La Forêt returned to Venice from the Ottoman Empire. They brought great news: Sultan Suleiman had agreed not to attack Corfu and would relocate more than a hundred of Turkish ships to Marseilles to assist France in the military campaign against the emperor. Andrea Gritti, Doge of Venice, signed the treaty with King François. Now France was allied with the Republics of Venice and of Sienna, and the Ottoman Empire against Carlos V, Holy Roman Emperor. The Duchy of Savoy and Piedmont were occupied by the French since 1536.

François and Anne were playing chess in the cozy room that had become the royal presence chamber at the Palazzo Montreuil. The walls were swathed in tapestries depicting various scenes from Ovid's Metamorphoses, Homer's Iliad and Odyssey, and Virgil's Aeneid. A golden floor mat and pieces of gilded furniture, including chairs and the desk, warmed the interior. Costly vases and statues were placed throughout the chamber.

Cardinal François de Tournon and Jacques de la Brosse bowed as they entered and paused at the doorway. The king and queen's chess match was interrupted.

In an official tone, Tournon began, "Your Majesties, we have news from England."

Brosse emphasized, "It is very important."

"Take a seat." The king gestured to the right.

The royals stared at Brosse and Tournon in anticipation, who landed in a pair of chairs.

King François cast a rapid glance at the chessboard and then trained his eyes on the two visitors. "I suppose you are going to share some findings about my wife's enemies."

Wings of apprehension fluttered in her stomach, and Anne looked out the window. The sky was a leaden gray tinged with roiling black, with heavy clouds rapidly moving towards overhead, showing whitish where the autumn wind stretched them into thin tails.

Tournon informed, "Your Majesties, Ambassador Philippe de Chabot has learned who made the most ridiculous claim amongst all the charges brought against Queen Anne."

At this, Anne's head snapped towards the cardinal. Her eyes were glittering with curiosity, but her voice was cold as she inquired, "What do you mean, Your Eminence?"

Tournon adjusted his crimson square-quartered cap on his head. "I refer to the charge of incest."

François rested his head on his steepled fingers; he often adopted this position when he was lost in thought or pondered a problem. "Was it Thomas Cromwell?"

Tournon divulged, "No. The main accuser was Lady Elizabeth Somerset, Countess of Worcester. She told Cromwell that George Boleyn had known his sister carnally."

Her mouth an O of shocked astonishment, Anne gasped, "What? Elizabeth and I were close!" With effort, she forced her expression into one of composure. "She had been interrogated by Cromwell. Perhaps he frightened her so much that she lied to him about me."

"Philippe cannot be mistaken?" queried François.

Tournon's response was accented by an unmistakable note of credence. "The information must be true. Monsieur de Chabot had his most trusted man look through the records of the case. Thomas Cromwell questioned several handmaidens, including Lady Margaret and Lady Anne Shelton. They said that several men visited the queen's chambers, although they did not accuse Her Majesty of anything improper. Lady Margery Horsman defended the queen. Lady Elizabeth Somerset was the main informant against you, Your Majesty."

"Did Philippe report anything else?" asked the monarch.

The cardinal commented, "Monsieur de Chabot wrote that there are so many loopholes in the case that if King Henry decided to examine it, he would undoubtedly discover that Her Majesty had been found guilty by the jury of peers without credible proof and a fair trial."

The ruler's gaze lingered thoughtfully on one, then the other of his two subjects. "Sometimes, friends betray us even if we are good to them."

"Elizabeth Somerset must be an evil woman," Brosse joined the conversation.

All eyes were glued to Anne, and a strained silence ensued.

The queen's crisp voice cut the pause. "I could never have imagined that Lady Worcester would be capable of spreading such an abhorrent lie. George and I were always close as brother and sister, but there was nothing more."

"This woman has sold her immortal soul to the devil with her filthy lies," averred Cardinal de Tournon.

The others dipped their heads in pious agreement.

Anne dropped her gaze to the chessboard. Although she admonished herself to stay calm, a flash of white-hot fury billowed through her like smoke through a chimney. She fiercely hated the Countess of Worcester. The queen clenched her fists into balls under the table, working hard to keep her neutral countenance. Royals were schooled to never display their true feelings, and as Queen of France, Anne would not make the same mistakes as she had done in England.

Her lips thinned as she stifled her ire. "When I was in the Tower, I was worried about Elizabeth due to her difficult pregnancy. The friendship, which I believed existed between us, must have lent credibility to all her accusations against me. Elizabeth must be delighted that so many innocent people were executed on the back of her falsehoods."

To defuse the gathering tension, François broke into a jesting tirade. "Most assuredly, this diabolical woman is pleased with what she did. But life is unpredictable, especially when you are caught up in life of crime. It is like playing a game of cards: you are convinced you have a good hand, but often you discover, too late and much to your horror, that someone else's hand is better. That will be so in her case, and the devil will come and take his payment for her lies."

Tournon and Brosse chuckled at their sovereign's joke.

With a thin-lipped smile, the queen retorted, "I have great admiration for crafty people, though only from a distance. Not when they seek to destroy me and my family."

François addressed his advisors.   "Thank you for the report; you can leave us now."

Brosse and Tournon rose to their feet, bowed, and exited.

The monarch sensed the disquiet that roiled beneath Anne's cool façade.   "Now we know the truth, and we are resourceful enough to circumvent the devil Cromwell, Lady Worcester, and even Henry Tudor."   His gaze flicked to her still flat belly.   "Anne, I do not want you to be upset."

"Your Majesty, how can we make that harpy confess?"

"I've contrived an artifice to entrap Lady Worcester."

"We are in Italy, and she is in England, sire."

"Anne, it was of benefit to France that my close and trusted friend, Philippe de Chabot, went to England at the beginning of 1536.   When I learned about King Henry's financial support of the emperor, I appointed Philippe as my ambassador so that he could watch Henry closely."   François rubbed his cheek.   "The criminal is often haunted by their crime."   He then outlined his plan to bring down Elizabeth Somerset.

The king wanted his consort to know something else. "You were imprisoned, and your future was highly uncertain at that time.   I enjoined Philippe to regularly report to me about your case as it progressed to its inevitable end."

"Why?" breathed the queen.

François elaborated, "It was clear to me that you were innocent.   Yet, I could not believe that Henry would go to such lengths so as to get rid of you to pave the way for his marriage to Jane Seymour."   He paused, weighing up whether he should admit his feelings.   "I've always quite liked you."

His speech astounded Anne to the core, and her heart thumped like a musician's drum.   The King of France had been concerned about her fate back then!   It was the last thing that would ever have crossed her mind, but it was yet another link connecting them. François observed her with an intensity that indicated deep emotion. A vivifying warmth was seeping into her veins, driving away the deadly cold that had reigned in her soul since her escape from England.

Yet, it was a moment's respite. She averted her gaze from his eyes, gleaming with amber fire. "In a blinding rage, King Henry is capable of killing anyone who even looks askance at him. Many of his actions are hardly believable at all."

François stood up and approached his spouse. Taking her hand, he gently hoisted Anne to her feet. His hands encircled her waist, and he gathered her into an embrace.

For the space of several heartbeats, they stood so in silence. He cupped Anne's face and gazed deeply into her dark eyes until a magnetic vibration seemed to link her to him, making her afraid. Before she could step away, the monarch kissed his queen with all the amorous yearning that was building within him. Suddenly, he parted from her and took a step back, leaving the queen aroused and baffled.

He sought to reassure her. "There are some seemingly insurmountable problems we are facing. Nevertheless, we will solve them and win the war against Henry." She started objecting, but he put a finger to her lips. "Please, don't worry. If you do not wish to do it for yourself, think of our baby."

"I'm absolutely calm," she lied in a flat tone delivered with a stony smile.

The ruler heaved a dejected sigh. "Someday, your name will be cleared. We will disclose to the world who you really are. You will be a great Queen of France! With God's help, you will be reunited with the children whom you left behind in England. Then you will have no time to be sad."

François had already learned how to gauge his spouse's mood swings and guess what caused them. Despite the many changes in her since her incarceration, Anne Boleyn still had a flair for drama, a healthy ego, and a passion for politics, even though she disguised them well with a courteous indifference. Had the king not possessed such exceptional observational skills, which had long been a source of pride for him, he would never have begun to understand this new Anne.

"That would be perfect, but it might remain a dream."

"No, it will not." He stepped to his wife and tightened his arms around her.

All of a sudden, an unpleasant remembrance sent Anne's mind spinning. As King of France, he championed what was advantageous to his country, his throne, and personally to him at any particular moment. *Sometimes, François does not keep his word despite his reputation of a chivalrous knight!*

He had supported her marriage to King Henry when she had met him in Calais, in October 1532. However, later, he had not acknowledged Anne as the Queen of England, and she had felt betrayed. She had been loyal to his first wife, Queen Claude, and had expected that François would have supported her rise to the English throne. Not only that, François had not given permission for a betrothal of her daughter, Elizabeth, to his son – Charles de Valois, Duke d'Orléans.

These memories unsettled Anne, alienating her from her spouse, even though moments before she had regarded him as her friend. Could he betray her a third time? Her position now seemed hazardous. She was subject to his authority and was not allowed to administer her own affairs without his approval and permission. François could do whatever he wished with Anne as her husband, lord, and sovereign.

She slipped out of his embrace and stepped back. His eyes darkened at these signs of a mute rebellion.

He surveyed her and guessed that she must be thinking of her uncertain future. "I shall not cast you off as my wife. I've told you what will happen if our plans fail, although I'm sure all will turn out as we desire."

As she didn't respond, François closed the gap between them and took her hands in his. He spoke half-savagely, half-tenderly. "Anne, do you reckon that I'm so heartless as to set aside the woman who is carrying my child?" He shook his head, as if in disbelief, that she could have such a low opinion of him. "I would never bastardize my own baby that was conceived and born in a true marriage blessed by God."

How strange this sounds! the queen cried in her mind. His words reached the deepest recesses of her heart. Henry had declared Elizabeth illegitimate and failed to acknowledge Arthur at all. As far as she knew, Henry had not even seen the boy she had given birth to in the Tower. Now François was saying the very words she had coveted to hear from Henry.

Nonetheless, she was silent. A blend of frustration and ire assailed François. Frustration, that she did not believe him; white-hot anger with Henry because the man's callous deeds had taught Anne not to trust men. However, François wrapped himself in an outward blanket of composure.

Still holding her hand in his, the ruler laced their fingers together. "What do you want, Anne?"

Anne tilted her head and narrowed her eyes, which blazed with an instantaneous burst of hatred. "I wish both Thomas Cromwell and Elizabeth Somerset dead. I also suspect that Charles Brandon, Duke of Suffolk, had his part in my downfall, and I want him punished."

His wife did not wish to talk about their relationship! A disheartened François stated, "Lady Worcester and Master Cromwell will be executed if our plan works. It will be difficult to discover how the Duke of Suffolk contributed to it all."

She remembered many offhand slights the duke had given her. "He has always loathed me, dreaming to bring me down."

"He might lose Henry's favor. If it does not happen when your innocence is proved, we will think of something."

The queen unlocked their hands. She seated herself into a nearby chair and directed a blank stare at him. "Yes, Brandon can be dealt with later, if needed."

The monarch settled himself into a chair beside her. "Your obsession with vengeance is blinding you to the truth: the greatest revenge is to be happy and forget your enemies."

"There is no joy for me anymore." Anne glanced down at her hands, feeling his gaze on herself.

The patient mask slipped from his face, and the king regarded her with a vexed expression. "Why are you hell bent on destroying yourself? I've told you several times that we will deal with your foes, and I mean it in all seriousness. Why are you making me repeat it again and again?"

All the color drained from her face. So many people had betrayed Anne! The memory of all her tragedies became a scorching fire that burnt the air and everything else in Anne's life. *How can I place my trust in François?* Anne agonized.

Yet, Anne writhed with shame, thinking of the French monarch's many kindnesses and generosity. He was willing to help her, even though he did not owe her a solitary thing – not his protection, his care, his interest, his money from the treasury of France, and, most importantly, not his name nor her new rank as his wife. Yes, he had made her his wife – she was now *Anne de Valois, Queen of France*! So far, François had given all these things freely and abundantly.

How could Anne not show her gratitude? Nevertheless, she reminded herself that François was still a king, and she was at best an accomplice in his schemes. One day, he would demand repayment, and she could not grow attached to him: it might be that in the future she would have to oppose him. The reality was that her future looked bleak if she displeased François, if he got tired of her, or if she stood in the way of his accomplishing what he deemed necessary for France.

Deep down, there were also the scars of the betrayals of her past marriage. King Henry of England! Only just over a year ago, Henry had almost succeeded in having her murdered. And now... *Christ in heaven! I'm married to Henry's long-despised rival, François. Due to a bizarre twist of fate, I find myself in an impossible situation: I'm caught between two powerful kings. How would Henry react when he eventually learned that I'm alive?* Anne must never show any weakness; one mistake could cost her everything, even her life.

With such thoughts, Anne directed her stony gaze on him. "I trust Your Majesty because we are allies."

A muscle twitched in his jaw, but other than that, François resembled an emotionless marble statue. "Not long ago, you were jailed in a tower made of stone. Now you are in a prison of your own making. You have let your adversaries become the sentinels standing guard at the door to your heart."

A pensive frown settled on her brow. "So?"

The king explained, "Your enemies have made their home in your heart and mind. They spend too much time there, which gives them power over you, Anne."

Her chin took on a defiant curve, and she bit back, "Sire, what about your own obsession with vengeance upon both King Henry and Emperor Carlos?"

His wife had a good point, but the proud ruler refused to acknowledge it. He shifted their discourse back to her. "I'm not the one whose life is sustained by hatred. There is more to my life than the pursuit of my many foes. I'm able to find happiness and peace beyond the plans I have for revenge." He raised his voice. "You might hate someone, but you should not be fixed entirely on it. What belongs to the past, must be left in the past. Think about this, Anne."

The monarch climbed to his feet and stomped out of the room without a backward glance.

The queen leaned back in her seat, her mind churning and her heart constricting in anguish. What did he want from her? A marriage or a political alliance? It was one thing to accept the bounty of such a useful arrangement, but there was a great risk in becoming more than an ally. Did he want friendship? What if her husband was developing feelings for her?

No, because of his infamous womanizing, King François can never love me. Anne was convinced of this truth. Could rulers love anyone, except for their narcissistic selves? Most importantly, Anne did not have the luxury to feel anything resembling amatory sentiments towards a man. With that, she steeled her resolve to resist her attraction for him.

§§§

During the next three days, King François prepared for his return to his army stationed in Piedmont. In Anne's presence he was reticent and, sometimes, even downright monosyllabic when she initiated a conversation. Sensing his sulky mood, Anne decided to avoid him; her heart was laden with sadness, for he was not as friendly towards her as days earlier.

At dawn on the fourth day, the ruler of France met with Jacques de la Brosse in the study. "Monsieur de la Brosse, I'm leaving in an hour. You will remain here with Queen Anne."

Brosse bowed in respect. "As Your Majesty commands."

"Fifteen of my most trusted guards will also stay in the city. Fortnight ago, I requested that seventy more guards arrive in Venice, so I'll be safe on my way to Turin."

"I'll look after everything in Venice."

The king heaved a labored breath. "My wife is pregnant. If you get any bad tidbits from England, think how to present everything to Anne. You know what stress might cause."

"I understand the situation."

François handed to Brosse a parchment stamped with the Valois royal seal. "This is a letter for Marguerite, Queen of Navarre. If something happens to me, you will deliver this missive to my sister and will safeguard Queen Anne until Margot takes my wife under her protection."

"I'll protect Her Majesty with my life," vowed Brosse.

A mischievous light sparkled in the monarch's eyes. "I'm ready to bribe you in order to ensure that you take the best care of my queen."

Brosse let out a smile. "Your Majesty, being entrusted to guard the Queen of France is the best bribe you could offer. It is a duty both precious and awesome."

"You will let me save money from the state treasury, then. Moreover, the king's policies must be steered only by his conscience, not bribes, so I thank you for your honesty."

They laughed in unison. The Valois monarch's subjects liked that their sovereign had a naturally good sense of humor, debonair manners, and a mellow temper. Yet, where politics was concerned, François could act in a cold, calculating, and even cruel manner if the circumstances demanded it.

CHAPTER 12

Incriminating Pamphlets

September 30, 1537, Hampton Court Palace, Middlesex, England

The Tudor monarch received Philippe de Chabot, Seigneur de Brion, Count de Charnay and Buzançois, Admiral of France and French ambassador to England, in the presence chamber, whose walls were covered with tapestries of hunts.

King Henry sat on his massive, carved throne on the dais under a canopy of gold. He was dressed in a dark gray velvet doublet covered with seed pearls and small diamonds, so it glittered like raindrops on gray ice. The sleeves were trimmed with ermine. He wore hose of gray silk, and his girdle of black velvet was covered with rich silver-gilt ornaments.

Charles Brandon, Duke of Suffolk, stood to the monarch's right. He was clothed in a slashed doublet of brown satin and hose of midnight blue velvet, embroidered with white satin.

The admiral's raiment contrasted with that of Henry and Charles in a discordant way. It comprised of Italian hose of yellow velvet, over which fell a short mantle of white and yellow cloth, the creases of which were gathered in at his waist with a girdle of diamonds.

Philippe de Chabot bowed with a flourish of his feathered cap. "I'm glad that Your Majesty has agreed to see me."

"The pleasure is mutual, Ambassador Chabot," assured the monarch as he viewed the other man from head to toe. "Why are you wearing the color yellow today?"

The Frenchman pointed out, "Actually, I'm dressed in a blend of lavender, white, and yellow."

"Mainly yellow; only some lavender and white," Henry corrected, smiling only with his lips. "In Spain, the color yellow is associated with heresy. Anyone who is accused of heresy and refuses to recant is compelled to come before the Inquisition dressed in a yellow cape." He sneered before quizzing in a mocking voice, "Did you develop an interest in Martin Luther? Or do you prefer John Calvin? Perhaps, fearing your master's wrath, you have clothed yourself in yellow in advance as a heretic before an inquisitor?"

The Duke of Suffolk suppressed a grin as he enjoyed his liege lord's jeering speech.

The diplomat did not take kindly to being the butt of such jokes and hints. "I'm a Catholic, but I'm interested in the ideas of reform out of curiosity. Unlike its meaning in England and Spain, yellow does not have any importance in France. It was sunny outside when I woke, and I decided to echo the sun."

Henry's fingers toyed with the collar of his doublet. "In contrast to you, Your Excellency, I'm not in the best of moods and, as you can see, do not wish to wear vivid clothes."

Chabot feigned apology. "I'm sorry for displeasing you."

The monarch smiled. "On the contrary. I should wear flamboyant attire to elevate my spirits."

Charles Brandon mocked, "The French are so uncreative these days. They think that if you speak French and have ever set foot on French soil, you are blessed by the Lord."

Philippe defended his nation with admirable courage and tasteful wit. "I've heard complaints about French eccentricity from the Imperial ambassador. The next time I hear this, I'll mention to him that he should talk to Your Grace more often."

Brandon reddened at this verbal parry, but he contained his indignation.

Henry redirected the conversation to the French agenda. "How fares my cousin, François?"

The ambassador answered, "At present, His Majesty King François is in Turin, Piedmont."

Henry broached the subject that had been playing on his mind for days. "It has come to my knowledge that François has married an unnamed woman in Venice. Who is she?"

Chabot shrugged. "There is no public information about Her Majesty. Even if I knew the queen's name, I could not tell you. Due to the attempts on King François' life, his wife's name is being kept confidential to protect her from all perils."

The King of England and the Duke of Suffolk shot each other bewildered looks.

Henry queried bluntly, "Who would want to kill François?"

"It is not a secret what my liege lord thinks," replied the diplomat. "The emperor wants to retaliate for the annulment of His Majesty's marriage to Infanta Eleanor."

"No further clarification is needed." The monarch looked between Chabot and Brandon. "The Duke of Suffolk will be our envoy to Italy." His gaze veered to his subject. "Charles, you will go to Turin and deliver our wedding gifts to François, passing on our congratulations to him."

The duke dipped his head in obedience. *In Italy, I'll have to work hard to find out the identity of the new French queen,* Suffolk realized. If he acted as the bearer of the gifts, the real reason for Brandon being in Italy would not be too obvious.

After dismissing the Frenchman, Henry and Charles discussed the Valois ruler's new wife. Henry was jealous that the Pope had speedily annulled François' second marriage; years ago, another Bishop of Rome had refused to terminate the English king's union with Catherine of Aragon.

A bubble of apprehension rose in the monarch's chest. "The story of François' wedding is so damnably secretive that a sense of foreboding creeps into my mind whenever I think of it. You must investigate the background of the mysterious Valois queen. Moreover, I need to know everything about the current relationship between François and the emperor."

Brandon acquainted him with the rumors about the French queen. "This lady is an enigma! She has become popular in northern Italy, including the Republic of Venice, the Duchy of Savoy, and the Duchy of Milan. King François is using the story of her taking a dagger for him to vilify the emperor. In Northern Italy and in Savoy, the new Queen of France is admired for her bravery. In France, the people worship her as their sovereign's heroic savior."

"They create a fuss about nothing," growled Henry.

"The French always act that way, sire."

"Is it not strange that François married so soon after the annulment?"

"That is suspicious," concurred the duke. "Perhaps I'll learn more in Italy."

"Charles, what will we gift to François and his queen?"

"A work of art," offered Suffolk. "The King of France loves paintings, so I'll find something exquisite in Piedmont."

Nodding, a pensive Henry surmised, "I believe that Emperor Carlos attempted to murder François. He must be furious at the speed of this marriage in light of the annulment of his sister's union with François. The French king has insulted both Spain and the House of Habsburg. No wonder the emperor wants to kill him."

"Then, maybe we should no longer work with him," Brandon said cautiously.

Daunted by the uncertainty, the king uttered in a distinctly troubled voice, "I hope that François has no idea I funded the emperor's campaign that resulted in his defeat at Pavia. If he learns the truth, he will go to any lengths to seek revenge."

"Do you mean his personal humiliation?"

Trepidation tinged the ruler's voice as he spoke. "Yes, I do; but there is something else. Although France paid a huge ransom for their king's freedom, the two princes spent almost four years in captivity. The boys lived in such poor conditions that the late dauphin's health was damaged, causing his early demise. François must be yearning to avenge his son's death."

The monarch breathed out a sigh of frustration. "Cardinal Wolsey favored England's alliance with France throughout many years. Because I could not resolve the Great Matter for so long, Wolsey secretly conducted negotiations with Emperor Carlos. It was agreed that we would finance his campaigns in Italy in exchange for his support of the annulment. However, Wolsey miscalculated: Charles got the funds, but he did not pressure the Pope, and we lost a fortune."

"I do not think His French Majesty knows the truth."

Alarm flashed in Henry's eyes. "François is not stupid. He must have his spies at my court, and they would have learned a thing or two." His brows shot up, and Henry admitted with distaste, "Doubtless François is a powerful king despite his defeat at Pavia and captivity in Spain. France has changed since then: François has created a large, well-trained army, and there is now the Franco-Ottoman alliance."

Charles Brandon shared his concerns. "King François is not to be underestimated, but we should not panic. Now he intends to establish an alliance with the Republic of Venice."

"I'll discuss this with Cromwell tomorrow. Enough about politics for now."

"How is Her Majesty doing in confinement?"

Worry gleaming in his eyes, the monarch revealed, "My dear Jane is feeling unwell and tired. Doctor Butts prescribed that she stay in bed until our child's birth." He effused, "Charles, I'm so happy that soon I'll have a son at last!"

Charles shared his sovereign's hopes, but he did not want to be in London should the child prove not to be a healthy boy. Perhaps it was a suitable time to travel. "I pray so," he said evenly. "As for my mission, I'll leave for Italy in a week."

October 8, 1537, Hampton Court Palace, Middlesex, England

Henry Percy, Earl of Northumberland, was in his spacious chambers when Philippe de Chabot paid him a visit. The wall tapestries of Christian martyrs reflected their tragic fates, but Percy radiated hope when the diplomat handed to him a letter with a nondescript seal – a disc without a signet.

An astonished Percy seated himself on a carved bench near the hearth, and unfolded it. At the sight of the familiar, beautiful handwriting, his heart palpitated with excitement.

Dear Henry,

I'm doing very well. I hope you are taking good care of yourself.

I know that you became close to Thomas Cranmer, Archbishop of Canterbury. Please ask Cranmer to keep quiet about my last confession at the moment.

Soon pamphlets vilifying Thomas Cromwell will create an uproar in England. Moreover, there is to be a book appearing soon about his role in the king's religious reform, which will wreak havoc in the country. This devil's name will be slandered and reviled until it becomes the blackest name in Tudor history. The common people will also blame Cromwell for my murder.

Wait for a few months after the pamphlets and the book appear on English soil so that the people have enough time to read them and digest the contents. Word of mouth will spread, and the commoners will pity the wronged Queen Anne Boleyn who was annihilated by Cromwell.

Amidst all this mayhem, Archbishop Cranmer will have a compelling reason to disclose my last confession to the king. He will want to ease his conscience by helping clear my name.

It has been discovered that Elizabeth Somerset, Countess of Worcester, has falsely accused me of adultery and of incest with George. It came to me as an utter shock, and I do not know why she betrayed our friendship, or if we had ever really been friends at all.

I thank you for your discreet financial support of my dearest Elizabeth, after her father refused to acknowledge her as his own. I'll never be able to repay you for all the good you have done for me, and I beseech the Lord to protect you from all the dangers that may lie in your path.

Philippe de Chabot can organize your departure to France should it become necessary.

Burn this letter.

With all my friendly devotion,

AB

Henry Percy read the letter until it was engraved upon his memory, then held the paper to the flame of a candle and watched it burn until it turned to ash. He then peered at the other man and uttered, "Monsieur de Chabot, thank you for delivering this. Who gave it to you?"

"You are welcome, my lord," replied Chabot. "But some things are better left unsaid."

"Where is King François now?" Percy questioned.

"His Majesty spent the summer in Venice, but now he must be in Piedmont. He often travels across Italy."

Later that evening, Percy paced agitatedly up and down, his emotions spinning wildly out of control. He was immeasurably happy to receive a note from Anne, awash in relief that she was all right. Finally, he settled on the bench, poured himself a cup of wine, and, raising a solitary toast to Anne's successful escape from England, drained it in one go.

Everyone in Europe was aware that there had been an attempt on the King of France's life. If Anne had been in Venice at the time, what could have brought her to François' notice? Percy's thoughts were whirling like leaves in an autumn wind. Had she been there, in the basilica? It was only a small leap, from there, to imagine that she might have been the one to foil the assassin's aim. And what of these enigmatic pamphlets, and the book mentioned in her letter?

Henry Percy poured another goblet. As he drank wine, he endeavored to piece together, with an ever-increasing sense of incredulity, some logical chain of events, which might support the bizarre conclusion taking hold in his mind. *Can it be that Anne is the new Queen of France? Why did King François marry her if it is so?* A perplexed Percy emptied his goblet.

October 21, 1537, Hampton Court Palace, Middlesex, England

In the past week, the Tudor temper had raged savagely, exploding like a volcanic eruption. King Henry was throwing things around his quarters, breaking furniture and anything else that came to hand. In the afternoons, the gloomy court seemed deserted as there were no feasts, no jousts, and no festivities. At times, Henry would summon someone to his chambers or reception rooms; the visitors reported that the ruler insulted them and threatened to banish them.

Today, the king had invited Thomas Cromwell, recently created Baron Cromwell of Okeham, to his rooms. Others were in attendance: Edward Seymour, newly elevated Earl of Hertford, and his brother, Thomas, now Baron Sudeley. Thomas Howard, Duke of Norfolk, was absent, having retired to his estates to recover his health in fresh countryside air.

Cromwell shivered. He could see the deadly rage flashing in his liege lord's eyes and the handsome royal features now contorted like those of a snarling animal.

An incensed Henry rose from his seat and walked the short distance, so he towered over his chief minister. "Master Cromwell! Why do many blasted pamphlets proclaim you the whore's murderer?" His voice boomed portentously throughout the chamber.

The minister remained silent, his face inscrutable, like a molded clay statue. But there was an odd gleam in his eyes as they beheld one another for what seemed like an eternity.

The ruler's smile was chilling. "I discern fear in your eyes. What you are trying to hide?"

Cromwell barely repressed a shudder. Henry tore his gaze from him and started pacing hither and thither. Everyone else was transfixed by the royal show of rage. The room's splendid interior, with costly oak furniture and arrases of picturesque panoramas of England, did not lessen Henry's rage.

Henry stomped over to his desk and grabbed the top pamphlet from a pile lying there. As he dropped his gaze to one of the poems composed by Mellin de Saint-Gelais, his expression was like that of an enraged ruler who was about to sign a whole sheaf of death warrants.

> *She was too a great woman to die*
> *An innocent victim of wretched lies*
> *An innocent tool of political struggle*
> *She was brought down by an ungodly liar*
> *A liar who belied his own queen*
> *A liar who fooled even his king*
> *A liar embezzling the king's money and treasures*
> *A liar shaming his king and his country*
> *And what is his name? What do you think?*
> *He is Thomas Cromwell, a knave and a cheat*
> *Born low, but climbed high through many dead*
> *He is Cromwell, the king's own right hand.*

Henry gripped the pamphlet and raised his scrutiny to the ceiling, as if beseeching the Almighty to counsel him as to the best course of action. His intense fury had rendered him speechless for a moment. He shifted his scrutiny to Cromwell.

The monarch barked with ferocious exasperation, "I've read many pamphlets printed in English. However, these are different. These were originally printed in French and distributed throughout France. Recently, they have been translated into English, and it is reported that they have reached every corner of my kingdom. These pamphlets can be found not only in London, but also in Dover, York, Manchester, Oxford, Norwich, Ipswich, Bristol, Exeter, and even as far as remote villages in the countryside. This slander is disruptive to the running of my realm as much as it is unpleasant to me." He swore virulently under his breath.

For this audience, the king was appareled in a shirt of white silk with a standing band collar, silver hose, and a doublet of black satin embroidered with gold. In his attire and with a crown encrusted with diamonds, rubies, emeralds, and sapphires, Henry looked every inch the absolute monarch, albeit an infuriated one. There was an air of sinister gloom about him, as if the darkness from the realm of Hades had cloaked the earth and dimmed the daylight.

Henry stepped closer to Cromwell and stared down at him, throwing the pamphlet at the other man's feet. "Cromwell, this poet is right that you are a clever and capable man. You have had the good fortune to make a brilliant career at my court in spite of your low birth. Since you are so talented, I demand that you explain the accusations and slurs in this pamphlet, because while they specifically target you, it is apparent that I'm the one they are really accusing."

Shrugging as if in uncertainty, Cromwell responded in a controlled voice, "Your Majesty, forgive me, but I have no idea why that French poet wrote these pamphlets."

Edward Seymour took the pamphlet from the floor. "I believe he is saying the truth, sire."

The Tudor ruler bellowed, "Who permitted the publication of these dirty falsehoods, and why?"

Cromwell eyed the parchment in Edward's hand. When he had first seen the pamphlets, a paralyzing horror had gripped him like a snake coiling around his throat and choking him. *Why do the French target only me? Or is it someone else's plot against me?* The minister was shocked and confused.

Thomas Cromwell voiced the unpalatable fact. "Mellin de Saint-Gelais has long been patronized by both King François and Queen Marguerite of Navarre."

"The King of France is now in Piedmont with his army," intervened Thomas Seymour.

Edward interjected, "Emperor Carlos is now gathering his forces and training his soldiers. The French are doing the same. Sooner or later, the war will break out."

Cromwell wanted to convince his liege lord into believing that he had been vilified solely for political reasons. "Perhaps King François asked Saint-Gelais to create the pamphlets in order to provoke England into declaring war on France."

Edward shook his head. "No. King François will not wage war against England while France is involved in the Italian wars. The French do not want the risk of fighting both England and the Holy Roman Empire on two separate fronts. That could mean the end of the Valois realm!"

Thomas nodded. "I agree."

Henry flickered his eyes over his subjects. "Then why did François let his poets write and distribute these scurrilous pamphlets throughout his country as well?"

Cromwell ventured, "Maybe the French king does not know about these things." Privately, he was convinced that François had been behind the pamphlet attack on him.

The monarch pondered the matter. "That might be true, but we cannot be sure until we talk to the French. Who is the regent of France in François' absence?"

"Queen Marguerite of Navarre," answered Edward.

Henry gritted out, "We must send our envoy to that Valois woman who imagines that she can rule kingdoms better than we men can. Ah, François has always been surrounded by clever ladies, and until his mother's death, he governed his realm together with Marguerite and Madame Louise de Savoy. What an effeminate man he is! A competent king ought to rule on his own!" His voice rose an octave. "I've digressed. Our envoy must demand that Queen

Marguerite have Mellin de Saint-Gelais hanged, drawn, and quartered."

"I can go to France," Thomas volunteered.

The ruler's irate gaze veered to Thomas Seymour. "In Paris, Lord Sudeley, you must convince the regent of France that it is her duty to execute the author of these pamphlets who dared slander a fellow monarch. You cannot fail me!"

Thomas bowed. "Sire, I'll carry out your instructions."

Edward chimed in, "We will do whatever Your Majesty wishes."

The monarch's expression was imperial. "Of course, you must do what I bid you – I am your lord and sovereign."

The Seymour brothers inclined their heads in obeisance.

Cromwell shut his eyes against the images of his own death running through his head. With a mirthless grin, he muttered, "Your Majesty, I'm always ready to serve you."

Henry regarded the disgraced man. "Cromwell, you are banished from court and all of your offices. Henceforth, Thomas Audley will assume these responsibilities."

Fear gripped Cromwell with its icy fingers. "I understand."

"Stay at home so far. Do not cross me." The king's voice was colored with overt threat.

Inwardly shuddering, the minister bobbed his head. "Yes, sire." An eerie premonition slithered down his spine.

§§§

Left alone, King Henry's thoughts drifted to the French ambassador. He nervously walked the room to and fro.

Although Philippe de Chabot had visited England twice on his diplomatic missions in 1533 and 1534, Henry did not think that he was the usual kind of courtier who would have been sent to live at a foreign court. The man was a member of François' so-called *Triumvirate,* which included Cardinal François de Tournon and Baron Anne de Montmorency.

242

Henry wondered whether François had enjoined Chabot to disturb the peace in his realm. Yet, according to the English ruler's reliable sources, the diplomat was not engaged in the distribution of the pamphlets, whose appearance in England was shrouded in mystery. Furthermore, King François had no reason to blacken Cromwell's reputation, or did he?

"Fetch the French ambassador!" King Henry demanded.

Within a matter of minutes, Philippe de Chabot came to the presence chamber. As Henry paced, he prepared himself for a repulsive audience. François had instructed him to deny everything and assured him that if Henry ordered him placed under house arrest and requested that Chabot be submitted to interrogation, no such consent would be given.

There is no proof of my involvement, the ambassador remarked to himself. Chabot's people had distributed the pamphlets through numerous intermediaries, who had been recruited by other anonymous people. Having done their job, those men had disappeared. Soon other mercenaries would arrive in England to distribute the book about Cromwell. The worst Chabot expected was to be declared 'persona non grata' and have to face his forced deportation from England.

At last, the English ruler stopped near the desk with the pile of pamphlets and picked up a handful, waving them in the face of the Frenchman. "Chabot, these scandalous pamphlets were brought to my kingdom from France." His eyes, which were shooting daggers, narrowed. "Does François know about them?" He threw the bunch of pamphlets back onto the desk.

Chabot's face remained devoid of expression. "Your Majesty, I read the pamphlets only after their appearance in England. How do you know they were issued in France?"

Henry pounced on Chabot like a wolf, grabbing the collar of his doublet. "Contact François and ask him why these pamphlets are popping up all over England!"

Chabot did not even blink. "Currently, few people are allowed to see His Majesty in Italy, because he and his queen must be safeguarded. Regular correspondence is limited."

The monarch released the Frenchman, who stepped back.

"I don't care how you contact your master. Or I'll imprison you in the Tower, where you will be put to the rack."

"Sire," pronounced the ambassador imperturbably, "I'm a subject of France. You must procure the permission of King François if you wish to arrest me."

Henry again gripped his collar, but Chabot did not even flinch. "Silence, you worm!" The king's eyes were now slits. "How dare you talk to me in such tones?"

"I'm sorry if my words offended you," Chabot said politely. His voice never wavered, he showed no fear. "Your Majesty knows such are the rules of international diplomacy."

"Leave!" screeched Henry. He pushed the other man away and forewarned, "For your own health, get a quick response from your master. Or is my cousin incapable of writing a letter, in spite of his far-famed Renaissance and education?"

Philippe de Chabot dropped a low bow to King Henry and exited. Truth be told, François' recent orders had unnerved and puzzled Chabot: he did not understand why his master had masterminded the plot against Cromwell and was also so strangely interested in the history of Anne Boleyn.

October 30, 1537, Hampton Court Palace, Middlesex, England

King Henry organized a feast in the hope of improving his frame of mind. He sat in a gilded throne under a canopy of state embroidered with Tudor arms, surrounded by the Duke of Suffolk and his favorites. The great hall was illuminated by a number of candles, shining with its resplendence. The walls were swathed with Flemish tapestries, portraying scenes of courtly love and medieval tournaments, which intensified the joy of the guests who all enjoyed the festivities.

Nonetheless, a touch of irritation festered inside Lady Elizabeth Somerset née Browne, Countess of Worcester, magnified by the grandeur of courtiers in expensive velvets, brocades, silks, and jewels, chatting merrily and dancing.

"I need solitude." Elizabeth longed to retire to the quarters she shared with her husband – Sir Henry Somerset, Earl of Worcester. These days, as a lady-in-waiting, she spent most of her time with the queen, who was now in confinement.

The Countess of Worcester steered her way through the throng, trying to find a place not overcrowded by people. Her accusations of Anne Boleyn had precipitated the death of the innocent woman, but she did not regret that. However, since Cromwell's banishment, her emotions were a tangle of despair and fright because their eventual fates were intertwined.

Finally, Elizabeth stopped and leaned against the wall. She glanced around, and her knees trembled under the penetrating stare of the French ambassador. Whenever their gazes intersected, there was an unfriendly smile on Philippe de Chabot's face, and her skin prickled with apprehension.

Her eyes flew to her husband, the Earl of Worcester, as if he could protect her from the eyes of Chabot. Nevertheless, her spouse was conversing with a pretty woman, who would surely become his new paramour tonight. Elizabeth's gaze then searched for her brother, Sir Anthony Browne, but the crowd was thick, and she could not see him.

A symphony of mellifluous laughter flowed from unseen lips. The throng parted for Lady Anne Bassett to pass, and men bowed to her, sparks of hunger in their eyes flaring into a bonfire. She exuded wanton heat in her revealing, eccentric gown of scarlet silk; it was the latest French fashion, trimmed with gold braid, intensifying her opulent appearance.

Anne Bassett strutted over to Elizabeth Somerset. "Lady Worcester, how are you doing?"

"I'm all right, Lady Bassett," answered Elizabeth.

The other woman intercepted her gaze. "Monsieur Philippe de Chabot is such a charming man." She giggled. "If I were not a royal mistress, he would have been mine."

Elizabeth experienced an overwhelming urge to run away. "You belong to His Majesty and cannot stray."

Anne glanced at Elizabeth as if she were a lunatic. "Chabot has many affairs; we do not need each other." Her eyes were full of mirth. "Ah, our king is such a wonderful lover!"

Elizabeth silently berated her for frankness. "I prefer not to discuss such intimate things."

"I recall that you were once His Majesty's paramour."

Three years ago, Elizabeth Somerset had been enamored of the king and eagerly given herself to him. She had tried to conceal her liaison, in particular from Anne Boleyn, to whom she had been a lady-in-waiting at the time. The vain Henry assumed that every woman belonged to him, and once he was bored with his mistresses, he easily discarded them.

Our sovereign is fickle in love and friendship, fickle in enmity, peace, and war. I was one of the many women whom he seduced and set aside, Elizabeth thought painfully. But her anguish was superseded by malignant gladness at the remembrance of how Anne Boleyn had learned about her affair with the monarch. The wrath of the distressed harlot had been frightening, to say the least, as Anne had screamed and thrown things. Elizabeth had apologized; yet, inwardly, she had been pleased with the former queen's sufferings.

"I'd rather not talk about it," the Countess of Worcester said evenly.

Yet, the king's paramour twittered in a poetic manner, "His Majesty is such a handsome man! Even though his leg troubles him a lot, he is as athletic in bed as a gladiator from ancient Rome. He has been generous to me and my family. Every time I see him, I always tremble with the sweet agony of my desire to surrender helplessly to his passion."

Elizabeth Somerset snapped sharply, "I'm happy for you."

"Look! Monsieur Philippe is staring at you right now!" giggled Anne Bassett. "Maybe he wants to bed you."

"What are you arguing about?" interjected a female voice.

Her brows arched in surprise, Jane Boleyn née Parker, Viscountess Rochford, approached the two women.

After her husband George's condemnation, all of her possessions had been confiscated by the Crown. Jane Boleyn had become a traitor's penniless widow, expelled from court. She had been powerless to save her innocent spouse, for the Boleyns had been beleaguered by countless foes. A year after the tragedy, Queen Jane Seymour had accepted Jane into her household; it was better to serve the new queen rather than be dependent upon her parents' charity for the rest of her life.

The women greeted Jane. "Good evening, Lady Rochford."

As her gaze fell on Elizabeth Somerset, Jane's eyes flashed with rage. This villainess had been the chief informant against Anne Boleyn, so she was guilty of her husband's appalling death. They had both been forced into matrimony, and at first, George had frequently indulged in affairs. Nevertheless, over time, they had come to love each other deeply, but Jane had failed to give George a child. Despite this, they had lived together in their marital paradise until George's arrest.

Oh, my dearest George! I'm still mourning for you, and I'll never forget you, my love, but I cannot speak about you to anyone, Jane Boleyn lamented mentally. Grief sprang from the depths of her soul, and she fended off the urge to weep. An instant later, her ire resurfaced as she stared into the eyes of her beloved husband's murderess, whom she hated.

Holding onto her rising temper by a thread, Jane glanced around and caught sight of the French ambassador, who was peering at the Countess of Worcester before tearing his gaze away from the woman. "Monsieur de Chabot seems to be quite interested in you, Lady Worcester, don't you think so?"

Elizabeth snorted. "Bah! That is not true!"

Jane remarked, "Lord Worcester is at the other end of the chamber. If he saw Chabot's stares, he would be jealous. This could lead to impulsive actions on his part."

Anne hypothesized, "Worcester is a good swordsman, one who is quite capable of challenging Chabot to a duel."

Elizabeth's stricken visage was such a pleasing sight to behold that Jane leered. "Jealousy sneaks into a man's soul and never sleeps; it shakes a married woman's security."

"It is not–" Elizabeth was interrupted.

Jane verbalized what everyone knew. "Lady Elizabeth, you are not the keeper of your husband's heart. Henry Somerset has two mistresses and many onetime lovers."

Lady Rochford viewed the Countess of Worcester from head to toe. Though of a short stature, Elizabeth was slender and pretty with brown eyes and long, dark brunette tresses, confined by a gable hood encrusted with precious stones. Her bronze velvet gown was ornamented with rubies, its sleeves decorated with strips of black damask. Elizabeth's stomacher was a silver cloth studded with gems.

Jane's gaze lingered on Elizabeth's diamond necklace before shifting back to the countess' face. "Your clothing and jewels are fashionable enough to tempt any man."

Recovering herself, Elizabeth sent Jane an acrid smile. "Lady Rochford, you are a wilting widow. Or do you wish Philippe de Chabot to become your lover?"

Jane blushed. "Why should you think that would be so?"

Elizabeth taunted, "Loneliness and being so unloved, with neither a husband nor a friend at court, is enough to kill any spirit, my lady. The most terrible poverty is loneliness."

Seething with fury, Jane Boleyn was in no position to defend either George or Anne. Elizabeth could make her words known through the length and breadth of the court.

Anne Bassett and Elizabeth Somerset perused the Boleyn widow. Unlike others, Jane did not wear luxurious gowns with elaborate designs. Tonight, she was clad in a gown of charcoal silk, with tight sleeves and a gable hood of black velvet that covered her light brown hair. Jane's plain face, with freckles and small hazel eyes, was not remarkable for comeliness. No, a notorious womanizer such as Chabot could never be interested in a woman like Jane Boleyn.

Anne opined, "The extravagant Monsieur de Chabot would rather bed you, Lady Worcester, than Lady Rochford."

"This is complete nonsense," mumbled Elizabeth, whose irritation was being exacerbated by this statement. "I need to go find my husband; enjoy the evening."

As Elizabeth stalked away, Anne Bassett laughed, and Jane Rochford frowned. Lady Bassett then joined her mother, Lady Honor Grenville, Viscountess Lisle, as well as her sisters.

§§§

Lady Somerset was crossing the great hall when she again intercepted Chabot's off-putting gaze – the kind of gaze a cat gives a cornered mouse. Her emotions swerved into all-encompassing terror, and she escaped from the feast.

An unnerved Elizabeth rushed through the antechamber and into the bedroom. All of the furniture was mahogany, and the carpet a deep maroon. Elizabeth lit several candles.

Her gaze landed on a sealed packet that lay on a table near the window. "No! Has *she* written to me again? No!"

Her nerves on the brink of shattering, she shuffled towards the table, grabbed the letter, and broke the wax seal that was neither stamped nor signed. The note included only one frightening sentence: "*Everybody pays for their crimes.*"

Elizabeth stifled a cry of horror. "It cannot be true!"

Yet, her mind was not playing tricks on her. The countess saw the lovely handwriting of the murdered queen. She threw herself onto a large bed canopied with burgundy taffeta curtains. The sight of the walls, tapestried with scenes of saints from the Old and New Testament, infused a sense of mortal dread into her soul. In her hand, Elizabeth grasped the dreadful letter, as if she could not be separated from it.

In April 1536, Elizabeth had aided the Duke of Suffolk to spread rumors about Anne Boleyn's infidelity to the king. She had first met Charles Brandon when he had been married to her elder sister, Lady Anne Browne. After Charles' marriage to Princess Mary Tudor, Elizabeth had renewed their acquaintance at court. Knowing Suffolk's animosity towards Anne Boleyn, the Countess of Worcester had not been surprised when Brandon had suggested discrediting Anne.

Suffolk had not told her anything, but Lady Worcester was certain that he and Cromwell had arranged together the dead queen's downfall. During her interrogation, Cromwell had bluntly asked her about Anne's incestuous relationship with her brother. Elizabeth had accused the Boleyn siblings of an unforgivable sin and lied about Anne's affairs with other men.

Elizabeth hissed, "I feigned my friendship with the Boleyn slut. I've always hated Anne and her family for Catherine of Aragon's dethronement and for her many woes."

Although she was a devout Catholic, she had signed the Oath of Supremacy, just as many others had done. In January 1536, her plot with Eustace Chapuys to destroy Anne had failed, so Elizabeth had seized another opportunity to bring the whore to justice, which Cromwell had given her.

Fingers of sleep unfastened a cloak of pitch-black misery. However, soon her victim came to torment Elizabeth: in her nightmare, Anne Boleyn, dressed in her coronation robes of ermine-trimmed purple velvet with a coronet of gold on her head, stood near the bed, smirking at her spitefully.

"Harlot!" cried Elizabeth as she woke. "Stop haunting me, you damned usurper!" On the edges of her consciousness, she heard someone knocking impetuously on the door.

The door jerked open, and Anne Bassett stormed inside. "Lady Worcester, I was passing when I heard your outburst. If others come, they might think that you have lost your mind." She scanned the room. "I see that Lord Worcester is not spending this night with you, as usual."

At the mention of her husband's famous unfaithfulness to her, tears misted Elizabeth's eyes. "What do you want?"

"To warn you for your own sake."

But the vision of another Anne, standing by the bed, would not leave Elizabeth, and a scream erupted from her mouth. "The witch was here! She shall never leave me alone!"

Anne quirked an eyebrow. "Who? What are you talking about? Such ludicrous behavior! Is your distress caused by your marital unhappiness? But why do you need to attract attention to your personal problems?"

Elizabeth shrieked, "Lady Bassett! Rot in hell, you whore!"

"Your odd conduct is not normal! It seems that I can do nothing for you. I bid you and your... ghost... goodbye." The royal mistress spun on her heels and dashed out.

Elizabeth flung herself face down on the bed and broke into loud sobs. Would her victim ever cease tormenting her? Anne Boleyn's death had brought her no respite.

Over the next week, the countess received two more notes from the 'deceased' queen. In one of them, Anne commanded Elizabeth to reveal the truth to King Henry, of her own accord or when she was asked by royal councilors. In the other, Anne had written that Elizabeth's soul was condemned to eternal damnation if she did not confess. The scared Countess of Worcester wondered whether she had plunged into madness; she always burned the letters after reading them.

CHAPTER 13

A Divine Punishment

November 10, 1537, Hampton Court Palace, Middlesex, England

"Dear God! Finally, England has a Prince of Wales!" cried an exhausted Queen Jane Seymour, as she reclined on a large bed curtained with heavy, wine-colored brocade drapes.

The Queen of England's bedchamber glimmered from the yellow and orange radiance of many candles. A cozy fire burned in the hearth, illuminating sumptuous Flemish gold-woven tapestries, and the hiss of the flames was the only sound for a few minutes. Awed, everyone trained their eyes on the midwife, who was now swaddling the baby boy in a blanket embroidered with the Tudor coat-of-arms.

An empyrean gladness filled Queen Jane, her expression eminently cheerful. Her face streaming with perspiration, she effused in a tired voice, "His Majesty will be very pleased!"

"Yes, my dear daughter," said Lady Margery Seymour née Wentworth with a smile. "After all the years of trying to have a male heir, the king will find the news the most joyful."

Jane smiled at Margery. She was glad that her mother was here to attend the birth of her child. After the death of her husband, Sir John Seymour, Margery had lived a quiet life at Wulfhall. Jane's mother had not been at court during the fall of the Boleyns, but she had attended her daughter's wedding to the Tudor ruler before returning to the countryside.

Margery looked content. A Catholic loyal to Catherine of Aragon, she had rejoiced in the plight of the Boleyn whore, but at first, Margery had not approved of Jane's marriage to King Henry. The fortunes of the Seymour family had depended upon Jane birthing the male heir so fervently desired by the monarch. *I feared that my Jane might have ended up like her predecessors. Now she is safe, and our family's future seems to be golden.* Such were Margery's thoughts.

Standing near the queen's bed, Lady Mary Tudor smiled brightly. "My father has a son, and I have a brother." She was genuinely delighted that she had a new sibling.

"It is the happiest day in my life." Jane could think only of her victory and her husband's gratitude to her.

Queen Jane had lost consciousness twice throughout the birth ordeal, which had lasted for two days. Margery had stayed continuously by her daughter's bedside, holding Jane's hand. Usually, only a midwife attended the delivery, but Jane's labor had been so complicated that Doctor Butts had come to examine her. As the contractions had been wracking her body, Jane had fulfilled the physician's and the midwife's instructions, while praying to the Lord to save her child.

Jane had the inclination to shout again and again that she had won so majestic a victory, but she managed to contain her excitement, for the queen's behavior must be dignified at all times. Her sufferings were not in vain because she was blessed with the long-awaited Tudor prince.   A festive thought bloomed in Jane's mind: *I'm the best wife Henry could ever wish for, and he shall love me for the rest of his life.* Now she and her family were safe, her position as queen secure.

In silence, the women watched the midwife hand the child to a taciturn Doctor Butts.

Jane addressed her stepdaughter. "Lady Mary, I thought about your sainted mother during my labor. This helped me endure the pain throughout many difficult hours."

Mary was moved by the mention of her beloved mother. Being a maid, she had not been allowed to attend the delivery. She had been summoned to the queen's presence soon after the labor. "Your Majesty has given England a precious gift."

Margery affirmed, "We all prayed for a son, and God heard us."

Doctor Butts passed the bundle on to Mary, who cradled the infant. As she eyed the silent child who stared at her with aquamarine eyes, Mary experienced such a strong motherly instinct that her eyes brimmed with tears. *I yearn to marry and have a family,* Mary mused. *Will I die an old maid?*

Mary glanced at the exhausted queen. "Your Majesty, this is your son."   She handed the newborn to her stepmother.

An unconditional love for this marvelous small creature filled Jane. "My dear baby!" She placed a kiss on his cheek. "You are England's hope for a prosperous and happy future!"

The door flung open, and Edward Seymour, Earl of Hertford, entered and walked over to the bed. He frowned at the sight of the infant's sickeningly white skin, attributing it to Jane's natural pallor. It was also alarming that the child was as silent as a tomb. Was something wrong?

"My lady mother and Lady Mary," began Edward, making a bow to them. "Did the baby boy cry when he was born?"

Margery veered her gaze to him. "No, he did not."

A terrified glitter appeared in the depths of Margery's and Edward's eyes, and a doom-laden sense of foreboding settled over them like a lethal cloud. Their gazes flew to Doctor Butts, whose expression was so very torn that Edward could not help but feel a shiver run down his spine.

King Henry stormed in like a giant vortex of winds encircling the area. When he had been informed about the prince's birth, a volcano of resplendent happiness had erupted in his chest. He had darted through hallways and hurtled down staircases as fast as he could, although his ulcerated leg had been causing him discomfort over the past few weeks.

The monarch stopped next to the queen's bed, short of breath. "My son! Thanks be to God!"

Jane smiled sweetly. "This is my gift to Your Majesty and to England!" She handed the bundle to him.

A triumphant Henry promulgated, "I've been waiting for years to hold my dear son in my arms! I'll name him Edward, for it is such a good name for a king."

"He will be England's finest prince," purred the queen, her smile widening.

The baby boy opened his eyes and stared at his father. As if spellbound by the glorious light of heaven, Henry stared at the infant while cradling him; his countenance evolved into ethereal delight. The child beheld him silently.

Puzzled, the ruler questioned, "Doctor Butts, why is my son so quiet?"

Butts sighed poignantly before answering, "The child has made no sound since his birth."

The king's brows knitted in surprise. "Why?"

Jane, Margery, Mary, and Edward all turned to the doctor, who was shuffling his feet. A pang of worry passed through them, ripping through their consciousness like a spear.

The fear of the monarch's unpredictable reaction did not deter the physician from voicing his suspicion. "Your Majesty, your son is healthy, though pale and rather small. However, I think there might be problems with the infant."

The queen asked, "What is wrong with my son?"

Lady Mary settled herself into a chair near Jane's bed and entreated, "Madame, please calm down. You have just given birth, and you should not overexcite yourself."

At the sight of tears in the queen's eyes, Margery tried to reason with her daughter. "Get a hold on yourself, Jane."

"What is happening?" insisted Jane.

The ruler's voice was apprehensive. "Doctor Butts, as the King of England, I order you to tell me the truth."

"Most likely, the child is mute and, thus, perhaps deaf," opined the physician. "I'm so sorry, Your Majesty. We need time to watch the baby in order to make proper conclusions. With God's help, his health might improve in the future."

"What?!" roared a shaken Henry, who blanched to the whiteness of marble. "What will change for the better? He shall not be named Edward! He shall not be my heir!"

The unfortunate prince stirred in his father's arms, but no cry followed.

Henry bellowed, "This is a cursed child!" He bundled the infant into Mary's arms, and burst out of the room, slamming the door behind him with a force that shook the walls.

Violent sobs rocked Queen Jane's body, echoing in the harrowing silence. A thought burned Jane's brain: as her child was born disabled, she had failed Henry and her country. Her heart-rending keening was that of a woman whose world had descended into a chaos of tragedy and brokenness.

Edward Seymour shot the queen a glare, blaming her for this misfortune. Meanwhile, Margery endeavored to console her. Appalled at the man's indifference to his sister's distress, Mary gave the child to the Lady Jane Rochford.

Margery quizzed with concern, "Doctor Butts, could you prescribe something to help my daughter sleep?"

At fifty-nine, Margery Seymour was a tall woman dressed in a high-necked dark velvet gown, which hinted at her slender figure. Having birthed many children, she had once been plump, but Margery had later lost her excessive weight. Her withered face – once beautiful with large gray eyes, high cheekbones, and lush lips – was now wet with tears.

The royal physician nodded. "Of course, Madame."

Despite the effect of herbs, it took Jane an hour to calm down. Even when she drifted into a restless sleep, she wept soundless tears, while Margery sat by her side, crying silently.

November 17-20, 1537, Hampton Court Palace, Middlesex, England

Sitting in sumptuous splendor in the middle of a huge oak bed hung with purple brocaded curtains, King Henry was contemplating the recent catastrophe in his life.

"How could this happen?" he spoke aloud, as if expecting the Almighty to respond. "Is it the Lord's will? Has Jane committed some unforgivable sin, so He punished our son?"

The biblical saints, depicted on magnificent wall tapestries from the great weavers of Flanders, could not answer any of his questions. The mahogany furniture, tastefully scattered about the royal bedchamber, depressed him further.

BETWEEN TWO KINGS

After the ill-fated birth, the monarch had spent the whole week locked in his quarters, seeking consolation in wine and crashing pieces of furniture and anything that would serve as a missile around his rooms. So overpowering and deep-seated was his grief that nothing could assuage it. Feeling cut off from the reality, a disconsolate King Henry did not attend the meetings of the Privy Council and canceled all audiences and entertainments. The country was ruled by Thomas Audley.

The newborn had been baptized Richard. *It is appropriate to name the cursed child after King Richard the Third, the Crookbacked Usurper,* Henry thought. At his wife's request, Elizabeth Tudor had been brought back to court. The Ladies Mary and Elizabeth had both attended the christening and carried the infant's train during the lavish ceremony. Shortly thereafter, the prince had been created Duke of Gloucester and sent away to his own household in Gloucestershire.

"Why has it all gone so terribly wrong?" inquired Henry, but no one could answer him. "Why is the Lord so cruel?"

At one time, the monarch had thought that Jane had been an angel sent to him from heaven to save England from civil wars. He had taken Jane's maidenhead on their wedding night and seen the proof of it – the bloodstained sheets. During her pregnancy, she had led a quiet and calm life. Her health had been watched over by the royal physician and the best midwives in the kingdom. Why had his wife failed him so utterly? What had caused his son's sickness?

A timid knock on the door interrupted his thoughts. "Who is it?"

The door opened slowly, and William Sandys, Lord Chamberlain of the royal household, emerged at the doorway. "Your Majesty, it is William. There is an urgent matter."

Scowling blackly, Henry snapped, "What do you want?"

"Lord Hertford has requested an audience with you," notified Sandys, a tinge of apprehension in his voice.

An indescribable rage simmered inside Henry until it boiled over like hot milk. He needed to take his anger out on something or someone, or he would choke on it. His gaze landed on William Sandys, who had dared name a member of the family he could no longer bear to think about – the Seymours.

The monarch grabbed a book from a bedside table and threw it at the chamberlain, who was barely able to duck in time. "Damn the Seymours to hell! Why don't they just vanish from the face of the earth? I do not know yet what to do with their accursed sister!"

Sandys backed away. "Forgive me, sire."

His fury somewhat abated, Henry growled, "Send Hertford away."

"As you command." Sandys dropped his frightened gaze to the floor.

When the man was nearly through the door, the ruler shouted. "Bring me wine."

"Just a moment. My sole purpose in life is to serve Your Majesty."

King Henry drank heavily throughout the whole evening. He could not remember a time in his life when he had been as devastated and helpless as he was at present. He was the absolute monarch of his country, yet he could not cure his son. His daughters, Mary and Elizabeth, were bastards by his own decree, and the succession was in jeopardy. A deep sense of loneliness enveloped the monarch, and he regretted that the Duke of Suffolk, his best friend, was away in Italy.

"There will be no English *Pax Romana*," lamented the ruler to himself. He drained his goblet in one smooth motion, then wiped his mouth with his sleeve. "Or am I mistaken?"

After days of remaining in his rooms, Henry ordered a banquet to be held. Courtiers attended out of duty, but a shroud of infinite misery cloaked the great hall, like a long night promising no dawn. Due to the information leaked from an unknown source, the nobles had learned about the troubles with the infant, and rumors circulated throughout the realm.

§§§

During the following days, Edward Seymour kept to his quarters, frantic with fear that all the power the Seymours had achieved was now lost to them. What should the Seymours do? Had the king lost all his affection for Jane? Could she re-ingratiate herself into his favor again? Would the ruler keep her as his wife? If he decided to discard her, how would that happen? Every hour of his waking day, these questions plagued Edward with a vulturine persistence.

Jane was confined to her apartments, waiting for the time to be churched. From their sister, Elizabeth, Edward knew that the queen frequently cried herself to sleep and even cried herself awake every morning; her weakness disgusted him. When Edward finally visited the queen, he dismissed all of her ladies-in-waiting, including Elizabeth and even Margery.

Jane watched her guest cross the bedroom. "Brother, why did you send our mother away?"

He settled himself on the edge of her bed. "We need to speak in private."

"When will Thomas return? Did he write to you?" She missed her second brother and hoped that if the family were united, they would survive the grief and the monarch's wrath.

"Thomas is still waiting for a private audience with Queen Marguerite of Navarre. I know not how long it will take."

"I want to see Thomas so much."

"Jane, we shall not talk about Thomas. Now you must stop weeping like a willow and concentrate on our problems." There was a sharp edge to his voice as he asserted, "Our only chance to avoid downfall is for you to get pregnant again as soon as possible. You must calm down and accomplish this!"

The queen was offended by his untactful words. "My son is disabled. No amount of tears in the whole world is enough to mourn for my baby. I shall never recover from this pain."

Edward sighed with exasperation. "You disappointed the king, and I fear the worst: he might no longer favor us and set you aside. As far as I can ascertain, Anne Boleyn's son is a healthy boy, who bears a strong resemblance to His Majesty."

The Earl of Hertford regularly received reports on little Arthur's life from his informant in Lady Mary Stafford's household. Edward had wanted to remind his sovereign who the child's mother was, but he had been denied an audience. *His Majesty might turn to the healthy bastard in consolation and proclaim him the heir,* Edward feared.

Jane shook her head. "That boy is a bastard of two traitors. Anne Boleyn slept with those executed men!"

He retorted half-sardonically, half-irritably, "My dearest sister, are you really unaware that if His fickle and dangerous Majesty wants something, nothing gets in his way? If you do not watch out, someone might take advantage of your naivete, so your family members must always guide you."

"Edward..." Her voice failed her. Her relatives saw her as a tool they could use in their plots until it broke, and that hurt her like a burn on the skin.

His brother's lips curved into a condescending smile. "At court, only Lady Mary, you, and King Henry believe that the harlot was guilty of her crimes."

"I don't understand." Confusion tinged Jane's voice.

"The Lady Mary hated the whore for taking her father away from her mother. Then later, the king had tired of Anne, and he saw her two miscarriages as the Lord's sign that their marriage was cursed. Anne outlived her usefulness. That is why she was found guilty by the peers of the realm."

Shock blanketed her entire being. "Henry would never have ordered her death if she had not betrayed him."

Edward elaborated, "Thomas Cromwell and Anne Boleyn became enemies. At court you have to eradicate your foes before they have a chance to destroy you." He paused, allowing the impact of his words to sink in. "The king coveted to wed you because he believed you could give him healthy boys. This gave Cromwell the opportunity to fabricate the charges against the strumpet and deliver you – a virgin – to our sovereign. Then the peers of the realm sat in judgment and gave their liege lord his legitimate freedom from her."

Disbelief was written across Jane's face. "No!"

"His Majesty chose to believe all the preposterous charges Cromwell manufactured in his crafty quest to get rid of Anne, without even examining any of the evidence against her." Hertford paused, waiting for his sister to comprehend that an innocent woman had been burned. "But if he ever realized that he had been misled, he would make everyone suffer."

Queen Jane moaned, "Oh my Lord!" Her expression was agonized, her world smashed into pieces, like a ship ruined by a gale. She had built her marriage on the blood and bones of people unjustly condemned! Her conclusion was borne out of this. "Did God punish my son for the harlot's unfair death?"

"You see, sister, you have to pray that the king continues believing that Anne Boleyn was guilty."

She regained her ability to think rationally. "Did you have a hand in her downfall, Edward? I must know everything."

"No, I didn't. Cromwell was her sworn adversary, and that was enough." He maneuvered the conversation back to stress the necessity of their future actions. "Jane, you must act as a good and docile wife and queen. Soon you will give His Majesty a healthy son. Do you understand me?"

At first, Queen Jane was silent and busied herself with examining the room's interior. Pieces of walnut furniture, all of them ornamented with leaves of acanthus and flowers, and gold-woven tapestries – the king's gift to her – irritated the queen. At least now no rooms in the Tudor palaces contained French furniture and frescoes depicting mythological themes in Italian and French styles, which Anne Boleyn liked.

Jane shifted her gaze to a window. The sky was a chill gray, full of leaden clouds that seemed to dissolve into the forbidding horizon, as if foretelling the storm brewing in the Seymours' lives. It would start raining in an hour, maybe less, as though signifying the mourning of nature for Anne.

Guilt rankled Jane's conscience, begging her to seek atonement. *But I did not know anything until today!* How could Jane stop her emotions from alternating between grief, fear, and contrition in the months to come? Nevertheless, Edward was right that they had to save themselves.

The queen turned to her brother. "Yes, I'll act as you say."

"Very well. Now rest." Edward then left her alone.

Jane asked herself whether she would have apprised Henry of Anne's innocence if she had learned about it in time to save her. The queen was not sure she would have, for she loved the monarch and wanted the crown. Instantly, a sour taste of self-disgust inundated her, and Jane berated herself for such unchristian thoughts. She comforted herself with the knowledge that at the time of Anne's arrest, neither she nor Henry had considered the possibility of her innocence.

Soon folds of darkness cloaked the city, mirroring the blackness in Jane's soul. Tormented by insomnia, the queen snuggled in the bed and covered herself up to her chin. It was raining heavily, and occasional gusts of wind wailed outside. Staring in the direction of the window, Jane thought that the heavens were weeping for the innocent queen murdered by the monarch's lust for her. *Dear Lord, I beseech you to take pity on my poor son and my family,* entreated Jane.

November 21, 1537, Newcastle-under-Lyme, Staffordshire, England

On Arthur's first birthday, Mary and William Stafford organized a celebration for all the children, including their own offspring – little Anne and Edward.

Thomas Boleyn, Earl of Wiltshire, and his wife, the Lady Elizabeth, arrived for the event. It was the first time the earl and countess had seen Mary and William since they had been married, and the first time that they had met any of their grandchildren. Everyone was in an exhilarated mood, and laughter rang out merrily through the parlor. Many fine gifts were presented to Arthur by his grandparents and his aunt, and the contemplative child smiled more often than usual.

A servant interrupted the festivities. He announced, "I am very sorry, but Thomas Howard, Duke of Norfolk, has arrived and requests a meeting with Lord Arthur."

Mary instructed the servant, "Escort him to the study until William sends word that we are ready for him." The man bowed respectfully and left the parlor.

Thomas Boleyn advised, "Do not alienate the Duke of Norfolk. He is a formidable foe, who is capable of destroying his adversaries with ease."

Elizabeth disclosed, "His Grace is cunning, and that poses a challenge to anyone, either on a political or personal battlefield. Through sheer craft and hypocrisy, he avoided any taint from the lurid scandals of Anne and George's shocking fall from grace. I refuse to call him my brother."

Mary paced the parlor, which was furnished with silver-brocaded couches and elegant tables. The walls were hung with tapestries depicting ancient Greek tragedies. As she halted in the middle of the room, she glanced at her parents.

Her face contorted in repugnance as she spoke about her uncle. "I don't wish to receive the duke, whom I despise. He is the Howard devil! He presided over Anne and George's trials as Lord High Steward and remained King Henry's prominent advisor, keeping his positions of Lord High Treasurer and Earl Marshal of England. Thomas Howard deserves to burn in hell for all eternity!"

"My disdain for my own brother is immense," confessed Elizabeth, her eyes brimming with tears.

Elizabeth's gaze locked with Thomas'. She still blamed him and her brother for their power games, which had resulted in two of her offspring meeting unfortunate ends. Her beloved son was dead, but at least Anne was alive. Anne's marriage to King François was like an incredible fairytale, and Elizabeth hoped that the Knight-King would destroy the architect of her two children's downfall –

Thomas Cromwell. *And I've not yet forgiven you either, my husband. I cannot,* Elizabeth mused ruefully.

Tearing his gaze away from his wife's eyes, which were full of silent condemnation, Thomas shifted his attention to their daughter. "Mary, I beseech you to be both polite and cautious with Norfolk and to conceal your antipathy towards him." His eyes flew to his spouse again. "Elizabeth and I will wait in the foyer until Norfolk has left the study. Then we will retire to the study until he leaves."

Lady Wiltshire tipped her head. "The duke should not see us. He ought to think that we are still estranged."

William Stafford chimed in, "Lady and Lord Wiltshire, I shall stay here with Mary and Arthur. I'll take care of them in case His Grace does something improper."

The Wiltshire spouses studied Stafford. A lean man of average height, William was handsome in a gentle way, with honest green eyes and an earnest expression, his personality a fusion of shyness, firmness, integrity, and intelligence. His old doublet of brown damask with matching hose contrasted with his fair complexion and wheat-colored hair, visible from beneath his toque of gray velvet. Stafford had no means to purchase luxurious garments, but he looked dignified.

Doubts stirred in Elizabeth Boleyn. She and Thomas had been shocked with Mary's marriage to Stafford because of his low station. They had planned to find a grand match for Mary after William Carey's death. At the news of Mary's pregnancy and elopement, Elizabeth had supported her husband's cruel decision to punish their eldest daughter for the shame she had brought upon them. Nonetheless, guilt was eating away at her, corroding her insides, for Elizabeth had abandoned Mary. *Perhaps I should not have protested against Mary's marriage to William Stafford.*

"Thank you very much, Master Stafford," said Elizabeth.

William sent her a benign smile. "I love Mary and will do anything to guard her happiness and peace."

Seizing the moment, Mary declared, "You see, Mother, wealth and titles don't make you a good person unless God endows you with kindness, chivalry, and honor."

"Indeed, daughter of mine," concurred Lady Wiltshire.

Mary tentatively smiled at her mother. Although Elizabeth had always favored George and Anne, which had wounded her heart, Mary loved her mother sincerely, considering her a model wife. Yet, Elizabeth's agreement to Mary's abrupt ejection from the family, without any means to sustain herself, had erected a thick wall of betrayal and coldness between them. Both women understood that today's reconciliation was superficial, but affection for each other shone in their eyes.

William reiterated, "Lord and Lady Wilshire, don't worry about Mary and Arthur. I'll not let anyone insult them."

Casting a skeptical glance at his son-in-law, Boleyn urged, "Let's go, Elizabeth." His wife nodded at him.

Thomas and Elizabeth hurriedly left, while William sent word that the servant should escort the duke to the parlor. Soon, Thomas Howard entered the room and greeted Mary and her husband.

§§§

Not wasting time, Norfolk began in the most courteous of tones, "My dearest Mary, I want to be introduced to the boy living in your household. He is my relative, after all."

"As you wish, Your Grace." Mary bobbed a shallow curtsey.

A man of average height and build in his mid-sixties, the Duke of Norfolk had a long, wrinkled face, which had once been quite attractive, despite his aquiline nose. His chilly, hazel eyes were like those of a hawk, piercing and powerful. Norfolk was dressed in a doublet of crimson velvet, wrought with gold and adorned with jewels, as well as a matching toque and hose of the same fabric. It was as if he were showcasing his wealth to his niece and her husband, who only scoffed at him. His boots were dirty from the mud outside.

William and Norfolk glanced at each other, and the duke then averted his arrogant eyes. Grudgingly, Mary brought Arthur to Norfolk, keeping Anne's son in her arms.

"The boy is one year old today," stated the duke.

Mary dipped her head as she cradled Arthur. "Indeed, Your Grace. He is growing into a big boy." She did not call him uncle, despite having known him since childhood.

The guest fixed his scrutiny upon Anne's son in his niece's arms, studying him closely and critically. Arthur peered back at the man who was taking such an interest in him.

A guileful smile lit the duke's wrinkled face. "Arthur, I'm happy to meet you, my precious boy," he uttered in a voice layered with fake friendliness. He patted the child's red-gold hair, delighted by the resemblance Arthur bore to the English monarch. Then he directed his gaze at Mary. "My niece, I'm pleased to see you, too. You are a Howard on your mother's side, and I'm seeking a reconciliation with you and your children." His eyes flicked back to Arthur.

The Staffords shared worried looks, knowing why the man beheld the boy so curiously.

Mary's upper lip curled into a derisory grin. "You did not wish to see me for years, Your Grace. Why are you striving to renew our kinship now?"

"Call me uncle." A glimmer of a smile warmed Norfolk's features, but failed to reach his eyes. "My heartfelt desire was to attend the first birthday of my great nephew."

She replied, "Thank you for making such a long journey."

If Mary did not wish to reconcile, Norfolk did not care. He was happy that Anne's son was the king's living image. Since Prince Richard was so sick, this boy could help him gain more power at court. "Mary, your household is not good enough for Arthur. I want you and the boy in London. Of course, your husband and children will accompany you."

William Stafford, who had been silently observing, interjected, "Your Grace, we are grateful for your offer, but we cannot accept it." There was a ring of finality in his tone.

The Duke of Norfolk moved his gaze to Mary, his mouth quirking in a lopsided smile. "Niece, are you certain that you don't need my protection and help?"

Mary said tautly, "Your Grace, you are indifferent to me, but I'm grateful for your desire to help Arthur." She kissed the child on the forehead. "When everyone forsook this innocent boy, William and I took him into our household. We love him as if he were our own."

Arthur started fussing, reacting to the rising tension in the room. His aunt gently rocked him to and fro, holding him to her chest and crooning to him until his crying ceased.

When the infant began playing with a strand of her hair, Mary continued, "The gossip about King Henry's ailing son has reached us. Some people say this misfortune is God's punishment for my sister's murder." In a granite voice, she challenged him. "Your Grace, I know why you want Arthur. I shall not allow you to use him as a pawn in your power games."

Norfolk taunted, "Mary, since when have you become such a genteel lady of principles? You were the mistress of two kings, and now you are pretending to be a proper wife and mother."

Mary blushed to the roots of her hair. She heard William sigh, and her heart skipped a beat. He was aware of her past affairs with both monarchs and her other liaisons, but he loved her, nevertheless. Her uncle's venomous remark caused her a great deal of embarrassment, just as Norfolk intended. Good breeding demanded that Mary be polite and composed, but she could barely bring herself to speak to the scoundrel who had deliberately insulted her.

"Your Grace, I request that you show my wife respect," demanded William harshly.

William's temper rose at the duke's insolence. His house might be humble compared to a ducal palace, but every Englishman's home was his castle, and Norfolk had ignored him as if he were a dead dog at the side of the road. *I'll not allow any man to humiliate my wife, regardless of his status,* an incensed William blustered in his mind.

The duke had absolutely no inclination to communicate with a poor commoner such as Stafford, so he turned to his niece and admonished, "Mary, you are robbing Anne's son of an excellent future because of your unwarranted fears."

"If His Majesty summons me to court, I'll obey." Mary's eyes narrowed warily.

Norfolk assumed an expression of pitying superiority. "As you wish, my stubborn niece. If you change your mind, you will have to write to me, and I'll send a reliable escort to bring you to wherever the court is. You will need me in the future."

I'll have to show Arthur to His Majesty, resolved Norfolk as he smiled nastily at Mary. *The king will have no doubt as to the child's paternity given their resemblance.* Everything he did in his life was driven by ambition, benefit, and greed. Without bowing, the duke departed shortly afterwards.

When her parents returned to the parlor, Mary recited the conversation with the Duke of Norfolk. Her father approved of her rejection of the duke's invitation, but the wily Boleyn patriarch realized better than anyone what Norfolk planned. *It is not yet the right time for the king to see Arthur, but we shall need Norfolk's support in the future to have Elizabeth and Arthur restored to the succession,* Thomas speculated pragmatically.

Mary admitted, "I was anxious during my conversation with the Howard devil."

With a scintillating smile, Lady Elizabeth Boleyn took Arthur from Mary. Her gown of beige brocade, ornamented with diamonds, accentuated the pallor of Elizabeth's face; a visage weathered and worn from fifty-seven years of life. Her blonde hair was streaked with grey and arranged in a chignon. Elizabeth's cerulean blue eyes shone with joy as Arthur's small hands wrapped around her neck. Her daughter, Anne, was her favorite child, and this little boy meant the world to her.

Suddenly, Lady Wiltshire noticed a flash of something akin to displeasure in her eldest daughter's eyes. *Mary does not want to see my love for Anne's son. But doesn't she realize that I adore her and William's offspring?* Little Annie and Eddie were merry children who had taken after their father. But Mary kept them both at arm's length from her mother, remaining aloof to Elizabeth as well.

Sighing, Elizabeth kissed Arthur on the cheek. "Thomas is my brother, but I do not want to ever see him again. I cannot condone what he did to Anne and George."

Thomas Boleyn told his daughter, "Mary, I know you have not forgiven me." His daughter was about to say something, but he waved for silence. "It is no use apologizing to you, but I want to say that I'm proud of how you handled Norfolk."

"Thank you." Mary was bewildered by his praise.

"We will need Thomas Howard soon," predicted Elizabeth.

"Why?" This time, it was William who spoke.

"Norfolk hates Cromwell." It was a flat statement of fact by Thomas.

Lowering her gaze to Arthur, Elizabeth brooded, "I wonder when Cromwell's misdeeds will come to light. That man is so evil that one day, God's wrath will surely descend upon him."

"In time, we will ally with the Duke of Norfolk and the Howard family," divulged Thomas.

Mary and William gaped at him in astonishment. They were aware of Cromwell's disgrace and had laughed at the pamphlets. However, they did not know the whole truth.

Thomas vowed, "I'll not let anyone harm my grandson." He then stated, "For Arthur's sake, it would be better if you all moved to Hever within the next weeks." His daughter started to object, but her father hurriedly explained, "Mary, since Prince Richard is chronically sick, Arthur's life could be in danger, and we must protect him."

Worry shadowed Mary's and William's countenances. Could their dear little Arthur be facing such peril? They had to acknowledge that despair from losing the king's favor might impel the Seymours to act against the boy. No one could guarantee that all the servants in the Stafford household were loyal to their master and mistress, so it would indeed be better to relocate to Mary's childhood home.

They seated themselves onto two couches, which stood on either side of a low oak table, where Arthur's gifts were placed. They spent the rest of the day playing with the children and talking about their upbringing. During all this time, Arthur never left his grandmother's arms, for the boy had taken a liking to Elizabeth, much to Mary's envious resentment.

December 8, 1537, the City of London, London, England

"Blasted pamphlets!" cursed Thomas Cromwell, unconcerned by the snowflakes blowing into his face. "How dare that French scum slander my name?"

The first snow had fallen, no more than a dusting, but the roads were slippery. Cromwell had already spent an hour astride his horse. Yet, his rage had not abated at all, and by the time he hauled the beast to a snorting standstill at the end of a long lane, he was in a flaming fury.

The king's *former* chief minister slid from his saddle and stalked back and forth across the snow-laden square while leading the animal by the reins. His mind was preoccupied with how to explain the unexpected attack on him. Since his banishment, he had been confined to his house; today, he had left it after dusk to avoid being seen by his neighbors.

Every day Cromwell read more in the stream of pamphlets written by the French poet Mellin de Saint-Gelais. They proclaimed that he had engineered the downfall of Anne Boleyn. There were more than ten pamphlets, each with a different text, but each declaring his guilt.

A fortnight earlier, his servants had given him a thick book entitled *'Thomas Cromwell: the Evil Genius of Religious Reform in England,'* which was printed in English. His spies reported that originally it had been written in French by Clément Marot, and that it was being distributed throughout England covertly. No one had been able to find out who was bringing the books into the country. This work crushed his usual indefatigable energy and confidence.

The book contained a painstaking analysis of Cromwell's role in and activities during the ongoing religious reform in England. "How did the poet obtain the information?"

According to Marot, Cromwell had insisted on the dissolution of the religious houses by removing some of the less important organizations within the Church. At first, only the smaller monasteries had been dismantled, and the monks sent to the larger institutions. Later, Cromwell began to claim that these monks had corrupted the larger houses, and, thus, he had closed them down as well. Marot accused Cromwell of manipulating the definitions of good and bad monasteries with the purpose of dissolving them all, both large and small.

The Frenchmen stressed several times in his work that Cromwell's ultimate goal was to destroy the whole Church infrastructure in England. The book declared that Cromwell did not support any of the ideas of humanism, including access to education, striving to confiscate all the money for the Crown. Marot emphasized several times that the monasteries had been an essential part of the national welfare and educational system, but Cromwell had taken them away.

The poet asserted that through all this, Thomas Cromwell had acted mainly for his own benefit and on his own motives, inventing false cases of corruption in religious institutions. Marot presumed that there was no enormous corruption in every of the liquidated monastic houses, and that Cromwell had stolen the wealth owned by at least some of them.

This reminds me of my arguments with Anne Boleyn, Cromwell thought, the icy fingers of dread running down his spine. In addition, Marot wrote that Cromwell wanted to legitimize his own radical Protestant beliefs, and in this, he was right. The author affirmed that Cromwell yearned to outlaw Catholic doctrines left in Thomas Cranmer's 'Ten Articles,' which was why he was nicknamed *'The evil genius of religious reform.'* The poet also declared him an enemy of enlightenment and all things progressive.

The sound of someone's footsteps intruded into his frantic thoughts. Cromwell jumped into the saddle and was off like a scared rabbit, heading to his home at Austin Friars. The gloom of twilight had settled, it was cold, and snow clouds were slithering across the horizon, but Cromwell did not care about the weather, breathing the frosty air in deeply.

"His Majesty is likely to have seen Marot's masterpiece," Cromwell said to himself. The fear of death blazed through him like a forest fire ripping through his consciousness, before giving way to a dismal certainty – he was doomed.

Cromwell brought his gelding to a walk when the two-storied brick house, with the imposing street frontage and the garrets, came into sight. He lived in an elegant and luxurious manor, suitable for accepting important guests, even royalty.

"This cannot be!" Cromwell ran his eyes over the mob near the entrance to his mansion. Since the publication of the pamphlets, there had been the occasional gathering of commoners, but this was a huge throng beyond anything he could have imagined. His expression fierce, he ordered, "Go away, you dratted scoundrels, and do not come back!"

As their initial astonishment at seeing him faded, an explosion of antagonism – curses, insults, indignant shouts, and death wishes – sounded around him. It grew louder and more brutal, melding into a crescendo of menacing, clamoring voices.

"Look at 'im! He must be Thomas Cromwell!"

"Yes, it's 'im! The blackguard!"

"Cromwell is a traitor to the king and England!"

"This devil killed an innocent queen, Anne Boleyn!"

A middle-aged, portly merchant lumbered past others and, glaring up at Cromwell and gesticulating irately, shrilled with loathing, "This heretic dares look at us without shame! He dissolved good monasteries and confiscated their property for himself, not for the Crown. He stole from the king and the people, and he has amassed wealth at our expense!" The man then spat on the ground to show his contempt.

"How dare you talk to me like that, you uncivilized and dirty mob!" Cromwell flung back, his gelding dancing on its hooves, disturbed by the tension of the assemblage.

An old, thin peasant in rags stomped up on his crutch towards Cromwell, and no one tried to intercept him. "You murdered Queen Anne because she weren't goin' to let you destroy our abbeys. She loved us, 'er people, and she wanted to 'elp us, and for that you killed her!" The old man's mouth had few teeth, and his infirmities made his speech all the more poignant.

The crowd pressed forward, and a rough, coarse-featured woman pointed directly at the mounted Cromwell. "This evil man should pay for 'is crimes! He is Lucifer!"

Cromwell felt the steady, increasingly hostile stare of the men and women. "This 'eretic must be burned, just as Anne Boleyn was." Someone at the back of the throng yelled.

"Cromwell murdered the wronged Queen Anne!"

"Anne Boleyn was innocent! He destroyed her!"

"Cromwell is a murderer and a thief!"

"A traitor! A 'eretic! Satan!"

"This damned man deserves only death! He will burn in hell for all eternity!"

As another enraged man lurched towards him, Cromwell steered his horse away from him, calling to his guards, "My men! Hurry up and deal with them!"

The captain of Cromwell's guard and several armed men came out onto the porch. At the sight of their master and the restive throng, they drew their swords and hastened to his aid.

Thomas Cromwell moved his girdling to the other side of the street, watching as the guards parted the mob, leaving Cromwell a free passage through. The folk would be forced to disperse. Cromwell was in a fever of impatience to gain the safety of his home and rode through the gates. For some time, he heard his captain's echoing voice issuing commands, then all went still.

There was a bitter taste of the people's hate in Cromwell's mouth. "Do they really loathe me so much?" He burst out laughing at the irony that today was the first anniversary of Anne Boleyn's burning at the pyre. His frazzled nerves snapped like dry twigs being broken underfoot.

CHAPTER 14

Royal Contests

December 2, 1537, Castello di Rivoli, Turin, Piedmont

The waging of periodic campaigns in Italy was not new for the French. The situation had become more complicated after the Battle of Pavia of 1525, which had led to a crushing defeat of the French and the King of France's capture. François would never forget his ignominious imprisonment and the humiliating Treaty of Madrid of 1526, which had made him relinquish his claims to the Italian lands and give up his Burgundian inheritance in favor of Emperor Carlos.

At present, King François had several strategic goals. He wanted the Burgundian inheritance of France back, but most of all he now desired to restore the Duchy of Milan to the House of Valois. The French had captured Turin and the greater part of Savoy over a year ago, and now he intended to reconquer Milan. François saw it as his kingly duty to return the territories he had lost to his subjects.

Since his arrival in Turin, François had been debating the military strategy with his councilors. As first light broke in the east, he convened his generals in the mahogany-paneled study, gathering beneath its crimson-silk battle tapestries.

King François took his seat in the wooden chair with gilded armrests, by the hearth. A fire crackled with a blissful heat contrasting to the bitter cold outside. Ever since the conquest of Turin, the Savoy coat-of-arms had adorned the door. The Valois coat-of-arms and the emblem of a salamander hung on the wall behind a desk piled with papers and rolls of maps.

Anne de Montmorency, Marshal of France, opened the meeting. "Your Majesty, let's send our envoy to the Holy Roman Emperor with an offer to sign a peace treaty."

François glowered at his friend, whose brilliant military mind often left him awestruck. As of late, the divergence of their opinions regarding the Franco-Spanish relationship was upsetting to him. The ruler then gestured towards Cardinal de Tournon, permitting him to speak.

Tournon emphatically delivered, "The Spaniards should never be allowed to insult our great nation again! We must restore the lands France lost after Pavia. Now our large army is strong, well trained and schooled in warfare. It is well equipped for high-intensity combats. We have significantly increased our military power in the past ten years."

The monarch turned to look out of the window; the sky was brightening as sunrise was only minutes away. "To make peace with Carlos would go against France's and my honor."

Montmorency understood his liege lord's feelings, because he had shared with the monarch the humiliation of the defeat and the hardships of the Spanish captivity. However, he was afraid that France could be vanquished again. *The next time, the emperor might order to mete out a slow, lingering death to François,* Montmorency feared. Furthermore, the English king could again enter into a secret agreement with Spain.

"How large is the emperor's army now?" inquired the King of France, his scrutiny on the cardinal.

Tournon reported, "About sixty thousand men in Spain and Flanders. Two thirds of them are well-trained."

François chuckled. "Our forces are almost equal."

"Our soldiers have a regular, rigorous training," chimed in Claude d'Annebault, who had been silent until then. "Soon we will be even better trained than our foes. The emperor needs more alliances to ensure that he will win the war against us."

Montmorency's lips curved in a semblance of a smile. "This is such a bold assessment of our army's combat capability. The emperor can also ally with England."

Suddenly, François stood up. In a half-sarcastic, half-reprimanding tone, he commented, "Monty, today you derive a sadistic pleasure from rubbing me the wrong way."

"Please forgive me, Your Majesty," muttered a pale Montmorency, who bowed low in apology.

The answer was his liege lord's booming laugh. "My subjects should not ruffle my feathers. Your punishment shall be a sparring contest with me."

François sauntered over to the door with the others trailing after him. They passed through the palace's labyrinth of corridors and mounted the steps, picking up their pace.

§§§

They emerged in the dimly lit, spacious armory, filled with a vast range of weaponry. On a long table near the fireplace, there were daggers and swords of different sizes. Shields, javelins, spears, lances, crossbows, and bows hung on the walls. The impressive assortment of armor of various styles and fashions, which the Dukes of Savoy had collected, was peculiar. The various pieces had once belonged to the most notable Italian and Swiss warriors of the past.

François strode over to the table with swords and rapiers. The monarch drew a rapier and motioned Montmorency to take a similar weapon. Tournon and Annebault watched in jovial amusement; it was not the first time that their sovereign had enjoined Montmorency to spar.

Smirking, the ruler spelled out, "Monty, you are such a skilled swordsman that it will be a pleasure to fight with you on equal terms."

"Ah, Your Majesty." Montmorency sighed meaningfully. "You are the best swordsman in Christendom!" That was an exaggeration, but not a falsehood as King François was a very formidable fighter, who displayed foolhardy courage on any battlefield, much to the worry of his generals.

"My victory is written in the stars! I'm the Knight-King!" François flourished his rapier, displaying his narcissistic streak. Tournon and Annebault smiled at his words.

Heedless of anything but the Marshal of France, King François leaped across the distance that separated them and thrust his rapier forward. Montmorency countered with a diagonal blow that was easily deflected by his royal opponent. The monarch lunged at him in a playful way, but in the next moment, his weapon flew in what seemed to be a deadly pattern, but it was not a dangerous blow. The clang of metal rang through the air as François unleashed an onslaught of attacks, and each time Montmorency blocked and parried, being exceedingly careful not to draw blood.

"We will not taste death today." François aimed the blade towards the other man's chest. "We will do it when fighting against the Spanish!" He nimbly avoided Montmorency's blow and continued, "Maybe I'll have a duel with the emperor and crush him. That would be my ultimate triumph!"

Montmorency was tiring as he was at a disadvantage to his liege lord, who was a head taller and stronger. "Aye, Your Majesty!" he cried, holding his blade in a defensive stance.

The sovereign of France stabbed forward, and his subject twisted away, causing his thrust to fall short. As his battle lust was not yet wearing off, François launched a new assault on Montmorency, intentionally missing the chance to strike the weapon from his hands. They danced nimbly across the room.

Expertly parrying his opponent's attacks, the monarch smiled, his amber eyes dancing with mischief. "Our victory over the Spaniards shall be the Lord's doing!"

Their rapiers continued clashing with a loud clang of metal in the morning sunlight, leaking in through the windows. The king's playful smile suggested that soon François would outwit his subject. The ruler feigned a movement to the right, and Montmorency automatically wielded his weapon in the same direction. In the next moment, François directed his blade downward before swinging back to the right and knocking the rapier from Montmorency's hands.

The King of France raised his hands, victorious. "Monty, you have lost! As usual!"

"Congratulations, Your Majesty!" chorused Tournon and Annebault.

Anne de Montmorency picked up his weapon from the floor. "Nobody can gain the upper hand in the battle with the Knight-King." It was a blend of flattery and truth.

"Enough," the ruler's strict voice resonated. "Let's continue our meeting."

They handed their rapiers to a minion, who approached them. The four men chatted animatedly on their way back to the study. The hallways were now humming with the early morning traffic of pages, servants, and maids.

§§§

As they seated themselves comfortably in the study, the French monarch eyed his subjects. He spoke again, a sardonic note underlying his jaunty tone. "Monty, I've punished you enough today. I refuse to brood over your offer to make peace with the emperor."

"With all due respect, I still disagree with Your Majesty's choices and counsel caution." Montmorency's opinion was firm and unshakeable.

François grumbled, "Your obstinacy vexes me, my friend." However, positive thoughts dissolved his annoyance. "We will not have enemies on multiple fronts. Carlos von Habsburg shall not be able to negotiate an Anglo-Imperial alliance anytime soon. My cousin, Henry, has many internal problems to address. I've been informed that there are demonstrations against the religious policy in England."

Tournon presumed, "A rebellion against King Henry and Thomas Cromwell seems to be brewing."

François and Tournon shared conspiratorial looks.

"It is highly likely." The monarch's reply was coy.

Annebault snickered. "The English king will have a hard time in the future."

Montmorency rubbed his beard before remarking, "Your Majesty, the French poets are the ones disgracing Cromwell. This might cast a shadow on your reputation."

François pronounced, a bit conceitedly and truthfully, "I'm a godfather of the magnificent cultural revival in France. If something inspires the imagination of poets, painters, and musicians, I'll never force them to forsake their ideas. I've embraced progressive values, and I support, not discourage, our artists in their endeavors to produce masterpieces."

Tournon, Montmorency, and Annebault all smiled. They admired their liege lord for his intelligence and his immense contribution to French culture. François was a capable king, who inspired loyalty and love in his subjects.

Montmorency was astounded at his sovereign's response, rising in his seat as if to challenge him. "Your Majesty, the works of these poets might be dangerous for France."

The king's lips lengthened into the thin line of a grim smile. "Monty, when did you start ignoring the values of our era? Freedom of expression is an essential condition to spread knowledge about intellectual things. I'll never prohibit our artists from producing works of art to enrich the minds of my people. I've ushered my kingdom into an era of enlightenment, and I shall not renounce it!"

François hoped that the marshal had caught the warning in his tone. He then moved to another topic. "Soon we will be ready for the war against Charles. Our Italian allies will provide us with many foot soldiers, and we may also form new coalitions. England will be too preoccupied with her internal problems." He became so enthused that his voice rose to a crescendo of confidence. "Our army is strong and does not lack morale, so I have high hopes for our triumph."

Annebault and Tournon bobbed their heads, while Montmorency released a sigh.

"We must be watchful for dangers," insisted Annebault. "It is only a matter of time before the emperor invades Provence or Piedmont. The question is when it happens."

Tournon underlined, "We must be constantly on the high alert for the emperor's schemes." His vast spy network was legendary, and they all realized that this seemingly innocuous phrase carried the weight of information supplied by agents embedded in the Habsburg Imperial court.

Montmorency reasserted his point of view once more. "Emperor Carlos will choose the most unexpected moment to attack us. I advise to follow a conservative foreign policy."

"I do not want to hear this." The monarch directed a hard glare at Montmorency. "Remember this well, Monty."

To avoid any friction, Annebault switched the topic. "Our people would appreciate it if they could see the queen who saved their sovereign from the emperor's assassin."

King François shook his head. "That is not possible. I treasure my spouse's life and that of my child above all else."

Three pairs of astonished eyes fastened on to the French monarch.

"Congratulations, Your Majesty." Tournon smiled benevolently.

Annebault exclaimed, "It is God's blessing, my liege."

"That is wonderful," added an intrigued Montmorency.

"Thank you." François' mind drifted back to the war. "With an enormous Spanish debt to clear and the Protestant movement in the heart of his realm, Emperor Carlos has many troubles to deal with. We must use this to our advantage."

They dipped their heads; this time, everyone was in perfect agreement.

Tournon coughed. "Remember how the emperor blocked the road near Pavia, and our soldiers starved as the supplies ran out. He succeeded in undermining our strength. Perhaps we can employ a similar strategy and set a trap in Piedmont or somewhere else to capture him." Tournon smiled at the ruler, who smirked in response. "We might also weaken the Spanish by causing them to suffer from some illness."

Annebault effused, "Cunning is the art of outmaneuvering your rivals and enemies."

Montmorency did not concur. "I prefer more traditional tactics."

"I approve of this genius strategy," endorsed the King of France. "We discussed it with His Eminence and my wife in Venice. Actually, she came up with some ideas."

Montmorency's eyebrows shot up in surprise; Annebault smiled in wonderment.

Tournon praised, "Her Majesty has an incredible mind."

The monarch and the cardinal smiled at each other.

Tournon had formed a favorable opinion of Anne Boleyn. At the same time, he was treading carefully around the woman for whom the King of England had broken from the Catholic Church. *I pray that His Majesty will not let his wife wrap himself around her finger. In this case, her influence over the king might become detrimental.* Tournon did not exclude that Queen Anne could become his enemy in the future.

December 10, 1537, Castello di Rivoli, Turin, Piedmont

"She does not care for me," King François lamented. He skimmed through his wife's letter, as if to reassure himself of its content. "Revenge has Anne Boleyn's face."

The Valois spouses maintained regular correspondence. He was happy and simultaneously anxious to receive her letters. As she had miscarried twice in England, he was worried for her health, but Anne assured him that she felt well.

The spouses discussed literature, art, culture, and politics in their letters, regaling each other with colorful accounts of happenings in Italy and France. François admired Anne's intelligence and shrewdness, and he was amused that Henry had discarded such a cultured lady to marry the simple and undereducated Jane Seymour. They deliberated the pros and cons of the Italian wars; François also shared tidings from the English court, reported by his spies.

The monarch re-read Anne's recent letter from Venice.

Your Majesty,

I am most delighted that our plan has subverted the established order in England, causing King Henry to banish

Thomas Cromwell. Henry Percy, Earl of Northumberland, will soon be able to speak to Archbishop Cranmer.

I'm not surprised that His tyrannical Majesty no longer favors the Seymour woman. She has failed to produce his much-desired prince, and now her position is weak, for the Prince Richard is disabled. Poor child, he does not deserve such a dreadful fate! Even having an army of princes, King Henry's son-obsessed spirit shall not be satisfied.

I hope that Your Majesty is doing well in Turin and is not exposed to dangers. God bless the Knight-King!

Written with the hand of your wife, Queen Anne

The letter was clasped in François' hands. "Damn Henry Tudor! Anne is more interested in him than building a future in France." This sent his spirits into a downward spiral. He tore the letter into pieces, but he regretted it forthwith.

"You have a troubled look, my liege," observed Anne de Montmorency as he walked in and bowed.

The monarch motioned him to a seat. "Nothing bad has happened."

His subject shrugged good-naturedly. "Can I ask you something?"

A brief smile flitted across François' countenance. "Of course, my friend."

"Who is the new Queen of France?" Montmorency inquired audaciously.

"Have patience, Monty. All things are difficult before becoming easy."

That day, everyone at the Valois court in Piedmont noticed the ruler's chagrined demeanor. Unable to concentrate on the military agenda, François dismissed his ministers.

§§§

BETWEEN TWO KINGS

In the evening, the French monarch sought to forget his troubles by abandoning himself to the festivities. Clusters of courtiers mingled at tables, wine flowed, and universal gaiety reigned. Eventually, a drunken haze settled over the guests, and some, including Claude d'Annebault, were so inebriated that they had to be carried away from the great hall.

Meanwhile, François brooded on his wife's attitude to his English archrival. Emptying goblet after goblet, he remained tight-lipped and withdrawn, a toxic blend of wine, cognac, and amaretto taking hold of his mind. His initial melancholy morphed into furious jealousy at the thought that Henry was always at the forefront of Anne's mind, despite all the atrocities the man had perpetrated against her.

After the banquet, the king and Anne de Pisseleu d'Heilly, Duchess d'Étampes, ended up in his apartments.

"Where are we now?" He stumbled over to a large walnut bed with a gilded canopy.

"In your bedroom." She helped her lover settle himself on the bed, lifting his legs and seating herself next to him. "This romantic place is ideal for lovemaking!"

Anne de Pisseleu was fascinated by this chamber's elegance tinged with a poetic shade. Two walls were frescoed with scenes from Horace's lyrical poems called *'Odes.'* A mural, depicting exotic birds frolicking amidst flowers, adorned the other walls. Marble statues of ancient poets were scattered around the area. The gilded oak furniture was ornamented with embellishments of Italian historical topics; the floors were covered with exquisitely patterned mosaics.

The duchess stroked his cheek and kissed his palm. "The feast was splendid, but I longed to be alone with you, *mon amour*. You and others drank a lot tonight." She giggled. "The drinking contest of Montmorency and Annebault was funny. Of course, Montmorency won and remained sober, for only Philippe de Chabot can outplay him in drinking."

"Philippe is in England," reminded the monarch.

"When will he return to France?" Soon she would need Admiral de Brion's help.

"I do not know." He shut his eyes as fatigue washed over him. "I need to rest."

Anne de Pisseleu removed all her hairpins, and her French hood fell to the floor. The mass of long, blonde hair tumbled around her shoulders and down her back. "If I might please Your Majesty in any way, I could surely stay with you."

François opened his eyes and eyed his lover, who bestowed a provocative smile upon him. *Her persistent attempts to coax me into making love irritate me*, he noted to himself. He emitted a sigh and closed his eyes to block out the sight of her.

She began unlacing her emerald brocade gown. "François, I want you! I crave to get lost in a river of enjoyment."

"I'm married," he objected.

A spontaneous titter erupted from the duchess. "It has never stopped you before."

"That was a long time ago."

Anne flirted with him outrageously. "François, you are a brilliant man who fascinates ladies. You have always been famous for your unparalleled gallantry, your artistic spirit, your intelligence, your flamboyant extravagance, and your overpowering charm. Besides, you are well-known for having a penchant for beautiful women. Passion is in your blood because you are a Frenchman and, even more so, a ruler."

With a half-hearted grimace, François admitted, "Many of my former mistresses loved me, but I broke their hearts and dismissed them as soon as I got bored. When I was younger, I was rather flippant and selfish, and I did not care about their feelings." He felt slightly dizzy from all the alcohol.

"You are too harsh on yourself, my majestic king." She finished unlacing her gown.

"I'm just being fair to myself."

She kissed his fingers, making mirthful sounds. "You cannot live in celibacy for long. As King of France, you are entitled to enjoy all the pleasures which make you happy."

The changes in François confused Anne de Pisseleu a great deal. Before his new marriage, the monarch had invited her to his chambers nearly every night, but they had not been regular lovers for months. She had a rich collection of lovers, one of them being Philippe de Chabot, although they both kept their liaison secret. During her separation from François, she had also slept with two Italian noblemen in Piedmont.

The ruler lifted himself into a sitting posture, and then pulled her gown down. "You have the soul of a courtesan! You are one of the best lovers I've ever had, Anne."

"I worship you." Anne pressed her lips to his.

At first, François did not respond to her sensual assault. However, at the remembrance of his spouse's unhealthy obsession with vengeance upon King Henry, red-hot anger spiraled in his chest, and, unable to contain it, he kissed his mistress back fiercely, bruising her lips. Instantaneously, she deepened the kiss, endeavoring to heighten the lust in him which they had shared for years in the past, but which he had lacked since his return from Venice.

Anne grinned wantonly. "I want you so much, my beloved François." She pulled the doublet from his shoulders and threw it away, and then started unfastening his shirt.

When they parted, François stared at her. His imagination ran riot: instead of this green-eyed and blonde beauty, he envisaged the dark-eyed, raven-haired Anne Boleyn.

He whispered, "Anne... Anne..."

His paramour chortled, thinking that he had meant her. "It is our royal passion contest! Tonight we will test our own boundaries, my king! Let me show how much I adore you."

They climbed to their feet, and her gown dropped to the floor. Anne de Pisseleu stood before him enticingly, her face split into a salacious grin. François tore open her chemise from the hem up to the waist. Then he slid his hands up from her hip and pressed his thumbs over the tips of her breasts. Laughing that he was finally in her grasp, Anne assisted him out of his shirt. They threw their clothes on the floor.

As they sat back on the bed, François drew his mistress against him, letting his hands glide over her curves. He kissed Anne with a devastating intensity as he had the desperate urge to claim her. As if the God Dionysus had blessed him for a drunken orgy, the monarch insanely craved to plunge into a lecherous ocean, where his negative emotions would drown.

All of her debauched nature aroused, she trailed feverish kisses along his cheek and down his throat. "Oh, my dear Majesty!" moaned the Duchess d'Étampes.

In the dim candlelight, King François perused Anne de Pisseleu. She embodied a tempting succubus, who again cast a spell upon his body, though not upon his heart. He unlaced his hose and sharply invaded her body. Instantly, they commenced moving, but they fell awkwardly from the bed. As they landed on the floor, the king started thrusting into her with a savage intensity and an almost ruthless force that he achieved in his current intoxicated state.

She wrapped her legs around his waist and clawed her nails into his back, arching herself deeper into him with every rampant thrust. Anne transformed into a French Messalina, for she was so much like that dissolute Roman matron as she was satisfying her royal lover's most wicked lusts.

Their copulating was far from an exquisite thing of love. The king's mind meandered to Anne Boleyn as he pounded into Anne de Pisseleu faster, more deeply, and harder. The tender lovemaking François had enjoyed with his secret spouse was a dance far more sensual than any court minuet, despite her restraint. Now he was with his mistress, and then the duchess smiled at him between kisses, he regretted that she was not the other Anne – *his* Queen Anne.

Soon the wildness within the two lovers exploded in a feeling of carnal rapture that was totally disconnected from emotions. Their bodies convulsed, heat and pleasure shooting through them like jolts of lightning. Satiated, François and his paramour climbed to the bed and again indulged themselves in their licentious adventures. Because of her years as the king's *maîtresse-en-titre* Anne de Pisseleu knew every inch of him, always offering him those intimate and indecent caresses which, she knew, satisfied François the most.

The ruler awoke at dawn, his head sore from the excessive amount of alcohol he had consumed the night before. Anne de Pisseleu lay near him fast asleep and naked, one knee up, the other dropped. Swimming in a vertigo of confusion, he labored to comprehend why she was with him, and then his befogged brain replayed the images of the past night.

François drew the covers over them both. Stretching his body across the sheets, he winced in pain from the deep scratches that she had left along his back. As he eyed the chaotic mess of their clothes on the floor, a twinge of regret ripped through him, and he wanted his mistress gone.

He shook her shoulder. "Anne, wake up."

Anne sleepily opened her eyes. "Good morning."

The king sighed in frustration. "I was drunk."

She snuggled closer to him, but he disentangled himself from her embrace. "We wanted each other." After a pause, she complained, "*Mon amour*, François, you have ceased paying attention to me since your return to Turin."

"I am very busy." His voice was tinged with ice.

"It is because of your new wife," she hazarded a guess. "How long have you known the woman you married?" Her tone changed from soft to a challenge, tinged with jealousy.

The monarch measured her with a vexed look. "Long enough to wed her; my personal life is none of your business."

A crestfallen Anne decided to test her theory that the reason why he avoided her was his new matrimony. "Your Majesty, we have lived in perfect harmony and happiness for years, and I greatly appreciate the honor to be with you."

A fleeting smile graced his features. "Those years are unforgettable."

François is so distant with me! The axe of his indifference removed the imaginary crown from Anne de Pisseleu's head. The devotion she was accustomed to hearing in his voice was missing. Was it possible that the king no longer loved her? This thought sparked a kernel of fear in the duchess, and her mind was awhirl with questions, the most painful one being that François could have fallen for his spouse.

She struggled to contain her rancor. "Your Majesty, the Queen of France must be an amazing woman if you married her only because she saved your life."

He smiled blissfully. "My wife is a unique woman."

She prodded, "Does she love you, *mon amour*?"

Unable to divulge the truth to her, François resorted to a skillful subterfuge. "Feelings do not matter in an arranged union. You know this from your own experience, Madame." His voice rose to a higher octave. "Monarchs do not marry for love, or they rarely do so. If Lady Luck smiles upon you, then you can become close with your wife at some point. It is a wonder in itself to find love, especially in a royal marriage."

The king's thoughts drifted to Anne Boleyn. *Marriage should be a union of body, mind, and soul, but it is not so in my and Anne's case.* For years, François had believed that any royal marriage existed for the sole purpose of procreation and continuation of a ruling dynasty. It surprised him that now he viewed it differently because of his English spouse. She had not had any amorous sentiments towards him when he had wed her. Months ago, François had not minded, but now this knowledge lacerated his heart like a thousand daggers.

"I love Your Majesty!" Anne's emerald eyes sparkled like diamonds. "You are the light of my life, and only you."

"I know." Her avowal did not please François.

The royal mistress determined a plan of action, which would be aimed at eliminating any rival for the ruler's heart and bed. *Woe betide all those who try to take François away from me, or turn him against me. He will forever be mine at any cost,* Anne de Pisseleu vowed silently.

She was about to kiss him, but he moved further away from her. "Why don't you permit me to stay?"

He turned a deaf ear to her question. "Soon I have a meeting with Monty." He had to take a bath and get dressed; he would not be able to eat anything with such a hangover.

She reluctantly left the bed and slanted a glance at his night robe of blue brocade. "Can I use it?"

Her very presence exasperated François. "Yes."

His paramour donned the robe, curtsied, and darted to the door. She paused and looked back at him. She hoped that he would ask her to stay, but he was staring at her with the same deadpan countenance he might bestow on a stranger.

The royal harlot remembered, "Monsieur d'Annebault mentioned yesterday that your wife is pregnant."

A smile lit up his visage. "That is true."

She mumbled forlornly, "Congratulations, Your Majesty." In spite of her dreams to give the monarch a child, she had never been able to do so. Anne accepted that her infertility was her punishment from God for her carnal vices.

"Anne, consider returning to France. If you choose to stay here, do not intrude upon my time." François experienced a momentary stab of guilt for no longer wanting her.

The Duchess d'Étampes nodded. "As you wish."

King François sighed with relief at her departure. After this night, he realized that Anne de Pisseleu could never give him the spiritual relationship he yearned to have so much. *Anne Boleyn, my wife and queen...* A vision of her exotic face invaded his thoughts. His wife was frowning at him, her eyes shining with disapproval and disappointment.

He had flagrantly dallied with other women throughout his two previous marriages. His heart had not constricted in remorse: as a ruler, he had the right to take any number of mistresses. Yet, now François was racked by pangs of guilt as acute as a sharp blade against his skin, while also conscious of his growing longing for Anne Boleyn, which fueled the ardent heat in him all day long, from sunrise until long after dark.

CHAPTER 15

The Fall of a Royal Mistress

December 15, 1537, Castello di Rivoli, Turin, Piedmont

Anne de Pisseleu d'Heilly, Duchess d'Étampes, rose from a throne-like chair near the fireplace and sauntered over to a looking glass set on a nearby oak table. She pinched her cheeks to give them a bit of natural blush, and then casually tugged at the very low décolletage of her sweeping gown of red silk, which was worked with gold and had long, open, pendant sleeves. She beheld her reflection in the glass for a minute, as if to reassure herself of her beauty.

The door opened, and King François entered the reception chamber. Anne smiled and rushed forward, but she stopped abruptly at the sight of his frosty countenance.

She collected her wits. "François! I'm so happy to see you, *mon amour*!"

The monarch sketched a mocking bow and stalked over to the fireplace. He settled in the same chair she had occupied earlier, and linked his hands loosely in his lap. "I've come because I received your note, Madame." His tone was formal, his eyes frigid.

The duchess smiled angelically. "Your Majesty, we should spend some time together; you have been working too hard." She came closer to him.

His laugh held no humor. "What do you want to discuss with me so urgently?"

Anne nearly choked on the rage that surged through her. "François, I must ask about your new wife. I know that she is pregnant, and that you care for your child, but you should not ignore that she might be using you. You do not know her well as you only met her in Venice."

François jerked to his feet and directed a withering gaze at her. "Listen to yourself. That is more than enough," he spat, and his gaze turned to the flames in the fireplace. "I no longer want you in Turin. You will return to France together with your sister and your household."

She braced herself against his anger. "I would leave, but I fear you will not be happy with your queen."

"That is not your affair." His voice was glacial.

Anne de Pisseleu looked at the monarch in such a way that spoke volumes of her jealousy. "I cannot give this woman the man whom I worship more than anything in my life. Even if you crush my heart and cripple my body, I'll still love you." Her voice rose to a high whine. "Your wife cannot mean more to you than I do. You and I belong together forever."

The ruler did not move, knowing that she hankered to see his emotional reaction. There was no passion for her left in him, for her outburst emptied his heart of the last drop of lustful sentiments he had ever harbored for Madame d'Étampes. François realized that what he had once felt for the duchess was sexual attraction, not love. For the first time, resentment of her wheedling ways reared inside him.

His countenance annoyed, he issued a stern reprimand. "Madame, never refer to the Queen of France in such a disrespectful manner. Never ever!"

"I'm sorry, Your Majesty." But she did not mean it.

§§§

Meanwhile, Queen Anne ascended the stairs, escorted by Jacques de la Brosse and several guards. They moved stealthily along dimly lit corridors; secrecy was paramount. They crossed a large hall with a high ceiling and strode down a paneled corridor, their footsteps echoing in the solemn stillness. For some time, they were lost in a labyrinth of stairways and corridors, where the lime-washed walls were lined with tapestries and torches, flickering in the torchlight.

§§§

The King of France flitted his gaze to one of the paintings on the wall, depicting the prurient Messalina, the third wife of the Roman Emperor Claudius, with her numerous lovers. He almost threw a jibe at Anne de Pisseleu, but suppressed it in time. *I cannot compare my mistress to Messalina because Anne has been faithful to me,* he assumed erroneously.

"Madame, leave Piedmont," ordered François. Now he was hardly able to bestow upon her the barest modicum of courtesy. "I've had enough of your snide insinuations about my queen, and of your pursuit of me to assuage your own desires." He then stomped towards the door.

Anne de Pisseleu emanated despair as she beseeched, "Your Majesty, do not leave me!"

The ruler spun around and fixed her with a severe look. "You will depart from Turin as soon as possible!"

The world of the Duchess d'Étampes lay in ashes, and her heart was breaking with the agony of her loss. Her lover behaved like the almighty God Zeus, whose word had once been law for mortals and the divinities of Mount Olympus, and she must obey him.

I cannot be like others! I am his Venus. Hasn't François called me so? However, the monarch had discarded Anne's predecessor – Françoise de Foix, Countess de Châteaubriant – to be with her. For years, François had favored his second official paramour so greatly that the duchess had never imagined she would ever be cast off as his *maîtresse-en-titre*. He could not be replaced in her life because she would lose not only the king, but also her power at the Valois court.

"Do not send me away! Please, let me stay with you!"

"Do not make me repeat myself, Madame."

At the same time, Anne Boleyn, newly arrived, halted at the doorway; she had sent her escort away. Seeing King François and another woman, a prickle of unease tickled her spine. *She must be the notorious Anne de Pisseleu d'Heilly, who managed to keep François' affection for more than a decade*, the queen guessed correctly. Then her attention focused on her husband, who stood with his back to her.

"Your Majesty," called Queen Anne in a high voice that resonated both loudly and musically, like the sound of rushing waters. "I hope I'm not distracting you."

King François swung his gaze to Queen Anne, who dropped into an enchanting curtsy. He flashed her a radiant smile and flourished a bow.

The queen viewed François from head to foot. As usual, he looked every inch the majestic ruler. His pale green satin doublet, slashed with gold, was encrusted with jewels and ornamented with sable. He wore it over a padded shirt of emerald silk embroidered in gold thread. His long, muscular legs were clothed in tight knee breeches of emerald velvet. On his head, there was a plumed flat cap of black velvet.

Galvanized into action, the ruler marched to the queen. "Anne!" He took her hands in his and kissed them. "Your appearance is like a magical sunrise in the dead of night."

A bemused Queen Anne riposted, "I'm not dressed in the color yellow or orange, sire."

François took time to look at his beautiful spouse. Her black and blue gown, loose enough to accommodate her expanding waistline, possessed an elegant train. Its airy sleeves were lined with gold fabric and trimmed at the cuff with ermine, as was her collar. Her head was adorned with a French hood edged in gold, and, fastened to it in the German fashion, an azure veil obscured her face.

He sent her a warm smile. "It matters not. You have brought light into a gray day."

The queen laughed. "Your Majesty is too kind to me."

The royal mistress watched the scene with distaste. *She must be the far-famed Queen of France, François' wife in the eyes of God and man,* Anne de Pisseleu hissed wordlessly. The monarch's eyes now shone with an eloquent yearning as he beheld his wife. The mistress longed to have such a look directed at her again, but instead, she was receiving only the king's arctic coldness. Hatred, fierce and inextinguishable, blossomed in the duchess' chest, seeping into her very pores.

Queen Anne requested evenly, "Husband, will you introduce me?" She referred to him in such a personal way to drive her queenly position home to the abandoned mistress. It was hilarious to see the puzzled face of the royal paramour, who labored to figure out who Anne was. Now masquerade was simultaneously practical and amusing.

François smiled at this form of addressing him for the first time since their wedding. Turning to the duchess, he declared, "May I present the Queen of France. I'm beholden to her for saving my life." His gaze slid to his spouse. "This is Madame Anne de Pisseleu d'Heilly, Duchess d'Étampes."

The duchess lowered herself into a deep curtsy before the queen. "I'm honored to meet you, Your Majesty."

The two Annes studied one another, making a show of civility. They both were seasoned courtiers schooled in power games, deviousness, and calculation.

"Likewise, Madame," answered Queen Anne flatly.

Anne Boleyn was glad that they did not see her stiff face under the veil. François did not always conduct his amours discreetly. In the past, she had witnessed the king parade some of his paramours, and his two long-term lovers had both become an ornamental decoration of his court. It was not surprising that her husband's *maîtresse-en-titre* was in Turin, but Anne wondered what had caused the rift between them.

"The duchess will depart for France," stated the monarch brusquely. "No excuses will be accepted if she fails to do so."

The queen found herself stranded in a fog of confusion. *Has François set his mistress aside, and, if so, why?* When Henry had taken mistresses, Anne Boleyn had not wanted to share him; each of his many affairs had been cutting her heart to pieces. But she was not in love with François! Then why, as the queen met the duchess' gaze, did she feel such a stirring of gladness that François was sending the Pisseleu slut away?

With a haughty air about her, the queen addressed the other woman. "His Majesty and I hope that your journey will be a pleasant and safe one, Madame d'Étampes."

Anne de Pisseleu compelled herself to smile. "I thank Your Majesty for your kindness." She curtsied in front of the royal couple. "With your permission, I shall retire."

François nodded. "Goodnight and safe journey, Madame."

As the *former* mistress exited, the royals were left alone.

"Your Majesty." The queen made a curtsey to the ruler.

The monarch stepped closer to her. "Anne, do not curtsey to me in your condition, especially not when we are alone."

"Thank you," she replied, amazed.

The ruler led his consort to a chair and helped her settle herself comfortably. He seated himself opposite her and leaned forward, his face inches from hers.

Raising her veil, he gazed into her eyes. "Anne, why didn't you send me a notice that you would come to Turin? The Count de Montreuil must be worried about you."

Anne elaborated, "Sire, I initiated my trip for important reasons. Don't blame Monsieur de la Brosse, who has been a wonderful companion to me throughout the past few months. Monsieur Jean was displeased, but he could not stop me."

"Of course, a count cannot give orders to the Queen of France."

Her face lost its embarrassed expression. "Indeed."

His gaze traversed her body. "How are you feeling, Anne? Did the journey go smoothly?"

"It was uneventful and not dangerous at all," assured the queen, touched by his solicitude. "All is moving according to God's plan, for it was the Almighty's will that I rescued Your Majesty." Anne had begun to believe the Creator had led her to St Mark's Basilica all those months ago. "Monsieur de la Brosse arranged everything. He also managed to get me into the castle undetected."

He touched her cheek gently. "I'm glad you are here."

Her lips arranged in a smile, Anne revealed the goal of her arrival in Piedmont. "Sire, we are allies, so the people must see their king and queen together. My appearance will make your men-at-arms totally united against the evil Spaniard."

His wife had not come to him, but for political motives! A storm of chagrin raved wildly in his blood momentarily, but then he realized that she was right. "Your presence will boost everyone's morale and confidence. It will motivate them to inflict a crushing defeat on the emperor."

She half-jested, half-claimed, "We will make everyone think that I strive always to be at the Knight-King's side."

François let out a laugh. "Yes, you are my heroic wife."

§§§

The queen's apartments were connected with the king's quarters by a hallway that in some places opened up and became a room. François had ordered that no one approach his wife's rooms on pain of death. Men from the Scots Guard guarded Anne's suite; only the King of France, Cardinal de Tournon, and Jacques de la Brosse were permitted access.

Anne pushed the sheets off her body and climbed out of bed. Her muscles were stiff after many hours in one position. She walked to a gilded sumptuous *cassoni*.

"It is for a bride's dowry goods," she said to herself, smiling. "Not for me."

As she strolled through the room, the queen examined its interior. The walls were hung with cream and yellow brocade, as well as rich jewel-toned tapestries. In the center was a huge mahogany bed, swathed in ivory covers embroidered with gold thread. Along one of the walls stood a collection of couches, upholstered in white brocade, and gilded chairs.

As he walked in, François saw Anne near the *cassoni*. Her white silk chemise enveloped her body, stressing the curves of her belly swollen with his child. She looked like an angel with her raven hair streaming down her back as a river at night.

"I'll help you, *ma chérie*." A torrent of warmth flowed into his soul like a stream of life-giving light.

The ruler aided his wife into bed. As he settled himself next to her, his gaze fell on a pile of parchments on a bedside table. "Poems in English! Read them for me."

Anne was bewildered, for they had spoken only in French since they had met in Italy. She complied and read a poem aloud. "Thomas Wyatt is a popular poet in England."

"I think it was written in your honor," he said in accented English.

The queen switched back to French. "Maybe."

"Thomas Wyatt was your admirer, wasn't he? He must have adored you, for he dedicated many poems to you. He was also arrested and imprisoned in the Tower for supposedly committing adultery with you." Something flickered in his eyes for a split second. "Why did Henry release him?"

"Thanks to his family's friendship with Cromwell, and the intervention of Wyatt's father."

The monarch elucidated, "My spies reported that he is not allowed at court and lives at Allington Castle."

Her face was a picture of astonishment. "You know even this!?"

"Yes, a clever king must keep fully informed."

Was his interest in the poet a sign of distrust? If it was so, Anne had to dispel his misgivings. "I swear that I never betrayed King Henry with anyone else. My enemies aspersed me with all the calumnies it is possible to invent. I was a true virgin when Henry took me to bed for the first time."

François discerned sincerity in her eyes. "Do not work yourself up, Anne. I believe you because I saw your feelings for Henry in Calais." A pang of envy cut deep into him at the thought of Henry being his wife's first lover. Such sentiments were fatuous, but he could not help himself.

She smiled faintly. "Thank you, Your Majesty."

"I've been honest with you, and I'll not tolerate falsehoods. If there is something that might damage our relationship, you must tell me about it of your own accord. If you ever lie to me, you will discover an unpleasant side to my character." His voice was without a note of threat, but the message was clear.

An annoyed Anne opposed the impulse to snap at him. "I've never lied to you."

"Very well." As François placed his hand on her stomach, his eyes filled with affection. "Will we have a girl or a boy?"

The startled queen blinked at the gentleness of this question. Henry had wanted only sons from her, and for him every pregnancy meant new hope for a male heir. François had two living sons to succeed him, so she was not under colossal pressure to produce heirs to the throne.

Curiosity glittered in her eyes. "Which would you prefer?"

François gauged her thoughts. His Tudor counterpart demanded sons from his wives, which was grotesque. "I'm not obsessed with begetting sons. It is God's will what a woman gives birth to. I'll be happy to have a daughter who is as beautiful and intelligent as you are. If the baby is a son, I'll be delighted, too. Just as long as you are both safe."

Anne was open-mouthed in sheer awe. *François does not mind having a daughter! It provides me with a sense of freedom!* Such an attitude, so unfamiliar and utterly amazing, made her feel as if a fairytale were unfolding before her eyes.

"Unfortunately, I do not have a history of many successful pregnancies." Her heart constricted in her chest.

"Anne, everything will be all right." François drew his fingers through her hair, marveling anew at the softness of her silky curls. "Relax! Any stress is not good for you."

"I'll try," promised the queen.

"My best physicians will take care of you, and I'll spare no expenses on your health and that of our baby."

François cupped her face and pressed a featherlight kiss on her mouth. It was the tenderest kiss they had ever shared; more tender than petals of a delicate flower blooming in the early spring. Nevertheless, when they parted, her eyes had a flicker of an icy glint as reality stepped in, crying for her not to allow herself to feel safe with another monarch.

Anne sighed as her mind returned to English matters. "I hope my foes will suffer in the months to come." She did not know that her husband's heart skipped a beat at her words.

December 16, 1537, Castello di Rivoli, Turin, Piedmont
Anne de Pisseleu walked out of the palace and paused on the front steps. She raised her gaze to the pink-tinted firmament, saying farewell to her life as the royal grand favorite. Her chin lifted arrogantly, Anne looked around and spotted several courtiers, who observed her departure.

The Duchess d'Étampes whispered, "I feel lifeless inside."

Yet, Anne would not show her heartbreak to those who had come to gloat over her. She had learned the art of pretense to perfection, and outwardly, she appeared unaffected. Confidence was essential to survive the whisperings and gossip, which would trouble the erstwhile mistress. Anne de Pisseleu had seen her predecessor's dismissal, and now she was following in Françoise de Foix's doleful footsteps.

Françoise and Anne had both taken what the position of an official mistress afforded them, holding their heads high in spite of all the reproving and envious whispers behind their backs. Madame de Foix had retained her friendship with the monarch, and they had often corresponded. The king had visited Françoise and her husband – Jean de Laval, Count de Châteaubriant – a few times in Brittany until her death in 1537. *But I shall never be discarded like an old dress!*

Swallowing the bile in her throat, Anne forced a smile at the courtiers. Then she mounted a fine palfrey, draped in cloth of silver, and led the group, which included her sister, Péronne de Pisseleu. The cast-off mistress ordered the column to move, and the horses trotted along the road. Two more rows of animals followed, pulling wagons containing her maids and luggage.

Péronne observed her sister as the miles took them away from Turin. A depressed Anne was more perilous if she were taciturn and calm than if she laughed hysterically or wept herself dry. After hours of silence, Péronne had had enough.

As she rode beside her sister, Péronne queried, "Are you sure that the king does not love you anymore?"

Anne pivoted her head to the other woman. "François looked at his wife with devotion and adoration. I suspect that he is in love with her." Gloomily, she pronounced, "He does not want me – now he needs only his Venetian savior."

"Speak more quietly, sister. Someone might hear."

"Most of our servants are Italians; they don't understand the French language."

Nonetheless, Anne nudged her horse into a trot ahead of the others; Péronne followed suit. Leading the column, they kept at a safe distance so they could talk in private.

Péronne broached the subject of her sister's future. "Anne, what are you going to do?"

The former royal mistress would battle for the monarch's heart like a lioness. "I'll not let François go. His wife is pregnant, and he will never allow her to stay in Piedmont."

"I hope you are not going to cause her to miscarry."

Anne shook her head. "Of course, not. It would be too dangerous and foolish. If the queen died from the bleeding, it would have tragic consequences for us. I would be one of the first suspects, and I do not need to land in that much trouble. We will play a more sophisticated game against

François' damned wife." She sighed grievously. "Besides, despite my hatred of the queen, I do not wish to have an unborn child dead on my conscience. I'm not that heartless."

The other woman nodded sullenly. "I know, sister."

The Duchess d'Étampes gripped the reins tightly as a rush of rage overtook her. "I hate Queen Anne! Evidently, she conceived quickly after their wedding. Some of François' former mistresses birthed his bastards. Although I've always dreamed of having a child with His Majesty, I could not get pregnant throughout the many years of our relationship."

"Calm down, Anne. What are you planning to do?"

"I have a contact in Turin and shall be notified where François and his spouse will travel from here." After a thoughtful pause, Anne enlightened, "I want to see the queen's face that was hidden beneath a veil. There is something familiar about her, as if I had met her in the past."

"Maybe you can find allies against her."

The duchess comprehended the complexity of the situation. "The king's spouse is carrying his baby, and those who declare themselves the queen's enemies cannot overlook it. I think his new queen is neither French nor Italian."

"Does her French have any kind of accent?"

"No, she speaks our language without any hint of a foreign accent, which means that she possibly grew up in France."

"I agree; otherwise her French would have been accented."

Anne slanted a glance at the passing countryside. "If François wed her for political reasons, she must be an enemy of the Holy Roman Emperor or of the King of England."

"I've always admired your quick mind," lauded Péronne.

The Duchess d'Étampes' cheeks glowed with heat from the festering loathing she felt for her unknown rival. "As soon as I learn who she really is, I'll devise a plan to crush her. I'll seek alliances with Emperor Carlos or King Henry."

Péronne was thoroughly shocked. "That would be high treason, sister." She lowered her voice that quivered with fear. "Contacting one of His Majesty's foes is an act of treason, and if you are discovered, you will be condemned to death."

Anne tittered, her head swaying slightly as she urged the beast forward. "King François does not imprison women, and his peers of the realm do not sentence them to death, bowing to his whims and caprices. François is not capable of inhuman cruelty – he is not like the despicable King Henry."

"No, Anne!" Péronne peered at her with consternation. She steered her horse closer to her sister's, and murmured, "No, I beg of you! If you betrayed the king to his enemies, you would be declared a traitor and have to stand trial. You would be reduced to pleading with His Majesty for your life, but he would not pardon you. Do you really want this?"

Her sister had a knack for saying just the right thing, and the duchess shivered as a clench of dread grabbed at her entire being. However, she swiftly pulled herself together and broke into a laugh. "Péronne, I'm not a fool. I'll not act until I have a complete understanding of all the circumstances which led to François' marriage. I'll think everything through."

"Oh my Lord..." Her sister's voice faltered.

"Queen Anne!" spat the former royal paramour, as though this name was a curse of the vilest sort. "She stole François from me, and I shall not forgive her for that."

Anne de Pisseleu spurred on her palfrey and set off at a gallop, leaving Péronne and the others behind. She rode the beast with an air of leadership and refined delicacy. Her cunning mind formed a guileful plan against the new queen.

BETWEEN TWO KINGS

One day, François will be mine again, the Duchess d'Étampes swore to herself, whatever the cost.

December 20, 1537, Castello di Rivoli, Turin, Piedmont
With the advent of dusk, the heavens darkened, as though a gigantic shadow had stretched over the earth.

Sitting in high-backed chairs near the fireplace, the royal couple were enjoying a game of chess. They had battled many times in Venice, both being exceptional players. Now Anne was greatly outnumbered after having lost her queen, several pawns, her bishop, and her knight. In contrast, François had only lost one pawn and one bishop; most of his pieces were untouched and centered around his king.

With a heartwarming concern, François enquired, "How are you feeling today, Anne?"

Her concentration broken, his consort raised her eyes from the board. "I'm fine, Your Majesty." She moved one of her pawns closer to his king. "How was your day?"

He countered with his bishop. "Routine. I had a boring meeting with Monty and Annebault."

She arched a brow, confused. "Monty?"

"Anne de Montmorency. I've called him Monty for as long as I can remember. A man needs a masculine name. Monty has been insistent that I tell him who you are, Anne."

The queen smirked. "They all know that I am in Turin."

Rumors about the queen's arrival in the city spread through the court like fire through dry woods. Courtiers wondered impatiently when she would be presented to them, almost desperate to see the woman who had saved their king's life and driven him from his long-time lover.

Anne spent several days in her quarters, resting after her arduous journey. She was a little more than five months along in her pregnancy and tired easily, so it became her routine to nap each afternoon. François spent a lot of time with his courtiers in the mornings, but he did not neglect his wife and visited her in the afternoons, staying until late into the night.

Moving her pawn, the queen chaffed. "Time erodes human lives and spirits more quickly than it does memories of them. Sometimes, only their names remain."

The monarch laughed, enjoying the queen's wit and verve. "That is why most people will remember Monty by the name his sovereign gave him." A frown marred his forehead. "Monty is still offering to make peace with the emperor."

"Your Majesty does not agree," deduced Anne.

"How can I sign a peace treaty with that half-Flemish, half-Spanish thug with a protruding lip? We are mortal enemies."

"Are you sure that the emperor tried to assassinate you?"

François blew out an exasperated breath. "Absolutely." He changed the direction of their talk. "After Christmas, we will go to Château d'Amboise where I grew up."

"I loved living in the Loire Valley!" Anne exclaimed in the most enthusiastic tones. Then her euphoria was replaced by befuddlement. "But why are we going to France?"

"It would be dangerous for you to stay here. After making one public appearance in front of the army, we will depart for Amboise. I've ordered to have the royal residence prepared for our arrival. I've also invited my sister, Marguerite, and Count Jean de Ponthieu there."

Anne smiled. "It is good that they will be there."

"I've always liked Monsieur Jean. He will be a pleasant companion for us."

"Will the court be at Amboise?"

"No. Although the court is usually where a king resides, this time only the four of us will be present at Amboise. We cannot risk disclosing your identity to the public, but it will not be long before things change in our favor."

"Soon Henry Percy will act. It is high time for Cranmer to talk to King Henry." She referred to the English monarch formally, which helped her keep a distance from the past.

François stared at the chessboard: his king was blocked by her bishop and her two pieces. He moved his free bishop to attack her king. She would not outplay him today: the chess contest would end in a draw. He raised his affectionate scrutiny from the chessboard to look at her.

"I hope the prospect of Cromwell's arrest pleases you."

"He deserves to taste the Tower's hospitality." A glitter of malice worked into her eyes.

"What pleases you pleases me, too."

This surprised her, and the queen permitted herself a smile. They continued playing until the game ended in a draw. He grinned, for his guess about the outcome had been correct.

§§§

As folds of night enveloped the castle, François retired to his chambers. Yet, sleep did not come, and Anne was anything but peaceful. In the grip of a heinous nightmare, the queen tossed and turned until the darkness in her mind, heart, and soul intensified and folded itself about her. This impenetrable gloom was a memento of her captivity in the Tower of London – each night dark, hopeless, and endless.

Her eyes flung open, the breath of mortality on her skin. "No! I'm not dead! I've escaped! No!"

The icy chill of death penetrated her entire being. When would these terrible dreams cease haunting her? Her heart began bleeding heavily again, like a lingering wound, and there was only one person who could aid her to find some peace.

Anne climbed to her feet and slipped into her robe of blue brocade ornamented with floral patterns. A moment later, she stalked out the door in bare feet and disappeared down the hallway, connecting her apartments with her husband's.

The queen gaped at the sleeping guards outside the king's door. "How undisciplined these men are," she muttered.

Anne pushed the door open. Driven by her desire to see François, she crossed the room and stopped near the bed.

After the queen's arrival, the King of France had relocated to new quarters. He slept soundly on a bed canopied with blue and white brocade, embroidered with fleur-de-lis. On a marble bedside table, a lonely candle was flickering, its dim light falling across the monarch's face. The gilded furniture was upholstered in dark blue, and the light from the candle illuminated it poorly. As Anne's gaze rested on the ruler, her whole being was suddenly invigorated, as if the mere sight of him had breathed strength into her. *I'm attracted to François, as any woman would be to a beguiling, magnetic man with an impressive physique,* the queen acknowledged to herself.

The sound of the door opening alarmed her and, as if she could hide there, the queen darted to a nearby wall. She would definitely die of disappointment if the person approaching was one of her spouse's mistresses. As she peered in that direction, a sense of confusion, blended with opaque foreboding, flowed through Anne when an Italian servant, clad in the king's livery, carefully shut the door behind him. The man then tiptoed across the chamber.

Who was the strange and cautious guest? In one sweeping motion, the man tore his blade free, his expression malignant, and fright speared through Anne's ribcage like a second heartbeat. *This servant is another of the emperor's assassins who has come to murder François. This shall not happen. There must be something I can do to save him,* Anne thought frantically, as the man approached the bed.

Despairing, she glanced at the desk. Amidst a profusion of parchments, books, and maps scattered there, she glimpsed a dagger. Desperately, she stole to the desk and snatched it up, her heart pounding. The hilt, encrusted with rubies and diamonds in the shape of a salamander, felt alien in her hand. Taking a fortifying breath, she firmed her grip on the blade.

The villain raised his weapon, poised to strike, and in that instant, Anne scampered across the room and lunged at him like a fury descending. A scream ripped from her throat as her dagger plunged down, pushing the assassin aside a mere moments before his blade plunged towards the king.

"Argh!" The man's howl of pain pierced the stillness and reverberated through the area.

Anne swayed, trying to force herself to move, to grab the villain's weapon in case he could still hurt the ruler. However, there was no need: bedsheets rustled as François bolted upright and leapt for the assassin's throat. Anne's strike had been enough. Gurgling, the man crumpled forward onto the bed. She froze like a fawn in the crosshairs of a crossbow, her gaze fixed on the blade protruding from the criminal's back.

"Anne!" The King of France's scrutiny oscillated between his ashen-faced wife and the sprawled body. "Anne!"

The queen did not respond, her shock as profound as that of a newly knighted warrior who had killed for the first time. Her vision was blurring, as if the corpse were floating past her eyes. Her universe transmuted into a realm of bloodshed, with all the impurity that came with murder. It was right there, in front of her eyes, the blood spreading across the sheets.

Her pale features whitened even further. "He is dead," she uttered in a shaken voice.

Instantly, the monarch was at her side. "It is over, Anne," he soothed as he gathered his wife into his arms. Holding her close, he kissed the top of her head and repeated, "It is over."

The door banged open, and the two guards, who had been asleep outside, rushed inside. They stopped in their tracks as they saw the royal couple and the corpse.

"Your Majesty!" they chorused, both scared.

Turning to them, an irate François growled, "Where have you been when your liege lord was under attack? If Her Majesty had not come, I would now have been dead. What are your names?" The two men murmured something inaudible, and François lost his temper. "You will both pay for your lapse! Wake Cardinal de Tournon and Monsieur Stuart!"

The two men bowed low in obeisance and scurried out.

The king drawled dulcetly, "You have rescued me again, Anne. God's ways are so enigmatic!"

"I've never... killed before," muttered the horror-stricken queen. A shuddering wave passed through her, and she would have collapsed if she were not in his embrace.

François briefly recollected the Battle of Marignano, where he had led his troops himself. It had been his first campaign in 1515, and he still remembered the nasty feeling in his gut afterwards. "It is not easy to take a human life for the first time, but a warrior gets accustomed to death."

She was still barely cognizant of her surroundings. "I had to stop the assassin."

"Anne," he murmured reverently, "I'm yet again in your debt." He asked worriedly, "You and the babe? All is well?"

She sobbed, "Yes."

He wiped a streak of tears tenderly from her cheek. "Do not weep, my queen! You and I are both alive!" As his gaze slanted to the dead servant, a frown creased his brow. "That

Habsburg scum has crossed a line tonight. I'll retaliate in due time, and I'll be merciless. I shall devise some trap for him."

"The emperor must be the perpetrator."

François lifted her chin with a finger, and enthused, "Your valor and courage equal your beauty. You are not only the Knight-King's savior, but also our French goddess Athena."

"I'll become more famous soon." She smiled as he nodded his affirmation.

"Do you realize what time it is? Why did you come to me?"

"It doesn't matter." Her face ablaze with embarrassment, she stepped out of his embrace. Anne would not tell him that she had wanted his company as a cure from her nightmares.

Almost immediately, the queen was again swept into his strong arms, cradled against his chest. His lips were on hers, firm and demanding, and her world receded into his warmth.

Yet, in the next moment, François pulled away from his consort. "You must rest. I'll walk you to your room." As they exited the chamber, he roared, "Guards!"

A commotion escalated in the corridor as more men arrived. Sir Robert Stuart, Seigneur d'Aubigny and captain of the Scots Guard, hollered, "Your Majesty, are you all right?"

Cardinal de Tournon flew into the hallway. "A new regicide attempt!" His steps slowed until he skidded to a halt beside the captain of the royal guard. "You are unscathed, Your Majesty! God save our great king and our brave queen!" He had been informed that Anne had saved the king again.

The monarch passed by them, his arm wrapped around Anne's waist. He threw over his shoulder, "God and my wife be praised! Take away the corpse and search the castle."

"Yes, Your Majesty," said Tournon and Stuart in unison.

The ruler enjoined, "Arrest those two soldiers who allowed that assassin to slip inside my rooms. I'm appalled that there are such incompetent scatterbrains in my guard."

Stuart's head dropped in shame. "As you order, my liege."

As the spouses walked down the hallway towards her quarters, Anne was thankful for the monarch's arms about her, being disoriented from the shock. His countenance was neutral, save tiny movements in his jaw muscles. François feared that there would be another attempt on his life in Italy, so he would accelerate their departure to France. The ruler refused to deliberately place Anne's life in peril; otherwise, he would not be a good king, knight, husband, and father.

CHAPTER 16

French Games

December 15, 1537, Windsor Castle, County of Berkshire, England

"It has been snowing since yesterday," complained Charles Brandon, Duke of Suffolk, speaking either to himself or to the captain of his guard, who rode next to him.

The King of England had arrived at Windsor Castle several days previously. Now the royal court was moving there before Christmastide. Queen Jane had been abandoned at Whitehall Palace with her ladies-in-waiting and Edward Seymour, Earl of Hertford, for the monarch did not wish to see her.

They squinted as snowflakes spun round them in thick flurries, obscuring their sight. Piles of snow were heaped along both sides of the road, shimmering in the bleak afternoon sunlight.

From afar, the huge castle resembled a sprawling stone giant, slumbering like a bear sleeping through the winter. It sat on the highest point of this stretch of the River Thames. They entered the lower ward through the Norman Gates and passed by St George's Chapel on its north side. The gardens, silvered by frost and loftily beautiful, came into view.

At the helm of the long procession were the Duke of Suffolk and his men. They crossed the bridge over the ditch and climbed the motte flanked by the walled bailey. Finally, they stopped near the imposing Round Tower that had been built by King Henry II in the 12th century to replace the original wooden Norman keep. Windsor was a formidable stone fortress and at the same time, an ancient royal palace, but it was not King Henry's favorite abode.

As they dismounted, Charles beckoned to the grooms, "Take our horses to the stables."

Turning his head, Charles Brandon saw a splendid litter draped with cloth of silver. It was drawn by four palfreys adorned with gold-embroidered silver damask. The supercilious Anne Bassett occupied this litter, her cheeks flushed from both the cold and excitement, her eyes shining with a triumphal light. Suffolk scornfully eyed the group that had assembled to welcome this woman, who had come from Whitehall at the monarch's behest.

The royal mistress garnered more influence on the back of the ruler's alienation from Jane Seymour. Therefore, many obsequious courtiers wanted to gain her favor, paying homage in case she became the next Queen of England. At the sight of the Lady Bassett's litter, men bowed to her, while women curtsied, nudging their children to greet her as well.

"This is the lovely Lady Anne Bassett!"

"Welcome to Windsor Castle, Madame!"

"Your beauty makes the court shine, Lady Bassett!"

"I've come to our majestic king at his request!" declared Anne impudently, waving at them. "We are always together!"

Acclamations burst forth with redoubled enthusiasm. "Welcome to court, Lady Bassett!"

As the crowd's cries grew more vociferous, a tide of abhorrence surged through Suffolk, and he averted his scrutiny. While the queen mourned for her hapless son, the royal paramour was hailed like a conquering heroine. Why was the king so hell-bent on hurting his wife?

Next emerged the Duchess of Suffolk's chariot covered with blue velvet embroidered with gold. Catherine Brandon was an attractive girl with hazel-green eyes. Sultry, lovely, and elegant described her accurately, conveying the vivid impact of her full ruby lips, high cheekbones, and a mane of blonde hair, today swept up in a sophisticated up-do. Dressed in an ermine cloak, his wife looked very lovey. *Catherine bewitched me the moment I first saw her,* Charles thought jocundly.

Another sumptuous litter, swathed in silver brocade, followed. It contained the relatives of the ruler's current mistress – her mother, Lady Honor Grenville, Viscountess Lisle, and her sisters, Ladies Philippa and Catherine Bassett. There were three more chariots occupied by Anne's maids.

Charles Brandon fought off the urge to screw up his face in repugnance. This woman had a team of maids to serve her every whim, yet she was just a whore, one who had set herself in the king's path at the behest of her ambitious mother. An eerie sense of foreboding coiled tight in Suffolk's stomach: would history repeat itself a third time? Could Anne Bassett conceivably supplant Jane Seymour on the throne? And what would happen to Queen Jane, then?

The procession stopped near the Round Tower. Suffolk spotted Thomas Seymour, Baron Seymour of Sudeley, who jumped from his saddle and met his gaze.

Thomas walked towards Charles. "Your Grace," he began, bowing.

Charles flourished a bow. "Your lordship, I arrived in London yesterday. I learned that the court is relocating to Windsor Castle, and that is why I'm here now."

Thomas' face darkened. "I returned from France a few days ago and found my sister and Edward in Whitehall—" His voice broke off as anguish gripped him. "Prince Richard..."

"My wife told me everything," Suffolk replied dejectedly. "I'm so sorry. I've been praying for the boy."

Charles and Thomas had both expected to hear stories of bells ringing to honor the Prince of Wales' birth. However, they had been met by the horrible news that Prince Richard had been born deaf and dumb. By now, in spite of Henry's attempts to contain rumors, the whole court knew that Jane Seymour had produced the king's son with defects.

"Thank you, Your Grace; it is noble of you," mumbled Thomas. "My brother and sister informed me that the king had commanded me to set off for Windsor upon my return."

"Lord Suffolk! Lord Sudeley!" a page called as he ran towards them. He bowed to the two aristocrats. "His Majesty demands that you see him immediately."

Sighing deeply, Brandon and Seymour braced themselves against the imminent gale of the Tudor royal temper.

§§§

The Duke of Suffolk and the Baron Seymour of Sudeley entered the keep and were helped out of their winter cloaks by servants. Although a large number of nobles had already arrived at Windsor, it was a despondent place: a solemn stillness, mingled with undertones of dolor and stress, seemed to blanket the castle. They made their way through elegant rooms and corridors; their anxiety peaked as they stopped near the monarch's presence chamber.

The herald announced their presence, and the heavy oak doors opened. They entered and heard the monarch's voice. "I hope you have brought me interesting tidbits."

After official greetings, the visitors neared the elaborately carved throne, behind which the Tudor coat-of-arms was painted on panel and hung on the wall. The arrases portrayed the history of the Tudor dynasty starting from the victory of King Henry VII at Bosworth Field in 1485.

In a black brocade doublet, its sleeves wrought with gold, King Henry looked thinner and pale. His eyes were bloodshot, as if he had not slept for days. His cap with a green plume was of black satin ornamented with emeralds. There was the indelible stamp of grief on his face, and an aura of melancholy about him. The ruler's appearance caught both men by surprise.

Henry concentrated his scrutiny on the Duke of Suffolk. "Give your report, Charles."

Brandon did not meet his liege lord's penetrating gaze, his eyes rooted to the floor. "Your Majesty, while in Turin, I talked to Baron Anne de Montmorency, Marshal of France. I was not allowed to see King François, despite my insistence." He then narrated his meeting with Montmorency and mentioned that the marshal had taken the wedding gifts.

"Did you travel to Venice after Turin?" questioned Henry, a scowl marring his features.

"Yes, I did," confirmed his subject.

Furrowing, the monarch queried, "Did you learn the name of the current Queen of France?"

His sovereign's hard gaze pierced Charles like an arrow. "No, I didn't. Her name is a closely guarded secret, according to Montmorency, to protect the lives of his king and queen."

Henry castigated, "Charles, you are utterly incompetent. I should have ordered a man of talent and skill in such matters to journey to Italy. You shall feel my wrath."

Suffolk responded stiffly, "Whatever Your Majesty puts me through, I'll obey."

The ruler jeered, "It behooves a subject who disappointed their sovereign to show obedience and repentance." His eyes flew to Seymour. "Lord Sudeley, how was your visit to Paris?"

Thomas was afraid to speak in the wake of the reprimand of Charles Brandon. "Sire, I was unable to meet with Queen Marguerite of Navarre for a long time. At first, I was informed that she had left Paris. In a fortnight thereafter, I made my displeasure known to her secretary, who told me that she was extremely busy and could not accept me. Finally, after more than a month of waiting, I was granted an official audience with Her Majesty at the Louvre Palace."

"What did she say to you?" The monarch's impatience was overriding his usual curiosity.

Thomas tensed. "Queen Marguerite deflected all our accusations against Mellin de Saint-Gelais, for she did not see him work on the pamphlets. She stressed that it is not a crime to write poems. Her Majesty cannot arrest a popular poet such as Saint-Gelais in her brother's absence."

King Henry howled with laughter. "I hate these French games! They are all lying foxes! Is François responsible for the mayhem in my country? Or is he is innocent?" He sucked in an irate breath. "Lord Sudeley, it is likely that Marguerite was not busy, but waited for instructions from her brother."

Sudeley's stomach twisted in knots of dread. "Your Majesty... I..."

The monarch glanced around. Induced by this talk of the pamphlets, flashbacks flooded his mind, sending a tremor of anguish and rage through his soul. In this very chamber, in September 1532, he had crowned Anne Boleyn with the gold coronet and placed on her shoulders a crimson velvet mantle, making her the Marquess of Pembroke in her own right.

A sense of nostalgia overcame Henry for a brief moment. *God's blood! That day, Anne was so enchanting in her jewels and ermine-trimmed velvet!*   After the lavish ennoblement ceremony, the monarch and she had journeyed to Calais to meet with the French ruler, his life-long rival François.

The king steeled himself against these painful memories of Anne. Those days were gone for good, and the adulteress was dead. "What do the French think of the harlot's crimes?"

Thomas Seymour blew out a frightened sigh, but his terror did not vanish. In France, most of the courtiers had read the pamphlets in the original language, which carried more nuance than their English translations. Sometimes, Thomas had heard nobles talk about Anne Boleyn's barbaric murder on the Tudor tyrant's orders. To them, King Henry's actions were an amusing, but horrendous, thing to behold from afar.

They say that the tyrant burned Anne, Thomas recalled. *They have no respect to our English Majesty.* Despite his hatred of the Boleyns, Thomas agreed with the French. King Henry had killed his second wife for adultery, while at the same time claiming their union was null and void – that was ridiculous as the ruler could not have it both ways.

Thomas contrived a seemingly plausible explanation. "The French are entirely focused on King François' wedding, and on many assassination attempts on his life."

The monarch climbed to his feet and stalked to the window overlooking the garden, where the snow-laden branches of the trees stood out stark against their black trunks. Nightfall would soon consume the light of day, and for a moment, Henry's mind diverted to his mistress, the Lady Anne Bassett, who would visit his bedroom tonight and take him to a world of carnal bliss. *I am relieved that Jane is not at Windsor, for I cannot bear to even look at her,* the king hissed mentally.

Refocusing on the present, Henry stomped to Thomas and Charles. "Many vassals have displeased me! I've elevated you so much in vain!" He shot the two men pernicious glances. "You will both leave Windsor at dawn and will not return on pain of imprisonment unless I summon you."

Not surprised by this decision in the slightest, Charles and Thomas bowed to their sovereign. Thomas hastily left; Suffolk followed him, but he briefly paused at the doorway.

Charles humbly uttered, "Sire, serving you is my pleasure."

The ruler's temper slipped its leash. "Leave my sight! Or I'll have you sent to the Tower!"

Suffolk's gaze fell on a tapestry showing a victorious Henry VII at Bosworth Field. Sir William Brandon, Charles' father, had served as a standard-bearer to the late king. *Henry the Eighth is his father's opposite,* Brandon observed. Although his liege lord was his best friend, it irritated Suffolk to see how swiftly and randomly people paid a price when the monarch lost his temper. It would be a relief to depart from the Tudor court, despite having been here for less than one day.

"I shall come whenever you need me," professed Charles before bowing again. He then strode out of the room.

§§§

The Duke of Suffolk was escorted to the spacious quarters, where his fourth wife, Lady Catherine Willoughby, was lodged. He found her in the antechamber furnished with silver-brocaded couches, carved ebony chairs and tables.

As Charles settled near the fireplace, his eyes locked with his wife's. "I've been ordered to leave the palace. It is good that we have not unpacked yet."

Not astounded, Catherine Willoughby inferred, "The king is angry with you because you achieved nothing in Italy."

"His Majesty is insanely furious, my Cathy," her husband confirmed. "He is greatly disturbed by the pamphlets and the prince's unfortunate situation that is unlikely to ever change." He clenched his fists and muttered, "Even though she is dead, the Boleyn whore still does not leave us in peace."

She settled in a chair beside him, and he took her hand in his, lacing their fingers. "The pamphlets and the book are causing a terrible outcry among the population."

"Cromwell is doomed. As soon as the king reads the book about Cromwell – and I'm fairly certain he has not yet – he will sign Cromwell's arrest warrant."

His wife hypothesized, "His Majesty might spare Cromwell in gratitude for his steadfast fealty."

Suffolk glanced away to conceal the troubled look in his eyes. "I do not think so. He plotted against Anne Boleyn."

As she clasped her fingers around his wrist, his gaze veered to her. "Was Anne innocent?"

"I do not know." That was a lie, but he could not say anything else.

She sneered. "Cromwell's disgrace makes me euphoric."

"Cromwell destroyed the lives of many people, and I'll rejoice in his death. However, if the king believes that Anne Boleyn was innocent, her children will be reinstated to the line of succession. And if His Majesty has two heirs, then it will be highly unlikely that the Princess Mary will ever be restored to her rightful place; you and I want to see it happen one day."

Catherine spat, "The harlot hated Queen Catherine and Princess Mary. Whether she was guilty or not, she deserved the agonizing death at the stake for all her awful deeds."

Like his deceased spouse, Princess Mary Tudor, Catherine had remained loyal to Catherine of Aragon and loathed the Boleyns. However, Catherine had secretly become interested in new religious ideas, and her husband had no idea about it. *Charles is a Catholic, so he does not need to know,* she mused.

A fire crackled in the hearth, and Charles stared into the flames, tiny fingers of red waving at him. He envisaged Anne's death in the flames. "The whore was a villainess."

Catherine did not know that the Duke of Suffolk had taken part in the coup against Anne Boleyn and the Boleyn faction. In March 1536, Cromwell had sought Suffolk out at a banquet and offered an alliance against the Boleyn strumpet. The two men had worked together to spread rumors about Anne's "misconduct" with many men in her chambers. Pretending to be dutiful subjects, they had both apprised the king of Anne's alleged affairs, as if acting independently.

As a result, an incensed Henry had ordered investigation into Anne's activities, and then Cromwell had falsified the charges against her. Brandon had not known that their plot would result in the deaths of several innocent men and Anne's execution. At first, he had truly believed that Henry would simply annul his marriage to the harlot and would have her ejected from court. After Anne's arrest, part of Charles had hoped that the monarch would send her to a nunnery.

To this day, Suffolk did not know whether he would have conspired with Cromwell if he had foreseen such a ghastly slaughter of innocents. His feelings over this sordid affair were rather conflicted, but he did not regret that Anne and her supporters had fallen from power, for in his eyes, she was a usurper and a seductress. *Despite everything, Princess Mary is still a bastard! Anne's death has not resulted in*

Mary's reinstatement to the line of succession, as many hoped.

"Did you participate in the slut's downfall?" She unclasped their fingers, studying him with her inquisitive eyes.

Charles flicked his gaze to her. "We will never talk of this again, my dearest wife." He shuddered at the thought of what would happen to him if his liege lord learned of Anne's innocence. Would Charles be executed then or not?

"As you wish, husband." Catherine scrutinized his face attentively, her suspicions about his secrets growing.

He managed a smile. "We will spend some time with the children at Westhorpe Hall. After the time at this gloomy court, it will be heaven to come home to them."

December 20, 1537, Windsor Castle, County of Berkshire, England

That night, the snowfall intensified significantly, and the gardens were a white swirling darkness. The cloud coverage was so obstinate that the rising wind could not blow it away.

A thick bank of clouds, which glowed brightly around the edges, passed over, as though a curtain had been drawn aside from a black canvas. A stream of moonlight lanced the darkness of the bedroom and illuminated two entwined lovers on a bed canopied with ochre silk. They were Philippe de Chabot, Admiral de Brion, and Lady Mary FitzRoy née Howard, Duchess of Richmond and Somerset, widow of the king's illegitimate son, Henry FitzRoy, and daughter of the Duke of Norfolk.

"Mary," Chabot whispered as he caressed her bosom. "I'm so happy to be here with you, away from courtiers plotting intrigues and downfalls. I am entirely free now!"

His mistress laughed as he kissed the tip of her nose. "And away from other women," she added, jealousy apparent in her tone. "Tonight, you are mine alone, Philippe."

His fingers played with her hair, creating a wonderful tune in Mary's heart that was infatuated with Admiral de Brion. "I'm faithful to you." The lie came easily to his tongue.

She stiffened in his arms and drew back slightly. "People talk about your and Sir Francis Bryan's escapades."

The Admiral of France feigned shock. "There is no dissipation on my part, and I only play cards with Sir Francis. In contrast to him, I do not like whores." This was mostly true: Bryan was an out-and-out libertine, while Chabot, though a womanizer, was far more selective.

A blissful smile lit up her visage. "Oh, I'm so happy, then!"

All the candles had long burned down to nothing, leaving the room lit by moonlight. The gentle light etched her lovely profile in silver, and Chabot kissed Mary briefly on the lips. He smiled in joy as he swept his hand through her long, golden hair, the thick waves curling around his fingers. As he enveloped her in his arms and placed her head on his shoulder, a sweet fire of remembrance about the beginning of their romance ignited within Mary's memory.

Once the Duke of Norfolk's daughter had been a virgin widow. After Mary Howard's wedding to Henry FitzRoy, King Henry had not wanted his bastard to have children before he could sire a son on Anne Boleyn. Thus, Mary and FitzRoy had lived separately despite being formally married. After the young man's untimely death in the summer of 1536, Mary had regained her freedom. Mary had surrendered her virtue to Philippe de Chabot just two months earlier.

She had first seen Chabot more than a year ago when he had appeared in front of the king to show his credentials as the new French ambassador to England. For months, she had watched him from afar, fascinated by his resplendent air of French gallantry and refinement, which none of the English courtiers possessed. Chabot had the reputation of a notorious philanderer, but Mary had still surreptitiously desired him, although she had not hoped that he would ever notice her.

When, at the end of the summer, Admiral de Brion had invited her to dance, Mary had been overjoyed. Since then he had lavished her with compliments, and they had had many pleasing conversations. Whenever they had encountered each other, he had smiled at Mary and bowed lower to her than he did to others, except for King Henry. Once Chabot had told her that Mary was the epitome of English beauty, allure, and intelligence – a rare flower at the Tudor court.

Her brother – Thomas Howard, Earl of Surrey – had lived at the French court and been part of King François' inner circle. Surrey had described to Mary how the French were different from the English: tremendously extravagant and elegantly passionate, as well as sweetly gallant and naturally inclined to courtly love. Mary saw all these qualities in the ambassador, to whom she was drawn beyond her will.

Flattered by and enamored of the charming Frenchman, Mary viewed Philippe de Chabot as her knight in shining armor, in whose arms she found refuge from her family's plots and her own loneliness. After one month of intensive letters and secret notes passing between them, Mary had been so smitten that she had consented to become his mistress. The inexperienced girl fancied herself in love with him, not caring that he had a family in France.

Mary groaned as he threaded kisses upon the slope of her neck. "Philippe, oh my Lord!"

Her lover leaned up on his elbow and stroked a strand of hair from her face. "How is your family doing?" he inquired, as if asking after their health. Audley and Norfolk were in charge now that Cromwell had fallen from the royal favor, and Chabot was curious to find out what the duke was up to.

"My father was at Mary Stafford's home. My cousin, Anne Boleyn, birthed His Majesty's son during her imprisonment in the Tower. Now the king does not have any legitimate heirs, and my father wants the next King of England to be a Howard. He wished to bring little Arthur to London."

This revelation piqued Chabot's interest. "I wonder whether he will deliver the boy to court, my lark."

Outside the wind howled, and Mary shuddered as if the chill of death had her in its grasp.

I admire my unique cousin, God bless her soul. Mary gave silent tribute to the "dead" Anne Boleyn. *However, I never approved of His Majesty's union with Anne.* As a Catholic, she had considered Henry married to Catherine of Aragon. Like others, she had signed the Oath of Supremacy for form's sake. Yet, Mary respected kinship ties and did not understand how her father could have found it in himself to preside over the fake trials of his niece and nephew. Since Anne and George's arrests, Mary had tried to be distant from Norfolk, who nevertheless controlled her life at the moment.

Philippe characterized the man whom he despised. "The Duke of Norfolk is an exceedingly ambitious man."

Her body strained in his arms like a string on a harp. "He is ready to sacrifice anyone, even his relatives, to accumulate more power." Bitterness was creeping into her voice.

"I'm sorry that you are in this miserable situation, Mary."

She sniffed in disgust. "At first, he planned to marry me off to Thomas Seymour when he thought that Queen Jane would have a son. After Prince Richard's birth, my brother suggested that I drive His Majesty away from the Lady Anne Bassett and become his harlot, hoping for my pregnancy."

"What?" Chabot's voice was tinctured with outrage.

With a sickening lurch in her chest, Mary commented, "I anticipated that my father would endeavor to use me in his games. However, I did not expect to receive such a degrading offer from my brother, Surrey. They are both too eager to taint their honor so as to obtain positions and privileges." She was acutely conscious of a bestial rage building up through her as she grouched, "I would never have slept with any monarch becoming their toy, especially not with Henry Tudor."

The ambassador sympathized with the girl. He could not imagine treating his own offspring so unscrupulously. "No parent should use their children as pawns."

In the shaft of moonlight, she glimpsed the concern in his eyes, and this warmed her heart. "Many fathers act that way. Thomas Boleyn pushed both of his daughters into the king's arms to elevate his status. Then he expelled one daughter after her marriage to a lowborn soldier and abandoned the other together with his only son in order to save his worthless neck. My father is no better than that cold-hearted Boleyn."

"With Cromwell gone, your family is once again at the center of court intrigues."

"The Howards are always scheming something."

Chabot nuzzled her hair affectionately and kissed her nose teasingly, then tangled his fingers into the silky strands. A moan escaped her throat, and her body tingled with lustful sin at his touch. His rich knowledge in intimacy assisted him in beguiling Mary into revealing her family's secrets.

He kissed her soundly and ardently before muttering, "The persistent gossip is that the king will discard Queen Jane." He then introduced the subject that interested him the most. "I've heard courtiers speculate whether His Majesty will launch a new investigation into Anne Boleyn's case."

"Our sovereign's temper is explosive and frightening," she noted, still dizzy from his kisses and caresses. "It would be good if Anne's name could be cleared of the phony charges."

Mary and Chabot exchanged a few comments about Anne's execution. He was astounded that she wanted justice to prevail for her cousin, despite being a Catholic.

She disclosed, "My father is certain that His Majesty will choose Sir Francis Bryan and him as investigators into the allegations in those pamphlets and the book on Cromwell."

Chabot smiled with satisfaction. His paramour often divulged interesting things about their king and the Howards. He did not have any influence over Norfolk, but there was Francis Bryan, and with this new knowledge, he could proceed to the next stage of his master's artful plan.

His arms closed around the girl, pulling her closer to him, and he murmured thickly, "Mary, forget about these trifles. Nothing matters when we are together."

Mary felt as if she were the queen of paradise. She bit her lower lip to stop herself from saying aloud that she loved him and wanted him to reciprocate her affection.

"*Chérie*," breathed Chabot. "You are such a beauty."

Tears misting her eyes, Mary flung her arm around his neck as though she would never let him go. "Philippe, I'll miss you so much when you return to France."

Shame cascaded through the ambassador like the torrent of a rampant sea. *Mary has no idea that I'm toying with her feelings, and that our romance is a carefully orchestrated charade.* In his letter to Chabot, King François had suggested that Admiral de Brion find at the Tudor court a mistress, one who was related to the most powerful English nobles, and use her as his informant. Norfolk's daughter and FitzRoy's widow, Mary had been an ideal candidate.

Philippe de Chabot did enjoy his romance with Mary. She was not a ravishing beauty like Anne de Pisseleu, and she did not possess Anne Boleyn's charisma and magnetism, but she was an attractive, tall, gracious girl, with an air of unblemished purity about her. Her enticing gray-green eyes and her heart-shaped face, framed by her glossy blonde hair, as well as by the gentle curve of her full, lush rosy lips, and the slender angle of her neck, mesmerized him.

The King of France did not approve of his subject's affair with the Lady Mary Howard. According to his spies, her virtue had been intact at the time of FitzRoy's death, so it was clear that Admiral de Brion was her first lover. In spite of his reputation as a philanderer, François had long outgrown a willingness to deflower maids, as he had done in his early youth when he had dallied with Mary Boleyn and others.

Everyone knew what this did to the marital prospects of such former maidens. However, François withheld judging Chabot, viewing their liaison as a useful means of collecting intelligence at the English court, but insisting that it remain a clandestine liaison for Mary's sake.

Shaking himself out of his reverie, Chabot heaved a sigh. "Mary, you knew from the very beginning that I'm married and at some point would return home."

His paramour disentwined herself from his embrace. "Philippe, I blame you for nothing; it was my decision to be with you." Yet, a pang of heartache shot through her chest.

"It is vital for your reputation to hide our relationship."

"Nobody will ever learn about us," she promised.

"Most women are fickle, like feathers in the wind, and fall for different men, then change lovers, but you are not like them." Chabot respected Mary Howard a lot, but he would never love her.   His heart forever belonged to Anne de Pisseleu d'Heilly – his cruel-hearted, smart, and beautiful idol.

Philippe kissed Mary hungrily until she was breathless, exquisite quivers running through her.   Lost in a vortex of wonderful sensations, she experienced celestial rapture in his practiced arms.   His mouth seemed to be everywhere at once, throat, earlobe, breasts, and stomach, and his brazen hands explored every inch of her body.   As he buried himself in her warm flesh, groans and cries filled the air as the lovers moved together until their bodies celebrated a festival of pleasure.

At dawn, Mary donned her robe and hastened back to her rooms, as she always did after their trysts.   A little later, Chabot woke alone, feeling content, and contemplated how being with her was like tasting the sheer innocence of life after experiencing the quintessence of unrestricted debauchery.

§§§

Clad in a brown brocade doublet with black silk slashing, an amethyst brooch clasped to the high collar, Philippe de Chabot sauntered through the castle corridors.

Torches blazed on the walls adorned with Flemish tapestries and carved wooden patterns.   Pausing at the top of the stairs, the ambassador scanned a crowd near the presence chamber.   Today was the first day when the King of England had begun accepting visitors, so many nobles wanted to see him, although the banishments of the Duke of Suffolk and of the Baron Sudeley had discomfited and even terrified them.

Chabot descended the stairs with the confident stride of a mighty lord.   The rich apparel of the assemblage represented the English court's splendor, but he thought that the grandeur of the French extravagant court far surpassed it.

He steered a path through the horde and requested that he have an urgent audience with King Henry; he was quickly permitted entrée.

As the ambassador saw the monarch sitting in the throne, he remarked to himself that he had chosen the right clothes. Henry was dressed entirely in black, reflecting his low spirits.

Chabot approached the throne, bowed to the king, and extracted a parchment from the inner pocket of his doublet.

The diplomat handed the letter, stamped with the Valois royal seal, to the monarch. "Your Majesty, I'm sorry that I was unable to deliver this missive earlier."

Henry's aquamarine eyes darkened in anger as he grabbed the parchment. "Ambassador, is François so busy that it took him many weeks to send his messenger to London?"

The Frenchman was as astounded at the ravages of grief apparent on the royal face as Brandon and Seymour had been. Henry's bloodshot eyes were sunk deep in his head, and he looked as if he could crack apart at any moment.

"These days, my sovereign does not accept any visitors, save his closest entourage. All the correspondence is checked by his most loyal and trusted people, so there might be delays. Everything is done to protect our king and queen."

"Is François still in Piedmont or somewhere else in Italy?"

"Yes, he is in Turin with the French army."

"Do you have any news about the Queen of France?"

Chabot shrugged. "Everything is kept secret."

"That is so odd. Something is happening." Henry broke the Valois seal, unfolded the paper, and skimmed through it.

Our most beloved brother Henry,

Currently, we must be too careful because a powerful lord of many lands has been persistently trying to kill us.

We were forced to establish a strict confidentiality of our life, both in France and everywhere else. We limited the number of people who may be granted access to us. Thus, we could not personally meet with your envoy – the Duke of Suffolk.

Philippe de Chabot, Admiral of France, wrote about the current disaster in England. I'm not sure that the pamphlets about your chief minister were written by some French poet. Maybe another foreign monarch wanted to disturb the peace in your kingdom, issuing works in the name of the respected poet, who is patronized by our beloved sister.

We regret to notify you that at present, we cannot personally look into the matter. After our return to France, we will have a chance to give you a more detailed answer.

Written with the hand of your cousin who is devoted to you. May God Bless you, Henry, and protect your realm!

King François I of France

Henry hurled the parchment to the floor and trampled it with his feet. "Ah, what a conundrum it is!"

This message shrouded everything in a pall of mystery. Henry's best instincts told him that his French counterpart was untrustworthy. Did François want to win more time by hinting that the emperor could be the culprit? Who was plotting against Henry – the King of France, the Holy Roman Emperor, or someone else? And why was Thomas Cromwell being targeted? This conspiracy was like a huge spider's web, which the Tudor monarch struggled to unravel.

"Your liege lord behaves strangely," the monarch ground out. "I wonder whether you really know nothing about these French games. You are a powerful man in France, Chabot."

"My master holds me in high regard," bragged Chabot with a smug grin. "I'm my king's friend and advisor since our boyhood, but in England I'm a mere ambassador."

His vainglorious boastfulness irked Henry. "When will François return to France? When?"

"I can contact my liege and ask him, sire."

The monarch bounced to his feet and sprinted to the desk, ignoring the pain in his leg. He grasped a dagger with a sapphire-encrusted hilt and rushed forward. Diving into the rampageous waters of fury, the ruler brought the weapon to the throat of Chabot, who did not show any terror.

"You lie!" Henry hissed, pressing the dagger to the other man's neck. "François' past duplicity has been detected and abundantly confirmed. He is playing with me!"

With deceptive indifference, Chabot protested, "There is no evidence to accuse my sovereign of this." Deep down, the fierceness of Henry's temper kept him in shocked awe.

An instant later, the king became aware of something in his palm. The irate blackness cleared in his head, and Henry realized that he was holding a knife to the throat of the French ambassador. In the space of heartbeats, he released Chabot, dropped the dagger, and stepped back.

The ruler hollered, "I understand nothing! Your master is a devious miscreant!" His words were so menacing that they sounded as if some beast from hell had been unleashed.

King Henry stormed out, leaving a roomful of shaken and scared courtiers. Whisperings arose, louder and louder.

Philippe de Chabot was virtually swooning with relief. He yearned to leave the court where no one was safe from the wrath of the frightfully volatile English ruler. Everyone had to employ the most subtle craft to survive, and despite his diplomatic protection, Chabot was no exception. It was extraordinarily difficult to navigate perils and pitfalls in these days of Henry's misfortunes, but Chabot was pleased that King François' plan had so far proven effective.

CHAPTER 17

The Mysterious Queen of France

December 25, 1537, Castello di Rivoli, Turin, Piedmont

"There is a plethora of guards here tonight," observed Queen Anne as she scanned the great hall. More than one hundred guests attended the grand Christmas banquet.

Soldiers from the Scots Guard stood vigilant, with drawn swords, along the chamber's perimeter. They also surrounded the high table on the dais where the royals were seated.

King François sipped wine from a jeweled goblet. "The security measures have been toughened significantly. Every guest was thoroughly checked before being granted entrée to the great hall. We are very well guarded, *ma chérie.*"

"It is necessary for Your Majesty's safety."

"And for yours, too," he corrected.

Twilight was falling, and several candelabra were placed along the table's length. Dressed in red damask, the tables were laid with fine cups, goblets, ewers, and finger bowls. Silver and gold platters overflowed with delicious foods, including wild boar, spit-roasted meat, heron, venison, roast tongue, pork, whale meat, roast eels with lampreys, salmon, loin of veal, mutton, and lark's tongue. The Savoy coat-of-arms hung above the fireplace, and portraits of members of this ducal dynasty adorned the walls. From the minstrel's gallery musicians played a collection of French chansons, the strains of music competing with the din of voices and laughter below.

François set his goblet on the table. "I've decided to further restrict the circle of those who can meet us. For some time, it is absolutely necessary for our safety. All the servants were interrogated, but nothing suspicious was discovered."

She stuttered, "So, the assassin I killed... worked... alone."

"It is all right, Anne," he soothed with a smile.

Anne fidgeted with her rings. "I suppose so."

Her husband placed his hand over hers. "Most likely, that thug didn't have accomplices, the same as that man in Venice. Forget about him: he is dead, while we are alive."

After the latest assassination attempt in Turin, everyone was engulfed in a fog of pervasive shock. Yet, tonight many curious eyes were riveted on Queen Anne of France. The impatience of all the courtiers to learn more about the king's savior was so palpable that the air was charged with it.

Much to the guests' chagrin, Anne wore a light green veil fastened to her bejeweled French hood that hid her features. The guests could only appreciate the queen's green velvet gown, fluffed at the pleats of a full over-skirt and ornamented with emeralds and pearls on the front. This gown had a high waist, hiding the queen's pregnancy, although rumors about her condition were already circulating. Diamonds and rubies were woven into her hair with gold thread.

It is entertaining to watch those who observe me, Anne ruminated, *but who cannot see my face.* Most of the courtiers were French and Italian nobles. Five Italian women sat at the table opposite them, looking spectacular in an array of velvet, silk, damask, and satin, with glittering jewelry on their bosoms. Their fashions allowed Anne to appreciate why Italian style, with its elegance and exquisiteness of design, influenced the way people dressed in England and France.

With a gleam of fascination in his amber eyes, François bent his head to his wife. "Anne, you are such a gorgeous creature. They are all charmed by you."

The queen's lips curled in a grin. "Even without seeing my face?"

"Of course! If you were not the Queen of France, all the gentlemen in this room would have attempted to woo you with compliments, gifts, poems, and vows of eternal love. When we come to my court, your brilliance will make it shine much brighter than burning flames of a thousand torches."

She let out a melodic laugh of the old Anne Boleyn. "Your romantic Majesty, you are flattering me, but I like this artistic streak to your complex personality."

François feigned an innocent look. "Exaggeration would be beneath my dignity."

"Frenchmen always lavish adulation on women," retorted Anne, a smile hovering over her lips; she regretted that he could not see it. "Gallantry is in your blood."

He pretended to be displeased, but his gaze glittered with mirth. "Madame, although I'm a Frenchman and a poet, I give compliments only when they are well-deserved."

"Can you prove that?" she challenged teasingly.

"Flattery corrupts both the receiver and the giver, but so far neither of us has been affected."

The queen chortled. As she ran her eyes over the guests once more, she admitted, "Their stares make me feel as though I were a butterfly emerging from a cocoon."

The king jested, "Most butterflies have colorful wings and flutter from tree to tree. Your place is with me because you are my queen." He peered at her on purpose. "Anne, I don't see a butterfly when I look at you.   I see the Goddess Despoina, whose sensuous charm and enigmatic beauty are irresistible." He lifted her hand and brushed it with his lips.

His spouse exuded gaiety. "Oh, no! No Greek mythology today, sire! Now we are in Italy! That is why I cannot be one of the central figures of the Eleusinian Mysteries.   And, please, do not compel me to take part in any religious rites of ancient Greece or Rome, for we are Christians."

"Our talk has amused you a lot," François surmised with a cocksure grin. "Wife, neither you nor I will ever participate in any pagan rites, save those amorous rites which happen under the cover of sweet darkness between husband and wife."

Anne was glad that he did not see her blush under the veil.   Suddenly shy, she glanced away from his look of affection, wondering what it meant.   There was an easy air between them, and she was conscious that being his spouse no longer seemed foreign to her.   Yet, Anne reminded herself – as she had often did lately – that their union was one of politics.

"Your Majesty possesses a good-natured sense of humor," she commended, but in a detached way.

His mouth tightened.   "That is generous of you to say that."

"Do you have any urgent tidbits from England?" quizzed the queen.

"Are you interested in the ailing Prince Richard?"

Having read his thoughts, Anne avouched, "I do not wish ill on an innocent boy, regardless of my attitude to his mother and her role in my problems."

The king's smile communicated that he believed her. "No, I have nothing to share, so we have to wait patiently."

During the next two hours, many courtiers approached the royals, heaping eccentric praises and prodigious blessings on them. The monarch introduced his queen, and her veil, which created an air of mystery, added to her allure.

§§§

Having greeted the royal couple, Anne de Montmorency, Marshal of France, returned to his seat at one of the tables and watched the queen from a distance. Her voice had been pleasant when she had spoken to him in flawless French, without the hint of an accent. Just like others, these were the only things he knew about his liege lord's new spouse.

"It is such an interesting evening," began Montmorency, looking at Claude d'Annebault, who sat next to him. "Her Majesty has exquisite taste in clothing and jewelry."

"The queen looks very breathtaking," effused Annebault, his eyes darting between Anne and Montmorency. "I'm very grateful to her for rescuing our liege lord."

"And so am I, Claude."

"But who is she in reality, Monty?"

"Tournon knows everything." The marshal envied that his sovereign did not trust him, his Monty, with the secret.

"Undoubtedly," Annebault concurred. "They are such a stunning couple attracting attention wherever they go."

"All of the king's mistresses were gorgeous, so the queen is bound to outshine his paramours." Montmorency thought that Diane de Poitiers, his ally, would be displeased. If the queen looked bewitching with her face hidden by the veil, she must be a rare flower of beauty without it.

His companion dipped his head. "I agree, Monty."

Montmorency's gaze slid to Anne's bosom. "Her Majesty's jewelry is too expensive – more sumptuous than Eleanor of Austria's jewels when the Spanish Infanta was our queen."

"What?" Claude d'Annebault shot a disapproving glare at Montmorency. "As Queen of France, she is entitled to wear the most fabulous outfits and jewels."

The marshal jeered, "I wonder whether those things are the Duchess d'Étampes' cast-offs."

Annebault fumed, "Don't you dare say such disrespectful things about Her Majesty! You are simply jealous that our monarch did not ask you to safeguard the queen." Claude respected and adored King François immensely, and, hence, his sovereign's choice of a wife must be right.

Montmorency expressed his attitude to the fashions of the day. "These elaborate gowns and jewels are such incredible lavishness. According to Diogenes, *'Modesty is the color of virtue.'* Wealth impresses, but modesty takes the heart."

"What do you mean, Monty?"

The marshal affirmed, "When François de Valois ascended the throne, his main goal was to usher France into a new era of culture and prosperity. That is why opulence and grandeur were needed. His Majesty achieved that, and now he is focused on maintaining a court which no other can outshine." He heaved a sigh. "Even so, sometimes I fail to understand the king's penchant for extravagance and spectacle. I do have ample wealth, but I'm a man of austere tastes."

"Our court is the most magnificent in Europe," evaluated Claude d'Annebault fairly.

"Claude, you know how much I love our sovereign, despite our different views on politics, luxury, and many other things. But this excessive lavishness is rather foreign to me."

Annebault sincerely believed him. "No doubt you are one of His Majesty's most loyal subjects and friends."

A sigh tumbled from the marshal's lips. "Whatever, but Her mysterious Majesty has unnerved me."

§§§

The musicians began playing a spirited Italian tarantella, and merry laughter fought to rise above the sounds of music and the dancing couples. The appetizing aroma of food and wine was powerful, but not strong enough to overcome the growing odor of human sweat and perfume.

Anne wanted to leave the stuffy chamber. Feeling a tug on her sleeve, she flicked her eyes to her husband. "Your Majesty, how can I serve you?"

François explained, "Anne, we will make a speech, and then retire for the night."

The king's wife nodded, pleased that soon she would play out this role in her marriage. Excitement burgeoned in her.

As the monarch and queen stood up, the hall fell silent. Then servants darted forward to help them dress in long warm capes of rabbit skin and ermine. François led Anne to the exit from the banquet hall, then through many hallways, and onto the front steps near the palace entrance.

From behind her veil, Anne peered out at the huge throng of people, all of them the monarch's men-at-arms, who had assembled to meet the King and Queen of France.

"My beloved subjects," François commenced in a majestic voice that could inspire minds. "You have been long impatient for this moment. And it is God's will that we are here today." He took Anne's hand in his. "I'm happy to introduce to you the Queen of France."

Cries of delight rang out, so loud that they seemed to displace the air.

Startled, Anne was not accustomed to being affectionately received by an audience. It was incredible and fathomless that now these people were *her* subjects, for she was the King of France's wife. For the first time, she was cognizant of the mystique of being a true queen loved by her people.

When she had been Queen of England, the people had loathed her. They had viewed her as a whore and a usurper, the villainess who had cynically driven King Henry away from the good Queen Catherine and the Catholic Vatican. They had despised the woman who had convinced their sovereign to execute those who had refused to sign the Oath of Supremacy. The people had considered Anne, not Henry, guilty for what he had done! Anne had endeavored hard to win their respect, including distributing vast sums in alms during Holy Week and on other occasions, but all of her attempts had been futile.

At present, everything was different, and Anne's face glowed with joy behind her veil. To the French, she was savior of the Knight-King and a living legend because of her feats. Her gown hid her small baby bump well, and she thought that her decision not to draw attention to it was correct.

The monarch raised his hand, calling for silence. As a hush ensued, he attempted to further fan their hatred for the Spaniards. "The criminal who tried to murder me in Venice was caught and executed. As you are all aware, there was another assassination attempt on my life a week earlier, in this castle." Shifting his gaze to Anne, he took her hand and raised it to his lips, then promulgated with pride, "My wife, the Queen of France, has now saved my life *twice*!"

Loud acclamations filled the air, as everyone expressed their devotion to the royal couple. Hailed almost like a saint, Anne was overwhelmed with exultant happiness.

"Our queen saved our king! She is our heroine!"

"Her Majesty is a defender of our lord and master!"

"God bless our great King François and our brave queen!"

"Our queen is as glorious as Jeanne d'Arc was!"

"Long reign to King François and his new queen!"

The ruler smiled at his spouse; their hands were still clasped together, their fingers entwined. Sweeping his gaze over the congregation, he proclaimed, "Our queen is a heroine of France and my savior from God! Her courage will lead France to our victory over Spain!"

Their liege lord's ebullient speech caused the soldiers to welcome the queen once more.

"For the queen!" the king's subjects chorused.

Raising his hand for silence, the monarch declared, "The sworn enemy of our great country – Carlos the Fifth, Holy Roman Emperor – might be implicated in these crimes. I must hope he is not responsible, but I cannot count on his integrity. Is a man of honor capable of sanctioning regicide?" A thunderous rumble was his men's answer. "Rest assured, my beloved subjects, that we will discover the truth. And when we do, we will act upon it, to the honor of France!"

This announcement produced a wild roar of vehement outrage, which reverberated through the cold air. Everyone was seething with abject loathing for the emperor.

Glowing with purpose, François and Anne descended the stairs, followed by the captain of the Scots Guard and ten men, all of them armed to the teeth. The French subjects all bowed to the royal couple in deep respect. The throng parted to make way for them, and they strutted forward and, finally, stopped, surrounded by the French men-at-arms from all sides.

The king, still holding his wife's hand, squeezed it as if he never wanted to let it go. "To confront the Imperial forces and win, we must be courageous, indomitable, and united against the emperor. We must have deep faith in the Lord." François stilled for a fraction of a second. "I ask you, my comrades, can we prove to our foes that France is mighty and strong, and that the Spaniards cannot defeat us? Can we defend the honor of our nation? God and truth are on our side!"

A sonorous roar of agreement echoed in the air like a song of belligerent spirit.

In these moments, Anne was impressed by the profound devotion of the French subjects to their sovereign. All the men beheld their ruler in reverent adoration, and so did she.

King François lifted his right hand. As everything quieted down, he affirmed, "We, the French, shall never allow the Spaniards, or anyone else, to undermine the power of our great country. We won the Hundred Years' War against the English invaders, having become totally united under the rule of my Valois ancestors. We can emerge triumphant from any war! We will not give the Spanish any chance to trample our magnificent historical heritage and our national pride. With every crisis, we have been learning to be more united, so let's keep on going in this direction, pushing ahead. The glory of France is in the valiant and intrepid spirit of our people!"

His speech was greeted by a burst of cheers. The ruler's plan was working like a spell.

"Long live King François and his queen!" boomed the soldiers.

The monarch tightened the grip on his spouse's hand, signaling that it was time to leave. The crowd parted to let them through, and they sauntered back to the castle's steps.

§§§

"That was quite impressive," declared Montmorency while observing the king and queen enter the palace. "I'm intrigued by Queen Anne, and I'd love to glimpse her face."

His gaze following the royals, Annebault hypothesized, "Perhaps Her Majesty can be a noblewoman from the German Protestant states. It would help our Protestant alliance, then."

Montmorency had a different opinion. "I do not think so. She is either French or Italian, or someone else."

In the next moment, Cardinal de Tournon approached them from behind. "My lords, you will learn everything in due time. I assure you that Her Majesty is a remarkable woman."

§§§

In the great hall, the royal couple were greeted by bows, smiles, and the whisperings of many courtiers. Knowing that his wife was tired, François bid everyone good night, and they headed to their quarters. Indeed, a depleted Anne was awash with relief that the day was finally over.

When safely inside her bedroom, François removed the veil from Anne's face. It occurred to him that her beauty had become eminently vibrant and fresh, like a snowdrop that had just burst into bloom in all its otherworldly delicacy. That could be due to her pregnancy, but he hoped that she had begun forgetting the afflictions that had beset her in England.

The king eyed his queen as he walked Anne to her bed.

"Anne, you must be tired." François planted a kiss on her forehead. "Do you want to retire to bed now?"

"Yes, I do." She was touched by her husband's concern. "Indeed, I would prefer to do so."

His eyes sparkled. "Anne, that was brilliant."

There was a mirthful chuckle from her. "Your Majesty has inspired them, just as most people who talk to you feel."

He amended, "They have been inspired and impressed by *us*, wife. Now it is not only my kingdom – it is *our* realm."

Anne flashed the cold smile that the Valois ruler had seen on her face many times. What was left of the old Anne Boleyn was battered, and her heart was too scarred like a mutilated corpse. But she was not dead, and at this moment, she could feel alive again, as a thrill of intense exhilaration bubbled up inside her. Nonetheless, François and Anne had *a political marriage*, and that gave her thoughts a mental shake.

"Your Majesty, I'm happy to assist you and fulfil my part of our bargain."

He feigned a smile. "Thank you, my darling."

François winced inwardly at the coolness emanating from his wife. His mind was churning with questions. Would Anne ever forget Henry and move past her obsession with revenge? Or were they doomed to live in a sham of a marriage until their dying days? A cloud of puzzlement swirled inside him. Why did the ruler's very soul hurt at the thought that his consort was still possibly pining after her almost-murderer?

The beginning of January 1538, Piedmont, on the way to France

Two days after Christmas, the French royal couple departed Piedmont, bound for France. They were escorted by the Scots Guard and, in addition, by over three hundred of the best guards from Turin. As Anne was faring well, they stopped several times in Savoy, Provence, Languedoc, Auvergne, and Guyenne to make an appearance before their subjects.

Her face covered with a veil, Anne always stayed at the monarch's side. While François spoke, they were surrounded by crowds, who greeted them cordially and condemned the emperor for his sins. The commoners were thrilled to see their king and new queen together, standing hand-in-hand beside them. Anne's far-famed heroism in Venice and Turin proved that if the queen could save the king, then the united French nation could crush the emperor and any invader.

Queen Anne both needed and yearned to be adored by the people, anticipating that most of the French aristocrats would have a lukewarm attitude to her. *The more the commoners love me, the stronger my position in France will be, and the more difficult it will be for anyone to bring me down,* she speculated. Anne strove to highlight her strength, boldness, and bravery, as she assisted her royal husband in his quest to inspire and unite his subjects against the Spaniards.

Understanding why his wife acted so, François admired her pragmatism and confidence, and he was pleased that his people adored her. He knew that in England, her behavior had often been emotional, but it was impossible to envisage Queen Anne of France, who was an epitome of reticence and detachment, throwing tantrums and fits. *We are working together as excellent allies, although each is simultaneously pursuing our own missions,* pondered François.

Once they stopped for the night at an estate owned by a French courtier absent in Paris, and, hence, nobody could see Anne without her veil, so she could not be recognized. As they readied for bed, the spouses chatted about the arts for some time, and then the conversation flowed to a serious topic.

François assessed, "Our tour of the provinces has been successful. We will continue developing your image as the queen who saved her king, and who is close to her subjects."

"Certainly, we will do as Your Majesty wishes."

A glimmer of an exhilarated smile pulled at the corners of his mouth. "You are a capable and clever woman, Anne. Is there anything you cannot make a man do?"

Anne quipped sardonically, "Sire, I'll let you know if I find something I cannot accomplish."

He internally flinched at the chill in her tone. "Of course."

This was typical of their interactions these days. During their journey to Amboise, Anne had become too reserved, her heart more closed than it had been in Turin. Only when they talked to the people, did a rosy bloom appear on her cheeks. Only in such moments would her dark eyes sparkle gaily, and a radiant smile warm her countenance. The ruler tried to write it off as circumstance: Anne was tired, and, sometimes, it seemed as though all of her energy had ebbed away.

Nevertheless, after watching his consort for days, François deduced that she had erected an emotional barrier between them. Clearly, Anne defended herself from the hurt he could cause her, for she was afraid of his power. Her entanglement with two monarchs terrified her beyond measure. *I wish Anne could see the man behind my crown. My wife would learn, then, that she has nothing to fear from me*, François mused.

Watching his spouse settle herself on the edge of the bed with a canopy of green silk, François commented, "Anne, your own thoughts are your main enemies." She frowned, and he quoted, "Heraclitus said that *'No man ever steps in the same river twice, for it is not the same river, and he is not the same man.'* Your English life is over, for better or for worse."

His hint was obvious: François was not Henry. Her gaze glued to the fresco depicting the ancient Greek Moirai, or the Fates, Anne declared ruefully, "According to Plato, *'For a man to conquer himself is the first and noblest of all victories.'* Maybe I am not capable of such achievements."

"Our destiny is in God's hands, but it is also related to your character, Anne. You are not a martyr by nature."

The King of France hurried out of the bedroom. How long would François have to watch the iciness of her demeanor every time he glanced her way? Queen Anne had pledged to devote her life to a quest for her vengeance upon King Henry, which was woven into her very existence.

The ruler didn't see his wife's eyes overflowing with guilt mingled with terror. Yet, Anne swiftly schooled features into blandness as her maids came to help her prepare for the night.

January 10, 1538, Palace of Whitehall, London, England

After the court had left for Windsor, Queen Jane kept to her bed, wallowing in heartbreak over her son's tragedy. Due to her daughter's troubles, Lady Margery Seymour had not returned to Wulfhall. Inside the palace, all the corridors and rooms were deserted, and the usual bustle had been replaced by a plaintive stillness of unspeakable thoughts, palpable and merciless.

Shortly after sunrise, the Seymours assembled in the queen's suite. Once her ladies-in-waiting were dismissed, the family settled themselves in matching mahogany chairs.

"We are treading in dangerous waters," began Edward Seymour, running his eyes over his mother and his siblings. "King Henry will not return to Whitehall until the end of winter." His gaze slid to the queen. "Jane, His Majesty cannot even bear to look at us and you. That is awful for us!"

Queen Jane dropped her gaze to her embroidery. Her mind detoured to her meeting with King Henry before his departure, the only one since the birth of Prince Richard. With a look of antagonistic aloofness, Henry had wished her a speedy recovery. This was more painful than if he had taken his anger out on her. Jane had beseeched Henry to permit her to visit their son in Gloucester, but he had prohibited her from ever mentioning the infant again and then stormed out.

Many physicians had examined the infant and said that the boy's condition was permanent. Thus, Prince Richard had been barred from the succession upon the king's orders.

Lost in thought, Jane did not listen. *I do love my son despite everything, but the king hates him. How can Henry be so cruel to me and our poor child? Does he not understand that my heart is broken?* Jane's musings weighed her down like stones, and her whole existence was a tottering edifice that could collapse under the rubble of her queenship.

Thomas' voice snapped Jane out of her mental trance. "Things may yet turn worse."

Margery claimed, "Strong families have a sense of loyalty and devotion towards family members. And we ought to be strong and loyal, so we must stick together."

The queen nodded at her mother. "Yes, my lady mother."

Edward, Thomas, and Elizabeth tittered in a peculiarly revolting way. In response, Jane sighed dolefully, while her mother frowned at her other children.

"We must act instead of talking," grumbled Edward.

Elizabeth, Gregory Cromwell's wife and Lady Cromwell, concurred, "Only some miracle of a plan can save us." Her eyes bore into the queen as she upbraided, "Jane, the king abandoned you and has made it clear to everyone that he prefers to be with the Lady Anne Bassett."

Jane's heart sank to her stomach. Henry's current callous behavior was incongruent with the image of the kind, just, and benevolent monarch she had fallen in love with. However, she uttered, "It was His Majesty's decision to move his court to Windsor, and it is his right to take a mistress."

Edward presumed, "The king might declare the whore's daughter and, perhaps, her son legitimate."

The Seymours nodded in unison, and Elizabeth whined, "Sister, your request that the harlot's daughter be brought back to court to attend Prince Richard's christening was foolish. This girl is dangerous for us and our power."

A frown formed on Jane's forehead. "Little Elizabeth was in exile for more than a year. Is that not enough?"

"She is Anne Boleyn's child," barked Edward.

"A child is free of its mother's sins, and the Lady Elizabeth is an innocent soul." A spasm of torment crossed the queen's face. "Look what happened to my hapless son. Maybe it is my punishment for the whore's unfair death."

Their mother tipped her head. "Innocents should not suffer for the deeds of others."

Margery's troubled thoughts were on the queen. *My poor Jane is no longer my bonny girl, who once dreamed of having a happy family while we lived at Wulfhall. If only King Henry had never set his eyes on her... Thanks to him raising them up, Edward, Thomas, and Elizabeth have all become hawks, and now they crave only power and wealth.* It was as if a nightmare had come into her life and would not pass, and now Margery felt like a stranger to her own family.

Her face tightened, and for a moment, Margery looked ferocious. That Henry Tudor! He was the ultimate cause of her daughter's misery. Only God knew how it would all end for Jane. To treat the warm-hearted Jane so terribly, to break her heart, to shame her by abandoning her in grief, to take away her baby, to destroy her zeal for life... Margery's ardent desire was to cut his beastly heart into little ribbons.

Edward scowled. "Mother and Jane, it is ridiculous to behave like nuns. Sainthood is acceptable only in saints."

"Don't speak to us so rudely," remonstrated Margery.

Thomas muttered, "Mother, we are sorry if we displease you, but if we are to survive, then we need to be canny and use every trick to vanquish our enemies." Nonetheless, in the next moment, he reproached further in a harsh tone, "Jane, your behavior undermines our already weak position at court."

The grief over her son's fate was lodged in the queen's soul. Why were they pressuring her so hard? "I know that." Her voice was subdued, her gaze downcast.

Edward voiced his concerns. "Now that His Majesty does not have any heirs, I repeat that the Lady Mary or the Lady Elizabeth, or even both, might be restored to the succession."

Thomas stiffened. "There is also Cromwell's disturbing situation." His gaze flew to their other sister. "What is that man doing now? Is he plotting to return to court?"

As Gregory's wife, Elizabeth knew more of her father-in-law's affairs than any of the others. "Cromwell is confined to his house and rarely leaves it after dusk. Demonstrations take place in front of his home almost on a daily basis. As you are all aware, my husband is not welcome at court, so he is now with his father at Austin Friars."

"Cromwell's execution is inevitable," asserted Edward.

Elizabeth glowered at Jane with a silent condemnation so fierce that Jane's skin prickled. Jumping to her feet and stomping over to the queen's chair, she tore the embroidery from her sister's hands and threw it away. "Jane, how can you be sewing when everything we have worked for is in jeopardy? What will become of us if the king annuls his union with you?"

"Mind your manners, Elizabeth!" Margery berated.

Elizabeth snorted. "Oh, please... Jane's conduct is idiotic, and it can harm our family." She earned her mother's glare.

Jane lowered her gaze, her hands trembling. "The king will not set me aside because he loves me."

Margery shook her head dejectedly. "Does he, Jane?"

As the queen sniffled, Margery regretted her words. It pained her that Jane would never truly be loved by her husband. Henry Tudor loved only himself and his throne. At the thought that they would never hear Prince Richard's happy giggles, her throat closed with a spasm of emotion. *Was my poor grandchild punished for King Henry's ruthless treatment of Anne Boleyn? Was she guilty or innocent?*

Edward sneered. "It is apparent that His Majesty takes mistresses who remind him of the harlot. You only have to look at them. They all have dark hair, sharp tongue, and that haughty tilt to their head. He has not forgotten Anne Boleyn!" Anger and fear warred in him; ire prevailed. "If he believes that the Boleyn slut was innocent, it might be our undoing. He has a healthy son with the whore, and he might legitimize the boy." Edward began pacing the chamber back and forth.

"So, the Lady Anne's son was fathered by the king," inferred Margery. "I did not believe it at first... Oh my Lord..." As this surely meant Anne's innocence, she crossed herself, causing her offspring to stare at her in befuddlement. It seemed that little Richard was doomed because of his father's sins.

"The harlot's child is a bastard," Jane countered.

Elizabeth returned to her chair. She hurriedly put in, "It is entirely within His Majesty's discretion to legitimize and bastardize. He has absolute power in England."

"We must do something so that you rejoin the court and sleep with the king to get pregnant again." Edward stopped beside Jane's chair.

"You must," Thomas and Elizabeth echoed together, their voices as hard as granite.

It was a daunting and virtually impossible task, and Jane lamented, "We cannot just appear in Windsor, for His Majesty commanded me to stay at Whitehall."

Edward promised, "I'll think of how to arrange it."

"Our meek Jane cannot be a temptress," interjected their mother, shaking her head. But no one paid her any heed, except for the queen, who smiled at her gratefully.

As the queen's mind drifted back to her son, her visage lit up with a smile. "My dream is to see my baby boy again. I hope His Majesty will let me meet with Richard in due time."

Elizabeth shot Jane a disgruntled look. "Sister, are you out of your mind?"

Edward stalked towards the queen and loomed over her. "Jane, forget about your son."

"Richard is my flesh and blood." Tears welled up in Jane's eyes. "I carried him in my body and almost lost my life in childbirth. How can you not see my love for him?"

"Ha!" thundered Thomas. "His Majesty named your child Richard because he viciously compared the disabled infant with Richard the Third. Don't you understand what it means? That perfectly shows the king's true attitude towards him."

Jane blustered, "I hate that my dear son was named in honor of that monster and usurper! I hate that he was taken away from me, and that I can do nothing to help him."

"Good Lord! Jane, stop!" Elizabeth rumbled. "Are you a fool?"

"Please, don't quarrel!" entreated Margery.

Edward Seymour grabbed the queen's shoulders, forcing her to stand up. He shook her so violently that her head flopped to one side. He then vented his spleen by slapping her hard across the cheek, as if that could annihilate the crippling power of her anguished emotions. He had to compel Jane to shift her attention to the urgent problem confronting them.

Jane gasped as he punched her again. "Edward..."

"Release her, Edward!" commanded Margery as she stood up from her chair and rushed to them.

Edward shook her once more before bellowing, "You shall do whatever it takes you to give the king a new child! Prince Richard does not exist!" At last, he stepped back from her.

In the next instant, Margery was next to her eldest son. Furious with the entire situation, she struck Edward across the cheek. "You ambitious, arrogant beast!"

A perplexed Edward blinked, while his siblings gasped in surprise. None of them had ever imagined that the gentle Margery Seymour was capable of violence.

Edward did not look ashamed. "I've done nothing wrong." He rubbed his check where his mother's slap had left a hand-shaped red mark.

Margery uttered, "Son, you need a lesson on principles. If you continue behaving in such a manner, I might bequeath all my wealth to the Crown. Do you want this to happen?"

There was such a deadly serious threat in Margery's warning that Edward's fists clenched impotently. "I'm not a fool, Mother." But he would not let any woman behave so.

"Good," said Margery, satisfied. Thomas and Elizabeth watched the scene in grim silence.

In a voice fraught with disdain and righteous indignation, Jane countered, "This is the last time you treat me terribly, Edward. A queen's life and body are sacred! And I'm the Queen of England, at least for now." She tumbled into her chair; tears spilled over and dribbled down her cheeks.

Now Edward was rather unsettled by his sister's rebellion. "Jane, you were on the verge of a breakdown, and I had to redirect your attention to our main mission of salvation."

Margery remained nearby in case one of them tried to hurt Jane again. "That does not justify you, son. It is within the law for a man to beat his wife regularly, but your father taught you that being aggressive towards a woman is not the right thing to do." She was dismayed to hear Thomas and Edward snigger, but Elizabeth nodded her agreement.

Thomas defended his brother. "Edward had no choice: he had to bring Jane back to her senses." He turned to the queen. "Jane, you have to think only about our current priorities and purposes. You must save yourself and your entire family. Otherwise, you will bring us all to ruin."

Edward eased himself into his chair. "Jane, we will ensure that you will soon go to Windsor Castle. You will do whatever is necessary to captivate His Majesty again. Your fate is to endure all hardships with dignity and to bear healthy sons for England." His upper lip curled in a sneer. "You became a queen because we, not you, arranged your royal marriage."

Jane inhaled sharply. "I'll never forget that I replaced a woman unjustly condemned."

Margery approached Jane, and put her arm around her daughter's shoulders. She sighed at the confirmation of the murdered queen's innocence. They had known the truth and weaved plots, while she had been misinformed. What else did Margery not know about her offspring?

A wave of anger swept over Elizabeth. "Stop this madness, Jane. The harlot had many foes and also alienated her former friends – her destiny was to die at the pyre."

Edward's expression twisted into a grimace of irate disgust. "Sister, the harlot is out of the way. However, her children are a threat to us, especially her son."

"Exactly," interjected Thomas.

Jane tipped her head hesitantly. She labored to persuade herself that her siblings were right. Even if the charges against the whore were all false, Anne Boleyn had never been a saint: she had pushed the king to break from Rome and destroyed Catherine of Aragon. By doing so, Anne had doomed her soul to the netherworld. Moreover, Jane loved

King Henry, while the Boleyn slut had lusted after the crown. *Maybe all I need to do is to conceive again*, Jane tried to console herself.

"Unlike Anne, you are alive, Jane," Elizabeth stressed.

Edward's features softened a notch. "The king is not going to condone your failure, and his anger with you will not abate soon. You must put your family's interests above all things."

Thomas snarled, "Anne Bassett is a real rival, damn her."

Elizabeth voiced the fear that haunted the Seymours day and night. "Pray that the Bassett prostitute does not fall pregnant. I'm certain that she is trying to convince the king she is able to bear his sons, and if that slattern succeeds, the consequences will be horrendous for us."

The queen assented, "I'll do whatever you want to return to my spouse's good graces." Her knees wobbled, and she would have fallen if her mother was not quick enough to support her. "Yet, now I can barely stand the sight of you. I want you all out! Leave me with our Mother!"

Edward bristled. "Jane, my weak sister, a queen must not look more pathetic than a sulking wench."

"Shut up, Edward!" shouted Margery, her usually quiet temper flaring again. "Get out and don't come back!"

The Seymours stood up. Edward and Thomas bowed, Elizabeth curtsied, and they exited.

"I do not recognize my own children," lamented Margery as she walked the queen to the royal bed. "God above, how could Edward turn out to be such a beast?"

Fresh tears clouded Jane's eyes. "Edward, Thomas, and Elizabeth have hungered for power since our arrival at court. But after my failure to birth a healthy son, their sense of safety has dwindled in equal measure. At present, they see their very way of life under threat, which makes them frightened."

Her mother hugged her close, just as she had often done in childhood. "I wish you had never left Wulfhall."

Jane extricated herself from Margery's embrace. "I'm beginning to think that my life was cursed the very minute I married the king. But don't tell anyone that, Mother."

"I will not, Jane." Reaching out, Margery brushed away the tears from her cheek.

"Please, invite Dorothy to court. She is not like them."

Margery gave a nod. Lady Dorothy Smith née Seymour, her youngest child, lived in Essex with her husband. As Dorothy had never been involved in any of the scheming of the other three, her presence at court would be like a breath of fresh air. Maybe if her other daughter joined the queen's household, they would be able to wage a quiet battle against their relatives' wickedness. *My dear Jane needs the support of those who truly love her,* Margery decided.

Queen Jane peeled off her green brocade over-garment and dropped it to the floor. Garbed in a white silk nightgown fringed with exquisitely wrought black lace, she fell onto the pillows and dissolved into tears, as a Tartarean depression shrouded her like a sanguinary fog. Margery stayed by her daughter's side and eventually calmed her.

CHAPTER 18

The Last Confession

January 14, 1538, Hunsdon House, Hunsdon, Hertfordshire

Saddened by the sullen environment at court, Lady Mary Tudor had retired to Hunsdon House, her favorite residence. Tonight, Mary and the Imperial ambassador Eustace Chapuys were dining in her private chambers, furnished with Flemish wall hangings and a fine walnut table positioned upon a dais. A decanter of red wine and two silver goblets stood on the table that was served modestly with roasted venison, chicken, mutton, and some fruit on silver platters.

"Your Highness, how fares the latest queen?" asked Chapuys as he sipped some wine.

Staring at her guest across the richly tapestried table, Mary responded, "Her heart is broken as the king distanced himself from her, and nothing can brighten her days."

The diplomat empathized with Jane's afflictions, but he also saw a positive implication of the infant prince's disability. "I'm sorry that your half-brother is not normal. At the same time, in the absence of legitimate heirs, His Majesty is likely to reinstate you to the succession."

Appalled, she slammed her goblet on the table. "I love my siblings, both Elizabeth and Richard. I would have died a thousand deaths if it could have made my brother healthy. And you dare speak about such unholy things!"

Chapuys regretted verbalizing his thoughts. "Please, forgive my bluntness. I know you have a heart of gold and a real concern for people in unfortunate circumstances."

She smiled at the ambassador, whom she deeply respected for his unwavering loyalty to her mother, Catherine of Aragon, and to herself. "Thank you, Your Excellency."

"You are welcome, Your Highness."

Mary brought a goblet to her lips and took a long swallow of wine. "The child was supposed to bring stability and prosperity to England, not grief and trouble."

"Queen Jane is still young and will bear more children."

She averred grimly, "Now everything is so unstable and unpredictable at court."

"Your Highness, what do you think of Master Cromwell's predicament?"

As a wildfire of rage burst through her, Mary balled her hands into fists. "Cromwell and his cronies are heretics, who are responsible for the country's break from Rome. They must all be burned like the harlot, and only this will purge the pagan wickedness from England."

"That would be the least of what that heretic deserves."

A murderous wrath welled up inside her, and she hissed, "Two French poets dare claim that the whore was innocent, even though she stood trial and was condemned to death."

Eustace Chapuys was fully aware that Thomas Cromwell had obliterated the concubine and diminished the rest of the Boleyn faction beyond hope of recovery. Moreover, *his own plot* with Lady Worcester against Anne had precipitated her downfall. *Princess Mary does not need to know the truth.*

"Of course, the concubine is guilty of her heinous crimes. She was capable of any villainy. It is a mystery why King François permits his poets to issue such works."

She was astounded beyond measure. "But why does he want to wreak havoc in England?"

The ambassador shrugged. "I do not have an answer."

"Maybe he is merely making mischief?"

Chapuys dived into politics. "To be successful, a monarch must deploy cunning and guile whenever necessary to achieve strategic objectives and aspirations. Kings profess love for their foreign rivals, but underneath the pleasant surface presented to the world, there is a lethal battle fought between them for power in Christendom and for territories."

"In reality, many rulers are adversaries," surmised Mary as she emptied her goblet.

"Indeed, Your Highness. Take King François and Emperor Carlos, two sworn foes." His lips thinned in a harsh scoff. "François was prone to making impulsive and rash decisions in his youth. However, the defeat at Pavia changed him, and now he is acting like the emperor."

Her brows shot up. "Like my cousin?"

"Yes. The youthful François liked showing off France's wealth and boasted of French culture being superior to that of all other nations. He has always been extravagant, but over time, he has become cautious and calculating. Dealing with him now is equivalent to opening Pandora's box: the outcome is unpredictable, and the consequences might be disastrous."

Mary speculated, "Maybe the King of France needs to bring Cromwell down because he supports an Anglo-Imperial alliance. Perhaps his motive is in creating tension in England to prevent our alliance with the Holy Roman Empire." After a pensive pause, she quizzed, "Your

Excellency, did my father mention an alliance with the emperor?"

"King Henry does not want to hear about it."

"He does not wish to be obliged to support an ally," she inferred.

"Your Highness, His Majesty frequently negotiates with the opposite side. If he signs a treaty, he might very well break it and switch sides later. In most cases, he prefers neutrality for the reason you mentioned. Now the king will observe and then act against either King François or Emperor Carlos. This is the best course of action for England because we cannot say with certainty that the pamphlets and the book were written by the French poets."

Mary blinked in confusion. "Why cannot we prove that?"

"The King of France wrote to your father, denying that the poets created the works against Cromwell. He suspects that a lord of some foreign lands has been trying to destroy the peace in England and could have used the poets' names because of their connection with the Valois court." The ambassador's spy had apprised him of the letter's content.

She blanched. "He hinted at the emperor, didn't he?"

Chapuys chuckled. "If it is a French plot, is it not a perfect underhand tactic?" As she nodded, he went on. "If François is set on destroying Cromwell, his best option is to shift the blame onto the emperor. The recent assassination attempts on his life are widely known in Christendom, which helps François play his devious game, if he is playing."

"The logic is that if Emperor Carlos attempted regicide at least once, then he is capable of committing any dastardly deed." Mary thought how François had managed to make the emperor appear guilty if he denied any involvement, and equally if he admitted it. This clever piece of misinformation placed her father between the devil and the deep blue sea.

The ambassador flashed a smile. With her intelligence and kindness, Mary would have been a great queen if King Henry had never met Anne Boleyn. "Exactly. François could have alluded to the emperor in his letter if his goal is to blacken your cousin's reputation. And if he wants Cromwell dead, he must have a serious reason to take such a gamble."

She finished a morsel of venison. "If King François is the architect of Cromwell's fall, he is a big liar and schemer." Like her deceased mother, she disliked France and the French.

"Your Highness, all monarchs are hypocrites on occasion."

"Indeed," acquiesced Mary, thinking of her father.

"In my opinion, Cardinal de Tournon wrote this missive. He is a competent and sly French diplomat with a brilliant mind for both strategy and tactics. His style is to reject or renounce something in order to create uncertainty, and then to launch an unexpected, deadly attack."

"Interesting." She poured some water for herself, for she had enough wine for the night.

Chapuys refilled his goblet and gulped wine like water. "French ministers are simultaneously wolves and foxes. As far as I'm aware, King François usually plots with Cardinal de Tournon. Claude d'Annebault, Anne de Montmorency, and Philippe de Chabot also have a propensity for scheming."

"The King of France has quite many mysteries, and one of them is his new queen."

The diplomat rubbed his cheek. "You know the official reason for secrecy around his new marriage."

Despite her inner turmoil, an animated smile graced Mary's features. "Well, King François is quite an eccentric man, like all the French are. Eccentricity has always abounded when and where strength of a person or a kingdom has increased. And France is now stronger than years ago."

The ambassador released a sigh. "Yes, my lady."

The rest of the meal continued in a lighthearted vein, laced with casual and merry laughter. All earlier traces of sadness gone, Mary laughed like a carefree girl for the first time in many months, and her face lit up with a burst of gaiety. No further matters of importance were touched upon.

January 16, 1538, Whitehall Palace, London, England

"Orange is the color of the sun," spoke Henry Percy, Earl of Northumberland. He drained a wine cup in a single gulp and refilled it. "Yet, I hate it." He emptied the goblet again.

"And so do I," concurred Thomas Cranmer, Archbishop of Canterbury. "This color elicits strong emotion. My heartache is so tangible that it hangs in the air like fog."

The two men sat a table laden with religious books such as 'The Ninety-Five Theses' and 'Small Catechism' by Martin Luther, as well as 'The Institutes of the Christian Religion' by John Calvin. With the king's permission, Henry Percy had gone to his estates before Christmastide; yesterday, he had returned to London to meet with the archbishop.

An iron chandelier with two rings of candles illuminated the earl's quarters. The yellow and orange brocade that swathed the walls usually created an ambiance of sunshine and cheer, but today, the flames dancing in the hearth and flickering in the chandelier transformed the colors into an unwelcome and traumatic reminder of Anne's execution.

They had become close when Percy had expressed interest in the religious reform in England and harshly criticized the Bishop of Rome. They often deliberated over the ongoing disbandment of monasteries, abbeys, and convents. Still mourning the loss of the condemned English queen, they also discussed her. *Our friendship is new and yet strong, so I pray that it will not waver when the archbishop learns the truth about Anne's survival,* Percy hoped in his mind.

Percy's expression cleared of its mournful clouds. "The sky takes on shades of orange during sunrise and sunset. It is when everyone hopes that the sun will set only to rise again. For some, it can ascend again even from the darkness of the underworld if God wills it."

Cranmer could not figure out this allegory. "But not for Queen Anne."

A twinge of guilt pierced the Earl of Northumberland, for his deceit was hurting the other man. "Perhaps, she is currently basking in the rays of *another* sun." He implied the Italian sun.

A good actor when necessary, Henry Percy had confided in Archbishop Cranmer that he had asked Thomas Cromwell in a joking manner why the king would not burn Anne as a witch. A horrified Cranmer insisted that the earl pray fervently for atonement, even if he had not foreseen that Cromwell would act so. Percy's frankness had solidified their friendship, and his stratagem was working like female charms on a lewd man: Cranmer trusted him more and more with every meeting.

The archbishop crossed himself. "May God let her gentle soul find peace in heaven."

Anne Boleyn was an essential part of Cranmer's life. Several years earlier, he had declared King Henry's marriage to Catherine of Aragon invalid, and he believed that it was true. He had stood as Elizabeth Tudor's godfather and baptized the girl. Three years later, with a heavy heart, he had annulled the monarch's union with Anne on Henry's orders. On the day of the queen's burning, a distraught

Cranmer wept in despair, watching the pitiless red flames lick her body.

Percy leveled a meaningful stare at him. "Your Grace, justice must finally be served." He appreciated Anne's advice not to move forward with the plan until the pamphlets and the book had gained popularity among the people of England. Until the scandal over the execution of the wronged Queen Anne had blown up and snaked its way to King Henry's door.

A knot of grief over Anne's tragedy in his chest nearly strangled Archbishop Cranmer. "Lord Northumberland, I've not been myself since Queen Anne's death. I voiced my doubts about her guilt in my letter to His Majesty and beseeched him to be benevolent towards her, but my efforts were futile."

"You did try to save her," stressed the earl.

"But I failed Queen Anne!" The archbishop was now wringing his hands in despair and anguish, his countenance doleful. "Cromwell told me that at times, someone must be sacrificed for the greater good. The king wanted her gone, and I resigned myself that her death was inevitable."

"Your Grace, we must ease our conscience," Henry Percy persevered. "God forgives sinners if they repent." Contrition etched into his features, he added, "I'll never forgive myself for giving Cromwell the idea to burn Queen Anne. Among her many enemies, that villain coveted her blood the most."

"That blackguard falsified the abominable charges against her." Cranmer's voice trembled.

The earl inclined his head. "That is true. Queen Anne did so much good for the reformers, including Cromwell. But that immoral bastard forsook and destroyed her!"

The surreptitious nature of Percy's scrutiny, directed at the archbishop, indicated that he waited for something to happen. However, Cranmer did not notice it, for he was completely engrossed in his thoughts of Anne's trials and tribulations. Northumberland pointedly and continuously appealed to Cranmer's conscience, convincingly and cautiously bringing to the other man's attention the fact that Anne had aided him to rise to the position of Archbishop of Canterbury.

A stinging guilt overwhelmed Cranmer. His eyes glowing with determination, he avouched, "Lord Northumberland, I'll travel to Windsor soon and meet with the king."

Percy's heart hammered with delight, but his façade was neutral. "I hope His Majesty is accepting visitors now. He has been depressed since the birth of Prince Richard."

"Maybe the prince's sickness is the Almighty's punishment for Queen Anne's iniquitous death."

"Maybe," drawled the earl. His heart bore the heavy weight of his guilt for manipulating the honorable archbishop into helping him clear Anne's name, but there was no other way to goad the man into action. "Your Grace, I pray that you will secure an audience with the sovereign of England."

Cranmer pledged with the utmost sincerity, "I'll serve Lady Anne and her memory well, Lord Northumberland."

Henry Percy breathed out a sigh of relief that his plan was working smoothly. His mind drifted to Anne, and an acute sense of longing throbbed deep inside of him for the future he would never share with her. *Soon Anne's adversaries will pay for what they did to her. But will I ever see her again? Now Anne is the Queen of France and again belongs to another man,* he lamented silently. He had no confirmation of Anne's second marriage, but his conclusion seemed logical.

January 23, 1538, Windsor Castle, County of Berkshire, England

BETWEEN TWO KINGS

The day was cold, crisp, and a bit cloudy. Wrapped in a winter cloak ornamented with gold and sable trimmings on the front, King Henry leaned over the terrace wall on the north side of the castle. To his right stretched the snow-laden park studded with trees and hills rolling to the river's edge. On the left many scattered houses formed the town of Windsor, amidst the picturesque windings of the River Thames.

I want my life to shine with colors as bright as the most gorgeous sunset. Instead, the outlook for my future is black... In her letters, Jane Seymour begged him to let her join him at Windsor. He would ignore her, for even being at this distance from his consort did not help him forgive Jane for her failure.

From this terrace, the monarch could see the deer in the park below, and sometimes, he had archery butts set up so that he could practice shooting at targets in privacy. It was not snowing today, and he would have gone hunting those deer, but his old leg injury was troubling him. Thus, Henry ordered to bring him everything for outdoor archery pastime.

"Shooting always lifts spirits, just as little pranks do," Sir Francis Bryan pronounced as he neared the ruler.

Bryan had arrived at the head of a small group of servants carrying everything necessary for archery practice.

A crafty turncoat, Francis Bryan wore a cynical expression that had long become habitual for him. Called the Vicar of Hell for his constant, outrageous debauchery, Francis sported a black eyepatch over his left eye, which he had lost in a tournament at Greenwich years ago. Clad in a sable cloak, Bryan had an oval and attractive face slightly wrinkled from age, while his eyepatch made him look like a pirate. There was an aura of sheer maleness around his muscular, tall body that caused women to flock to him and his bed.

His liege lord turned away from the breathtaking white scenery around them. As their eyes met, Henry's face split into a wide grin. "Welcome! You have come in time."

Bryan bowed. "Your Majesty, forgive my intrusion."

"I'm glad to see you, Sir Francis."

After the Duke of Suffolk's banishment, the monarch had taken a liking to Francis Bryan's company. The man often entertained him with wanton stories about French and Italian brothels. They also covered political and intellectual topics, and the king's trust in Bryan was growing day by day.

Henry took a longbow and an arrow from a servant. "This is my favorite bow."

Bryan commented, "Your Majesty started making annual payments to the Fraternity of St George at the beginning of your glorious reign. You sagely ordered that all able-bodied men under the age of sixty practice shooting regularly. As a result, now all Englishmen have a basic training with bow, and they can defend our country in case of invasion."

"My decisions are always just and wise," stated the ruler haughtily. Now fully equipped for archery practice, Henry bragged, "Most definitely, I'll make a better shot than the illustrious archer Robin Hood ever could."

Spectators had assembled behind them. They stared at the monarch, whose aquamarine eyes focused on the red circle, emblazoned on the white board at the center of a series of numbered rings. Henry took aim and released an arrow that landed in the middle of the red circle.

The whole terrace rang out with applause. "Bravo!"

As Bryan handed to him two more arrows, the monarch drew his bowstring. In a fraction of a second, he let an arrow fly again. The arrows created a drum-like sound as they all hit home, in the red circle close to the first arrow.

The courtiers cheered wildly, "Bravo, Your Majesty!"

"Nobody else can shoot like me." The King of England swaggered with self-congratulatory arrogance. "My martial prowess with bow and sword is legendary."

"Our liege lord is a majestic archer!" complimented Bryan.

As Henry turned his head, his gaze landed on Archbishop Cranmer, who stood nearby. He lowered his bow and beckoned, "Archbishop, it is a great surprise to see you here."

Cranmer came closer and bowed. "I seek an audience with Your Majesty."

"Are you intending to discuss the introduction of shooting practice for priests in the Church of England?" The ruler laughed at the ludicrous idea of churchmen taking up archery.

This joke triggered an explosion of laughter. The audience was pleased that the monarch's mood was improving. Since the court's relocation to Windsor, the king's tantrums had been more frequent and horrible than ever, so intense that everyone was afraid of angering him.

The archbishop shuffled his feet. "I... I..." he stammered.

An alarmed Henry consented, "I'll send my page to bring you to my apartments tonight."

"Thank you, sire," Cranmer mumbled.

Suddenly, the wind gusted, lifting snow from the trees and the ground, filing the air with ice crystals. The temperature was plummeting, and the wind rising, so the ruler abandoned his archery, and everyone retired to the palace.

During the day, the monarch attended to state affairs. Then Henry held a private dinner with Francis Bryan, eagerly listening to stories about his subject's notorious escapades with aristocratic lovers and whores in houses of ill repute. At sundown, Cranmer was summoned to the King of England.

§§§

"Genius is like a fire," the Tudor monarch pronounced as he scrutinized the volume in his hands. "Can Cromwell's religious genius really burn my entire kingdom?"

An array of Venetian candelabra glowed, burnishing the gilded furnishings throughout the vaulted study. They provided much light for Henry, who sat at his mahogany desk reading the book *'Thomas Cromwell: the Evil Genius of Religious Reform in England'* by Clément Marot. It offered an incisive and exhaustive critique of Cromwell's role in the ongoing religious changes in the country.

"Enemy of enlightenment!" Henry was studying page after page. "Marot calls Cromwell so." A headline caught his eye. "According to the poet, Cromwell murdered Anne Boleyn."

He glanced around. The far wall was lined with shelves from floor to ceiling. On the other walls, the tapestries on the lives of Saints Peter and Paul summoned visions of Anne and him attending matins at St George's Chapel. *Despite Anne's wickedness, many of her talents received their direction and impulse from her piety,* the king acknowledged to himself.

The book consumed the king's evening until the herald's announcement interrupted him.

As he froze at the doorway, Thomas Cranmer dropped into a deep and ceremonious bow. "Your Majesty."

The monarch did not even look up at his guest, his eyes on the book in his hands. "Your Grace, tell me what it is you want and leave. I have much business to attend to."

The archbishop crossed the room and stopped near the desk. "I'm sorry for intruding." His gaze landed on the book.

Henry rested the volume on his knee, marking the page with his index finger. "This is an intriguing masterpiece."

"Having read it, I can attest to the truth in it."

"Is that so? Elaborate, Cranmer."

It was high time for the archbishop to open the ruler's eyes to Cromwell's treason. "I believe that Master Cromwell dissolved many good monasteries that were not as corrupt as he reported. I inspected several large monasteries he insisted be dissolved and met the monks living there. Some of them were well run, so there were no grounds for disbanding them."

"Master Cromwell has been carrying out my orders," huffed the king in irritation.

"Sire, I'll never do anything to jeopardize our reform."

"Why are you telling me this?"

Cranmer divulged, "There was a split in the reformers' faction. I thought that the swift and utter disbandment of the corrupt religious houses was not the most judicious course of action." He sighed. "Another person shared my opinion, and was worried about the people of England."

A baffled Henry put the book aside. "Pray continue."

"Master Cromwell and... the late Qu–" The archbishop abruptly trailed off. Anne had been a queen in his eyes, but to refer to her in this manner could send his sovereign into a fit of rage. Choosing his words carefully, he proceeded, "Master Cromwell and the late Lady Anne Boleyn had a disagreement over the suppression of the religious houses, which could not have been fixed. Lady Anne wished to use the collected money for charity purposes, and to finance educational institutions in order to advance enlightenment in England."

Henry felt a throbbing in his temples; something akin to an excruciating tune devoted to his romance with Anne Boleyn. An unbridled ire stirred in the pit of his stomach, and a ripping pain at Anne's supposed betrayals commenced racking him nerve by nerve.

"I don't wish to hear about the harlot." The king's face darkened like the earth's shadow swallowing the face of a moon in a lunar eclipse. "The whore sinned against God, me, and England, so she merited her ignominious death."

Cranmer gathered all his bravery. "As a man of God, I feel it is my duty to disclose the truth, even if I have to break the seal of confession." He dragged a deep breath before stating, "The Lady Anne Boleyn has been falsely accused."

The ruler's eyes flared with a bestial fire. "That is absurd."

"While making what was supposed to be her *last confession*, she swore her innocence." In a voice colored with the utmost sincerity, Cranmer promulgated, "Lady Anne asked Master Kingston to be present during her confession in order to allow the world to know the truth."

Henry flashed him a fulminating look. "Anne was always a consummate actress."

"It was Lady Anne's *last confession*," underscored the archbishop. "Despite her pregnancy, she thought that you would probably execute her the next morning."

Gnashing his teeth, the ruler spat, "Did she give you the names of all the men whom she had fornicated with? It would have been a long list of lovers."

"Lady Anne confessed her innocence before God. She did not betray her marital vows." Cranmer paused, waiting for a reaction, but his liege lord seemed momentarily stunned.

At first, the monarch thought that he had misconstrued or misheard Archbishop Cranmer, but the other man's earnest expression indicated his seriousness. Henry clenched and unclenched his fists, as an impervious cloud of red-hot anger entered all the vacant spaces in his mind.

"How can that be real?" Henry's voice reflected his furious disbelief.

A flood of supreme confidence rushing into him, Cranmer communicated the gospel truth. "Lady Anne said that she had not always treated Your Majesty with the obedience, humility, and respect a wife ought to show her king and husband. She submitted herself to your will. Lady Anne swore upon her eternal soul that she had never sinned against you with her body, so she believed she would find peace in heaven."

King Henry got to his feet, every bone in his body ached with horrified consternation. His mind raced back to the days before Anne's arrest, and he moved a hand to his chest, pressing it over his heart thundering inside like cannon fire. The visions of Anne entreating him to believe her that she had not betrayed him, and proclaiming her devotion to him, flashed in the monarch's mind like a Greek tragedy.

At the time, the ruler had wanted her dead with every fibre of his being because he had been convinced the woman was a treacherous adulteress. Whatever he did to try and banish Anne from his head, he would never succeed. She would always be with him; her image would be engraved upon his memory forever. His world tilted and span out of control, his thoughts whirling like a cyclone. The king stood rooted, staring into space, and abject terror painted his visage.

So enormous was the shock that the monarch was unable to move, speak, and even breathe for a brief moment. The concept of Anne's innocence was like a colossal physical blow, and he recoiled as if the harrowing truth had slapped him in the face. A rampageous river of alternating sensations – abashment, surprise, fright, despair, and agony – all commingled, submerging his previous ire. The air seemed thin and stale, his lungs struggling for their next breath.

His raiment of crimson silk, wrought with gold, created a homicidal air about Henry. His gaze darted to a nearby tapestry portraying St Peter's death by crucifixion at the hands of the Roman heathens. The king pictured Anne's lovely face in his head, and in a flash, he envisaged the gruesome end of her life at the pyre that had been kindled at his behest. If the Romans who had killed a saint in such a heinous way were unholy barbarians, who was Henry, then?

Cranmer was dizzy with immense relief as he watched his sovereign's inner struggle with the acceptance of the truth the ruler had been unwilling to admit before.

"It was Lady Anne's *last confession* before she was to be executed in the early morning," reiterated Cranmer, his voice emphasizing each word. "On the morning before her burning, I was unable to come to her. I know that she confessed her sins to another priest, who can be summoned to court. As Supreme Head of the Church of England, Your Majesty has every right to command this man to reveal the confession to you. I'm sure he will tell you the same."

The archbishop lapsed into silence. There was a subtle stirring of guilty emotion behind Henry's shaken façade.

The Tudor ruler remained quiet, but his lips twitched. It dawned on him why Cranmer had repeated several times that it was Anne's *last confession*. She had sworn her innocence upon the damnation of her soul, and that could mean only one thing – *Anne Boleyn was indeed innocent*.

Thoughts tumbled through Henry's mind in the same way as a herd flees from hunters in a wild stampede. If Anne were not guilty, then the birth of Elizabeth and the boy in the Tower of London, whose name the monarch did not know yet, were the Almighty's signs that their marriage was blessed. *In that case, my union with Jane must have been cursed, which was proved by the birth of a disabled child,* Henry surmised.

This conversation instilled dread in the king, whose world was now in turmoil. He feared the consequences of these macabre revelations for England, the Tudor dynasty, and himself. The selfish part of Henry screamed to ignore the possibility of Anne's innocence and to dismiss Cranmer. Yet, a small voice in his head entreated him to learn the truth.

Henry mandated, "Your Grace, go back to London, find the priest who listened to Anne's second confession, and send him to Windsor." His voice was quivering with emotion.

"I feared to speak up and displease you," uttered Cranmer. "But as an honest man, I could not turn a blind eye to the grave injustice perpetrated towards the Lady Anne Boleyn."

The pallid monarch flinched. "Leave!"

Thomas Cranmer bowed to his liege lord and exited.

The king trudged across the room and sank into a chair by the fireplace. A blizzard of questions rushed through his head. Was Anne really innocent or not? Had Cromwell committed such perfidious acts, as Cranmer claimed? There was a ring of truth to the archbishop's denunciations.

The perplexed ruler spent the rest of the day in his rooms, drinking wine, as if it could give him a repose from his woes. Holding a goblet in his hands, Henry sat quietly staring into the flames of the flickering fire burning in the hearth. *The roaring fire reminds me of Anne's death at the stake,* the king moaned silently. *I ordered to have her executed as a witch!* He felt as if he were being burned alive from the inside out.

January 25, 1538, Windsor Castle, County of Berkshire, England

"The Lady Anne Boleyn swore her innocence. She was resigned to her death and regretted only that she would never see her children again." The old churchman finished his story about Anne's last confession on the day of her burning.

A portly, grizzled man in his late sixties, Father Esmond Belcher served at the Chapel Royal of St Peter ad Vincula at the Tower of London. He had arrived at Windsor at dawn and corroborated Cranmer's account of Anne's last confession.

Henry halted in the middle of the presence chamber. Agitation thrummed from the walls, coincidentally swathed in tapestries of biblical saints, as if by the Creator's command to judge the monarch for his mistakes and wrongdoings.

"You are dismissed," barked the ruler. "Thank you."

Father Belcher dropped into a bow. "I am always at Your Majesty's service." He was relieved to leave the palace.

The calamity that had befallen the Tudor monarch was destroying him like a slow-acting lethal poison. Cranmer and the priest from the Tower did not know each other, and neither had any reason to lie. Could Anne have told both of them a falsehood? *Whatever her faults, Anne was a pious woman, and she would not have risked eternal damnation.*

If Anne had been faithful to Henry, then George Boleyn, Mark Smeaton, Henry Norris, William Brereton, and Francis Weston had all died innocent for their "villainies." The thought of Anne's burning was like a mortal blow to his soul, for Henry had even reneged on his word to bring a French swordsman for her execution. *At least, Anne was given some poison. It was the only act of mercy I could have granted her at that time.* Now it was the monarch's only consolation.

With effort, King Henry clawed his way out of his shocked trance. He invited Thomas Howard, Duke of Norfolk.

The ruler lounged in a gilded mahogany chair. He snarled savagely, "There is one important matter to discuss."

Norfolk bowed. "Yours to command, Your Majesty."

An ominous glint in his eyes, Henry studied the other man closely. "As Lord High Steward, you presided over the trial of your niece, Anne Boleyn. The jury of peers found her guilty, but she confessed her innocence to two priests. She had nothing to gain by lying because it would not have prolonged her life or saved the others. To save her soul, Anne would have said the truth to her confessors. What do you think?"

Norfolk realized his predicament. His only chance of surviving the obvious outcome was to shift the blame onto Cromwell. "You and other nobles were informed by Thomas Cromwell that Mark Smeaton had admitted to having an illicit affair with Lady Anne. The evidence presented by Cromwell was enough for the peers to deliver a guilty verdict."

The monarch rose to his feet and hobbled towards a window. As ill luck would have it, the pain in his right leg intensified, as if in punishment for his sins. The winter sun was shrouded behind gray-black clouds, scudding low on the horizon. *The stress of the past months must have aggravated my liege lord's health problems,* Norfolk assumed.

Henry gazed back at the duke. "I recall Smeaton was tortured."

The duke dipped his head. "Mark Smeaton was the only one among the accused who did not bear the status of gentleman. He was subject to the cruelest treatments in the Tower." After a short pause, he added, "As he went to the block, Smeaton said that he deserved death. Maybe Smeaton repented of lying to Cromwell in the hope that by saying what the man wished to hear would save his skin."

"His words are not a testament to Anne's guilt, then." Henry beheld the duke with a sort of mute resentment before demanding, "Why did you pronounce Anne guilty?"

"Master Cromwell presented seemingly compelling proof of her crimes." Norfolk's façade was impenetrable.

"Do you believe that she committed all the crimes ascribed to her?" Now the monarch wanted to know everything.

Norfolk could not say aloud that the king's lust for Jane had doomed Anne. "I prefer to abstain from drawing any conclusions. Perhaps, in view of her last confession, it would clarify exactly who was to blame if a new investigation into the allegations against Anne was made."

His countenance unforgiving, Henry glared at his subject. "You sentenced your own niece and nephew to death. Now it is your duty to sort out the mess created by Cromwell."

The implied threat was not lost on the duke. "I'll not fail you, sire. Cromwell doesn't deserve to resume his former life."

"Arrest that mendacious bastard," enjoined the king.

Norfolk suppressed a smile. "It shall be done."

Henry contemplated what else was required. "Thomas Boleyn, Earl of Wiltshire, and Lady Mary Stafford, together with her ward, must come to Windsor as soon as possible."

The duke was overjoyed that Anne's son would be brought to court. "Your Majesty's wish is my command. What are the charges against Master Cromwell?"

The ruler seated himself in a nearby chair. "High treason and heresy. You and Francis Bryan will lead the investigation. I myself will look through the original evidence against Anne."

The Duke of Norfolk clutched the collar of his emerald silk doublet. Now the king believed that Cromwell had tricked him into killing many innocent people. If Henry saw the materials prepared against Anne, he would realize her innocence. *Arthur and Elizabeth will then be reinstated to the succession,* Norfolk effused wordlessly. *I want a Howard monarch on the English throne regardless of their religion.*

The duke pledged, "I'll ask my secretary to gather the papers, but it might take some time, sire."

Another royal order was issued. "Thomas Audley will be my chief minister. As he is at court, I'll speak to him today."

"I hope Sir Thomas will be worthy of your trust." Norfolk was privately disappointed with Audley's promotion. Audley already was Lord Chancellor of England!

Henry's thoughts drifted to his exiled friend. "His Grace of Suffolk must return." His voice was unusually calm.

"As you wish." Norfolk swept a bow and was dismissed.

This time, there were no tantrums of rage, threats, and violence, nothing being thrown across the room to herald the arrival of Henry Tudor's explosive temper. An aloof Henry, his mind cold and clear, was not easy to manipulate, and he exuded both sinister aggression and overwhelming brutality. It might foreshadow the barbarous slaughter of Anne Boleyn's foes – a fate Norfolk emphatically hoped to avoid.

January 27, 1538, Austen Friars, London, England

Thomas Cromwell was dining with his son in the richly decorated great hall. Their table was overflowing with all kinds of delicacies, including venison, pork, pheasant, stork, gannet, fish, and vegetables cooked with fish and spiced with garlic. The hall was richly appointed, and tapestries portraying the lives of Martin Luther and John Calvin, who were two highly esteemed figureheads of Reformation, lined the walls.

Without warning, the Duke of Norfolk and Sir Francis Bryan arrived; they were accompanied by a squad of guards.

Although the *former* chief minister was full of mortal dread, he labored to maintain an unemotional façade as he stood to face his unwelcome guests, along with his son, Gregory.

"Father," Gregory Cromwell began, his expression colored with a trace of terror. "Why have they come?"

Thomas demanded, "Leave us, my son. Now."

Gregory cast a desperate glance at his father, who maintained a steadfast expression that compelled the young man to comply.

Gregory's scrutiny veered to their unwanted guests as fearful anguish nearly overwhelmed him. "What do you want from us, Your Grace and Sir Francis?"

The Duke of Norfolk pointed a scornful finger at the elder Cromwell. "We are here for the traitor Cromwell – not you, lad."

"Go to your room, son," reiterated Cromwell.

Francis Bryan jeered, "Disobedience is essentially a power struggle against someone in authority." He sneered, "Your father has long lost his influence and privileges."

Gregory defensively argued, "Don't insult my father, my lords! You loathe us because we do not belong to the old English nobility. However, my father has done a great deal of good for England: he liberated the country from Roman slavery and brought the reformed faith to the realm. Regardless of what the king will do to him, his name will never be forgotten."

At this moment, Thomas Cromwell was immeasurably proud of his smart, courageous son. Young Gregory was only seventeen, but he was a man of principles and integrity. Yet, Gregory was not for politics: he exuded dignity and softness flowing from the nobility of his heart. Gregory had no propensity for plotting and manipulating, so he would never be able to become a wily and seasoned courtier.

My son should lead a quiet life in the countryside, Thomas thought. *I hope he can find happiness with his Seymour wife.* His only surviving son's appearance reminded him of his dearly departed wife, Elizabeth. Gregory's plain, light yellow brocade doublet, as well as his matching hose and his toque emphasized his pale skin, blonde hair, and blue eyes. A man of tall and lithe stature, Gregory had an air of endearing and poetic elegance about him.

"That is enough from you," Norfolk growled, glowering at Gregory. "Get out!"

As his father nodded again, Gregory bowed and reluctantly exited the chamber.

Thomas Cromwell looked from Bryan to Norfolk, striving to keep his features impassive. Anne Boleyn's prescient words echoed through his mind menacingly: *'Eye for an eye, tooth for a tooth, and blood for blood.'* Was this retribution for his crimes against the dead woman? Would he die soon?

The prisoner inquired tightly, "On what grounds do you wish to apprehend me, my lords?"

A cynical smile of sadistic pleasure illuminated the Duke of Norfolk's visage. "Master Cromwell, you have been accused of high treason and heresy."

Francis Bryan leered at him. "We are here to escort you to the Tower on His Majesty's orders."

Cromwell responded with dignity, "If it is His Majesty's command, I'll gladly obey."

Donning his sable cloak, Cromwell recognized that he would never wear such garments again. Then he was led out of the mansion by guards. A throng of enraged people, who had been outside his house for months, awaited him in the street. The propaganda against Cromwell had awakened their bloodlust with a ferocity that horrified him to his core.

The mob reviled Cromwell, and no doubt would have killed him had he not been surrounded by soldiers.

Hateful cries boomed through the cold air like thunder.

"Traitor! Wretched criminal!"

"Death to Thomas Cromwell!"

"He destroyed our monasteries! 'eretic!"

"You deserve death at the stake like Queen Anne Boleyn!"

"You are the devil! We want your blood!"

Someone threw a stone at Cromwell's back, causing the prisoner to gasp in pain.

Cromwell staggered backwards, but he was supported by guards who rudely pushed him forward. Others endeavored to disperse the crowd, whose exclamations of approval of the man's arrest and curses were still abundant. Sadness seized his heart as Cromwell jumped into the saddle and watched several soldiers attempt to pacify the commoners' fury.

As they departed, the former minister closed his eyes, fighting off the terrifying images running through his head. *I shall never see my Gregory again,* Cromwell realized. *The courtiers will view my downfall as a triumph of the English nobility over a baseborn man who, to their envy, amassed many privileges. Don't they understand that Henry Tudor can send any of them to the scaffold regardless of their status?* Cromwell comprehended that all of his wealth and lands would be confiscated, and he prayed that Gregory would retain at least a couple of estates.

Unbeknownst to him, the Duke of Norfolk had similar thoughts as he rode at the helm of the small procession. If Anne Boleyn and Thomas Cromwell, who had both once been loved by King Henry, could fall so dramatically from grace, no one was safe. A sense of uncertainty was gnawing at him, and the duke struggled to push aside the serpents of fear circling his throat. *I'll have to be far more careful from now on because His Majesty has become so unpredictable.*

Between Two Kings

The firmament was a gray blanket of clouds, and it began snowing. The roads were slippery, so they traveled at a slow pace. Patches of ice cracked beneath the hooves of the horses, and snowflakes danced in the air, falling and forming a blanket of white on the ground. Cromwell had a detached countenance as they discerned the outlines of the Tower of London in the distance. Norfolk was somber while Bryan snickered devilishly.

CHAPTER 19

Seeds of Future Happiness

January 29, 1538, Château d'Amboise, Loire Valley, France

"We are very close to the town of Amboise," announced Sir Robert Stuart, captain of the Scots Guard, breathing steaming from his nostrils in the chilly morning air.

Inside a splendid litter, swathed in cloth of gold with the finest ornaments and drawn by four palfreys caparisoned in purple damask and adorned with the Valois escutcheon, King François and Queen Anne both sighed with relief. Although they made stops at various châteaux and royal houses, their journey through southern and central France was arduous. On the Feast of Brother Juniper, one of the original followers of St Francis of Assisi, the day was chilly and windy.

"We have almost arrived," the king told his spouse.

Anne smiled at him faintly. "I'm weary, but my mood has brightened."

A frown marred his forehead. "Sometimes, I regret leaving Italy, although I obviously could not let you be exposed to perils from the emperor's assassins and armies."

"I'm so very glad to be in France again!" Her excitement quivered in the air in subtle waves.

"Wife, that is excellent," drawled the monarch.

"Yes, Your Majesty." The queen did not miss how he had referred to her. This personal dynamic between them was a testament to their growing bond.

Anne pulled back the curtain and looked out of the litter's window. The forest of Amboise was cloaked by a glistening mantle of fresh snow. A blast of icy wind tossed the upper branches of snow-capped trees, causing cascades of frozen flurries to rain down upon the travelers. As it subsided, a peaceful quiet settled over the valley, and the only remaining sounds were the rhythmic crunching of snow beneath the horses' hooves, the braying of trumpets, and the creaking of wheels straining to transport wagons filled with luggage.

In a matter of minutes, the woods were left behind. Many peasant houses were scattered across the rolling hills and barren fields, and each passing village was dominated by a church. The pallid sun peeked through the clouds, casting lean shadows across the land. At this time of the year, the Loire Valley was a place of majestic beauty, where winter's fragile loveliness filled the chilly universe with a sense of timelessness and eternity, unifying humanity and nature.

The monarch commented, "Amboise is one of the busiest towns in the Loire Valley."

"One of the most picturesque, too," his spouse added, and he nodded his agreement.

The terraces of Château d'Amboise rose up out of the snowy carpet like a mirage. When the cortège stopped in a courtyard near the château, François and Anne wrapped their winter cloaks tighter. As they stepped out of the litter, a long row of servants waited to greet them and dipped with bows and curtsies as the couple walked towards the entrance. Nodding at them briefly, François intended to lead Anne inside the palace, but she motioned for him to pause.

There was an uncertain expression on the king's face. "Anne, don't you want to rest?"

BETWEEN TWO KINGS

The queen's thoughts meandered to the golden days of her youth in France. The major events were etched indelibly upon her mind. During her service to Queen Claude as one of her ladies-in-waiting, Anne had seen the births of the gentle queen's many children. She had also attended sumptuous banquets in the rare moments when Claude had not been in confinement. Anne remembered the shattering heartbreak when her father had recalled her back to England.

Years ago, I left Amboise unwillingly, Anne remembered. *I've always wholeheartedly adored France, French culture, and the Valois court.* Anne associated France with a golden and happy era of her life. Maybe the queen was even more French than English, and her enemies in England had called Anne a Frenchwoman in the most derisive tones.

Her smile radiated a lively energy. "I'm never better and wish you to stroll with me."

A grin creased his mouth. "It will be my great pleasure."

The royals crossed the courtyard and entered the vast garden, laid out in carefully planned symmetrical lines. With its parterres, groves, alleys, and mazes, the park was both breathtaking and eerie, in spite of not being vibrantly green and its lack of colorful blossoms. They walked along the snow-covered paths in the midst of this romantic whiteness. Eventually, they stopped in a grove of trees by a small frozen stream, their guards keeping a discreet distance.

Anne exclaimed, "The garden is magnificent! It must be wonderful for Your Majesty to visit this place, where you spent so much time in your childhood."

"Yes," confirmed François, his eyes pensive. "Years ago, my sister, Marguerite, and I would run around the park and pluck flowers. We played a hide-and-seek game together, disappearing from our governess. Our mother would come to the gardens and call for us, but we would not answer, and when she heard us laugh, she would join in our merriment."

The queen could easily envision her husband and his sister in childhood, for she had known them in her adolescence. "Do you have any other heartwarming memories?"

"Sometimes, Marguerite and I went to one of the towers to enjoy the amazing view. My sister liked watching barges and ships plying the river, and so did I." His smile revealed a bit of sentimentality. "Back then, I was not burdened with affairs of state and nation. I'm lucky to look back at my childhood with affection, for it was a great time without anxiety."

"Memories of my childhood are precious to me as well."

François enveloped his arm around her waist. In silence, they beheld the dazzling views of the Loire River, cognizant of their spirits soaring weightless, like souls of brilliant light.

Anne thought back to her early childhood at Hever Castle, before her departure to the Low Countries. She remembered how she and her siblings had adored each other, and had been loved by their parents. At the time, their father had not used his offspring in his power games. Visions of George and her running and playing in the Hever gardens flickered through her brain, and warmth seeped into her soul. Anne had always been closer to George than to her sister, Mary.

Images of her brother's execution pierced her whole being like a javelin. King Henry of England had murdered George! Her face twisted in immeasurable repugnance and enmity, but she rapidly disguised her rage with aloofness. Yet, François had noticed the shift in her expression.

"Would you mind if we return to the palace, sire?"

At the sight of the arctic coldness in her eyes, the ruler sighed, but he still compelled himself to smile. "It would be better for you to be indoors because of the cold."

"Indeed." She pivoted to leave, but he placed his hands on her shoulders, stopping her.

François gazed at her meaningfully. "Anne, I'm aware that your previous life is mired in too much hurt. But now you are the Queen of France, and the past is gone forever."

She pondered his words. "It will be as God wills it."

February 5, 1538, Château d'Amboise, Loire Valley, France

During the next several days, Anne's spirits lifted to a state of reverent elation. Perhaps the improvements in her mood were down to her love for France and the French court.

"How much I admire this place!" enthused Anne as she wandered through the castle.

Queen Anne had always admired Château d'Amboise. As a member of Queen Claude's household, she had often stayed at this palace, which had not changed significantly since then.

Despite remembering it well, Anne toured this place with the enthusiasm of someone seeing it for the first time. The Gothic hallways were rather narrow, and some were tastefully frescoed with versatile religious and mythological scenes. Light filtered through the large and sharply-arched stained-glass windows, throwing rich-colored patterns around.

The ceilings were vaulted with stone ribs holding the weight. There was so much volume in the height of the chambers that a loud word, a small noise, or the sound of footsteps resonated through the hallways. Orderly arrangements of columns, pilasters, and lintels, semicircular arches, niches, and aedicules exhibited the traits of Gothic and early Renaissance architecture.

The queen encountered the king in the great hall. It boasted marvelous frescoes and white marble fireplaces, carved with fleurs-de-lis and kneeling angels.

Cardinal de Tournon and Jacques de la Brosse were with the monarch. The French queen's identity was still being kept secret, and the château was well guarded. As Tournon and Brosse knew the truth about her, in their presence the queen did not have to hide her face with a veil.

François flourished a bow to his wife. "Anne, come here!"

His advisors both bowed and chorused, "Your Majesty."

Standing at the arched doorway, Anne sank into a gracious curtsey, although it was rather difficult for her to move her body down because of her growing belly. Her husband strode towards her and instantaneously raised her up.

"Anne, my wife, I've told you not to curtsey to me in your condition," reminded the king in the gentlest accents.

A grateful smile shone on the queen's visage. "I promise to never do that again."

François led her to the large hearth, where a fire blazed briskly. "How are you enjoying Amboise, wife?"

They stopped, and she chortled before professing, "I take a great pleasure in these lavish surroundings."

He was gratified to glimpse his spouse's sunny disposition. It had been one of her most distinctive features before she had endured tragedy. "I hope you are enjoying the touch of our marvelous French culture. Our great art is timeless."

"*I'm the most happy!*" cried the queen. "I've always admired the splendor and culture of France. Euphrosyne, the goddess of joy and mirth, must have blessed this country."

François and others all grinned at the mention of Anne Boleyn's famous motto.

Haughty pride burgeoned in the ruler. "Beauty, elegance, and culture merge together in my kingdom. My hospitality to poets, architects, painters, humanists, musicians, and other intellectuals reflects the enlightened nature of my kingship, in contrast to that of my predecessors."

She nodded vivaciously. "Your Majesty's court is the envy of all nations!"

"Well, my queen, I'm sorry, but I must go you as we have business to attend to." François bowed, and the three men left Anne to explore more of the castle on her own.

Queen Anne strolled through rooms and hallways, where the walls were painted in rich colors of gold, royal purple, crimson, lavender, and blue. Corridors were lined with paintings depicting battle scenes in opulent hues and famous cities such as Rome, Milan, Venice, and Florence. It was almost impossible to tear the eye from the fabulous frescoes devoted to religious topics, including the dramatic episodes of Jesus Christ's crucifixion and resurrection.

Salamanders – the King of France's personal emblem – were omnipresent in the château, engraved upon the walls, ceilings, and fireplaces. The furniture was adorned with architectural forms and ornaments in a bold color palette, including gold, blue, charcoal, grey, lavender, green, purple, and crimson. Many pieces were gilded, each elaborately carved and intricately decorated. Some rooms exhibited marble sculptures of gods, goddesses, and ancient heroes.

Magnificent Flemish tapestries bedecked the walls of chambers, galleries, and halls. They depicted the lives of Christian saints and scenes of chivalry, courage, and courtly love. Several rooms were adorned with Italian wall hangings, showing the striking paintings of Giovanni Bellini, Leonardo da Vinci, Filippino Lippi, Jean Clouet, and others. There was a spacious room profusely decorated with portraits of the Capetian dynasty and those of the Valois kings.

By the time Anne appeared in the long, spacious gallery that contained a great deal of paintings, she had been tired.

After surveying her surroundings, Anne said to herself, "I will soon return to make the acquaintance of the arresting artworks collected by King François throughout his reign."

Before leaving, the queen examined her husband's portrait by Jean Clouet. François I, sumptuously attired in the Italian style, was depicted without crown or scepter, facing the viewer and casting a noble gaze. Anne imagined that the monarch was now staring at her with his affable amber eyes, flashing her a captivating smile. *God above, I feel a faint stirring of warmth within my breast, which a woman feels when her beloved enfolds her into his arms. Oh, no!*

"I cannot have such thoughts," Anne persuaded herself.

She hastened away from the gallery. Yet, on the way back to her quarters, the queen had a rapturous smile, overawed by the unparalleled luxury, glorious beauty, and tremendous sophistication around her, still reminiscing about his portrait.

February 10-11, 1538, Château d'Amboise, Loire Valley, France

A euphoric Anne bloomed like a sweet-scented flower. For the first time in many months, she unlocked her heart, and, unexpectedly, she felt closer to her French husband than ever before. The palace's grandeur also evoked a sense of philosophical wonder, and sometimes, she meditated upon the ephemeral and fragile nature of life.

Her advancing pregnancy had recently started sapping her energy. Tonight, she went to bed as soon as the yellow disc of the winter sun commenced its downward journey.

The maid aided the queen to change into a golden silk nightgown with a high waist. The girl brushed her hair in long, even strokes until it shone, and now it streamed down Anne's back and shoulders in a charming mass of raven curls.

Queen Anne lay back on a large bed that dominated the room and was raised on a small dais. It was canopied with copious lengths of ochre silk, which was embellished with floral motifs. She snuggled beneath the covers and stared into the flickering flames in a marble hearth, decorated with a salamander emblem. A collection of massive ebony furniture inlaid with precious stones, ivory, and gold was tastefully arranged throughout the chamber. The walls were frescoed with scenes of the Greek Aphrodite and her son, Eros.

"François," whispered the queen in a dreamy voice.

Soon the numbing fingers of sleep started creeping over Anne. She dozed off, but only for a short while. At the creak of the door, her eyes flew to the sound. The king walked in, and their gazes intersected, the blazing fire in his amber eyes reigniting the dying embers in her dark pools.

The spouses were lodged in the apartments of the Count and Countess d'Angoulême, which had once been occupied by François' parents. Their bedrooms were separated only by the door, so she was not surprised to see her spouse at this hour.

The queen's countenance glowed with a welcoming light before turning impassive. His mere appearance had begun arousing in her a delicious blend of delight and fulfillment, but she reminded herself of the ghastly price she had paid for her Tudor queenship. Anne had to guard herself against emotions such as tenderness, and just hope that her second marriage could be different from her dreadful union with Henry.

"Are you well, Anne?" inquired the monarch.

Despite her efforts to maintain an indifferent exterior, her eyes twinkled. "Good evening, Your Majesty. You are most kind to me, but I assure you that everything is fine."

"I received a message from Philippe de Chabot. Thomas Cromwell has been imprisoned in the Tower. The English court is buzzing with this news, and the nobles are happy."

A vitriolic satisfaction gushing through her, Anne reveled in the villain's plight. Yet, in an instant, her glee waned, leaving hollowness in her heart. With unsparing truthfulness, she discovered the barrenness of her soul and the sensation of piteous heaviness that weighed her down like a traumatic bereavement. *Has my thirst for vengeance done this to me?*

She smiled half-heartedly. "That is excellent."

François eased himself onto the edge of her bed. "Tell me if you are feeling unwell. If you need something, you will have it." He kissed her hands and held them to his chest.

Anne regarded him with amazement. Henry had been so worried about her only when she had been pregnant with Elizabeth, but Anne had disappointed him by giving him a useless girl; during her two failed pregnancies, he had not doted on her. Tonight, François gave her a new memory to cherish – his deep concern about her and their child.

She squeezed his hands. "I've been thinking back to my years in France."

"I remember the lovely and young raven-haired girl, who was fascinated by my court and who Claude liked a great deal." He bestowed upon her an exuberant smile.

"I'm most honored," she said sincerely.

"I have something for you."

The ruler leapt to his feet and marched to his bedchamber. In a minute, he returned and settled himself on the bed with a cryptic smile, his hands behind his back.

"What is it?" quizzed the queen impatiently.

"Here. Take it." The king presented Anne with a red rose.

A beaming Anne brought the flower to her nose, enjoying its fragrance. Arousing in her a tangle of mystical, aesthetic, and creative emotion, François intrigued her in the same way as the works of Leonardo da Vinci entranced an audience. Discovering new facets of his character, which made him irresistible to women, was like a never-ending journey.

A sense of elation swept through her. "Thank you very much, Your Majesty. Where did you get it in the winter?"

"We have an orangery at Amboise, and my gardeners work magic, even at this time of year."

François could be immensely romantic if he wants to be, thought a beaming Anne. Most definitely, her husband's care and attention were far more than she had anticipated having in a political union, and they constituted a treasure for her.

"Thank you very much, sire." Her voice was toneless.

A strange silence, pulsating with unspoken words, ensued. Only the fire, crackling and popping, disturbed the peace.

I'm intoxicated by my queen's unfathomable charm and her unconventional beauty, the monarch thought as he gazed into her eyes. The sophistication and grandeur of his consort's personality enthralled him, just as Cleopatra had hypnotized Marc Antony centuries ago. Oblivious to everything but his wife and driven by the need to touch her, François captured hers lips in a searing kiss and embraced her.

Anne responded with an astounding eagerness. She had a fleeting sensation of something akin to a lush, yet doleful, ode about great love and its loss. Nonetheless, the little voice in the back of Anne's head continuously warned her about the danger of developing any emotional ties to the Valois ruler.

When they parted, the king's gaze lit with the fervency of his emotion. "I'll take care of you, wife," pledged François. His lips brushed hers with the softness of a feather. "Perhaps I cannot endow you with the idyllic happiness a woman fantasizes of finding in her marriage. However, I give you my word that nothing bad will happen to you and our child. Don't fear anyone – neither Henry nor any foe of yours."

Anne was ensconced in a cocoon of his benignity and fire. "My gratitude to Your Majesty is unbounded and unfading." The rose was still clasped in one of her hands.

He gazed at her reverently. "You are not in debt to me. I'm glad that I met you in Italy, and that it was you who saved my life. As you say, we are helping each other."

François tilted his head and showered Anne with more kisses, each of them like a present wrapped differently. Some were of almost lyrical tenderness and bright like a fresh spring morning, while others were so exotic and so passionate that they took her breathe away. At this moment, there were no ghosts of the past between the spouses.

§§§

The next morning, Count Jean de Montreuil arrived at Amboise. He had been a frequent visitor to the château in the lifetime of the Count d'Angoulême. After his death, Louise de Savoy had invited Jean to Amboise or Cognac. Queen Marguerite of Navarre was expected to come soon.

Having greeted the old count cordially in the great hall, King François and Queen Anne went to the Church of Saint-Florentin to attend a private Mass. Part of Château Amboise, it was a spectacular church, with an interior adorned with frescoes and stained glass in every direction.

In the aisle, the spouses both genuflected and crossed themselves. Then they went to royal pews and knelt again, bathed in the orange light cast by burning candles.

Despite being a reformer at heart, today Anne listened to the priest with a reverence that she had not felt for long. As she so frequently did, the queen contemplated her past. Her mind drifted to the late Catherine of Aragon and her daughter, Mary Tudor, and her mood was anything but tranquil. A shard of guilt pierced her, and she could not shove it away.

The queen had once fiercely despised 'the Spanish woman' for refusing to step aside and allow Henry to wed a young and fertile lady. After Catherine had been expelled to Kimbolton Castle, Anne had despised Mary for her stubborn refusal to accept her bastardy status and her, Anne, as Queen of England. It was King Henry's idea to compel Mary to serve little Elizabeth, but Anne had approved of it.

It surprised Anne to a significant degree that her erstwhile loathing for Catherine and Mary had vanished like smoke in the wind. *Now I regret my cruel treatment of my predecessor and Mary,* she surmised silently. However, the sands of time had run out for Queen Anne Boleyn of England, and she had "died" in the Tower of London. Queen Anne of France was a new woman, one who would have to live with the knowledge that she had no way to rectify her past mistakes.

As Mass concluded, the priest announced the benediction over the royal couple, and then left them alone.

The queen's attention was caught by a beautifully worked stained glass window, one which portrayed the Virgin holding the baby Jesus in her arms. The winter sun illuminated the window, and this elicited a misty smile from her.

"It is lovely, isn't it?" Her husband's hushed voice spoke in the stillness of the church.

Anne veered her gaze to the king. "Yes, it is. This window possesses an ethereal beauty."

François smiled serenely. "It is a blessed beauty that originates in our love for the Lord."

She shifted her scrutiny back to the superbly wrought window. "Our love for God is a result of Jesus Christ calling to us through the power of the Holy Spirit. It opens His children's minds to understand the greatness and goodness of the world and our lives."

The ruler nodded. On occasion, he had been worried about his spouse's religion. Anne was notorious for her role in England's break from the Vatican, and, François knew, she still sympathized with the Protestants. Nonetheless, having spent months with her in Italy and especially now, when he saw her genuine devotion to the Creator, his earlier doubts dissipated. *Anne will make a dignified, pious Catholic queen in France, or, at the very least, she will play this role well.*

It took Anne a long moment to tear her gaze away from the window and glance back at her husband. As their gazes met, time seemed to freeze, and the rest of the world faded away.

His heart drummed in his chest like the consistent cadence of marching troops while he was drowning in two dark pools of mysterious allure. All at once, François realized that although Anne and he had entered into a political marriage and joined their forces in their quest for vengeance, his wife had long ceased being only his ally. What exactly did he feel for Anne Boleyn? A sense of clarity was settling over him.

The King of France coveted revenge on his Tudor archrival for their old political conflict. At first, his wife had been a useful tool for fulfilling that wish. François had arranged Thomas Cromwell's downfall, and it entertained him to watch events in England from afar. At present, the situation there was not far from a possible revolt against King Henry's religious policy. With her name cleared, Henry would be compelled to officially announce Anne's innocence.

You will never have Anne back, Henry, François swore in his mind. *You must still be obsessed with her, but Anne is my wife until death do us part.* François experienced a sadistic pleasure envisaging his English counterpart's reaction to the news of Anne's new status in France.

Anne and François had a great deal in common: they were both pragmatic and ambitious, able to rule with firmness, honor, and integrity. The spouses were impeccably educated and superbly intelligent, each of them highly influenced by Renaissance humanism. They craved greatness for France, and had an unquenchable love of all things progressive and intellectual. François also enjoyed their intimate encounters, even if there was no wild fire between them; he hoped that passion for him would awaken in her heart over time. Without a shadow of a doubt, Anne would be useful to François as his consort. He was proud that Anne Boleyn, whom he endlessly admired and adored, was his queen.

Like a mighty stream gushing forth from the mountains, it dawned upon François that the lush blend of his adoration, fascination, and respect towards Anne had evolved into a feeling that was wholly new for him – love. It was highly likely that his spouse was the first woman for whom he felt a pure, real love, not just primitive lust. Anne was his queen, his lover, his wife, and the mother of his unborn child, and now, most importantly, he realized that she was *his true love.*

I really do love my Anne, King François concluded with supreme confidence. *I love my wife with all my heart.* This understanding made him soar on the wings of divine elation.

The monarch murmured, "The church is a symbolic place for us, Anne. You saved my life in St Mark's Basilica in Venice, and it was clearly God's will. Now another important thing has happened to me in the church."

Her brows arched. "What is Your Majesty implying?"

"Something that is not of importance to you."

He gestured towards a chapel in one of the aisles. As they stood up, François strode forward, and Anne trailed after him.

As they walked, the ruler made up his mind: he would not reveal his love to her. Henry's treatment of Anne had left his wife's heart trampled and beaten; to raise it up again would take both tender hands and loving patience. If Anne was ever able to reciprocate his feelings... To conquer her heart, he suspected he would have to be patient for a very long time.

Anne was no longer Henry's wife: she belonged to François by law, and in God's eyes. Yet, a fear in the back of François' mind tormented him that part of Anne could still yearn for Henry, despite all the misery the man had caused her.

As they stopped near a tomb, the king informed, "This is the resting place of the illustrious Leonardo da Vinci. It was the maestro's wish to be buried in this church."

This inflamed great interest in the queen. The epitaph stated that the God-gifted painter, inventor, scientist, and all-around genius was laid to eternal rest in this place.

"Did Your Majesty compose this epitaph in honor of the great Maestro da Vinci?"

"Yes, I did. I gave him the honors he deserved. His death was a huge loss for me." Melancholy colored his voice.

At the sight of such deep sadness etched into his face, Anne had the urge to console him, but refrained. "You admired the maestro as a man of superior intelligence. You invited him to work at the French court, and he was your friend. I'm sure that Leonardo was pleased to die in France."

François was perplexed with her behavior for an instant, but then he sighed. "Indeed, you are right." A rueful smile on his mouth, he murmured, "Once Leonardo told me that *'Life without love is no life at all.'* It is as true as the fact that day follows night. I hope you understand that."

To his chagrin, his wife answered unhesitatingly, "Love is a lethal poison that creates suffering. It slowly, but surely, consumes one's mind, body, and life until eventually it kills."

Unreciprocated love keeps you alive, but kills every day. How long will I have to hide my feelings from Anne? Or will she ever drink from the waters of Lethe, which will leave her with nothing to reminisce about Henry? Anne would surely not welcome the monarch's confession at this time. Now she did not even believe in love anymore. He wondered if, unreciprocated, his affection for her would eat away at him like the poison Anne believed love to be, little by little.

François touched his neck and felt cool metal under his fingers. After the wedding, he had contacted Philippe de Chabot in England and asked him to secretly talk to Hans Holbein in order to produce Anne Boleyn's miniature, for the artist had sketches of her in his workbooks. While in Turin, the king had received the small portrait from England and placed it in the locket he always wore on a fine gold chain around his neck. His spouse did not need to know about it.

"One day, the past will be where it belongs: in the past."

Anne said wretchedly, "Maybe yes, maybe no."

Her reserve apprised him of her unhappiness. "Don't be so forlorn, Anne. In due time, you will be free of all ghosts, alive or dead. Time and the Almighty heal all wounds."

Annoyed that her misery was so plain, she riposted, "The past always influences the present and, thus, the future, too."

François did not respond straight away. He simply stared into her eyes, and she deciphered a flicker of something that looked unmistakably like melancholy. But she said nothing.

Anne thought of her first husband and their doomed romance. To her surprise, she did not care whether Henry was married to Jane Seymour or anyone else, and she was not jealous at all. There was no amorous yearning for him in Anne's universe, not even in the deepest recesses of her soul, as if the winds of fate had eroded their love away.

I'm no longer caught between two kings, Anne concluded. *My love for Henry was dying during my imprisonment in the Tower, writhing in agony for months. It drew its last breath on the day I learned about Henry's order to burn me.* Henry's barbaric cruelty had destroyed Anne's fervent longing for him, leaving the romance that had once seemed to her the greatest possible love story in the ruins of tragedy.

At present, Anne's hatred for Henry possessed her whole being, and a pitch-black darkness ruled her inner realm. She abhorred Henry Tudor for murdering her brother and the other men unjustly condemned, for bastardizing their children, for nearly murdering her twice, and for forcing her to be separated from Elizabeth and Arthur. Perhaps Anne would not see them again. *I do not love Henry*, Anne repeated to herself, now cognizant of her feelings more than ever.

Knowing nothing about his consort's conclusions, François sighed. He quoted one of Leonardo's maxims, "*In time and with water, everything changes.'* I agree with it."

Anne rewarded him with a smile. "Perhaps Maestro da Vinci's words will come true."

"They will." It was his only hope.

She foretold, "This church shall always have a special meaning for us."

"It shall." He cast a glance at the genius' tomb.

Anne could no longer use her old badge of a crowned white falcon. In France, she needed a new personal insignia. "When it is over, I want to use the phoenix as my emblem."

François flitted his jolly gaze to her. "That is an excellent idea, my clever wife! We will choose for your royal crest a crowned golden phoenix rising from the ashes. It would be a powerful symbol of your triumph over the past and your resurrection as the Queen of France."

A chuckle slipped through her lips. "The King and Queen of the French realm! The golden crowned salamander and the golden crowned phoenix! That would fit our story so well!"

His mood soared to heavenly heights. "That is what I want, Anne. Our joint emblem will be the salamander and phoenix in the flames, which can withstand any devastating fire."

Anne marveled at the strange workings of fate, which had made her the Queen of France. She envisioned her life as consort to François, and her chest swelled with gladness. Her new royal status was a heavenly reality, and the queen did believe that God had led her to him in Venice.

She viewed her union with King François as something profoundly awe-inspiring and remarkable. His respectful and caring treatment of Anne was gradually healing her shattered heart, causing the ice in it to thaw. Her husband had sowed the seeds of future happiness in her soul. Yet, the arctic cold of her antagonism towards Henry and her fears remained the only impediments to the blossoming of her fledgling affection for François, which she resisted with all her might.

Her husband's voice snapped her out of her reverie. While the monarch was reciting another of his many poems, the beautiful words delighted the queen's senses.

> *O Anne! My Muse for my poetry and life!*
> *The loftiest Muse! You are now my queen*
> *Reborn on this night! My phoenix of a wife!*
> *Of heaven on the spiritual air we both breathe.*
> *Of earthy existence, that is a torment for me*
> *If I imagine it to be spent without my Muse.*
> *Your dark eyes and luxuriant hair entangle me*
> *Into the web of passion described in ancient odes,*
> *My pulse of life, letting me dream of glory,*
> *One who will help us write our love story.*
> *Down my mouth comes to yours, and down*
> *Your dark eyes descend like a fiery wind*
> *Upon my mind: my lips meet yours, and a flood*
> *Of celestial fire sweeps across me, so I drown*
> *Within two brown pools, enchanted by my Muse.*

Anne's smile was scintillating. "That is apparently a lovely ode about me, François." She addressed her spouse in such a personal manner for the first time. The sound of his name was for her as gorgeous as a wave slowly curling in the sun.

François drew his consort to him and hugged her carefully not to hurt her growing stomach. "Oh God," he whispered as he buried his head in her neck. "I am a creature of something divine when I'm close to you, Anne. Your enigmatic spell over me is passion, and it is your art, for no other woman has ever had a magical effect upon me such as you have."

"I... don't know..." She trailed off as her emotions whirled like mist in the evening air. "Your Majesty has a great talent in poetry." That was all she could say to him now.

As they parted, he told his wife, "I'll write many poems in your honor, wife. We have a whole life ahead. As the Muse of my life, you fill it with a great deal of sense, Anne."

Suddenly serious, Anne uttered, "I'm most honored to be your Muse."

He kissed her hands. "Heaven has granted me the grace of having you as my queen."

"Is it a blessing or a curse, Your chivalrous Majesty? The Knight-King must know that."

"The best God's blessing possible, Your brave Majesty." François brought her hands to his lips again, the jaunty gleam in his eyes. "You are my most magical Muse, Anne de Valois! Pericles said, *'What you leave behind is not what is engraved in stone monuments, but what is woven into the lives of others.'* We can create a wonderful world together."

In his gaze, Anne saw the reflection of many stars and a golden future that they could build together in France and her domains. "As Plato rightly said, *'Man: a being in search of meaning.'* We are both thirsty for discoveries."

François and Anne gazed into each other's eyes most cordially. An incredibly tender smile flicked across the king's features, revealing the depth of his emotions for his wife. He extended his hand to her, and she took it with a luminous grin. Hand-in-hand, they strolled out of the church, and outside, the bright sunshine of an otherwise chilly February day bathed them in a golden light, as if prophesying a glorious future for the magnificent French royal couple.

THE END

COMING SOON ...

The Anne Boleyn Alternate History Series, Part II: The Queen's Revenge

Queen Anne Boleyn perseveres in her quest for justice and vengeance upon the narcissistic, volatile, and homicidal King Henry. At last, she is officially declared innocent of all the phony charges leveled against her by Thomas Cromwell.

Her odyssey takes Anne from a world of gloom, across the barren landscape of ruin and the tempestuous waters of peril, to a realm of unexpected, heavenly happiness in her marriage to the flamboyant, cultured, and chivalrous King François. Meanwhile, politics and disquieting intrigues abound...

Author's Notes

In **Between Two Kings** and all the other instalments **in the Anne Boleyn Alternate History series**, Anne Boleyn is portrayed as close to historical reality as possible.

The historical Anne Boleyn was an epitome of grace, charm, elegance, wit, and, of course, intelligence. Raised at the magnificent French court of King François I and at the splendid court of Archduchess Margaret of Austria, she was impeccably educated and well learned in the arts. Anne was exactly what today we would call *a true Renaissance woman*. She also had a practical, cunning, and conniving mind; the Boleyn family were ambitious and hungry for power.

In my fictional account, the erstwhile Anne Boleyn has become a different woman after her dreadful experience in England, when King Henry VIII of England almost had her murdered. She has died at the pyre of Henry's brutal narcissism. Rising from the ashes of unfathomable ruin, Anne has learned a tragic lesson, and she has realized that she committed many mistakes in the past. The new Anne is a smart, cold, reticent, and calculating woman, one who never acts without reason, controls her emotions masterfully, knows how to play her cards well, and who tailored her personality to fit into her second marriage to King François.

Undoubtedly, Anne was not a treacherous adulteress to King Henry. Most definitely, she was a dignified and intensely religious person, one who could not lead a promiscuous life. Anne was clever and perspicacious enough to comprehend that she could not betray Henry during their long courtship and their tumultuous marriage. In this series, Anne is a true maid when the Tudor monarch takes her to bed for the first time in Calais, and it is highly likely to have been true.

There are things and historical tidbits I wish to share about this instalment.

I changed the method of Anne's execution for a compelling reason. Anne could have been either beheaded or burned according to the king's pleasure. I chose the second option because this made it easier to stage her death and smuggle her out of England. Moreover, there was an ancient prophesy of unknown origin that a Queen of England would be burned.

Anne narrowly escapes her destined tragedy in England. In the city of Venice, she starts her life in the shadows under a secret identity, becoming Anne Gabrielle Marguerite de Ponthieu, the only granddaughter of Jean Frédéric Roger de Ponthieu, Count de Montreuil. Jean is a fictional character, but his title is linked to history. In the 16th century, the county of Ponthieu was part of the French royal domain, and, hence, there were no nobles holding the title of Count de Ponthieu. So, I was free to use these name and title for my character.

The first important change to history is that King François' marriage to Eleanor of Austria, Emperor Carlos' elder sister, was never nullified. In my novel, François travels to Rome and has his union with Eleanor annulled because he was compelled to wed her after the devastating defeat of the French at Pavia in 1525, and his subsequent captivity in Spain.

In reality, François did not discard his second wife, although he disliked her and preferred to spend time with his mistress, Anne de Pisseleu d'Heilly. In some books, it is said that François and Eleanor never consummated their marriage, which seems unrealistic to me. Most likely, the monarch rarely shared a bed with his unwanted spouse. In this instalment, they never engaged in intercourse, and this is an additional ground for the annulment of their union.

The fateful meeting with François de Valois is a turning point in Anne's life. Striving to have a political advantage over the Holy Roman Emperor, the French monarch arrives in Venice to negotiate an alliance with the Doge of the Venetian Republic. By a twist of fate, Anne saves his life in St Mark's Basilica, where François made a stop for a prayer and was almost killed by an assassin. Carlos V, Holy Roman Emperor, is the perpetrator, and François understands this, although there is no evidence of his sworn foe's involvement in the crime. This did not happen in history despite the life-long enmity between these two monarchs, who could never be friends.

François realizes that Anne and he have foes in common – King Henry and Emperor Carlos. He takes a foolhardy step and offers Anne a marriage deal. Understanding that it is her only chance to extract vengeance on Henry for her sufferings and for George Boleyn's death, Anne accepts his proposal, despite her misgivings and fears. She does not love François and has lost faith in love – he knows about it from the beginning, but he still weds Anne in secret. As political allies, they join forces in their quest to take revenge on King Henry.

Anne and François are not joined in matrimony under her secret identity. The queen's identity is kept secret only until her name is cleared of the false charges leveled against her by Thomas Cromwell. Henry officially declares her innocent throughout England in the next installment. Otherwise, Anne's second marriage would have been implausible.

Unexpectedly, another assassination attempt on François' life happens in Turin. Rescuing him once more, Anne becomes the legendary heroine of France, who is hailed by her subjects as the Knight-King's savior. Obviously, both regicide attempts are fictional events for drama.

In this fictional series, Henry of England secretly financed the emperor's Italian campaign that resulted in his French counterpart's capture. In history, François was taken prisoner after the Battle of Pavia of 1525 by the Imperial troops, but Henry was not involved in that war and in other conspiracies against his Valois archrival. These twists were necessary to make François perceive Henry as his mortal adversary.

After weighting various scenarios, I decided to take an original approach to Jane Seymour's fate. Jane births Henry's disabled child, and she does not die of childbed fever. The hapless baby boy is named Richard at Henry's behest, for it is an unfortunate name for English kings. Given the significant amount of inbreeding in royal and aristocratic families back then, it is entirely possible that not all of their offspring were born healthy and normal. King Henry VIII was related to all of his wives, including Jane Seymour. Through her maternal grandfather, Jane was a descendant of King Edward III's son Lionel of Antwerp, Duke of Clarence, which makes her and Henry VIII fifth cousins. Henry himself was a son of cousins – a product of generational inbreeding. King Henry VII of England and Elizabeth of York were third cousins, as both were great-great-grandchildren of John of Gaunt.

King François I and King Henry VIII were distant cousins. Henry was descended from his great-grandmother Catherine de Valois, who was a daughter of King Charles VI of France, known as the Mad (*le Fou*) and his wife, Isabeau of Bavaria. Moreover, Henry also shared Capetian blood with François through the marriage of King Edward II of England to Isabella of France, the only surviving daughter of King Philippe IV of France called the Fair (*le Bel*). François was descended from his murdered great-grandfather – Louis I, Duke d'Orléans, who was a younger brother of Charles VI and the youngest son of King Charles V of France called the Wise (*le Sage*). Henry and François shared part of the Valois ancestry tree and part of the Capetian ancestry tree starting from Charles V of France and down to Hugh Capet and even Charlemagne.

Anne Boleyn and François I were very distantly related as well. Young Marguerite de France, a sister of Philippe IV of France and a daughter of Philippe III of France called the Bold (*le Hardi*), married King Edward I of England known as Edward Longshanks. The couple had two surviving sons. One of them was Thomas of Brotherton, Earl of Norfolk, whose daughter and eventual sole heiress – Margaret, Duchess of Norfolk – was an ancestress of the Howard family. As Anne's mother was Elizabeth Howard, Anne had Capetian blood coursing through her veins, being a descendant of Marguerite de France. The House of Valois, including François, were descended from Hugh Capet, and Philippe III of France was François' direct ancestor. Thus, Anne and François shared part of the Capetian ancestry tree starting from Philippe III of France and down to Hugh Capet and Charlemagne. This makes François and Anne very distant cousins.

There are reasons why Jane Seymour's son was named Richard. Some might say that Richard is an unlucky name for royals. King Richard III had a visible spinal deformity, which was proved by the recent discovery of his bones. He could have murdered his brother's two sons – King Edward IV – in the Tower of London. One of those boys was Richard of Shrewsbury, Duke of York. Yet, Richard III's involvement in the boys' deaths cannot be proved. Later, Richard III was killed at Bosworth Field. Richard II, son of Edward the Black Prince and grandchild of Edward III, could have suffered from a personality disorder: he had been deposed and soon died in captivity. These three Richards all had unfortunate endings and died without leaving any legitimate male heirs.

The Franco-Ottoman alliance between King François I and Suleiman the Magnificent was established in 1536. It is true that Mary de Guise married King James V of Scotland to strengthen the Auld Alliance between France and Scotland.

The Franco-Venetian treaty is a fictional event that gives François more power to further propel his political fortunes.

Although King François is portrayed as an inveterate libertine in some anecdotal textual depictions and literary works, his amorous reputation is highly exaggerated. A friend and colleague of mine has the memoirs written by his ancestor, who had been a seasoned courtier at François' court. The information in this book proves that the king had many affairs, especially in his youth, but he was not as lecherous as he is sometimes shown by Anglo-Saxon historians.

The Valois ruler had only two official chief mistresses – Françoise de Foix, Countess de Châteaubriant, and then Anne de Pisseleu d'Heilly, Duchess d'Étampes. Françoise de Foix was dismissed after his return from Spanish captivity in 1526; Anne de Pisseleu was his most illustrious favorite. He also had flirtations and other mistresses such as Claude de Rohan-Gié. At the same time, Anne de Pisseleu seems to have been the greatest love of King François' life, for they were devoted to each other for the rest of the monarch's life.

Most of the facts about the families and entourages of the English, French, and Imperial monarchs are true, but at times, the author's interpretation of historical facts has been altered to suit the plot. The names and biographies of the famous French Renaissance poets, who wrote the pamphlets and created the book about Thomas Cromwell, are historically correct; I myself composed the content of one pamphlet.

The exact date of Anne's birth is unknown. It appears that she was born at Blickling Hall in Norfolk, England, sometime between 1501 and 1507. I assume that her date of birth is in the summer of 1507. I did not want to make Anne significantly older than Jane Seymour and Anne de Pisseleu d'Heilly. Anne also needed to be young enough to bear François' children.

In history, François I was born on the 12th of September, 1494. In this alternate reality, he has the same date and month of birth, but a different year – 1498. For fictional purposes, he has to be nearly a coeval of Emperor Carlos since the rivalry between them is at the forefront of this series.

I tried to make the appearances of the main characters close to those in history. Yet, there are some divergences; for example, the French and English kings do not wear beards.

Some historical events were altered on purpose, but I did my best to portray them as close to real history as possible. The descriptions of Renaissance clothes, meals, and traditions of the era, as well as those of French, English, and Italian royal palaces and châteaux, are historically correct. The poems, which François composed for Anne, were written by me.

According to many accounts, Anne was courted by Henry Percy, Earl of Northumberland, in her early youth, and they were in love. The information about her meeting with King François I of France in Calais in October 1532, mentioned in Anne's and François' memories, is historically correct. The facts about Leonardo da Vinci are true as well, except for the assumption that he died in François' arms, which was a myth; we do not know how the maestro passed away.

I pray that you have enjoyed this novel. From the bottom of my heart, I thank you for coming along on the journey, and I hope you will continue with our beloved Anne into the next installment, which is going to be full of intrigue and drama.

Olivia Longueville

GLOSSARY

Achilles' heel

In ancient Greek mythology, it was a small, but fatal, weakness of an otherwise invincible opponent. It can refer to any type of weakness, not just a physical vulnerability.

Aphrodite

The Greek goddess of love, beauty, pleasure, and procreation. In Hesiod's Theogony, Aphrodite was born off the coast of Cythera from foam. In Homer's Iliad, she was the daughter of Zeus and Dione. Venus was her Roman counterpart.

Athena

The Greek goddess of wisdom, handicraft, and warfare. She was believed to have been born from the head of her father, Zeus. Minerva was her Roman counterpart.

affiquet

A brooch pinned to the upturned hat brim in France in the Renaissance era.

affinity

In Catholic canon law, affinity is an impediment to marriage due to the relationship which either party has as a result of a kinship relationship, or extramarital intercourse.

ambrosial

Succulently sweet or fragrant; balmy or divine.

antechamber

A chamber that serves as a waiting room and entrance to a larger room.

arcade

A structure made by enclosing a series of arches and columns.

arras

A wall hanging made of a splendid tapestry fabric, typically used to conceal an alcove.

arquebus

A form of long-barreled gun that appeared in Europe during the 15th century.

arquebusiers

Soldiers armed with an arquebus.

bailey

It is a courtyard of a castle, enclosed by a curtain wall. Outer bailey is the defended outer enclosure of a castle. Inner bailey is the strongly fortified enclosure inside a fortress.

bodice

A tight-fitting, sleeveless garment covering the torso and frequently stiffened with boning and cross-laced, worn over a blouse or chemise.

bow *(bōh)*

A weapon that propels projectiles (arrows).

bow

1) Bending at the waist towards another person as a formal greeting.

2) The front of a ship.

brocade

A class of richly decorative shuttle-woven fabrics woven with an elaborate, raised design or pattern, typically with gold or silver thread.

brooch

A decorative jewelry item designed to be attached to garments, a testimony to their owners' wealth and status. Brooches were also popular gifts.

butterfly

An insect with large, often brightly colored wings. It is a symbol of change, joy, and color, as well as a powerful representation of life and resurrection.

Catholic canon law

Ecclesiastical law made and enforced by the Roman Church's hierarchical authorities.

chariot

A type of carriage driven by a charioteer, usually using horses.

chemise

A full-sleeved blouse worn next to the skin to protect clothes from sweat and body oils. It was the basic foundation garment of all women's Renaissance clothing.

chignon

A woman's hairstyle where the hair is arranged in a knot or roll at the back of her head.

clandestine marriages

They were not performed with the rites and banns of a public ceremony. In Catholic canon law, clandestinity is an impediment that invalidates a marriage performed without the presence of three witnesses, one of whom must be a priest or a deacon. In England before 1215, a couple could announce their intention to marry in front of witnesses, and if this was followed by consummation, canon law considered the couple to be legally wed.

Chronos

The Greek god of empirical time, who was sometimes equated with Aio, the god of eternity. Not to be confused with the Titan Cronus (Kronos), the father of the God Zeus.

Clotho

She was one of the Three Fates or Moirai, who was spinning the thread of human life.

column

An upright pillar supporting an arch, entablature, or other structure.

courtesan

A woman who seeks financial support and security from noblemen and men of wealth in return for companionship and sexual favors.

courtier

An attendant at court, especially a person who spends a great deal of time attending the court of a king or other royal personage.

curtsy

A formal gesture of greeting and respect made by women and girls, consisting of bending the knees to lower the body while slightly bowing the head.

dais

A raised platform for a throne and seats of honor.

Dionysus

The Greek god of the grape-harvest, winemaking, wine, ritual madness, religious ecstasy, and theatre. He was also known as Bacchus, the name adopted by the Romans.

ditch

It is an obstacle in a castle, designed to slow down or break up an attacking foe.

Despoina

The Greek goddess of mysteries of Arcadian cults. She was described as the daughter of Demeter and Poseidon and one of the central figures of the Eleusinian Mysteries.

doublet

A chief and expensive upper garment worn by men from the 15th to the 17th century. This close-fitting jacket was hip length or waist length and worn over the shirt or drawers.

dowager

A widow whose title was obtained from her deceased husband. Adding this modifier to a title distinguishes the widow from the wife of the man who currently holds the title.

dowry

Money or land given by the bride's family at the time of her marriage.

dryad

A nymph of oak trees, but the term has come to be used for all tree nymphs in general. In Greek mythology, they were typically considered shy creatures.

Eros

The Greek god of sensual love and desire, who was said to be the son of Aphrodite or a primordial god. His Roman counterpart was Cupid.

empyreal

Heavenly; pertaining to the highest heaven.

epitaph

a short text honoring a deceased person, especially as an inscription on a tombstone.

escutcheon

a shield or shield-shaped emblem bearing a coat of arms.

Euphrosyne

The Greek goddess of joy or mirth, as well as the incarnation of grace and beauty. She was one of the Charites, minor goddesses of beauty, nature, creativity, and fertility.

fealty

Loyalty that a vassal owes to his lord. This often refers to the actual loyalty oath, as in "an oath of fealty."

Feast of the Immaculate Conception

This is the solemn celebration of belief in the Immaculate Conception of the Virgin Mary. It is celebrated on the 8th of December. It is one of the most important Marian feasts in the liturgical calendar of the Roman Catholic Church.

fief

Land granted to a vassal for his use. In return, the vassal provided loyalty and service to the owner of the land. A fief could also be a payment instead of land.

fiefdom

Land owned by a noble or knight.

field

In heraldry, the background color of a coat-of-arms is called the field.

fleur-de-lis

In heraldry, a stylized representation of an iris, consisting of three petals. This heraldry represents the royal family of France in gold on a blue field.

forthwith

An old word that dates to the 13th century. It means immediately, at once, without delay.

fortnight

A period of two weeks, or fourteen days.

French hood

A woman's headdress popular in Western Europe in the 16th century. It was rounded in outline and less conservative, displaying the front part of the hair.

Gable hood

It was an English female angular headdress worn between 1500–1550. It was called so because of its pointed shape that resembled the gable of a house.

genuflect

Briefly dropping to one knée before rising. This was a formal greeting performed when in the presence of social superiors. It is also performed towards the altar when in church.

girdle

A piece of underwear worn around the waist and bottom, which stretches to shape the body.

great hall

Known as the heart of the living space in a castle, it was the location of feasts, and often the area where business was conducted. In earlier times, it was also where people slept.

gown

A long, fashionable over-garment that could be sleeveless, have cap or pendant sleeves, or could feature decorative hanging sleeves. Styles could range from close-fitting to loose.

halberd

A two-handed pole weapon that came to use during the 14th and 15th centuries.

halberdiers

Troops which used a halberdier.

Hades

1) In ancient Greek religion, he was the god of the dead and the king of the underworld. He and his brothers, Zeus and Poseidon, defeated their father's generation of gods – the Titans. Then Hades received the underworld, Zeus the sky, and Poseidon the sea.

2) A name for hell. This use is not capitalized.

headdress

A head covering worn for protection against weather conditions, ceremonial or religious purposes, safety, and as a fashion accessory.

Hebe

The Greek goddess of youth or the prime of life, the daughter of Zeus and Hera.

Hera

The sister-wife of the God Zeus, who ruled Mount Olympus as queen of the gods. She was the goddess of women, marriage, family, and childbirth. In some myths, Hera showed her jealous and vengeful nature against Zeus' numerous lovers and illegitimate offspring.

Heracles

The son of Zeus and Alcmene, he was the greatest of the Greek heroes.

heresy

Adherence to a religious opinion contrary to church dogma. In the Catholic Church, those who continuously displayed obstinate heresy were frequently excommunicated. From the early 11th century, many people accused of heresy were burned at the stake.

high table

An elevated table in the great hall where the lord, his family, and important guests were seated during feasts.

hilt

The handle of a sword or dagger. It is comprised of the cross guard, grip, and pommel.

homage

A declaration of loyalty from one person to another. The man declaring his loyalty would receive a fief in return. The first step in becoming a vassal is to pay homage to the lord.

hose

A close-fitting men's garment for the legs and lower body. It was worn from the Middle Ages through the 17th century, when it fell out of use in favor of breeches and stockings.

humors

The fluids in the body. In ancient Greece, Rome, and the medieval period, humors were thought to be closely tied to health. Balancing your humors was vital to good health.

jousting

A tournament competition where two mounted knights rode towards each other with the goal of unhorsing their opponent using blunted lances.

Jupiter

The Roman king of the gods, as well as the god of the sky and thunder. He was the chief deity of Roman religion throughout the Republican and Imperial eras.

keep

The living area inside of a castle complex. It was a heavily guarded and fortified building or tower. The great hall would be located in the keep.

lapis

A blue metamorphic rock consisting largely of lazurite, used for decoration and in jewelry.

Lent

A Christian season of fasting and penitence in preparation for Easter, beginning on Ash Wednesday and lasting 40 weekdays to Easter, observed annually.

Lethe

One of the five rivers of the underworld of Hades. As it flowed around the cave of Hypnos, all those who drank from it experienced complete forgetfulness.

litter

A type of transport for one or several aristocratic passengers. Unlike a wagon or a carriage, it had no wheels and was drawn by horses and a horse at the front.

liege lord

A feudal lord who is entitled to allegiance and service from his vassals.

lord

A landholder, typically a noble or the monarch, who granted fiefs to vassals.

matins

The nighttime liturgy, ending at dawn.

Mass

A Catholic Church service which includes Holy Communion.

maître-en-titre

The King of France's official chief mistress. This position came with its own apartments. The title came into use during the reign of King François I.

Messalina

Valeria Messalina was the third spouse of the Roman Emperor Claudius. This powerful woman with a reputation for promiscuity, and now she is often associated with dissolution.

men-at-arms

A general term for trained soldiers. Typically, they were trained like knights, but not all men-at-arms were knights.

minstrel

A medieval entertainer. Some wrote their own songs, but most sang songs composed by others. They also performed acrobatics, juggled, told jokes, and recited poems.

moat

A moat is a deep, broad ditch, either dry or filled with water, which surrounds a castle.

motte

A mound, either natural or artificial, forming the site of a castle or camp.

Morpheus

The Greek god of sleep and dreams. The phrase, "in the arms of Morpheus" simply means that the person is asleep. Today, the narcotic morphine can trace its name to Morpheus.

Mount Olympus

In Greek mythology, the location where the gods and goddesses lived.

Nemesis

The Greek goddess of divine retribution and revenge, who meted out punishment for evil deeds and arrogance before the gods. She was the daughter of Oceanus or Zeus.

nymph

A Greek mythological divine spirit of nature. It was usually depicted as beautiful, young nubile maidens who love to dance and sing.

obeisance

Giving proper respect and deference to someone of superior rank. Typically this would require kneeling (see genuflect), bowing, or curtsying.

page

A boy in training to become a knight. He would progress from page to squire to knight.

palazzo

a large imposing building, especially in Italy.

palfrey

A horse used for everyday riding. These smaller horses were often ridden by women.

parchment

Animal skin that has been processed to use as a writing surface. It was typically sheepskin, and it was also used to cover windows before the widespread use of glass.

piazza

a public square or marketplace, especially in an Italian town.

pillar

a tall vertical structure of stone, wood, or metal, used to support part of a building.

plafond

An ornately decorated ceiling.

Persephone

The venerable Greek queen of the underworld. After her abduction by Hades, the god of the underworld, she married him. She embodied a type of life-death-rebirth deity, whose eventual return signified new life and the change of seasons.

physician

A university educated doctor.

poniard

A long, light thrusting knife with a continuously tapering, acutely pointed blade. It was worn by the upper class, noblemen, or knights during the Middle Ages and the Renaissance in Europe, in particular in France, Switzerland, and Italy.

relics

Sacred objects associated with a saint or holy person.

rapier

A type of slender, sharply pointed sword. It was mainly used in Europe during the 16th and 17th centuries. It can be called a man's Renaissance weapon.

salamander

An amphibian typically characterized by a lizard-like appearance. According to legends and mythology, this creature could live in fire without being consumed. In heraldry, salamanders symbolized fire and represented the virtues of courage, loyalty, chastity, and impartiality. King François I chose salamander for his personal emblem.

scabbard

A rigid sheath for sword or dagger made of wood, metal, or hardened leather.

sire

The form of direct address used for royalty.

Sisyphus

The cruel Greek king condemned by the gods to push a large rock up on a steep hill, only to find it rolling back on nearing the top, so he had to repeat this action for eternity.

slashing and puffing

Slits cut in a garment with fabric from the undergarment pulled through to form puffs.

stomacher

A piece of decorative cloth worn over the chest and stomach by both men and women in the 15th and 16th century. Later, it was used only by women.

Styx

The Greek mythological river forming the boundary between earth and the underworld, often called Hades. The souls of the dead were ferried across Styx by Charon.

surcoat

An outer garment worn in the Middle Ages worn by both men and women.

Tartarus

In Greek mythology, it was the deep abyss of torment and suffering for the wicked, as well as the prison for the Titans.

tapestry

It is woven decorative fabric, the design of which is built up in the course of weaving. In the 14th and 15th centuries, tapestries were produced at Arras in northern France. In the 16th century, Flanders became the center of European tapestry production. Elaborately woven and sumptuous tapestries were a common art form in the Middle Ages and the

Renaissance, a testament to their owners' wealth, erudition, and taste.

Terpsichore

One of the nine Muses and the Greek goddess of dance and chorus. She was considered a mother of the sirens and Parthenope.

titan

An important and powerful person who stands out for greatness of achievement. In ancient Greek religion, the Titans preceded the Twelve Olympians.

The Eleusinian Mysteries

The most famous of the secret religious rites in ancient Greece. They were held every year for the cult of Demeter and Persephone based at Eleusis.

The Pax Romana

It was a famous long period of relative peace and stability in the Roman Empire between the accession of the Emperor Augustus and the death of the Emperor Marcus Aurelius.

The Moirai (the Three Fates)

The Greek incarnations of destiny: Clotho, Lachesis, and Atropos. Clotho was spinning the thread of human life. As the measurer of the thread spun on Clotho's spindle, Lachesis determined destiny. Atropos chose the mechanism of death and ended the life of mortals.

The Sirens

In Greek mythology, they were dangerous creatures, who lured sailors to shipwreck on the rocky coast of their island with their enchanting music and their bewitching voices.

The Scots Guard (the Garde Écossaise)

It was an elite Scottish military unit founded in 1418 by King Charles VII of France, known as the Victorious, to be personal bodyguards to the French monarchs.

troubadour

A poet and songwriter. Troubadours sometimes performed, but they were primarily seen as composers. They were sometimes from noble families.

vassal

A man swore loyalty to a noble landowner in return for use of that land (a fief).

Venus

The Roman goddess of love, beauty, desire, sex, prosperity, fertility, and victory. She was the mother of the Roman people through her son, Aeneas, who escaped to Italy after the fall of Troy. Aphrodite was her Greek counterpart.

Vesta

The Roman virgin goddess of the hearth, home, and family. The daughter of Saturn and Ops, she was among twelve of the most honored gods in the Roman pantheon.

ward

A person who has been placed under the control and protection of a guardian.

Zeus

The ruler of the Greek gods who lived on Mount Olympus, as well as the god of the sky and thunder. He was married to Hera, by whom he fathered Ares, Hebe, and Hephaestus. According to Homer's Iliad, he fathered Aphrodite. Zeus was infamous for his erotic escapades which are mentioned in many myths. Jupiter was Zeus' Roman counterpart.

About The Author

Olivia Longueville

Olivia Longueville has an artistic and academic mind with a natural inclination for research and constant learning. She earned several degrees in finance & general management from London Business School (LBS) and other world-wide prestigious universities. At present, she helps her father run the family business. Olivia has always loved literature and fiction and been very passionate about genealogy, historical research, philosophy, literature, and the arts, in particular painting and sculpture during Tudor and Renaissance eras.

During her first trip to France years ago, Olivia had a life-changing epiphany when she visited the magnificent Château de Fontainebleau near Paris and toured its library. This truly transformed her life as she realized her passion for books and writing, foreshadowing her future career as a writer. In early childhood she began writing stories and poems in various languages. Then Olivia wrote some fan fiction stories, which taught her to create plausible, vivid, engaging characters and plots. A passionate fan of Anne Boleyn, Henry VIII's second wife, Olivia finds her more compatible with another monarch of the era – King François I of France, at whose court Anne grew up and developed the sophistication of her personality and her French manners. As a result, she wrote a novel about the alternate life story of Anne Boleyn – ***"Between Two Kings"***, the first installment in Olivia's Anne Boleyn series.

If You Enjoyed This Book
Visit

PENMORE PRESS

www.penmorepress.com

All Penmore Press books are available directly through our website.

THE ALTERPIECE

BY

SARAH KENNEDY

It is 1535, and in the tumultuous years of King Henry VIII's break from Rome, the religious houses of England are being seized by force. Twenty-year-old Catherine Havens is a foundling and the adopted daughter of the prioress of the Priory of Mount Grace in a small Yorkshire village. Catherine, like her adoptive mother, has a gift for healing, and she is widely sought and admired for her knowledge. However, the king's divorce dashes Catherine's hopes for a place at court, and she reluctantly takes the veil. When the priory's costly altarpiece goes missing, Catherine and her friend Ann Smith find themselves under increased suspicion. King Henry VIII's soldiers have not had their fill of destruction, and when they return to Mount Grace to destroy the priory, Catherine must choose between the sacred calling of her past and the man who may represent her country's future.

PENMORE PRESS
www.penmorepress.com

A BLACK MATTER FOR THE KING

BY

MATTHEW WILLIS AND J. A. IRONSIDE

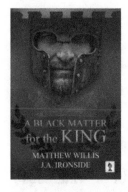

TWO POWERFUL RIVALS -- ONE DECISIVE BATTLE

Now a political hostage in Falaise, Ælfgifa forms an unlikely friendship with William, Duke of Normandy. William has been swift to recognize her skills and exploit them to his advantage. However, unbeknownst to the duke, Gifa is acting as a spy for her brother, Harold Godwinson, a possible rival for the English throne currently in the failing grip of Edward the Confessor. Homesick and alienated by the Norman court, Gifa is torn between the Duke's trust and the duty she owes her family.

William has subdued his dissenting nobles, and a united Normandy is within his grasp. But the tides of power and influence are rarely still. As William's stature grows, the circle of those he can trust shrinks. Beyond the English Channel, William has received news of Edward's astonishing decree regarding the succession. Ælfgifa returns to an England where an undercurrent of discontent bubbles beneath the surface. An England that may soon erupt in conflict as one king dies and another is chosen.

The ambitions of two powerful men will decide the fates of rival cultures in a single battle at Hastings that will change England, Europe, and the world in this compelling conclusion to the Oath & Crown series on the life and battles of William the Conqueror.

"I loved these books. Sweeping history, battles galore, treachery, a cast of glorious, well-depicted characters - all in all, a fabulous story told brilliantly." - Michael Jecks, author of the Templar series

PENMORE PRESS
www.penmorepress.com

Mistress Suffragette

by

Diana Forbes

A young woman without prospects at a ball in Gilded Age Newport, Rhode Island is a target for a certain kind of "suitor." At the Memorial Day Ball during the Panic of 1893, impoverished but feisty Penelope Stanton draws the unwanted advances of a villainous millionaire banker who preys on distressed women—the incorrigible Edgar Daggers. Over a series of encounters, he promises Penelope the financial security she craves, but at what cost? Skilled in the art of flirtation, Edgar is not without his charms, and Penelope is attracted to him against her better judgment. Initially, as Penelope grows into her own in the burgeoning early Women's Suffrage Movement, Edgar exerts pressure, promising to use his power and access to help her advance. But can he be trusted, or are his words part of an elaborate mind game played between him and his wife? During a glittering age where a woman's reputation is her most valuable possession, Penelope must decide whether to compromise her principles for love, lust, and the allure of an easier life.

PENMORE PRESS
www.penmorepress.com

A Falcon Flies

by

James Boschert

The fifth book of Talon

Talon returns to Acre, the Crusader port, a rich man after more than a year in Byzantium. But riches bring enemies, and Talon's past is about to catch up with him: accusations of witchcraft have followed him from Languedoc. Everything is changed, however, when Talon travels to a small fort with Sir Guy de Veres, his Templar mentor, and learns stunning news about Rav'an.

Before he can act, the kingdom of Baldwin IV is threatened by none other than the Sultan of Egypt, Salah Ed Din, who is bringing a vast army through Sinai to retake Jerusalem from the Christians. Talon must take part in the ferocious battle at Montgisard before he can set out to rejoin Rav'an and honor his promise made six years ago.

The 'Assassins of Rashid Ed Din, the Old Man of the Mountain, have targeted Talon for death for obstructing their plans once too often. To avoid them, Talon must take a circuitous route through the loneliest reaches of the southern deserts on his way to Persia, but even so he risks betrayal, imprisonment, and execution.

His sole objective is to find Rav'an, but she is not where he had expected her to be.

PENMORE PRESS
www.penmorepress.com

Penmore Press

Challenging, Intriguing, Adventurous, Historical and Imaginative

www.penmorepress.com

CPSIA information can be obtained
at www.ICGtesting.com
Printed in the USA
LVHW041304201120
672144LV00001B/8

9 781950 586578